Shakespeared
IN THE PARK

Joy Ann Ribar

BAY BROWNING MYSTERY SERIES

The Medusa Murders
BOOK 1

Shake-speared in the Park
BOOK 2

COMING NEXT!

Poetry Slammed
BOOK 3

DEEP LAKES COZY MYSTERY SERIES

Deep Dark Secrets
BOOK 1

Deep Bitter Roots
BOOK 2

Deep Green Envy
BOOK 3

Deep Dire Harvest
BOOK 4

Deep Wedded Blues
BOOK 5

Deep Flakes Christmas, A Nisse Visit
PREQUEL

 Follow Joy on Substack

joyribar.substack.com/about

 Joy Ann Ribar Wisconsin Author

Shake speared
IN THE PARK

Joy Ann Ribar
A Bay Browning Mystery
BOOK 2

Wine Glass Press
U.S.A.

Wine Glass Press, U.S.A.

Shake-speared in the Park: A Bay Browning Mystery, Book Two

© 2025 by Joy Ann Ribar

Published in the United States by Wine Glass Press.

GENRES: Mystery, Amateur Sleuth, Women's Fiction.

ISBN: (paperback) 978-1-959078-27-2

ISBN: (ebook) 978-1-959078-26-5

EDITED BY: Kay Rettenmund
COVER AND INTERIOR: Terry Rydberg, Fine Print Design

First Edition: 2025

PRAISE FOR

IN THE PARK

BAY BROWNING MYSTERY SERIES • BOOK 2

"It's not just about who was 'speared' and why,
but who is hiding behind the various costumes
and masks, how many hats and names can
be donned by one character, who has the rein
(or reign) well in hand... Ribar's latest mystery is
an exciting ride through gardens and stages of
a college town being terrorized. Is your favorite
character the killer? *Or the next victim?*"

~ J. Ivanel Johnson
   Author of the award-winning JUST (e)STATE Mysteries

"Something wicked this way comes in
Shake-speared, book 2 of Joy Ann Ribar's
Bay Browning Mystery series. A university summer
theater production is difficult enough, but when
a rich family's son is killed during rehearsals, the
trouble is only beginning. Ribar effortlessly pulls
the reader into academic, theatrical, and family
worlds, each with unique behind-the-scenes
dangers. Shakespeare, college politics, old
family money, and a hunky policeman make
this novel an irresistible read. Throw in a little
psychic ability, and you have a magical novel!"

~ Sharon Lynn
   Award-winning author of A Cotswold Crimes Mystery series

Shake speared
IN THE PARK

Cast of Characters
WITH BRIEF DESCRIPTIONS

The Principal Players

Bay Browning: Literature Professor at Flourish College, a private college specializing in fine arts, located in Prairie Ridge, Wisconsin.

Casandra Browning: Bay's older sister. An ex-WWWW, reformed grifter with paranormal powers. Cass specializes in the field of apothecary.

Barrett Browning: The sisters' father. A semi-retired anthropologist who is currently working the college lecture circuit.

Diana Poulin: Bay's and Cass's half-sister. Works at the reference desk at Flourish College Library.

Jen Yoo: Bay's colleague and friend. Professor of Art History at Flourish.

Stasia Andino: Associate Dean. Bay's immediate boss. Stasia is caught up in helping extended family by insisting Flourish employees patronize their businesses.

Pamela Foyt: Dean of Humanities.

Gabriel McNelly: Religious Studies Professor at Flourish and a thorn in Bay's side. Ex-priest with a mysterious aura.

Bryce Downing: Prairie Ridge police detective. Chemistry exists between Bay and him.

Nolan Harris: Detective Downing's partner.

Flourish Theater Players

Desmond Carver: Flourish head of theater department and director of summer show.

Maya Leary: Props Mistress for the summer production. No nonsense, meticulous.

Talon Hunt: plays lead role of Shakespeare in the summer show. Arrogant, ladies man, legacy student.

Jackson Lange: plays multiple roles in summer show. Talon Hunt's best friend and legacy student. Jackson's father is part of the law firm The Lange Group.

Adam Lee: third member of the legacy peer trio with Talon and Jackson. Plays various roles in summer show.

Nora Stroud: plays multiple roles in summer show. Part of the legacy peer group. Her parents are equestrian experts who work on the bluff.

Cher Devane: plays various roles in summer show. A spoiled diva and legacy student. Her parents house expensive horses at their stable on the bluff.

Logan Thorne: Talon Hunt's understudy and adversary.

Henry Knight: part of the summer show tech crew. Clever, shy, suffers from low self-esteem.

Aria: Stasia's niece. Works backstage with Maya as a volunteer.

Robert, Rowan, Kitt, Tamara, Daniel, Dylan: Flourish students playing various roles in summer show.

Ginny Knight: Henry's mother and professional seamstress in charge of costumes.

Evan Barnes: Technical director for summer show, from UW-Madison

Bluff Birds: members of the wealthy crowd and founding families who live on Bird-Angel Bluff.

Posey Hollingsworth: Single, age fifty. Cassandra is her personal assistant. Practicing apothecary with a troubled past.

Malcolm Hunt: Wealthy, heir to the Hunt fortune. Warm at times, aloof at other times.

Corrine Hunt: Wealthy wife to Malcolm and rich in her own right. Cool and calculating.

Edison Hunt: Malcolm's and Corrine's oldest son. Bumbling, careless, considered a fool by many.

Lincoln and Julia Lange: Jackson's parents. Fair and down-to-earth.

Monroe Lange: Attorney at The Lange Group with his brother, Lincoln. Monroe is a player.

Bianca Lange: Monroe's much younger fourth wife; pregnant.

The Ex-Ladies Lange: Monroe's ex-wives in order: **Suzanne, Gretchen and Heather**. Each has a daughter with Monroe. Now they make him miserable.

Other Players

Ophelia Kingsley: ostracized from the Bluff Birds.

Marva, Fanta, and Sage: the Sweet Sisters, collectively. Marva is Posey Hollingsworth's housekeeper; Fanta is employed by Malcolm and Corrine Hunt; Sage is employed by the Devanes.

Joyce Strost: Posey's friend.

Joanna Stengel: Diana's boss and head librarian at Flourish.

Anthony McGann: Posey's personal attorney.

Cheers to The Bard and to every educator out there
brave enough to teach and discuss meaningful literature
from diverse voices in every era.
America owes educators a debt of gratitude.
We preserve history and story through literature
and discourse, and that must not change.

CHAPTER 1

By the Pricking of my Thumbs
~ MACBETH

"What about a garden-themed party? Didn't you say Posey is an accomplished botanist?" Bay Browning jabbed a handheld rake through the soil. Her sister, Cassandra, decided their apartment balcony needed a garden, of all things.

Cassandra gave the soil an affectionate pat after potting the chocolate mint in place. She already imagined the tea blend she would later concoct with the herbs now bedded in the long rectangular planter.

"No. Posey always hosts a garden party in September. Her way of saying a fond farewell to the blooming season."

Bay raised curious eyes towards her sister. Cassandra was happier than Bay remembered since they were children. Had it only been a few months since their awkward reunion? Cass arrived on Bay's doorstep after a three-year stint in a Florida prison for larceny and fraud. As a condition of her parole, she needed a responsible supervisor. That was Bay.

Cass waved a hand in front of Bay's face. "Did you hear me? I think a Shakespeare costume party would be perfect. What a complement to your summer theater production!" Cass clapped her garden gloves together, scattering dirt all over.

Bay smiled. She recently partnered with theater professor Desmond Carver to write a parody featuring some of Shakespeare's famous characters dishing the dirt on each other and The Bard himself. The result, *Shakespeare's Couch*, was well received by the humanities department, who unanimously deemed it perfect for a summer production in the park.

"Oh really? Are Posey and her aristocratic set Shakespeare fans?" Bay had met Posey Hollingsworth once since Cass became her personal assistant in March, and Posey seemed down-to-earth for a descendant of the Prairie Ridge founders.

Cass pointed to a flat of colorful pansies. "Why don't you plant those in the three red pots there. You can't hurt pansies. They're the hardy ones of the flower world."

Bay stuck out her tongue at the jab.

"Didn't I tell you Posey is the head of the Twenty-first Century Club and Literary Society? The club sprouted from the Ladies Home Social Club that founded the library here. Posey serves on both the city and college library boards. She's well-read, Lulu."

Cass typically reverted to calling Bay by her childhood nickname when she was feeling tenderhearted or when schooling her. This time it was the latter.

"Many of the people Posey invites to her parties are from the college, you know. She rubs elbows with more than just the stuffy founding families." Cass potted a final tomato plant in the round whiskey barrel, surrounding it with basil and bright yellow marigolds. The three garden staples were suitable companions for successful results.

Bay arranged the pansy pots between the whiskey barrels and the long planter boxes and sat on her heels to admire their work. They still had some herbs in starter pots to contend with, and Cass insisted they needed to place hanging baskets along the edges, but that would have to wait for another day.

Bay sprang upward and brushed off her jeans, then shoved the garden tools into a canvas wagon. "Time for me to change for rehearsal. After a week of read-throughs, tonight we're rehearsing on stage at the park. There will be plenty of starts and stops with blocking. It's going to go long."

Cass nodded. "I'm grabbing dinner with Diana then going over to Posey's. She and I are comparing notes on botanicals." Cass and Bay descended from a long line of women apothecaries on their mother's side. Cass honored her penchant for botanical medicine, as Bay embraced literary pursuits while enjoying the tea blends her sister concocted.

"Say hello to Diana and tell her we'll catch up soon."

Diana was their half sister, who was currently living in the second-floor apartment owned by Bay's and Cass's father. Barrett was currently on the college lecture circuit after deciding he needed something more fulfilling than retirement.

Bay smiled at Cass. "Just thinking how far we've come in six months—you and me. I'm glad you found Posey."

Cassandra drove up the famous Angel Bluff Road toward the oldest side of Prairie Ridge overlooking Lake Spindrift.

The bluff was home to the original and wealthy end of town, frequented by gawking visitors perusing the decorative homes built between the 1870s and 1930s.

Cass found the well-preserved homes an architect's dream, even if some inhabitants exercised superiority she often found disgusting and puzzling.

"Why do the wealthy find entitlement in their status?" She spoke out loud despite being alone in the gray Subaru she'd been gifted from Bay. "Well, not all of the wealthy do." She self-corrected, knowing Posey Hollingsworth didn't fit the description.

Cass had her half sister, Diana, to thank for the introduction. Diana switched jobs from glorified gofer in the humanities building to working at the reference desk in the Flourish campus library. Posey frequently visited the library and warmed to Diana, seeing her as a wounded bird in need of tending. Diana suggested Posey and Cass meet to discuss their shared passion for gardening, and the women bonded immediately.

Since Posey's diagnosis of multiple sclerosis, she found herself becoming more reclusive. She needed help dressing at times, driving long distances, and sadly, tending her beloved gardens. In Cassandra, she found a single person who could assist with all three and more. She offered her a substantial salary to be her personal assistant.

Cass remembered how easy it had been to leave her job at Outfitters; the difficult part was revealing her ex-con-on-parole status to Posey. Instead of shuddering and dismissing Cass, Posey smiled warmly, thanked her for being forthright, and said the offer still stood.

Now she arrived at the gates of Spirit Gardens House, its majestic Queen Anne turrets rising toward the heavens as if defying Cass's amended opinion of the rich. Posey's father, Dr. Lionel Hollingsworth, a respected ophthalmologist, inherited the home his grandfather built in 1885.

Posey was an only child, like her father and grandfather before her. In fact, Lionel was forty-eight when Posey was born, and the community declared her a miracle baby since her mother, Ramona, had given up on motherhood years earlier.

Now the driveway welcomed her with its alternating red maples and Japanese lilacs. It was the lilacs' turn to show off their whipped cream blooms and sweet scent. Cass rolled down the window to catch the heady fragrance before curving around the circle drive to park on the stone courtyard.

Spirit Gardens had a back door and servant entrance, but Posey insisted everyone should use the main door, even her housekeeper, Marva. The driveway had ample parking spaces on both sides, but Posey's large parties required guests to park around the back.

Posey opened the door as soon as the outside lamps lit the courtyard and ushered Cass inside, their arms linked. The petite woman was well endowed, not slim and not plump. Dressed in jeans and a chambray shirt, she led Cass through the sunroom to one of her three greenhouses. Half of it included plants wintered over for replanting outdoors, while the other half was reserved for Posey's pet plants from tropical climes.

Posey's eyes were bright stars when she pointed to the coffee bushes. "Look, they're blooming, and the coffee cherries will be coming." Her genuine smile could melt ice. "I know there's not a lot, just enough to harvest, roast, and give away to my closest friends."

Cass appreciated anything nature produced, except mosquitoes and poison ivy. The fact anyone managed to grow coffee successfully in Wisconsin was a marvel. "So cool. I hope you'll let me help with harvesting and roasting. I'd love to help."

Posey nodded, her brown hair swaying with enthusiasm. She wore her do in a modern style with layers from crown to shoulders, framing her high forehead and wide cheekbones. "Absolutely. Just a couple new blooms to show you and then let's talk about your party ideas."

The two botanical enthusiasts wowed over the Jamaica pepper berries, ready to use whole or grind into allspice powder, and the budding marmalade bush, a South American species primed to show off its array of orange to pink to yellow blooms in the front gardens.

"Oops. I almost forgot," Posey paused beside a work area equipped with garden tools and gloves. "Here, put these on. I want to show you something special." She handed disposable gloves to Cass and put on a pair herself.

Cass trailed Posey to the far corner where tropical trees towered over shorter plants, shading them from sunlight. Grow lights coaxed the shaded plants to blossom. Posey stopped behind a bush with oval serrated leaves trailing along a stem in pairs. Several cranberry-colored stalks protruded from the foliage. Their tiny branches ended in waxy round white berries with a black dot in the middle.

Posey carefully lifted one of the stalks into the light, sending the berries into an unearthly dance. "White baneberry, also called Doll's Eyes. Every part of it is toxic, the berries most of all. Cardiac arrest could ensue after one taste." She waggled her eyebrows sharply.

Cass held her breath and moved back a step. "I wondered if you were ever going to show me the good stuff." Her smile conveyed mystery and approval.

Posey relaxed. "I hoped you'd feel that way. What can I say? Botanicals are alluring. Once you master the easy plants, you move up a level. Sooner or later, poisons are the next thrill."

"May I?" Cass ran one finger along the leaf cluster of the baneberry, before gently lifting one stem, heavy with berries. She wondered how close she dared go, whether she should hazard a sniff. The thrill of danger enticed her. She bent nearer, close enough to detect a heady fragrance.

"Roses," Cass stated.

Posey snorted. "Cassandra, you're a true compadre."

The women tossed their gloves into a biohazard bin and proceeded to camp out in the study where Posey typically planned events. The two sat at the oversized rosewood desk, their heads together.

Cass explained her idea of a costumed masquerade with guests dressed as famous Shakespeare characters. "I thought you'd enjoy making a game of it, like twenty questions."

Posey clapped. "I love it. We'll have music and dancing. Guests will ask questions while they mingle and keep track of their guesses. The guest with the most correct identities will win a prize. I've never had a live action role play party." She giggled in anticipation.

Marva, Posey's long-term housekeeper, stuck her head in the door. "Everything okay in here? Can I bring you something?" Marva Presley, a sixty-something widow, wasn't certain about Cass at their first encounter, but soon accepted her presence after watching her interactions with Posey.

"Tea, please." The two said together.

Posey checked the time. Almost seven p.m. "Marva, go home. No need to stay late because of Cassandra. We can make our own tea."

Minutes later, Marva carried in a tea tray with the ladies' favorite evening blends before saying good night. Naturally, she'd added shortbread cookies to the tray.

Cass crafted a sample invitation from Posey's assortment of decorative papers and stamps while Posey made a guest list. "I hope you'll bring your sister. A Shakespeare party will be right up her alley. Besides, she'll know the college folks, and what a great opportunity to meet some parents of her students."

At the mention of Bay's name, something knocked inside Cassandra's stomach making her jolt. The paper piercer she was using to make an embossed border bumped her thumb, a precise poke that formed a bead of blood. Her thumb throbbed in pain, and she sucked on it to stop the blood flow. Posey's suggestion still hung in Cass's orbit. *You don't know my sister. She wouldn't like this kind of party at all.*

Carillon Tower Park was buzzing with activity when Bay arrived for rehearsal. Desmond Carver, the director, was only steps ahead of her, so she dashed to catch up. Bay smiled at his signature bobbing walk on those extra-long legs that might belong to a pro basketball player instead of a theater professor.

"Desmond, hey. Looks like the students are psyched about the show." Bay nodded toward the outdoor theater area where a portable tech booth had been set up. People inside were testing spotlights and sound effects.

The stage was midway through set construction showing false stone walls and two framed second story balconies. Someone was sweeping the stage free of pine needles, while a couple of others were taping the floor where furniture would go. Bay waved at Jen Yoo, her art professor friend, who was painting a flat with some students.

"It's a positive sign when they show up early. Believe me, once we're in the trenches, some will find reasons not to show up at all." Desmond set a stack of scripts on one of the seats near the middle of the theater. "Actors," he said using air quotes around the word.

Bay's optimism didn't dwindle. She was pleased with the turnout for auditions, considering it was a summer production, meaning many students were gone or working. The fact she and Desmond had backups for the main roles revealed enthusiasm for the show.

Desmond handed her a theater badge and key for the rooms beyond the stage. "By the way, in case I forget later, thanks so much for volunteering to help with the play. It can be a thankless job."

Bay grinned but wondered why Desmond was being so pessimistic. He wasn't close to retirement, maybe ten years older than Bay, and she'd pegged him as carefree and upbeat. Then again, in the two years she'd been a Flourish professor, she'd had a handful of short conversations with him.

At seven p.m. on the dot, the clock tower bell rang out the hour and Desmond spoke through a megaphone he'd brought to rehearsal. "Let's get going. We start on time. We end on time.

That's my number one rule."

To Bay's surprise, every student hushed without delay. She'd heard Desmond was respected, and he knew these students from past plays. Many were seniors doing a final postgraduation show before entering the real world.

"For the first few rehearsals, we're going to need to work around the set builders and the tech crew setting up lights and testing sounds. This isn't a typical show. Summer theater is a shortened schedule, so we're putting an entire production together in short order." Desmond handed printed schedules to Bay, who passed them out to the actors and crew.

It wasn't quite June, thankfully, because performances were marked for the last week of that month, just past the celebration of Midsummer on June twenty-fourth.

"You'll notice on the schedule that all lines must be memorized by June tenth. That's two weeks, my friends. Let's make it happen." Desmond used his teacher voice. Even Bay snapped to attention.

"Places everyone. We'll start with the prologue and go straight through from act one as far as we can until eight-thirty. The script notes some introductory music, but we won't add that for a couple of weeks. Proceed, Kitt."

Bay and Desmond watched from the back third of the theater, taking notes as lines were delivered, stopping when necessary to help with enunciation or cadence. At the end of the second act, Desmond announced a seven-minute break, then headed to the tech booth to talk about lighting.

Bay noticed he seemed nervous about the tech crew being run by an intern. His normal production partner, Leo, another theater professor, was spending summer break in New York

City at a Broadway intensive master class. Leo recommended a theater grad student from Madison to take his place.

As lights flashed on and off in different positions, Bay watched the techies at the booth.

Desmond pointed at the script as intern Evan made notes, then flashed the light Desmond asked for. Bay noticed Evan's body posture: alert, attentive, like a golden retriever eager to please. In contrast, Desmond alternated running a hand through the twists on top of his head, placing his hands on his hips, then rubbing the back of his neck before repeating the moves again.

"That looks intense." Jen Yoo was sitting by Bay, a clean paint brush in one hand.

"Hey, Jen. Yes, I've never seen this side of Desmond. How about you?"

Jen shrugged. "I haven't worked on a summer production in some time. The younger Desmond was laid-back. But some of us lose our patience as we age. Thankfully, I don't have that problem." She snickered.

Bay turned her full attention to Jen. "Why are you working on this production, anyway?"

"Two reasons. One: It fulfills my volunteer hours for the whole year. Two: It's a show you wrote. I'm proud of you and want to see how it turns out." Jen leaned her head over to meet Bay's.

With break wrapping up, chatter from the stage echoed around the quiet outdoors.

When a commotion ensued, Bay chalked it up to high energy from a new show, the honeymoon period. But then a loud thud sounded, someone began shrieking, and a cacophony of shouts and running feet ensued.

Bay, Jen, and Desmond ran to the stage, with the tech crew close behind. The adults vaulted onto the stage where the lead actor, Talon Hunt, lay crumpled in a twisted heap.

"Everybody back up," Desmond shouted.

"He fell off the balcony," one of the students called out.

"I didn't mean to. We were goofing around, practicing a duel." Jackson Lange knelt over Talon, his chest heaving, his face distraught.

Desmond, Jen, and Bay knelt beside Talon too, and Jackson stood up and looked away. Desmond checked Talon's pulse, shook his head, listened for a heartbeat, and shook his head again. Bay called 911.

"Let's straighten him a bit so I can do CPR." Desmond motioned for Jen and Bay to get on either side of his legs and they gingerly turned him.

Desmond was still administering chest compressions and breaths when the emergency team arrived to take over. Thirty minutes later, the EMTs pronounced Talon dead. ✣

CHAPTER 2

With my sword I'll prove the lie thou speak'st.
~ MACBETH

The lead EMT motioned for Desmond to follow him to the ambulance. Minutes later, Desmond returned to the stage, his face ashen.

"What's next?" Jen asked.

"We wait for the police. The EMTs said it's protocol. Everyone needs to stay put until the police dismiss us." Desmond looked like he might cry.

Bay scooted closer and put an arm around his shoulder. "It's going to be okay. But we need to corral these kids."

Desmond, hands over his face, peered into his lap, rubbed his temples, and nodded. "Can you, please?"

Bay stood and faced the semicircle of onlookers, frozen in the moment. She could hear murmurs among some, but most appeared to be in shock. Here she was, the authority figure, the youngest of the three adults on stage.

"Everyone. Can you look up here, please?" She clapped her hands in the air, a sound that echoed like gunfire in the theater space.

Students raised their heads in alarm.

"Curses," Bay said under her breath. "Sorry about that. We need everyone to stay put. I'm sorry to tell you the police will be here soon and will need to speak with each of you about… the incident." She spoke haltingly, sometimes in search of the right word.

"What you're saying is we can't go home until the cops talk to us? Can we sit in the theater seats?" One student asked.

Bay wasn't sure if it was okay for the students to move about. Her recent participation at a crime scene still rocked her memory. It would be so easy for this scene to be contaminated between the actors and crew. *But this wasn't a crime scene. It was an accident.*

"Right, you can't leave until the police clear the scene. And I'm sorry, but let's just stay where we are until the police give us instructions. And please don't go near the—Talon." Bay hoped she sounded both sympathetic and commanding.

Two squads raised dust on the gravel road near the theater, red and blue beacons flashing, thankfully without sirens. Bay didn't recognize the two officers from the first squad, but her stomach seized when Detectives Downing and Harris emerged from the second.

The four walked as a unit toward the stage, spoke to the EMTs, then split up. One stayed to take statements from the EMTs while three climbed onto the stage to address the wary huddle.

"I'm Officer Moore. Let's get you all off the stage now. Before you move, step lightly and look around carefully. Don't pick anything up—even the smallest crumb could be evidence. Pay attention to your surroundings so you don't disturb marks or debris of any kind. Follow me, single file."

Officer Moore turned to face the line of students and pointed to the seats. "Sit down there with at least two seats between you and the next person. Don't talk to anyone. You will be called individually to speak with one of us."

He pointed to the other two men. "Detectives Downing and Harris will be talking to some of you. We all appreciate your honesty and cooperation."

After the officers supervised the students' movements, Moore nodded at Downing, who assigned him to Desmond with a wave. It was clear to Harris he'd be speaking to Jen when Downing stared down Bay, allowing a momentary smile to grace his face.

"Professor Browning. So soon?" Downing shook his head.

Bay arched one brow. "Seems like only yesterday, Detective." The crisp exchange was enough to break the ice and quiet her butterflies. "What do you need from me?"

Downing surveyed the scene. "What's your role here?"

"Assistant director. Desmond is the director. Jen is set director." Bay nodded toward each one as she spoke.

"Sit tight. I'm going to assess the vic, gather evidence there, then start talking to them." Downing waved a hand over the audience. "Blast it all, this is a big production. Just perfect." He grunted.

Harris stopped to say hello to Bay, then went to assist Downing. Moore garnered a copy of the cast list from Desmond and began interviewing them in order. Bay noticed the EMTs remained on the scene, standing outside the ambulance to watch the students.

Please let this be ruled an accident, was the sole thought in Bay's mind as she watched the detectives at work.

Soon the medical examiner arrived to attend the victim. Her face held a mixture of grim curiosity and care as she studied every detail of Talon Hunt's body. Bay remembered that she and Jen moved Talon's legs and decided it was important to say so.

"Excuse me," she stayed as far back as possible from the body. "I thought you should know that Professor Yoo and I untwisted Talon's legs to lay him face up so Desmond could perform CPR and resuscitation."

The ME raised her face to Bay's. "Show me how you found him, please. Can you lie on the stage over there in the same position?"

Bay complied, trying to mimic the crumpled version of Talon Hunt, lying on his side, legs sprawled away from his torso like a pair of bent scissors, one arm lodged beneath his left side, the other stretched outward to the right.

Downing snapped photos of Bay from every angle and the ME thanked her.

When she returned to the stage apron, Jen Yoo whispered, "Wow, that was weird. Did it feel weird, playing a dead body?"

Bay glared at her friend, a spirited individual who lived nearly filter-free. "Of course, it felt weird, Jen." She changed the subject by pointing at the two unfinished balconies.

"You helped design the set. What's the status of the balconies?"

Jen shrugged. "We've had a lot of help building the set

because of the short turnaround time. The actors helped, too. Anyone who knows how to use a drill, hammer, staple gun, or paint brush has been put to use. As far as I know, the balconies are framed up, but not reinforced with supports."

Bay scanned the structure. "Can someone stand up there safely?"

"Yes and no. The balcony can support some weight, probably not two people if they were moving around. Movement caused it to fail."

Both squinted to study the platform. The floor had held, but the side railing hung open like a gate.

"The students knew the balconies weren't finished. Everyone was told to stay on the stage floor," Jen added.

The detectives moved to the audience and called off two names, then took each student to another seating section to question them.

With four officers conducting interviews, Bay thought time would pass quickly, but she was wrong. They were about halfway through the thirty odd interviews when she heard the clock tower chime ten. She yawned and Jen followed suit. Desmond was sitting in his truck and appeared to be dozing off.

Jen shoved Bay's arm. "How come Desmond gets a comfy seat?" She pointed to the black truck with its driver's side door ajar.

Bay yawned again. "Maybe he asked. I'm sure one of the officers is babysitting Desmond's phone. That was probably the trade-off."

As if in response, Bay's phone alerted her to a text from Cass wondering where she was. Bay waved her phone in the air to get attention. Officer Moore motioned her over.

"Could I please call or text my sister to let her know where I am?"

Moore nodded. "Keep it short. Tell her you're still at rehearsal and there's been an accident, but you're okay."

Bay snorted. "I assure you, if I text that, my sister will be here with reinforcements. How about I write the text and show it to you before I send it."

Bay typed: *Rehearsal is running late. Problems with actors. Don't wait up. I'll fill you in later.*

Moore read the text and scrunched his lips to meet his nose. "You're just going to lie to her then? Well, okay. Go ahead and send it. She's not my sister." He held both hands in the air in surrender.

Moore took Bay's statement, moved on to Jen, but Downing interviewed Desmond, which took much longer. Desmond could offer further insights about the theater folk.

Another hour passed and interviews were wrapping up. The park was empty now, except for the adults, and a few remaining actors, including Jackson, who tussled with Talon on the balcony before he fell.

Downing interviewed Jackson again, while Harris spoke with Maya Leary, the props master and costume manager. In a small college production like this one, there would be an overlap in the people handling costumes and props, but why interview Maya again? Costumes and props didn't factor into the initial rehearsal.

Bay surveyed the remaining students and gasped when she spotted Aria, her boss's niece. Aria was a high school senior, one of those handpicked to help with the show. High schoolers with a connection to the college were allowed to apply for volunteer work at Flourish. Assistant Dean Stasia Andino was the boss of the three directors, and their relationship with her was complicated.

Downing brushed Bay's side and pointed toward Aria. "She looks familiar," he said.

Bay swallowed a nervous lump. "My boss's niece. You remember Dean Andino—Stasia? Her niece, Aria, helped with the Medusa investigation."

Downing remembered. "Ah, she works at the dry cleaners. Do you still take your clothes there?" He didn't miss a beat.

"Once you've had Giorgio's Tender Touch, you'll never go anywhere else." Bay quipped, referring to the name of the dry cleaning service all of Stasia's employees were expected to use.

Despite the situation, Downing chuckled. "Professor, you're with me. I think the young lady might be more open with you there when I question her."

Bay was happy to have something productive to do. Approaching Aria, Downing and Bay stood side by side. Her shoulders slumped, but she willingly stepped away to a nearby bench with the two.

"Hello, Aria. Do you remember me?" Bay asked.

"Duh-uh. I see you every month at the dry cleaners." Aria's salty retort made both adults grin.

"Yes. I'm sorry I didn't know you were helping with the show. What's your role, may I ask?" Bay's tone was polite and cautious.

"I'm helping with props and costumes. Organizing them, making sure they get to the proper actors, checking if any need repairs."

"It sounds like you know what you're doing, which is great, because once we're using them at rehearsals and performances there's a lot to keep track of." Bay hoped her message was a vote of confidence.

Aria beamed. Score one point.

"What about tonight, Aria? Did anyone use props tonight?" Downing took over.

"Nobody was supposed to mess with props tonight. Maya was going over props with me. We made notes on the script, so I would know which props were used for each scene and where to place them."

"And who is Maya?" Downing asked.

"The props master."

"Okay. Nobody was supposed to use props, as you said. But…" He prodded.

Aria's cheeks reddened and she looked at the ground. "Someone took a sword and fencing saber."

"Do you know where these items are now?"

Neither Aria's face nor posture changed. "Maya and I found the saber on the floor under the balcony, but we didn't touch it. We looked everywhere for the sword. It's disappeared."

"Did you see the person who had the sword, Aria?" Downing's voice was gentle.

"It was Jackson Lange. Maya and I heard Jackson and Talon stomping around on the balcony during break. They were playing at sword fighting. Talon used the fencing saber."

"Are you certain Jackson used the sword?" He moved his phone recorder closer to Aria.

"Jackson faced our direction. I'm sure." Aria lifted her face briefly.

Downing searched the teen's face. "Did you know Talon Hunt?"

Aria blushed as she shook her head. "Only by reputation. He's older than me."

Downing remained stone-faced. "What about Talon's reputation?" He considered illegal activity might be an option.

"Talon Hunt is a smooth guy. You know?" Met with the detective's blank expression, Aria looked to Bay for comprehension. "He's a hottie? Popular, always looking for a new conquest."

Bay nodded. "I think Aria's saying Talon is a player. Maybe goes from one conquest to another?"

Aria nodded. "Am I in trouble, and are you going to tell my aunt about this?"

Bay stared at Downing, arms crossed, hoping he would make Aria feel better.

"This isn't your fault, Aria. You know that, right? You and Maya were on break. If you're being honest with me, you have nothing to worry about. I may need to talk to you again though, but you're free to go now." He smiled in encouragement and handed her his card. "Call me if you think of anything else."

"Do you think Talon Hunt was killed with a prop sword?" Bay's voice shook.

Downing shrugged. "It's too early to tell. The ME thinks he broke both legs in the fall. He has an inflamed mark on his neck, close to his jugular."

"But there wasn't any wound, was there? I mean, he wasn't bleeding. The sword wasn't a real sword." Bay insisted.

"Probable internal bleeding. He hit his head. But he might have been dead before he hit the floor. We'll know more when the tox screen shows up." Downing pressed his index finger to his lips.

"I won't say anything. Don't worry." Bay assured him.

"Did you learn anything interesting from Jackson? He was the last person to see Talon alive." Bay's dramatic proclamation made her shiver.

The detective grimaced. "Nice one, Professor. Thought you'd catch me off guard. Let's talk soon. Maybe swap recipes or do each other's hair?" Downing broke into a burst of laughter and Bay joined in. ✿

CHAPTER 3

There where my fortune lives, there my life dies.
~ KING LEAR

Cass was sitting with her legs curled up underneath her bottom in Bay's favorite reading chair, writing in her plant journal, when she heard the door lock open with a snick.

"What kind of actor trouble did you mean in your text, Bay?"

Bay heaved a sigh and plopped onto the couch, grateful to accept the mug of tea Cass handed across to her. She lifted the cover to take a calming whiff of orange and lemon. On the first sip, she savored the honey Cass added, a blanket for her weary mind.

"About that? It was code for one of our actors fell from the balcony and died on stage tonight." She took a larger sip of the tea and let its warmth soothe her.

Cass appeared unfazed. "I knew something was amiss. I felt it when I was at Posey's house crafting party invitations." Cass had extraordinary perceptions that defied logical explanation,

31

a gift dispersed among the family, but not Bay. "What happened?"

Bay shared what she knew, which wasn't much.

"Detective Downing, huh? I don't imagine you had a chance to catch up at all."

Leave it to Cass to raise a personal issue. Since Bay worked with the detective on a murder case a few months back, she hadn't spent time with him. Although it seemed the door might be open for them to see each other, she wondered if the prospect was something she imagined.

"No, it wasn't the time to share a beer and talk about old times, Cass." Bay smirked, but the two sisters giggled.

Cass moved on. "Talon Hunt. I believe he's the son of Malcolm and Corrine Hunt." She silently perused her memory from time spent with Posey. "Exactly," she mumbled.

"Malcolm and Corrine Hunt?" Bay's curiosity was piqued.

Cass set down her pen and journal and sipped her tea. "They live on the bluff. I've met them once or twice. They were guests at Posey's Maypole social. I remember Corrine talking about an elaborate graduation party they were hosting for their son. Once Corrine circulated, she left, but Malcolm stayed until the end." In fact, Cass recalled that Posey and Malcolm spent the bulk of the evening together.

Bay didn't know which question to ask first. "Talon graduated in May. Many of the senior thespian club members auditioned for *Shakespeare's Couch* as a last hurrah. About the Maypole party. I'm picturing people half-dressed dancing in drunken revelry. Is that how the bluff dwellers live it up?"

Cass stuck out her tongue. "No, not quite. To be honest, I stayed in the background, observing. Posey likes to host a social soiree every month if she can pull it off. She loves flowers and folklore, so celebrating spring with Maypole dancing in the garden courtyard behind her house became a tradition. She lights contained fires all around and hires an ensemble to play Celtic music. It's a breathtaking sight."

Bay smiled at the picture that came to mind, then heaved a sigh. "I'd hate the job of telling the Hunts about Talon's death." Bay's stomach clenched.

Cass agreed. "The question is, was it horseplay or was it murder? Do you know the other student, Jackson?"

Bay waved one hand in a so-so gesture. "I had both Jackson and Talon in two of my courses. Neither of them majored in English. Jackson was a better writer and thinker than Talon. I got the impression Talon went through the motions of being a college student. He was arrogant, maybe even had a chip on his shoulder." Bay tried to recall specific examples but came up empty.

Cass flashed a grin. "Or maybe he just didn't like English courses. Not everyone's cup of tea, Lulu."

Bay took the empty tea mugs into the kitchen to rinse them out, then pulled the cast list out of her work bag and tacked it to the fridge with the hula dancer magnet Aunt Venus sent them from Hawaii.

"Did Talon have a major part in the show?" Cass saw her sister peering out from the pass-through between their kitchen and dining room. The apartment communal space was an expansive area that included a sunken living room below the entrance and dining area. The kitchen was partially walled in, but the pass-through was usually kept open.

"You could say that. He was The Bard himself and had lines

in nearly every scene," Bay bit her bottom lip. "Never fear. Like the scouts, Desmond and I were prepared for anything. Talon's understudy will assume the role."

Cass smiled. "You are the epitome of preparedness. Who's the understudy?"

Bay stopped, assaulted by a sudden memory. "Logan Thorne." She grabbed the countertop to steady herself.

Cass stood up and ran to the pass-through. "Are you okay?"

"I just remembered that Logan and Talon didn't like each other. Talon wouldn't run lines with him. He thought he was too talented to help Logan. And there was something else, too."

Bay came out the kitchen door and leaned against it to think. "They were rivals over the show's Juliet." She went back into the kitchen to take the cast list from the fridge and trotted over, waving it at Cass.

"Cher Devane. She took my Shakespeare course last fall. Smooth." Bay laughed to herself, recalling Aria's earlier words.

"What's funny?"

"Oh, something Aria said to Detective Downing. She called Talon Hunt smooth. It's like playing the field, but maybe with added entitlement." Bay frowned. There was no love lost between Cher and Bay. She reviewed the cast list, committing it to memory as if it might soon matter.

Cass snatched the list from Bay for possible name recognition. "Some of these are familiar to me from the Bluff Birds. That's what people who live in the real world call the bluff dwellers. I wouldn't be surprised if Cher is related to the Devanes from Posey's gatherings."

Bay switched tracks in her head. "Oh, I get it. Angel Bird Bluff is the official name of the place. So, Bluff Birds makes sense. Clever. Did you know the bluff is named for two of its famous founders—Augustus Bird and Colonel William Angell? Somewhere along the way, the Angel name lost its last letter l. I guess people associated the name with a winged angel."

Cass knew the history from working for Posey but was surprised to hear it from Bay.

Bay's smile concealed her smugness. "Before I interviewed for my post at Flourish, I read up on the history of Prairie Ridge and the college."

Bay was a precocious child and an overachiever. Thanks to dedicated tutors and her passion for learning, she began college at sixteen and earned her doctorate at twenty-three, making her the youngest Flourish College department chair at thirty.

"Of course you did. Well done, Lulu. Most people just shorten the name to Angel Bluff."

Flourish was a private college specializing in fine arts. Its founders included the old money Prairie Ridge citizens, many of whom occupied Angel Bird Bluff. Just miles down the road from the renowned University of Wisconsin, the community wanted something all its own that townsfolk could point to with pride. Bay wondered how the university reacted when some of its benefactors pulled their resources to build Flourish in 1925. But the Goliath university couldn't be too concerned and maybe viewed the college like a pesky little sister. Still, nobody wants to lose big money donors.

"Hey, did you hear me?" Cass snapped her fingers.

"Maybe you should call Detective Downing with your new information while it's still fresh," Cass smiled brightly, pleased with the notion.

Bay snorted. "I was thinking the same thing."

"Hello Bay." Downing sounded sleepy. *Did she wake him with her call?*

"Hello," she faltered. She became uncertain when he used her first name. "Detective, I thought of a couple things of interest."

Downing shook himself to be more alert. *Oh, this is a business call.* "Sure, go ahead."

Bay told him about the understudy. "Logan Thorne didn't get along with Talon. I'd say it was because of Talon's attitude, but still. Then there's Cher Devane. I think she was leading on the two of them."

"I see. She's your Juliet, isn't she? Cher Devane?" He said.

Bay was caught off guard. "Oh well, I guess you have a cast list and…"

"Desmond told me about the rivalry between Talon and Logan. Logan didn't mince words about his feelings either. He said he hated Talon, called him a 'priggish jackass', but stopped short of saying he didn't care Talon was dead."

"What's your take on Cher Devane?" Downing added.

"She was in my Shakespeare course. She spent the bulk of her time pretending not to be on her cell phone, flirted with the male students during class, and once she texted a breast pic to several people during an exam. I had to zero her exam and take it up with Stasia, and eventually the head dean. Cher was a numpty bugbear."

Bay remembered her annoyance at having to prove Cher's disruptive behavior. In the end, the head dean reprimanded

Cher but allowed her to take a makeup exam. Of course, she was distantly related to Simon Devane, the linguistics professor in Bay's department. That relationship may have been a factor, too.

"A numpty what?" Downing's loud chortle interrupted the memory. Bay laughed, too. "Basically, she was a stupid pain in my arse."

"Did you weigh in about casting Cher in the show?"

"It's a big show, Detective, and Cher is talented. Besides, she's primed to play the leads for two more years, so Desmond made the call." Bay vowed not to hang on to the Cher experience yet hoped she wouldn't be in any more of her courses.

"I guess I wasted your time. I should have figured you knew about Logan and Cher. I guess your main suspect is Jackson. He was the one sword fighting on the balcony with the victim." Bay wished she had a follow-up question about the case.

"Call me anytime you have information you think is important. You should…" Downing stammered.

"We should catch up sometime, maybe…" their sentences crisscrossed. "Okay, we'll talk soon," He spoke in the awkward silence. "Good night." ✿

CHAPTER 4

Foolery, sir, does walk about the orb like the sun;
it shines everywhere.

~ TWELFTH NIGHT

Bay and Cass were halfway through their morning yoga on the garden deck when Bay's cell sounded off for the third time. She opened her eyes, straightened her leg, and set her foot down on the mat to descend from tree pose. She glanced at Cass, who wore a serene expression.

"I guess my phone won't wait," she whispered, padding into the living room.

All three missed messages were from Desmond. She swiped his name in her contacts.

"Bay, listen. I need to talk to you. I think we better get on the same page with this Talon situation. Can you meet me at Sunrise Café for a quick bite?" Desmond's voice held panic.

Bay checked the time. "Half hour, okay?"

Cass stood at the open sliding glass door. "Detective Downing?" Bay couldn't decide if she approved of the lilt in her sister's voice or her dancing eyebrows.

"No. Desmond Carver. He sounds like a nervous wreck. I'm meeting him at Sunrise in thirty minutes."

Sunrise was a local favorite for breakfast. When Bay arrived, she found Desmond sitting with coffee in a front corner booth near the kitchen, away from other diners. He drummed his fingers on the Formica table while scrolling through his phone.

Bay slid in across from him. "Desmond, what's up?"

Desmond set the phone aside and raised worried eyes. "Talon Hunt's parents. They've got access to the best lawyers money can buy. I think they're going to sue the college, and that means we have a big problem."

"Whoa, back up. Why would his parents bring a suit?" Bay asked. "We told everyone twice to stay off the second story and away from the balconies. The students knew it wasn't safe."

Desmond ran one hand roughly through his dark hair twists, a gesture that was becoming his signature move. "I don't think making an announcement is enough to free us from liability. The college is expected to keep the safety of students its number one priority."

Bay paused to flag down a server. "Can I please get coffee and cream? And one of those multigrain raspberry muffins from the pastry case. Desmond, you should eat something."

"Yeah. Cinnamon oatmeal muffin please."

"Does that mean we shouldn't rehearse until the set is complete?" Bay wondered if Desmond had taken shortcuts in the past through the college policies concerning productions. Every campus event faced a time crunch.

Desmond shooed away the comment. "That's not what I'm saying. When push comes to shove, somebody has to take the fall for Talon's death. I doubt the deans are going to support us, Bay. They'll wring their hands, apologize, and offer the Hunts whatever they want."

Bay grimaced. "Our heads on a platter?"

Desmond nodded. "That's why we need to unite on this. Write an exact script of how last night went and stick to it."

Bay fidgeted in her seat. She wouldn't make up a story to save herself or Desmond. "Why don't we each write down in detail what we remember from the beginning of rehearsal until Talon fell. We can exchange them tonight and talk after practice."

Desmond's knitted brow and heavy frown spoke volumes. "That's not what I had in mind. Also, I'm trying to decide about cancelling practice."

Cancelling made sense to Bay. The cast and crew must be reeling from the shock of Talon's death, along with being delayed by the police for hours. "We should cancel, Desmond. It's the right thing to do."

The server brought Bay's coffee and refilled Desmond's mug. She also set two plates on the table with the warmed muffins and a dish of soft butter.

Bay wound her way back to the lawsuit topic. "Do you know Talon's parents? Have you spoken with them?" She wondered what brought on Desmond's paranoia.

Desmond blew out a long breath. "The Hunts are part of the old money crowd perched on Bird Bluff in a ridiculous monstrosity of a house. Talon was the baby of the family, their pride and joy."

"Sounds like you disagree," Bay said.

"Talon was a spoiled jerk. He was a frat boy, mean, conceited, and he used people. I heard he purchased his diploma through contributions his parents made to the college. I've known Talon since his freshman year, and I always hoped he would grow up. I guess I'll never know." Desmond stared at the coffee, lost in thought.

Bay let the silence hang while she broke off buttery chunks of the muffin and popped them into her mouth, savoring their sweetness. She stirred cream into the dark roast coffee and watched it create swirly designs on the surface.

Desmond resumed the conversation like a doll whose batteries had been replaced. "You know, there's plenty of people who won't miss Talon. He's made as many enemies as friends at Flourish." He crouched over the mug and spoke in a low tone.

"What are you saying? You think he was murdered?" Bay asked.

Desmond's mouth gaped. "I guess I buried the lead, no pun intended. I thought you'd heard. The police think Talon was murdered."

Bay swallowed hard. "What? Already? They couldn't possibly have those answers yet."

Desmond was scornful. "You don't know the Hunts or what money can buy. I bet they stood over the ME while she did the autopsy."

Bay scoffed. "You're not telling me anything specific, like cause of death. Why did the police bother contacting you?"

"A professional courtesy, so I'd have time to prepare for the tidal wave. Perfect timing. Just when the Universe seems to be raining down fire in my world." Desmond stared at the muffin as if it were a pile of ash.

Now we're getting somewhere. Bay remembered Desmond's pessimism and stressful manner from last night before Talon fell from the balcony. "What are you talking about?"

"My life. Nothing's going as planned." One hand paused its path through his hair twists, caught in a pair of beads.

Bay waited; her eyes never left his face.

"It's Claire. She's done with her graduate work and has a job offer."

Bay had met Claire at a few college events. She smiled with pleasure. "That's wonderful."

"Is it? A college in Ohio wants her. O-hi-o." Desmond gave every syllable its due.

The light dawned. "So, Claire will be moving. Are you going with her?"

Desmond nodded, shrugged, then shook his head. "I can't leave without a proper reason. I have tenure and free reign of the theater department. At least I did, until Talon Hunt died."

Desmond was distraught. Bay reached across the table and clasped both hands over his trembling ones.

"We're going to deal with Talon's parents and the college, come what may, Desmond. You're not going through this alone. Let's talk to Jen and Evan, too. They're both responsible adults in this production." Bay smiled in encouragement.

Desmond was grateful and squeezed both of Bay's hands, feeling some relief. And that's when Detective Downing walked up to the pastry case to pick up an order, pure astonishment covering his face as he witnessed the emotional tableau of Bay and Desmond, hands clasped across the table.

Bay let go of Desmond's hands in time to see Downing's retreating figure, at least the familiar gait and back of the man's head. Bay rose from the booth to excuse herself and follow him out the door.

When she recognized the detective's car, she called out to him. "Hey, Detective Downing!"

The man turned on his heels and met Bay's eyes with an accusation. She shrunk back momentarily, uncertain about his mood.

She moved forward as she spoke. "I heard your department is looking into Talon's death as a murder?" It was her turn to wield an accusation.

Downing motioned her closer to his vehicle.

"Shh. That's not public information. Did you hear that from your boyfriend?" Downing nodded toward the diner.

"Yes, and Desmond isn't my boyfriend. We're colleagues and directing the show together, remember?" Bay folded her arms, but a beguiling smile registered on her face. *Is the detective jealous?*

"Yeah, sure. You looked pretty cozy in there." He looked down, embarrassed. "What's your beef, Professor?"

"I'm just wondering why someone didn't contact me. My butt's on the line just as much as Desmond's is." She backed off. "How did the ME reach that conclusion so fast?"

Downing leaned against the car door after setting the bagged order on the hood. "The rich can move mountains, Bay. They know the ME. They publicly donate big money to the police department."

"Naturally. Can you tell me the cause of death?"

"It's pending the full report so I can't. I'll give you a heads-up, though. Your deans are calling a meeting today, and you'll be part of it. Be ready, because the Hunts will be there, running the show."

Bay sighed. "Will you be there? Or Harris?"

He shrugged. "I'm waiting for my orders." He kicked the asphalt with one boot keeping time with the small tick beating on his jawline.

"What about Jackson Lange? Is the investigation heating up against him?" Bay asked.

Downing laughed in derision, angry for being at the Hunts' beck and call.

"You talk like a character on a cop show. Seriously, anyone involved in the production is under investigation at the moment. Including you, Professor." He retrieved the bag from the hood and opened the car door.

Bay was smug. "Looks like you'll be busy." *Shakespeare's Couch* has fifteen cast members, plus the crew, and directors.

He hoisted the bag up like a trophy. "Brain food, a detective's best friend. Talk soon." ✤

CHAPTER 5

All the world's a stage...
And one man in his time plays many parts.
~ As You Like It

An hour later, Downing's warning proved true. Stasia called the four directors to inform them a required meeting would be held at one o'clock in Dean Pamela Foyt's office.

The four directors pledged to rendezvous at noon in the break room on the sixth floor near Desmond's office, away from their bosses. Desmond looked ill, while the other three wore a mixture of concern about the show's future and Flourish students, and annoyance that their futures may be dictated by the Hunts.

"Desmond, you need to get a grip," Jen Yoo admonished. "You act like someone with something to hide. Whatever happens, we'll deal with it. But we need to be calm and professional."

Bay agreed. "Let's keep our comments to a bare minimum. Answer questions with short responses. We can suggest ways to keep tabs on the students during the rest of production."

Evan, the graduate student, looked bewildered, as he nodded along with Jen and Bay.

Desmond was sullen and silent.

"Best feet forward, Desmond. All for one. One for all!" Jen mustered out the crème de la crème of clichés.

Desmond laughed and relaxed a bit. "Tally ho," he said weakly.

Dean Foyt's office occupied the back corner on the sunny side of the gray stone humanities building. The large office suggested stately authority and respect for the position, with floor to ceiling black shelving, gray hobnail wingback chairs, and paintings depicting the campus throughout its one-hundred-year history.

The four entered the dean's office, heads held high and surveyed the room. Dean Pamela Foyt looked polished and serene as usual, not a frosty hair out of place. Her steel gray power suit matched her demeanor. Behind the dark mahogany desk, she was at ease and in control.

Stasia, the assistant dean whose office occupied the same floor as Jen's and Bay's, sat beside the dean at one corner of the majestic desk. Stasia was a foot shorter than Pamela, so she sat as straight as possible, her chest and chin forward. Bay decided Stasia must be nervous despite wearing her game face, as she continued shuffling the papers on the dean's desk. And Stasia avoided making eye contact with the directors, not a good sign.

The Hunts were seated in two wingback chairs some distance from the dean's desk. Bay noticed both looked at the wall clock when the directors entered, as if to convey they were kept waiting, when in fact, the directors were a bit early.

A gulf of space separated the Hunts from the four chairs the directors would occupy after they made an uncomfortable walk past Talon's parents.

Dean Pamela wasted no time, beginning as soon as the four sat.

"Mr. and Mrs. Hunt, do you know all of our summer theater directors?" She didn't wait for their response, so she must know the answer from an earlier conversation with them before the four arrived.

Each director nodded when introduced but said nothing, choosing to see what the barometer registered once the real business began.

Pamela faced the directors. "I'm sure you're aware that Mr. and Mrs. Hunt are grieving over their loss and are here to discuss a reasonable way forward." She stopped to clear her throat and sip from the glass of water on her desk, an invitation to the directors to consider her words.

Mrs. Hunt used the vacancy to speak and directed her full attention on Pamela and Stasia. "Of course we're concerned for the safety of Flourish's students. It's come to our attention there are simply not enough adults for adequate supervision." The voice was clear and pointed, but quiet as if it came from a tinkling bell.

Inwardly, Bay objected. *These college students are adults, after all.*

Pamela acknowledged Mrs. Hunt with a simple nod. "I know our four directors are responsible professionals. However, it wouldn't hurt to have added adults involved in a production of this size."

Another pregnant pause ensued as the four held their collective breath, which allowed Desmond to dive in impulsively.

"Mr. and Mrs. Hunt, are you volunteering to assist with supervision during rehearsals?" Desmond's voice shook with tamped down irritation.

Malcolm Hunt shifted in his impeccable light gray suit, a perfect match for the office color scheme. "I, for one, certainly cannot spare the time to supervise a summer play." His voice dripped with disdain.

Mrs. Hunt still faced forward, her pale face made whiter by the soft yellow ensemble she wore. She looked fragile, as if turning her head might break her neck, or break her composure,

Bay mused. *How would I feel if my son just died? I wouldn't waste my time at this kind of meeting unless…*

Pamela searched Mrs. Hunt's face, waiting for her to weigh in. "Mrs. Hunt?"

The woman raised her eyes, as she ascended from a reverie. "Oh, that is not what my husband and I have in mind at all, Mr. Carver," the smooth controlled voice tinkled.

"Dr. Carver," Pamela addressed Desmond respectfully. "You remember Edison Hunt? He graduated a few years ago, but I believe he took part in our theater productions." Pamela paused for the statement to register.

Desmond couldn't conceal his disapproval. "Ah, yes. I believe so." Jen Yoo had settled one hand on Desmond's forearm to curtail his speech. She too, remembered Edison Hunt.

"Edison has graciously volunteered to join the summer

theater staff for the duration of the show. I know Malcolm and I will feel greater assurance with an extra adult overseeing the students." Corrine Hunt produced a semi-satisfied smile.

Corrine rose, signaling the meeting was over. "Thank you for seeing reason, Dean Foyt, Dean Andino." She nodded stiffly to both women. "We'll keep you abreast about plans for Talon's memorial service, won't we, Malcolm?"

Hunt grunted and entwined arms with his wife, then pivoted like a military sergeant, turning his back to the four directors. The couple left without a word to any of them.

Once the office door closed, Stasia and Pamela both blew out a sigh as their posture deflated.

Desmond went off like a firecracker. "Edison Hunt? You've got to be kidding me. That's what the Hunts wanted with this meeting? A job for deadbeat Edison!"

Bay and Evan looked at each other and shrugged, out of the loop on the subject.

Pamela regained her posture and waved a hand toward Desmond. "Please calm down, Desmond. The college is lucky the Hunts aren't suing us—yet. Giving Edison a summer job is apt to be just the beginning of their demands."

"Can you please enlighten Evan and me? We're not familiar with the Hunt family," Bay said.

Pamela stood, in need of movement after a day filled with meetings: first the police chief, then a lengthy session with the Hunts before this meeting. She circled to the front of her desk and stretched her back against it, then rocked forward, closer to the directors.

"Edison Hunt barely graduated from here. Let's just say that academics aren't for everyone. The Hunts are both from legacy families, so there was no question regarding Edison's admission, even though his high school grades were dire. Since graduation, his track record speaks for itself. He can't keep a position, even at his parents' companies."

Bay felt an emotional surge. "Are you telling us the Hunts are using Talon's death to secure a position for their older son?"

"So it seems," Pamela put it plainly.

Desmond prickled. "Having Edison at rehearsals makes one more kid to supervise. I wouldn't trust him to move stage furniture." Desmond rubbed his hand through his hair.

Pamela stood straighter, towering above the seated directors. "I trust the four of you will handle this situation. Or should I shut down the show altogether?" The dean was formidable, a burning ember that could ignite a fire if necessary.

Bay, Jen, and Evan turned to Desmond for the response. He was the lead director, after all.

"We've got this, agreed?" He looked left and right at his colleagues. They nodded emphatically.

"Does that mean we should continue rehearsing?" Desmond asked.

Pamela held up her hand. "About that. Because of time constraints, I had my assistant contact your students to cancel tonight's rehearsal. I'm sorry I had to take matters into my own hands, Desmond, but I wanted to show the Hunts that things were being managed. You can resume rehearsals tomorrow."

"Please see the set gets finished before tomorrow's rehearsal. Whatever it takes." Pamela added, "Oh, and I want all four of you to attend Talon's memorial, whenever it happens. We have to put on our best faces."

As the directors headed to the door, Stasia followed on their heels, tugging on Jen's sleeve.

"Jen, Bay," Stasia's voice was a loud urgent whisper. "Can we meet in my office? It won't take long."

How could they refuse?

Stasia's fifth-floor office sat on the north end of the building where the sun was largely blocked by columns of evergreens. Her office resembled a souvenir shop in a Grecian market with every type of knickknack advertising Stasia's pride in her heritage. If a visitor had any doubt, a blue and white tapestry featuring gods, goddesses, and the Greek alphabet occupied the wall behind her desk.

Stasia swayed behind the white desk and gestured for Bay and Jen to sit opposite her. She removed her modern black metal glasses and cleaned the lenses with a microfiber cloth from her desk drawer. The glasses replaced the oversized frames from a past decade and complimented her new softer hairdo.

Leaning forward, hands clasped on the desk blotter, she stared from Bay to Jen. "I would appreciate it if the two of you would quietly investigate this matter."

When the women blinked without responding, Stasia added, "As you did during the winter when that Medusa killer was stalking about."

Bay and Jen stared ahead, each waiting for the other to answer Stasia's odd request.

"Well," Bay said, "we'll keep our eyes open, Stasia. We don't know the cause of Talon's death, though."

Stasia bobbed her head. "Yes, yes. I know. But the college shouldn't suffer any negative publicity, and I know you two possess a talent for crime solving."

Bay's brows scrunched together. "Do you have information you care to share with us?"

She did not. "No, but before your meeting, Pamela and I met with the Hunts and Police Chief Sessions. The Hunts came down hard on the chief. They promised to make a spectacle of the police and the college if Talon's murderer isn't found lickety-split."

"Speaking of the Hunts, what can you two tell me about Edison?" Bay hadn't been at Flourish long enough to know him.

"I'm glad you mentioned Edison. The Hunts wish to hire you to tutor him, Bay," Stasia handed Bay Mr. and Mrs. Hunts' phone numbers.

Bay stared at the paper, mouth agape. "Excuse me, but why? Didn't he graduate?"

"He did, but he's applied to graduate school at the UW, and he needs to brush up on grammar and vocabulary to pass the entrance exam," Stasia said. "I'm certain they will pay top dollar for your services."

Jen couldn't believe it. "UW–Madison? Just how does Edison expect to get into grad school? He couldn't even earn an honest degree here."

"What do you mean?" Bay asked.

Jen gave Stasia a pointed look as if to say she owed it to Bay to level with her.

"Rumor has it Edison had an appetite for drugs as a teenager. He injured his head his senior year, and it appears he never recovered full cognitive function. The Hunts played the legacy card, though, so Flourish couldn't turn Edison away.

His grades were poor, well below average." Stasia stopped with the bare-bones version of the story.

"Flourish invented a degree for Edison. Music appreciation." Jen scoffed. "That was six years ago. Edison must be thirty now. How in the world will he get into the UW?"

Stasia pursed her lips and puffed out her cheeks. "Corrine Hunt's uncle is a retired provost at the university. I believe he's calling in a favor."

Bay folded her arms across her chest. "I understand a private college bending rules, but the UW? I just can't believe it."

Stasia nodded. "Will you please tutor the boy? He's going to need all the help he can get."

Bay placed the information in her purse. "This is about appeasing the Hunts, right? They seem comfortable throwing their weight around. The college. The medical examiner. The police department."

"Speaking of the police, what do they know so far about Talon's death, Bay?" Jen asked.

The remark annoyed Bay. "How should I know?"

Stasia caught on. "Oh, you're still friends with that handsome detective. Use him to help you and Jen," her head bobbed along in the affirmative.

Bay blew out an audible sigh. "I can try. I can't promise anything. But Jen and I will be watching."

"Ah good. Well, keep me informed. And Bay, thank you for protecting my niece." Stasia's glowing smile was on full display. "By the way, here's my cousin Nico's business card. He operates a food truck, makes superlative kebabs. I know he'll be happy to park by the ticket booth during performances."

Flourish employees in the humanities building could count on Stasia's expectations that they all patronize her family's business ventures. It seemed more of the extended family moved to the area from Chicago all the time. Cousin Nico was a new add-on to the family circus.

Outside Stasia's office, Bay pushed Jen down the hallway toward the art professor's corner office.

"What's up?" Jen asked.

"Ever since Desmond told me this morning that Talon was murdered, I've been replaying the scene of the students circled around Talon's body on stage. Can you sketch it out if I describe it to you?" Bay's penchant for remembering visual details had been part of her makeup, even in her childhood.

Jen brightened. "Just let me get a sketch pad and pencils." In January, Bay had relied on Jen's prowess about art history to help catch the Medusa, a crafty killer who left behind a trail of clues connected to art and mythology.

"This is exciting. Another puzzle to solve, and the dean wants us to investigate," Jen's enthusiasm for the macabre gave Bay pause.

"Apart from a student being murdered, I mean." Jen said. She fished a fresh sketch pad from a closet and sharpened two graphite pencils, a medium and a fine point, then settled into her chair with one pencil poised over the paper.

Bay closed her eyes in meditation, recalling the scene following Talon's fall. Students arrived from every direction since they were milling around the stage at the end of the break. She knew that Desmond, Jen, and herself climbed onto the stage about the same time, having proceeded from the same direction. She recalled the tech crew stood below the stage, watching from a distance.

Jen interrupted Bay's visualization. "It seems like you and Stasia are getting along well. I mean, you seem more at ease around her lately."

Bay cocked open one eye and puckered her lips. "Yes. I've had a change of heart toward Stasia. She's not the enemy, and I was wrong to see her that way."

"What brought that on?" Jen asked. "I thought our take on Stasia matched. The woman is such an opportunist. Now we need to add Cousin Nico's food truck to our list of places to patronize."

Bay opened both eyes in surrender and sat back into the chair. "I guess so. You have to admire the woman's nerve, though. After talking with her, I see her in a new light. For one thing, she's the glue holding the family together. Stasia is the oldest one living here, so the rest rely on her for support."

Jen's wide smile showed admiration. "Good for you, Bay. You're clearly a better person than me. I still quake at her fashion choices."

"Well, you are the fashion maven around here. I, for one, think she's brave to dress in those bold designs. She's unapologetic about who she is, and I'm trying to learn from it. Starting with the new nameplate on my office door." Bay checked for Jen's reaction, wondering if she'd noticed.

Jen scrunched her face and laughed. "I saw it. You eliminated the LL. You're just Bay now." She noticed her misstep. "I mean, that's great. You're comfortable in your own skin. It takes some of us decades to feel confident."

"Yes, one name's enough for anybody. I tore a page from your confidence handbook, Jen." Bay still tolerated her family using her Lulu nickname. "Let me get back into the zone now, please." She tapped the sketch paper to get Jen's attention then closed both eyes, sat up straight, and tried to connect with her mind's eye.

"The first person on the stage was Nora Stroud. I see her switching between shrieking and covering her mouth. Several students run to center stage, reacting to Nora's shrieks. Maya comes from backstage and stands under the balcony, looking around. Aria follows her but hangs back, uncertain or maybe afraid."

Bay stops to let Jen work. "Let me know when you're set."

Jen sketches with agility. "I'm placing figures around Nora, but you'll have to describe the ones I don't know, and I'll fill them in later. Okay. Go."

"I remember seeing Jackson. He must have run down from the balcony, because he was already there when we climbed onto the stage. He's horrified. He's kneeling beside Talon and checking for a pulse. He's sobbing and out of breath. I think he's sweating, too. I see perspiration on his forehead and arms."

Jen sketches it out. "Didn't Jackson call for help? Or was it Nora?"

"I think Jackson did. Nora was incoherent," Bay recalled. "Jackson's right arm has a red welt on it. Maybe Talon poked him with the saber."

"What else?" Jen asked.

"The three of us are kneeling around Talon. You and I are at his feet. Desmond gives chest compressions and breaths. I'm looking around the circle. A lot of shocked faces. Still scanning faces." Bay concentrated hard now, visualizing the students.

"Logan Thorne is standing on the edge, a bit apart from

the group. His arms are crossed, and he's looking directly at Talon, calm, almost smiling like he doesn't care." She inhaled a big breath. "Cher Devane. Similar to Logan. Except Cher is watching the bystanders, looking around, smug, like she just won something."

Bay stopped and opened her eyes to regain her composure as Jen sketched. Bay rubbed her temples, feeling a thimble full of pain pulsing between her eyes. She willed it away, so she could help Jen complete the stage picture.

Jen looked up. "You ready?"

Bay closed her eyes, breathed in and out to a count of six, and summoned the figures to materialize. The rehearsal would pick up at the third act, and now the actors filled in around the distraught Nora.

"Daniel is standing next to Nora, consoling her. Kitt is on the other side of Nora, also trying to calm her. Kitt holds Nora's hand. Robert is next to Kitt, glaring at Nora. He says something to her I can't hear but it seems sharp by the disgusted look on his face. Adam…"

"Hold on a sec and let me catch up," Jen said. "What about Adam?"

"Don't you remember? Adam thinks it's a joke. He kicks one of Talon's feet and calls his name aloud. Tamara buries her face into Rowan's shoulder as he strokes her hair. He seems to be in shock, too. Dylan is next to Rowan, his hands cup his face and partly cover his ears. He wears a pained expression, like someone punched him."

Jen finished the grouping. "Keep going."

Bay opened her eyes. "That's all. There must be people standing behind us. The tech crew never came on stage. Did you see any of the stagehands? The high schoolers?"

Jen shook her head. "It's all a blur. I can't get the vision of Desmond working nonstop between pounding Talon's chest and giving him breaths. It was awful."

"I understand. Let's look at the sketch together. So?" Bay turned the paper around then back again.

"If I were trying to pare down suspects, I'd start investigating Logan and Cher. They don't seem surprised or sad, and I wonder why." Jen stared at the figures she'd brought to life.

"Yes, but what about Adam acting like Talon is playing around?" Bay asked.

"Typical. If you know that trio. Jackson, Talon, and Adam were like pack leaders, always the life of the party, with a reputation as practical jokers." Jen said.

"Jackson can't be ruled out, though. The mark on his arm. The mark on Talon's neck. Maybe their fighting wasn't all pretend. And, the sword Jackson used is missing."

Jen held the sketch up. "Are you taking this to the detective?"

Bay considered. "I guess I should. But let's make a photocopy of it. Just in case we remember anything else. We should ask Desmond and Evan. Evan's said little to nothing since the incident."

Jen copied the sketch and handed it to Bay. She folded it, placed it in her purse, and bumped into the Hunts' phone numbers. "Ugh. I guess I'll call the Hunts to talk about tutoring their son. Which Hunt do you suggest I call? Mr. GQ who has no time to slum with the summer theater folk? Or Mrs. Arctic Freeze?"

CHAPTER 6

Well, whiles I am a beggar, I will rail and say there is no sin but to be rich; And being rich, my virtue then shall be to say there is no vice but beggary.

~ King John

Cassandra and Posey were finishing lunch al fresco on the eastern patio when Marva rushed in, whispered something to Posey, then began to clear away the crystal salad plates. Posey stood, wiped away a stray bit of berry balsamic dressing, and moved slowly toward the sliding doors. A buzzing arc surged through Cassandra's chest. Something was amiss.

"Who's here to see Posey?" Cass asked, startling Marva.

The housekeeper righted the tower of dishes she carried just in time and frowned at Cass. "Stop that, Miss Browning. It's not natural."

"Marva, I told you to call me Cassandra. Well, whoever is here, he's making Posey upset."

Marva focused on steadying the dishes and walking to the double doors. Cass followed.

"Here, let me get the door for you. I'll clear away the rest of lunch, Marva. You don't need to pick up after me." Cass didn't see the necessity of being waited on when she was perfectly able-bodied.

She collected the remnants of lunch: a crystal bowl with a smattering of field greens with strawberries, pecans, spring onions, radishes, and shaved carrot coins; a half-filled cruet of balsamic dressing; and a pitcher containing a splash of iced hibiscus tea.

Behind the double glass doors, Cass heard raised voices down the hallway, so she settled the armload on a decorative table and walked in the direction of the voices. Outside the library, Cass could hear Posey.

"What does she want this time, Anthony? I thought we'd reached an agreement." Posey's irritation was obvious.

"Nothing's changed, I'm afraid. You know there's no satisfying that one." A man spoke in a tired voice, but conveyed a familiar tone, as if he and Posey were well acquainted.

Posey's muffled reply included a few audible words. Something about the old stables. Cass imagined she heard a pen scratching across paper and paper being torn from a book. The man called Anthony replied with a groan, and the words Cass could hear didn't add clarity to the conversation. His footsteps were close to the door.

Cass scurried to the hall table, retrieved her armload, and scuttled toward the kitchen with the serving dishes. Marva glared when she bounced through the swinging door.

"Who is Anthony?" Cass asked.

Marva's scowl crossed her whole face now. "You may ask Posey that question. Hmph."

At Carillon Tower Park, the four directors found outlets for their frustrations after the meeting with the Hunts in the dean's office. Bay and Jen painted the set while Evan and Desmond finished the balconies and secured stage structures.

They seldom spoke, choosing to channel their feelings into hard work, so they barely noticed when a group of volunteers showed up with tools in hand until they climbed onto the stage.

Detective Downing and two officers in plain clothes approached Desmond to ask how they could help finish the set. Desmond showed them plans for two moving walls and pointed to the half-completed stairway he and Evan were building.

Some Flourish professors were behind the officers, toolboxes at the ready. Behind them, Bay recognized Mandy Harris, the new police officer who taught her self-defense at the cops- only hangout known as The Pig Squeal.

"Mandy, it's nice to see you." Bay slid the paintbrush into the water cup and greeted her.

"It's been too long, Bay. Call me anytime you want to get some sparring in." Mandy's dimples were a sly disguise for her fierceness. She could kick anyone's butt on the force, Bay imagined.

"Anyway, I'm great at painting. Just point the way."

Jen led Mandy to one of the black flats that would serve as the scene for act three of the show. The wall appeared blank, but on closer inspection, an outdoor scene of woods, fields, and the sea was outlined.

"How do you feel about landscapes, Mandy?" Jen smiled. "It's either this or the city scape flat." Jen pointed to stage left where another flat was leaning.

Mandy shrugged. "I'm kind of an outdoor gal myself."

Jen brought paints, brushes, and a jar of water over and wished Mandy good luck.

Bay groaned. Even with the extra hands, it was going to be a late night. But to her surprise, stage construction materialized in short order thanks to skilled helpers and power tools. Instead of leaving, the builders switched gears to help with the slower labor of painting the flats.

Downing claimed a spot near Bay, who was painting a library scene, the individual books beginning to blur before her eyes. He waited until she printed the last letter onto one spine, then nudged her, a big grin on his face.

She laughed, stifled a yawn, and bent to rinse her brush. Downing's hand met hers and he gently pulled the brush away.

"Let's trade. I'll paint books for a while. Maybe you can paint these arched windows." His hand lingered on Bay's fingers until she released the brush.

Her eyes rose to meet his as the world dissolved around her. Was she dazed from the stress of the past twenty-four hours or was she under Downing's spell? The detective leaned in closer. She could smell the scent of fresh washed linen mingled with wintergreen on his skin.

Bay closed her eyes but was jolted to reality by Jen Yoo.

"Hey look! Food!" Jen pointed behind the seating area where a food truck, painted in blue and white stripes like the Greek flag, pulled into view.

A young man with a dark beard and mustache flipped open the side of the truck, cranked out a striped awning, and called out through a speaker mounted to his roof. "Hello, I am Nico. Welcome to Ambrosia, my little food truck loaded with goodies for you. Come and get it!"

The stage emptied in a flash and soon everyone was indulging in pita bread, kebabs, hummus plates, falafel, and other Greek specialties. Stasia Andino knew the park would be busy with volunteers helping to finish the theater set and called Nico to show up to feed them, courtesy of the college.

Downing squatted next to Bay, using a pita wedge to scoop hummus, then settling cucumber slices and olives on top. He made a wedge for Bay and offered it to her with a smoldering smile. She laughed and gobbled it up, her physical hunger replacing his hold on her for now.

Dinner renewed the volunteers' spirits and gave them energy to surge ahead. Before dark, Desmond declared it was quitting time and clean up began. Most of the flats were painted to some degree, and the construction was completed. The tech crew hung all the stage lights, and the ladders were stowed away in the park utility shed.

Bay helped Jen cover the paints and carry them into the makeup room, which was just off stage and easy to access for finishing the painting details. Now that the electricity was working, Bay flicked on the light switch in the dark room and shifted makeup cases from the floor onto the vanities.

Something caught her eye, and she jumped, thinking the flash was a rodent of some kind. She moved the vanity away from the wall and gasped. Lying on the floor was a prop sword. She bent down for a closer look when Jen walked in.

"What are you doing?" she asked.

"Look at this. Could this be the missing prop sword that Jackson used?" Bay turned her cell phone screen light onto the object, as Jen crouched to pull it from its hiding place.

"No, don't touch it, Jen. I'll see if Downing is still here."

Bay glimpsed the detective near the tech booth talking to Desmond and called out. "Downing, can you come here please? We found something."

The detective hurried to the makeup room and squatted to view the space where Jen pointed. Bay handed him a paper towel from the countertop and he wrapped it around the hilt and pulled it out from behind the vanity.

"It looks like a prop. Do you think this is the sword Jackson used last night?" Downing looked at both women.

"I guess you should ask Maya or maybe Aria. They're in charge of props. Their contact info is on the paper Desmond gave you."

He nodded. "Stay here and watch this. I'll grab an evidence bag from my car."

When Downing returned to bag the prop sword, Bay handed him the drawing Jen had sketched that afternoon. "This is the scene following Talon's fall. What I remember anyway. You can see where everyone was standing."

He perused the sketch, noticed facial expressions, and postures. The name of each person was labeled over their head. "Who drew this? It's a dead ringer for a professional courtroom sketch."

Jen sat on one of the vanity stools and raised her hand. "I'll claim it. I drew while Bay dictated from memory. I'm afraid I couldn't recall the details Bay did. I guess I was too shocked to notice."

Downing thanked Jen, then turned to Bay. "Anything stand out about these characters?"

Bay pointed at two figures on the drawing. "Cher Devane and Logan Thorne didn't seem surprised about Talon's death. In fact, I'd say they radiated satisfaction." ✣

CHAPTER 7

I have no words. My voice is in my sword.
~ MACBETH

After being greeted by the housekeeper, Bay was led into the library to wait for Corrine Hunt. The property, Fox Hollow, was nestled in a cozy valley between two of the distinctive rock formations that formed Angel Bird Bluff. Bay peered at the lush woods that fronted the Fox Hollow estate, where she could imagine the Hunts and their neighbors outfitted in equestrian garb on the chase behind fox hounds, like a scene from a regency story.

Corrine glided into the library dressed in riding clothes, as if reading Bay's thoughts. The clacking black leather boots and riding crop made Bay sit up at attention. A young man trailed behind Corrine. If this was Edison, he achieved a younger than thirty look with his careless ripped jeans and well-worn T-shirt.

Corrine walked to an alcove to sit behind a polished ebony

desk and gestured for Bay to take a seat nearby. The young man remained standing beside Corrine, resentment etched on his face.

"Professor Browning, this is my son, Edison Hunt. I do appreciate you coming here for his lessons. As you can see, we are well equipped, and this environment is essential for Edison's progress." Corrine's velvety voice contrasted her steel composure. Bay noticed she grasped Edison's hand before she spoke and gave it a rough squeeze.

Bay's mouth was cotton and her tongue seemed to have doubled in size. She swallowed hard and a raspy voice emerged. "I look forward to getting acquainted with you, Edison." She addressed the man directly, avoiding Corrine's flinty stare.

Bay cleared her throat and turned to Corrine. "Since time is short, I suggest we begin immediately." She hoped she sounded professional, but not too eager. After all, she wasn't here by choice.

Corrine blinked twice. "Yes, I agree. You and I will work through your contract while my son changes into proper learning attire. Professor Browning will see you in ten minutes, Edison."

The dismissed man-child slunk away, shoulders drooped.

The corners of Corrine's mouth twitched, barely concealing her satisfaction. Bay signed the agreement to tutor Edison for four weeks, lessons geared toward passing the college entrance exam for a business management program. The pay was generous, but if Edison successfully passed the exam, a substantial bonus sweetened the deal.

Edison returned to the library dressed in casual slacks and a button-down, short-sleeved shirt. His light brown hair curled over his ears and collar, making him look boyish, and his pout added to it.

Corrine stood, seemingly primed to walk the red carpet at a gala. Bay wondered if the woman was a past beauty pageant queen; she glided with perfection. She nodded stiffly at Bay while placing a firm hand over Edison's balled up fist. There was that crushing squeeze again. Edison winced and pulled away. Corrine snapped the riding crop into the palm of her hand and guzzled air. Bay wondered if Corrine wanted to smack Edison or if she just needed to feel something apart from the pain of losing her other son.

When the library door closed, both Bay and Edison heaved a sigh and smiled in relief.

"To start with, I'd like to hear you read aloud from this book. The first two pages if you don't mind." Bay handed him Neil Gaiman's *American Gods* and opened it to chapter one.

Edison's eyes widened at the swear words that jumped from the sentences; he paused a moment then continued. He didn't stop until he finished three pages. Bay marveled at his oratory skills, thinking he possessed better stage presence than his brother had.

"Why did you want me to read this book?" he asked.

Bay hesitated. "My college students enjoy the book. It's an optional read in my mythology course and is a real hit with the male students. I think they can relate to it. Plus, it reads well out loud."

Edison sneered. "And you think I can relate to this? That my parents control me like a prisoner? That I know what it's like to hit rock bottom?"

Bay bristled. "No. I don't even know you or your family,

Edison. I would never presume…"

He laughed and slapped one hand on the library table. "Ha! I'm just kidding. But hey, I think I'd like to read this book. May I keep it for a while?"

Bay nodded, uncertain what to make of her pupil's mood swing. "Of course. I'll get it back from you at the end of our session. Now, let's move on. I want you to write an essay, five paragraphs in length, describing your goals for the graduate program you plan to study."

Bay handed him three pieces of lined paper and a black pen. She took a portable timer from her bag and placed it on the table in Edison's view. "You have thirty minutes as soon as the timer starts. Feel free to use one sheet of paper to brainstorm or outline your essay."

Edison's expression traveled from incredulity to defiance to sulky as Bay spoke. Since she never wavered from her instruction nor asked if he had questions, he succumbed. The timer ticked away several seconds, and Edison picked up his pen.

Time was about up when a ruckus ensued in the foyer outside the library. The housekeeper entered the room red-faced and flustered. "I'm sorry but you must leave at once, Professor."

Loud voices continued, then were muffled when the parties must have continued the fray in a closed room.

The housekeeper picked up the timer, stuffed it into Bay's tote bag, then tore the pen out of Edison's hand. She gathered the pages and shoved them at Bay, reiterating, "Please. You must leave. Now."

Like a butting goat, she pushed Bay toward the library door, through the foyer, and out the formal entrance, shutting the heavy double doors with a bang.

A bewildered Bay stood stock still. Had she heard Detective Downing's voice in the foyer? She gazed around the circle drive and noticed a squad car idling under the carport left of the circle. Downing must be in the house, conveying the autopsy results to Corrine and Malcolm Hunt.

She reached in her bag for her cell phone. Should she text Downing now asking him to call her later? That seemed presumptuous. It didn't matter, because all her digging turned up empty. "Bangers, my phone's in the library."

Bay sneaked toward the main entrance and peered into the front room windows where she glimpsed Downing with an unfamiliar officer, and Corrine. The three were standing poised for defense. This wasn't a friendly gathering.

She tried the double doors. Both were locked, so she skirted around the side where dappled willow and ninebark hugged the south walls. When she rounded the extra wings of the manor, she found a tiny back entrance with a carport large enough for a single vehicle where an older model compact car was parked. "Must be the housekeeper's car."

She tried the nondescript door, and it opened. She was in a mudroom with steps leading upward to a kitchen. She could smell food cooking, so encountering the housekeeper was a certainty.

Bay climbed the steps and looked around. She didn't see the housekeeper and the stovetop was empty, so there must be something in the oven. She took two or three tentative steps into a restaurant-sized kitchen, bright with shiny black tiles and white cabinetry, très chic.

Bay took the main hallway that she hoped would lead to the library but stopped near an open room when she heard Corrine Hunt. Corrine's words rooted Bay to the spot.

"Edison, look at me. Were you involved in this?" Corrine's voice rose word by word, then abruptly fell. "He's your brother, Edison. Your brother." Corrine sounded tearful but controlled.

Bay waited, but Edison didn't say anything. Where was Malcolm, she wondered? She held her breath, about to tiptoe into the room across the hall, but Corrine resumed, her words coated in acid.

"I swear Edison, if I hear that you were anywhere near that stage. Anywhere near that sword. Anywhere near campus that night, so help me…" Then something shattered and Bay didn't know who knocked over what, but she knew she needed to get out of that house.

Bay hugged the wall and crab-walked into the room across the way, which appeared to be an office. The room had a second door on the far wall and Bay prayed it led to the library or at least out.

The door opened onto a grand formal dining room, connected by a short hallway that led back to the kitchen. The dining room walls were glass, and she could see an atrium beyond them where she recognized the shrubs that lined the outer walls. At least she knew which direction to go now. Beyond the formal dining area she saw a hallway and a staircase. The hallway led to a set of impressive doors.

"If this were my house, those would open into my library," she said to nobody. She tried the handle, and the library swallowed her whole, dark, but inviting. She scampered to the desk, retrieved her cell phone and went to the opposite wall leading to the foyer. But someone was there, sitting in the darkness, staring at the cold fireplace.

She made it to the side door before a tiny whimper caused her to turn around.

"I didn't hurt my brother." The scratchy whisperer was Edison.

"I'm so sorry," Bay murmured, crept out the door, and scurried out the main entrance after unlocking the dead bolt. *If Edison was in the library, who was Corrine talking to in the other room? Or had she overheard a rehearsal?*

Either the late May sunshine or the Hunt house ordeal made Bay perspire, and she cranked the air conditioner as soon as she started the Land Rover. The circle driveway was empty and the idling squad car was gone, but she waited until she reached the end of the Fox Hollow property before tapping Downing's name on her cell phone contacts.

"Hello, Bay. Did I see your car at the Hunt's?" His tone was serious.

"Yes. I've been contracted to tutor Edison, so he can pass the UW–Madison entrance exam before fall. My turn for a question. What the blazes is going on with the Hunts?" Bay couldn't decide if she was more rattled by pathetic Edison or hellcat Corrine.

"Can you be more specific, Professor? Or should I just stick with no comment since this is a private matter?" Downing didn't waver or sound playful.

"I guess you left before the show was over," Bay breathed in some cool air to steady herself. "Corrine railed at Edison, then threatened him. Or maybe not. But I think she intends to do both."

Downing picked up a pen and paper on his end of the call, his brow a trough of confusion. "Back up, Bay. I don't understand."

Bay repeated what she heard Corrine say in one of the rooms, while discovering Edison in the library moments later. "Corrine used Edison's name. She acted like she was speaking to him, so maybe she was gearing up for it. Meanwhile, Edison looked like a lost child, huddled into himself on the library sofa."

"Talon Hunt died from an overdose of fentanyl, and there was fentanyl residue on the prop sword."

Bay heaved a sad sigh. "So that's the news you were delivering to the Hunts. I know how Corrine took it, but what about Malcolm?"

Downing hesitated. "I shouldn't be telling you anything, Bay. Malcolm wasn't home. He's away on business. Corrine's reaction was shock and denial. She said Talon never used drugs, but she also denied that Jackson could be involved in harming Talon."

Understanding began to dawn. "Jackson and Talon were like the dynamic duo, at least in my classes. Always joking around and playing off each other. I can't recall a time when I saw either one show animosity to the other. Drug use—who knows? Recreational drugs are common. Desmond knows the theater students much better than I do though."

"Did Logan or Cher have access to the prop sword?"

Bay wasn't surprised the detective had anticipated her plan to drill him for details. "I think anyone in the show had equal access to the props. But Maya runs a tight ship as props master, so maybe not. Don't forget that Logan was the understudy for

Talon's part. With Talon dead, Logan will take the lead role of The Bard. The highly coveted part."

"Noted. I've got a full plate here, so I need to run. Thanks for calling me." Downing was gone.

The Land Rover sat on a level shoulder south of the Hunt property, about to pull away. In the rearview mirror, Bay spotted two people on horseback trotting along the quiet roadway. As they loomed closer, she recognized Cher Devane and Nora Stroud, both summer theater cast members.

Cher reined her horse alongside Bay's window and peered down toward her. Bay obliged by lowering her window. "Hello Cher and Nora. Such beautiful horses." Bay's terse greeting was all she could muster.

Cher tossed her head back, a swish of blonde locks flowed over her shoulders. She laughed, a cackle. "Yes, my father is a champion breeder. I've been riding since I could walk. I'm surprised to see you on Angel Bluff. I thought you lived near the college." Cher's statement might have come from a seasoned prosecutor.

Bay bristled. "I have business. I'll let you continue your ride. I don't want to spook your horses." Bay raised the window, shutting out Cher, although she had no bone to pick with Nora.

Cher pulled too tightly on the reins, causing her horse to momentarily rear before she righted it again. Both forward feet landed with a thud and kicked up a cloud of dust that bathed the Land Rover. Bay resisted the urge to swear and confront Cher. Nora walked her horse past Bay's window, an apologetic look pasted on her face.

Bay waited for the two to gain distance before she drove away, crawling along Secret Spring Road behind the horses.

Finally, she saw Cher and Nora turn down a paved driveway at the corner of Secret Spring and Angel Bluff roads. Rising above the black iron gate, an ornate sign proclaimed Vanity Ridge: Devane Thoroughbreds. Perhaps it was time to know her enemy better. ✤

CHAPTER 8

*The web of our life is of a mingled yarn,
good and ill together.*
~ ALL'S WELL THAT ENDS WELL

Cass entered the back door of Spirit Gardens House to find Marva kneading dough as if offended by its existence. Each thump landed on the butcher board was accompanied by muttering, and she didn't notice Cass standing nearby, waiting for the storm to pass.

Cass interrupted the beating. "Marva, are you making hard rolls?"

All four and a half feet of Marva just missed hitting the polished kettles hanging from the overhead pot rack. "Lordy, you shouldn't sneak up on a person, Cassandra." She held one hand to her chest to still its pounding.

Cass laughed. "I'm sorry. You were engrossed in beating up that dough there. Is anything wrong?"

Marva examined the dough, which held a satin sheen despite the abuse. "Looks quite all right, I guess. I shouldn't say a word until you talk to Posey. She's on the phone with the Hunts." Marva raised a finger to her lips and crept to open the swinging kitchen door where she could hear better.

She shrugged and resumed cutting the dough into fist-sized balls. "I imagine she's in the study or greenhouse. I can't hear her at any rate."

Cass shrugged, too. "Do you want to talk about it?"

Marva greased the tops of the dough balls with a generous amount of cold butter. "The police were at the Hunts' home with news about Talon's death." Her voice dropped to a whisper. "Drug overdose."

"If Posey's on the phone with them now, how did you know about this?" Cass asked. "Oh, your sister called you." Cass jabbed a finger toward the woman, who stared at the countertop.

"Of course she did. Fanta and I tell each other everything."

Fanta was the housekeeper for the Hunt family the past few years, a post Posey helped her acquire after Fanta moved to Prairie Ridge.

"You and your sisters have your own network up here on the bluff. You all must keep the Birds on their toes," Cass giggled. She didn't like to use the word *servant*, but the staff on Angel Bluff reminded her of the historical novels she read where the wealthy nobility often forgot their servants had eyes and ears.

Marva frowned. "Never mind. We look after our families and each other." She huffed and strutted around the corner to the walk-in pantry.

Cass proceeded through the door and waited for Posey in the study. She didn't have to wait long.

Unlike Marva, Posey didn't appear a bit ruffled by the

Hunts' news, although Cass noticed her irregular gait, step, catch, step. Her disorder must be acting up today. Posey reached for Cass and held one hand.

"Good morning, Cassandra. I'm happy to see you. Before we proceed with party plans, I want you to reply to my emails and file this stack of papers over there." She pointed to the large wooden cabinet where tax, charitable foundation, and legal documents were locked away.

"But you've never had me answer your correspondence before, Posey," Cass faltered, surprising herself and her employer.

"It's time to go beyond the basics. You're capable and I trust you, so we will go through some emails and letters this week together, until you get the hang of it," Posey reassured her.

The two women read emails and responded in kind for an hour before Cass felt like a bubble about to burst. "Posey, I know about Talon Hunt. Marva looked vexed as a cat in the bathtub, so I made her tell me what was wrong. She said drug overdose?" It was an invitation to fill in the blanks.

"Yes. But it seems as if the drug in question—fentanyl—was on the prop sword that poked Talon at rehearsal. The Hunts never showed concern Talon was using drugs. Now Edison... maybe."

Posey opened an envelope from a law firm and slid it into a red file folder. Cass noticed her glowering expression and wondered how the contents of the file was related to Anthony McGann, Posey's visitor from the day before. Somehow, as her extra sensory gift dictated, she just knew.

"Who's Anthony McGann?"

Posey flushed pink and her eyes fluttered to the red folder.

"I suppose I shouldn't be surprised, knowing you have the gift of extra sensory perception," she said.

Cass half-frowned. "I overheard the two of you in the library yesterday. Nothing specific, but I know there's something there. It made me suspicious and well, nosey, I guess."

Posey looked tired now, as if she held the weight of the world in her hands. "I'm not feeling my finest today, Cassandra. A driver is coming to take me to therapy, and I'm going to rest now. Please make the phone calls on this list for me, send a floral arrangement to the Hunt family with my sincere sympathy, and schedule my next three therapy appointments."

Posey locked the red folder into the middle desk drawer and rose with great difficulty, wincing as she did so. She held onto the desk edge for support and pushed away Cassandra's offer to assist her.

"No need. The therapist is teaching me modifications for movement and pain. They're not going to help much if I don't practice using them." Posey glanced out the window and saw the driver pull up to the formal entrance. "I'll see you tomorrow. Poor Talon Hunt. I just received his thank you note yesterday for the graduation gift. Just imagine, he had his whole life in front of him."

Cass knew it was more than Posey's multiple sclerosis making her rigid. The mention of Anthony McGann and the contents of the red folder were partly to blame, and Cass knew her prying question added to Posey's woes. That, and she wondered about Posey's conversation with Talon's parents. Maybe Bay would have firsthand information about the Hunts. After all, she was there now, tutoring Edison, the wayward son.

Cass must have telegraphed her thoughts because her cell rang with Bay on the line.

"Bay, I'm glad you called. Are you still at the Hunt house?"

"No. I left right after the police did. I'm at the college doing research."

"Research? You're on summer break, remember? What's up?"

"A couple things. Talon Hunt's autopsy showed an overdose of fentanyl, and the prop sword had residue on it. That's not the worst though. Corrine seems to worry that Edison might be involved. I'm trying to look through the archives to find out anything I can on Edison."

"Yes, I heard about Talon, and I'm no help. Posey is mum on the subject, but I know she spoke with Malcolm and Corrine. At least, that's what Marva said."

"Hmm. Malcolm's out of town on business. Maybe she spoke with them separately? That's bad news about Posey. I was also hoping you could find out the scoop on the Devane family. I don't trust Cher, and I'd like to be armed with information, just in case."

Cass sighed; she wanted to be helpful. "Posey's not feeling well, so I doubt I'll get a chance to find out anything useful today. Maybe I'll pick Marva's brain instead." Cass's tone was devious.

"Speaking of Marva, how did she know about Talon's autopsy?"

"Fanta. Marva's sister. She's the Hunts' housekeeper."

An image of Fanta popped into Bay's head. Yes, the two shared resemblance in their short stature and curly hair. One long curly strand of Fanta's hair was dyed bright orange, and it framed one side of her face like a birthday ribbon. She couldn't form a clear picture of Marva but wondered if she also sported some color.

"Are you still there, Bay? Let's catch up at dinner." Cass disconnected.

―――――――――――――――

Bay and Cass ate dinner on the apartment deck, surrounded by pretty pots of flowers. A hummingbird zoomed in and out while they enjoyed chicken and grape salad on the Parker House rolls Marva sent home with Cass. The sisters started a weekly cooking ritual, so they made the salad together along with sautéed fresh peas and mushrooms, too.

"I hate to admit it, but I'm enjoying learning to cook. There's an art to it, and I appreciate your patience, Cass."

"It's fun teaching you. It's no surprise that you're a decent student. Changing the subject, did your research yield anything worthwhile?"

Bay set down the overstuffed roll. "I'm no computer hack. The best I could do was find Edison's transcript, since I'm faculty. He eked out passing grades every semester and was never placed on probation, even though his GPA was low enough. He earned a BA in music appreciation. Strange, because he's now trying to get into a business grad program."

"I guess I should talk to the faculty, but nobody's around at the moment. Desmond Carver's under pressure as head director, plus he's having relationship problems since his girlfriend was offered a post in Ohio. Jen Yoo only knows about Edison by proxy. She never had him in class."

Cass continued the conversation. "Marva wasn't in the mood to shed light on anything today. I think she follows

Posey's lead. If Posey has a bad day, so does Marva. Then again, I admire her loyalty."

Cass munched on a crispy pea pod and grinned. "I can't figure out why Cher enjoys tormenting you. I bet she's never been called out by any of her teachers before. You know, the Devanes moved here from Chicago." She flourished her fork in the air like a laser pointer. "She might resent small town life."

Bay stared at Cass. "I thought you didn't know anything about the Devanes. Spill the tea, Sister."

"Nothing buzzworthy. Cher's father is a horse breeder from Texas who met his wife at an equestrian conference. Mrs. is from Chicago and didn't want to live south of the Mason-Dixon, so Mr. landed a fancy position in Chicago with the help of his wife. Mrs. Devane's family runs an equestrian products company. After Cher's sister finished high school, her father found a defunct stable and property on Angel Bluff, and they relocated Cher's junior year."

"Oof. Nobody wants to move at that age. I can understand the resentment. Look at how much we were shuffled around between Dad's anthropology locations and Auntie Vee's places all over Chicago." Bay felt some empathy for Cher.

Cass remembered the time too well. As a teen, she'd often run away from wherever they called home and perfected her grifting skills. She wasn't proud of leaving Bay behind, and she sure wasn't proud of her descent into the company of criminals.

Bay reached across the table and took her sister's hand, clasped it with tenderness, a gesture that brought Cass back to the present with tingles and a trickle of tears. The two held hands and Cass felt Bay's forgiveness surge through her. Then the current broke as Cass pulled away.

"Whew, that was a little much, but thank you, Lulu." Cass was an unfinished creation, and still worried that rehabilitation had not quite won her over.

"I saw Cher riding today with Nora Stroud. They're both in the show. The horses were beauties. Do most of the Bluff Birds keep horses? I mean, they have space. In fact, Corrine Hunt was wearing riding clothes when we met this morning to go over my contract." Bay cringed remembering Corrine's snap of the riding crop against her palm.

"Maybe," Cass said. "I know Posey used to ride until the MS made it impossible. She sold her horses a couple of years ago. I guess her mother was an accomplished rider."

"I wonder if it's too late to learn horseback riding. Could be useful going undercover." Cass's eyes slid sideways slyly.

"Undercover? I doubt I could accomplish that in Prairie Ridge. The people I'm currently worried about all know who I am." Bay's shoulders slumped. "No, I need to find people who know these Birds better than I do." She giggled at her pun. "Speaking of birds, it's time for me to fly off to rehearsal. We're back on schedule."

Bay arrived to find the tech crew going through paces with Intern Evan. Desmond and Jen weren't around, so Bay opted to learn about the technical pieces of the production.

"Hey Evan. Can you show me the new tech notes for the show? I know Desmond's added a lot since he and I wrote the script."

Bay regretted the interruption seeing Evan's stressed expression.

"I'm running checks on the system before rehearsal starts. Maybe one of my crew can go through the notes with you. Any specific scene or act you want to review?"

Great, Evan thinks I'm here to check up on him. "No, just interested. That's all. Please continue. Sorry to interrupt." Bay smiled to offer encouragement.

Evan waved one of the tech crew over. "This is Henry Knight. He's a freshman at Flourish, and he's a quick study. Why don't you show Professor Browning your project?"

Henry pointed toward the stage, and they began walking. Bay noticed Henry still looked like a gangly middle schooler with youthful features. His too-long hair hung into his eyes and whooshed off to one side where a couple of cowlicks pitched upwards like random fence posts.

"Nice to meet you, Henry. Are you from Prairie Ridge or a transplant?"

Henry faltered and almost ran into the arm of a theater seat. "Transplant, sort of. My mother and I moved back about a year ago from Chicago. She wanted me to attend college here. You'll be meeting her. She's sewing the costumes."

Henry led Bay to mid stage and clicked the remote control he removed from his pocket. A piece of the stage floor lifted upward at a slant. Bay could see a ladder leading to the ground below the trap door.

"This is going to work well for people to come and go, especially the ghosts. Did you design this yourself?"

"I did. I like to tinker with electronics and stuff. In most scenes, the couch will be blocking the audience's view of the trap door, so actors can come and go without being noticed. We're putting a fog machine below the stage, too, so the trap door will raise letting in the fog for the ghost scene." Henry spoke with great pride.

"Will the actors be stuck there until the scene changes?"

"Come here, let me show you. Can you climb down?" Henry held out his hand for assistance.

Bay grimaced at the idea that thirty was too old to descend a ladder. "No, no. I've got it." Bay descended after Henry, who waited at the bottom with his cell phone on flashlight mode.

When she reached the ground, Henry shined the light upward and turned on a switch. Dim Christmas tree lights made a pathway under the stage leading to a narrow exit out the back. Bay applauded.

"Nice idea." The exit led straight to a tented area where the actors could gather unseen while they waited to go on stage. "Excellent work, Henry. In fact, the trap door will be a perfect device for Shakespeare to come and go. You know, he shows up as a surprise guest when the characters least expect it."

Henry nodded. His enthusiasm made his hair look like a twirling alien saucer. Bay wondered how he fit in at Flourish, which seemed to appeal to the affluent. Henry wasn't hoity-toity, that was certain.

Back on stage, Henry's smile faded when he saw Edison Hunt. Bay sat on the stage edge and watched Henry as he avoided Edison by trailing down the aisle furthest away, then going into the tech booth. Edison, meanwhile, stood gawking around the theater, hands in pockets, waiting for someone to give him orders.

Bay jumped from the stage and met him behind the last row of seats. "Hello Edison. How are you?"

"Fine, I guess. What am I supposed to be doing here?"

Edison glared at her.

Bay blinked and remained stone-faced. She understood this man was having some issues, but the jury was still out about her involvement with him. Being a paid tutor was one thing, being a true mentor was something else. She bit back a snippy retort. It wasn't up to her to figure out what Edison's job in the show would be.

"Well, let's ask Evan, he's the technical director."

Evan wasn't happy to see Edison either, and he didn't even know the guy. "Oh, blast it, I forgot about you." Evan sounded like he was talking to an unwanted stray that showed up out of the blue.

Bay spotted Desmond walking their way and she waved to get his attention. "Hey Desmond! Can we have a quick directors' meeting over here?"

Evan looked relieved and Edison skulked away from everyone and sat down, his legs draped over the seat ahead of him. He pulled his ball cap over his face and pretended to sleep.

"Oh great. Edison. I forgot we had to contend with him," Desmond exchanged scowls with Evan. "Ideas about something he can do?"

The three batted about suggestions, shooting each one down with fear Edison would screw something up.

"I think we should assign him to be the prompter. He can read, so he must be able to follow a script." Bay remembered the quality of Edison's reading vocals from yesterday.

Desmond frowned. Evan nodded, thankful he wouldn't have to be in charge of the guy. "I suppose we can try it out," Desmond relinquished. "Here you go, Bay. He's all yours." He handed her the prompting binder, which she pushed back in protest.

"Please, Bay. You're tutoring him anyway."

She took the binder and stuck out her tongue at Desmond.

By now, everyone else had arrived and hung out in clusters around and on the stage. Bay observed that nobody approached Edison, not even to offer their condolences. ✣

CHAPTER 9

Were it my cue to fight,
I should have known it without a prompter.

~ OTHELLO

Best foot forward, Bay gathered the cast and introduced Edison Hunt as their prompter during rehearsal. "Edison will be seated there, so just look at him and raise your hand so he knows to prompt your line." Bay pointed to the audience seating left of the stage.

She scrutinized their reactions. Cher and Logan glared, and so did Jackson, which made Bay wonder why Talon's closest buddy seemed to despise the brother. Adam chuckled and elbowed Jackson, who frowned and stared at the floor. The others looked straight-faced as far as Bay could tell, except maybe Maya, who looked a bit sad.

Bay stepped off the stage and sat beside Jen Yoo, who just arrived carrying a box.

"What's in the box?" Bay asked.

Jen rolled her eyes. "Just arrived from my mother. Look at

this garbage." Jen muttered something in Korean.

Bay peered into the box and guided her fingers along the spines of books, reading their titles one at a time. *"Dating and Waiting, Mom Life for Geriatrics, How to Cook Everything*— what's your mom trying to say, Jen?"

Jen blew a raspberry at her friend. "She's trying to say she supports my workout routine by sending me weights to haul to St. Vinny's. That's where this box is going," Jen fumed.

"Hey, how's it going with your pupil?" Jen indicated Edison.

"Undecided. It's only been one session. I had him read aloud and he's gifted. He could be on stage, maybe a politician. Our writing lesson was interrupted when Downing arrived with the autopsy report. The housekeeper tossed me out like a bad penny. Which reminds me…"

Bay reached into her tote bag and pulled out the folder with Edison's essay inside. "I better review this before tomorrow morning." She flashed the paper toward Jen. "A sample of Edison's writing."

"Never mind that. What did the autopsy show?"

"Fentanyl overdose and there was residue on the prop sword. So, I'm glad we didn't touch it."

Jen gasped. "So, Talon was murdered?"

"It looks that way. It was the only drug in his system. And get this, I think his mother suspects Edison was involved."

Jen dug her fingers into Bay's arm. "You better be careful around him, Bay. You're already a killer magnet." Jen's reference to the serial killer Medusa, who targeted Bay last winter, wasn't easy to dismiss.

"Stating the obvious, we're surrounded by suspects, Jen. We both need to keep our eyes and ears open."

Jen shuddered. "You're right. Anybody at the top of your list?"

Bay shrugged. "I'm not getting warm fuzzies around Cher Devane. But that's nothing new for me."

The conversation ended abruptly when a scuffle flared on stage. The scene in progress featured Shakespeare's tricksters at a picnic conversing about their favorite pranks and arguing who was the champion trickster Shakespeare ever created.

Jackson played Puck, the prince of mischief among the *Midsummer Night's Dream* fairy kingdom. In the scene, Puck argues with Ariel, a spirit enslaved by Prospero in *The Tempest*, played by Kitt. The climax is a magical duel between the two fairy figures. It's up to Logan, The Bard, to settle the duel. The Bard proclaims Ariel is the best because he has mastered poetic speaking. Of course, Shakespeare values words over actions. Puck's response is to turn Shakespeare into an ass, much as Puck does to Nick Bottom in the *Midsummer* play.

Bay and Jen didn't know where the scene went wrong, but Edison was pushing apart Jackson and Logan while Cher shouted expletives at Logan, and Kitt looked ready to cry. Since Cher wasn't in the scene, it was a mystery why she'd inserted herself in the ruckus.

Nora, who was in the scene, plopped on the couch, arms crossed, staring daggers at Cher.

Desmond leapt onto the stage with Bay and Jen.

"Stop it, now." Desmond was graced with the vocals of James Earl Jones. "Jackson, sit over there. Logan, over there." He pointed in opposite directions. "And Cher, go back wherever you came from." He ran his hand over his twisted locks.

Desmond glared at them. "Logan, what's the deal?"

"Jackson's an ass. He jammed this thing on my head too hard. On purpose. Look at my ear." Logan was still holding the donkey head piece, but pointed to his ear, which was scraped and flaming red.

Desmond turned. "Jackson, what gives, man?"

Jackson sneered, hot under the collar. "Talon was my best bud, and this idiot killed him." He pointed at Logan.

A cacophony of voices erupted. Desmond blew a shrill full-throated whistle. "Enough of this."

Bay placed her hand on Desmond's arm. "What proof do you have, Jackson?" She couldn't bear to use the word *murdered.*

Jackson sputtered. "Everyone knows they were rivals. He wanted Talon's part in the show. He could care less that Talon's dead." He gained confidence as the accusations continued. "I know the police think he did it."

Logan lunged forward, but Desmond blocked his path. "You don't want to do this."

"I didn't kill Talon." Logan stared daggers at everyone on the stage, eyes pleading.

"You're crazy if you think I'd kill someone for a show."

When his gaze reached Cher, she flinched and drew back a step. Kitt grabbed her elbow, afraid she might swoon, and steadied her.

"We don't know what you're capable of, Logan," Cher spewed through gritted teeth.

Logan sneered back at Cher, his face a mask of anger and anxiety. "I wonder what the cops think you're capable of, Cher." He stomped offstage, disappearing behind the curtain.

Now several people looked at Cher Devane with new eyes.

Bay could tell what they were thinking: Cher was a suspect. What did that mean? Bay imagined Cher's peers knew she behaved like a spoiled diva, but could she kill someone? Bay wished she could question them, but they were students, at least until the play's final curtain.

Desmond broke the spell with loud clapping. "Let's move on to a new scene. Unless you all want to scrap the show?"

The murmurs suggested the students did not.

"Okay. Let's see. Go to act two. I need Prospero, Miranda, Fernando, and Caliban. Stat!" He hopped off the stage and sat behind Edison. "Did you find it in the script?" Desmond asked him and Edison nodded.

Act two was all about family life, the good, the bad, and the dysfunctional. The act opened with King Lear and his daughters, fighting over their inheritance and accusing their father of being mad, but since Cher and Jackson played Lear and Goneril, Desmond wisely opted to begin in the middle, with characters from *The Tempest*; Prospero, the power-mongering magician; his innocent daughter Miranda; the handsome love interest, Fernando; and Caliban, a native islander lusting after Miranda but kept in a cage.

"I'm not sure which makes for better theater, Jen. Shakespeare's characters or Flourish College's." Bay's delivery was lighthearted, but inside, she wondered if the show would survive. ✀

CHAPTER 10

Who shall be true to us,
when we are so unsecret to ourselves?

~ Troilus and Cressida

"Good morning, Cassandra. I have a special project for us to work on if you'll agree to help me."

Cass found Posey sitting in the sunroom with her eyes closed; an Arnold Palmer sat on the low table beside her. Today's Posey was quite different from the bedraggled, suffering Posey of the day before, and Cass couldn't wait to find out why.

"You're in good spirits this morning. Are you feeling better?"

Posey smiled and patted the sofa's floral cushion. "Yes, I spent much of the day shifting from electromagnet treatment to massage, to meditation, to behavior therapy, and I'm working on my outlook on life."

Cass accepted the invitation to sit and laid her hand over Posey's. Warmth instantly spread between the two women. "Happy to hear it. Speaking of outlook, I left a Sweet Cheeks box in the kitchen with Marva." Cass knew that both Posey and the housekeeper were obsessed with the tasty macarons from the local bakery, and she hoped to cheer up Posey with the offering.

Posey's face lit up. "I hope they'll be safe in there until lunch," she teased. "Thank you. That was thoughtful."

"You know Posey, since we've met, I've always believed our relationship works when we're both being honest. You know it isn't easy for me to trust someone, but I trust you. And I admire you." Cass felt a sudden electrical jolt surge from Posey's fingers to hers and she yanked her hand away.

Posey crinkled her nose and brows. "What just happened?"

Cass lost her luster for a moment. "I know you're keeping something from me. Something that's tormenting you."

Posey's eyes darkened and she moved closer to Cass. "I admire you too and appreciate how honest you've been with me about your past. But there are some skeletons not worth rattling. At least, not now." She patted Cass's knee and smiled.

"On the subject of skeletons, I would like your help going through my closets. It's time to donate some items for the mission summer rummage sale. Would you mind?"

She clapped her hands in delight. "That sounds like a dream come true. I adore going through other people's stuff." She set aside her worry about Posey to embrace the project.

On the second floor, Posey led Cass into the bedroom her mother used to occupy. The walk-in closet extended an entire wall and was stuffed with costumes and custom-made clothing. Posey sat on an overstuffed chair while Cass brought out items and laid them across the bed for Posey's assessment.

Renaissance fair laced-up dresses, bustiers, hair wreaths,

slippers, and tall button-style boots were stacked on the plush carpeting against one wall. Posey figured they might be useful for the upcoming Shakespeare character party, where her guests could borrow from her stash. Cass was surprised to find men's costumes in the mix. She giggled, holding up a pair of royal blue brocade breeches complete with an ornate boxy codpiece.

"Whoever said a man purse is something new, never explored one of these," Cass gave the codpiece a playful squeeze and opened it. "You could fit a handgun and a snack in here and still have room for the manly equipment it was designed to cover."

Posey burst out laughing. "I imagine a huge entourage of Shakespeare characters wearing those. This party is going to be a hit."

Assorted Halloween-themed costumes formed a new stack after the witch, fairy, and wizard garb was moved into the Shakespeare pile. Christmas and New Year's outfits were next, and Posey chose some items to donate to the sale, stashing them in a corner of the room.

"Before we continue, let me go through the Halloween costumes and make some donations. Nobody needs this many outfits, do they?" Posey moved to a chair near the assortment of goblins, celebrities, French maids, vampires, and various creatures from the animal kingdom. Cass's favorite was a flamboyant peacock ensemble.

"Whatever you do, never give away the peacock. It's stunning. You should wear it to the Shakespeare party. There must have been a peacock in one of his plays."

While Posey sorted items, Cass perused the final rack in

the closet, a variety of clothes for horseback riding, tennis, golf, sailing, and even snow skiing. "Are these costumes or real-world clothes?" Cass stood by Posey, a pair of fawn-colored breeches and black competition jacket in one hand and a nautical jumpsuit in red, white, and navy in the other.

Posey looked up, a wistful expression on her face. She leaned into the nautical jumpsuit and fingered the stiff white off-the-shoulder collar and anchor buttons on the waist. Cass noticed tears forming in Posey's eyes and wondered what memories the jumpsuit held.

"My father bought this for my mother. They planned a sailing trip together, but it never came to pass. He loved this jumpsuit and hoped I would wear it one day, but I never have."

"Why not? I think it would make you feel closer to her, wearing something of hers."

Posey inhaled the fabric and sighed. "It smells like her. Honeysuckle and mango. I'm afraid if I wear it, her scent will disappear."

Cass understood. "My dad still has a bottle of my mother's signature perfume. After she died, he bought every bottle he could find. He spritzes a little on his pillow every night."

"Anyway, the jumpsuit is such a fun piece. I can see you out on a sailboat, your face in the wind. What about these riding clothes? Do you miss riding?" Cass knew she was treading into the past, a murky messy place, but what good were unspoken memories?

Posey looked far away. "I miss my horse, Dorado. When we rode together, we were like one being. We understood each other. But once he died, it was hard to ride again. Five months later, I was diagnosed with MS, a sign I think to close the stables permanently."

"What happened to your horses?" Cass asked.

Posey was still somewhere else. "Malcolm Hunt bought them. By that time, I had two left. Sweet quarter horse sisters; Flora and Fauna." Her reflective look disappeared. "Do you ride, Cassandra? If you do, you may borrow any of these riding clothes. I was thinner then and I'm sure they'd fit you."

Cass paused to consider; a devious idea forming in her head. "Maybe. I know how to ride. Would the Hunts let me take one of your horses for a spin?"

Loud footsteps sounded on the stairs mingled with Marva's scolding voice, interrupting the conversation. "Excuse me but you cannot just barge in…" but Marva's attempts to waylay the intruder were useless.

Kelly Weber, Cass's parole officer, loomed large in the entrance, wearing a determined expression. Marva tried to squeeze in beside the officer while Posey presented a tiny smile and Cass looked mortified.

"It's all right Marva. Officer Weber is welcome here." Posey settled the matter, and Marva left in a huff, muttering.

"Thank you, Ms. Hollingsworth. I'm just checking in on my charge here." She gestured toward Cass with a meaty thumb. Kelly Weber was a no-nonsense officer, gruff on the surface, but fair and supportive underneath.

"Hello Officer. I'm surprised to see you. You were just at the apartment, what—last week?"

Kelly crossed her arms over her chest. "Is that so? You know how this works by now. My checkups are supposed to be a surprise. I stopped in to talk to your employer." Kelly turned toward Posey. "Ms. Hollingsworth, I want you to know that

Cassandra is keeping up with all of her requirements. In fact, if she continues to act responsibly, I may recommend an early release." Kelly bit the insides of her cheek to maintain her stern composure, while Posey nodded and did the same.

Kelly assessed the mountains of clothing littering the bedroom. "I'll let you get back to whatever the Sam Hill is happening here." She spun on her heels and left.

With Posey's blessing and a flurry of giggles, Cass drove from Spirit Gardens to Fox Hollow, a leather satchel filled with party invitations. When Fanta opened the back door, she jumped backward, her mouth open in shock.

Cass was unrecognizable dressed like a nineteenth-century footman in silk stockings, breeches, and a fancy coat. The look was completed with a top hat and powdered wig. She held out one hand to Fanta with the Hunts' invitation, then bowed with a flourish.

"An invitation for Mr. and Mrs. Hunt to a Shakespeare party celebrating Midsummer, hosted by Posey Hollingsworth on Sunday, June twenty-second." Cass disguised her voice with a British accent.

Fanta blinked and stared at the cream envelope embossed with a butterfly, Posey's seal. "Is that you, Miss Cassandra?" She moved closer to Cass's face and squinted to examine it.

Cass chortled. "Well done, Fanta. Posey thought hand delivering the invitations would be an authentic touch, but I wonder if you can help me to make the experience even better?"

Fanta tucked the bright orange strand of hair over her ear. "What is it you want?"

"I wonder if I might borrow one of the horses to ride around the neighborhood. I understand Posey's two horses live here now." Cass leaned in closer to the small woman.

Fanta faltered. "Well, I'm not sure. I think we better check with either Mr. or Mrs. Hunt. Wait here."

Fanta returned minutes later and motioned Cass to follow her. The Hunts were having a late breakfast in the solarium and appeared to be reviewing some papers. Both wore casual clothes, dressed for a golf outing, Cass guessed.

Corrine's impassive expression didn't alter when she raised her eyes to take in Cass, but Malcolm looked amused.

"To what do we owe the pleasure, Ms. Browning?" Malcolm asked.

"Thank you for seeing me," Cassandra cast her eyes downward, prepared to kowtow to these two if need be. "I'd like to borrow one of your horses, if I may, so that I might accomplish delivering my satchel of invitations for Lady Hollingsworth, my good sir and madam." Cass was talented at vocals, and she was a natural at the English servant accent.

"Oh, for heaven's sake, what is all this?" Cass's performance had nicked Corrine's composure.

"My apologies, Mrs. Hunt. Ms. Hollingsworth is excited about her upcoming costume party, but I understand what a sensitive time this is for your family." The anticipation of the party caused Cass to forget about Talon's death for a moment.

Corrine raised her teacup to her lips. "Do you, honestly? I wonder. Of course, Posey would put you up to this. It's like her to ignore protocol."

Malcolm cut off his wife to avoid a scene. "Never mind, Ms. Browning. Let me take you to the stables where you may choose a horse. It's a clever idea." He offered Cass his arm.

"I'll be back soon, Darling, and we can finish the paperwork," he said to the sneering Corrine.

"Make it quick. We must leave for the country club soon." The controlled Mrs. Hunt was back in form.

Soon Cass was trotting around Angel Bluff, delivering Posey's invitations to the enjoyment of the residents. She was pleased to ride a horse again, grateful for one as lovely and gentle as the golden-cream mare, Fauna.

A dash of guilt flared inside Cass, knowing her purpose in making the deliveries was to observe and gather tidbits of information about the Bluff Bird families involved in Bay's Shakespeare production.

Her satchel was almost empty, and she hadn't accomplished much in the way of espionage, until she rode up to Vanity Ridge in the middle of a dustup between Cher Devane and Nora Stroud.

Each young woman walked a horse toward the stables, facing away from Cass, but their sideways exchanges were easy to hear.

"Honestly Cher, I think it's mean of you to lead on guys the way you do. It's just a game to you." Nora kicked a piece of stone on the path.

"It's none of your business. I don't know why I let my dad talk me into hanging out with you. It's a waste of time." Cher lifted her chin and spat the words without any thought.

Nora walked ahead of her, urging the horse forward. "Don't worry. I'll just put away Bunny and you won't be seeing me again."

"Ha, that's a laugh. We're stuck in this stupid show together for weeks." Cher called at Nora's back.

Nora kept walking.

Cass tucked herself and Fauna behind a tall stand of arborvitae. A surge of adrenaline coursed through her blood. Hiding in the shadows, spying on people, bathed her in familiar comfort. Some people cuddled puppies; Cass cuddled danger.

She saw Cher dash forward to catch up to Nora but couldn't hear them. She could read their body language though, and it gave her pause. Cass waited for them to take the sloping path that led to the stables below before she sent Fauna walking again to the back door of the Devane house. She presented the invitation to Sage, the third sister of Marva and Fanta, a trio of housekeepers to Bluff Birds.

"You look so funny, Cassandra," Sage burst out laughing. She was the youngest sister and didn't follow many of the unspoken rules applicable to staff. "Maybe you should visit the stables, so the Devanes can see you."

"No, I don't think so. I just saw Cher and Nora Stroud arguing. It looked quite dramatic." Cass gave Sage space to comment.

"They've been riding together every day. Mr. Devane pays Nora so the horses get exercised, but she and Cher are not close friends."

"I wonder why. They're the same age, go to the same school..." Cass tossed out more bait.

"Nora used to be close friends with the Kingsleys: The family that lived here before the Devanes. Cher isn't the nicest person. That girl has a mouth on her." Sage puffed her cheeks out and wagged her head in four directions to make her point.

"Of course, I won't take what she dishes out, so she doesn't give me any attitude. You should see the way she talks to her parents though..."

Cass excused herself to make her final delivery, about a mile ride to the outskirts of Prairie Ridge at the law firm of Anthony McGann. This time, she hoped to solicit details from the attorney to understand his relationship with Posey.

Now there was a second confounding mystery to solve. Two invitations would be left with Attorney McGann, one for him and one that bore the initials J.S. Cass was curious to know who J.S. was. A relative? A secret lover? The person causing Posey so much grief?

The offices of McGann, Crick, and Crooks occupied a converted stone Greek Revival house. Cass knew there wouldn't be a place to park her lively steed, but she didn't have to worry.

The office receptionist, a middle-aged woman dressed for casual Friday, hopped down the front steps to meet her.

"Are you taking part in a reenactment? They do those in the summer by the riverwalk, but you're the first one I've seen today."

Cass laughed. "No, I'm dressed up to deliver invitations for Posey Hollingsworth's Shakespeare costume party. We thought this would make it authentic." Cass pointed to the horse and her outfit. By now, the sun endeavored to roast her, and she was happy to near the end of the trail.

"Oh, I see. You must be hot and your horse, too. Let me get you both some water. Are you here to see Mr. McGann?"

Cass nodded.

"I'll send him out."

The receptionist returned with a filled water dish and large iced water for Cass. Both horse and rider drained their containers. The receptionist went back for more.

Anthony McGann grinned ear to ear when he saw Cass. "I see Posey is up to her old tricks again," he chuckled. Cass didn't mention the idea was hers.

"I don't think we've met. I'm Cassandra, Posey's personal assistant."

"Ah, the indispensable Cassandra I've heard so much about. It's good to meet you. I understand you didn't attend Posey's recent affair."

Cass spent most of the Maypole party hiding around the garden, observing and assessing. She didn't mingle with the guests and left early to help Bay get their half sister, Diana, settled into Barrett Browning's apartment.

"Right. Family business. But here, I have two invitations for you." She held out her hand and bowed as she'd practiced.

Anthony McGann didn't look at all surprised or confused about the second envelope. "Are you bringing a mystery guest?" Cass volleyed.

He stared at her, not comprehending, then said, "Oh, the second envelope."

Cass's question managed to derail the attorney. "I've never seen a speechless lawyer before, Mr. McGann."

"I'm afraid I can't comment, Cassandra. I'm not at liberty." The practiced remarks rolled out with ease.

And we're back. Same old worn-out arguments. She studied Anthony McGann from head to toe. He was handsome in a business way and dressed for success. His gray suit indicated he might have been in the courtroom that day. Although he wore a serious expression on his chiseled face, the tiny crinkles around his eyes suggested he had a side that might invite mischief.

McGann shifted from foot to foot, aware he was being assessed by this woman dressed as a man in nineteenth-century livery. The scene would be worth photographing by passersby if there were any.

"You rode all the way here on this horse? It looks like one of Posey's." McGann broke the silence.

"It is. Fauna. I asked the Hunts if I could borrow her."

"They said yes? Wait a minute. Did you talk to Corrine or Malcolm?"

Cass smiled and waited a beat. "Both of them. But Malcolm wins the warm personality award. I'm afraid I'm not Corrine's type."

"To be fair, not many are. Corrine's type, I mean." He grinned and Cass noted a suggestion of playfulness on his face.

"My turn to ask a question. Are you Posey's personal attorney?"

He studied her face, wondering whose side she might be on. "It's complicated. I do legal work for her and her foundations, yes."

"There now, that wasn't so hard, was it? I respect her privacy, but I did notice that she's been vexed since your visit the other day. I care about her and want to keep her as healthy as possible." Cass was telling the truth mixed with an ulterior motive.

"That's a relief. You strike me as someone quite capable of handling my...Posey." Again, the lawyer's eyes crinkled in a teasing way.

She would have loved to continue the ping-pong game the two of them were playing, maybe dig deeper into the man underneath the suit, but she was hot, and the powdered wig was scratchy.

"It was nice to meet you, kind sir," she recited in the voice of a noble lady, even waving the top hat like a fancy fan. "I must go, I'm afraid. I'm out without a chaperone and am expected at home." She lowered her eyes in mock timidity.

McGann chuckled, then stepped forward and took her hand. He held it up to his lips and placed a warm kiss on her palm. "Until we meet again, dear lady." McGann hoped he'd be able to recognize her without the wig and costume.

Back at Fox Hollow, Cass rode Fauna to the stable where one of the hands helped her down and walked the horse back to its stall for a rub. Cass found a sack of treats and fed the mare a carrot before leaving.

When she rounded the corner by her car, she saw Bay waiting.

"Cassandra Phoebe, what in the world is going on?" Bay pretended horror but her smile gave her away.

"Posey and I decided it was a cool twist to deliver the invitations to her costume party in style—well, old style, I suppose. This getup is something, huh?"

Bay stuffed her hands in her capri pockets. "And by you and Posey, of course you mean it was your idea. You must be wilting in that."

"I am, but it was fun. Plus, I rode Fauna, Posey's horse. It felt great to be riding again." Cass gazed upwards, catching the sun and a light breeze.

"Again? How did you learn about horses?" The large absences between the sisters were telling. Bay realized the unknown details about Cass's past may be for the best.

Cass bit her bottom lip, deciding on her answer. "Let's call it on-the-job training." She switched subjects. "Are you busy later for dinner? I want to share some information with you."

"Dinner? No, I'm not busy but I have to be at rehearsal before six. Detectives Downing and Harris are meeting with the directors. Maybe there's news."

"I'll text you with dinner plans later."

Cass drove off and Bay headed toward the Land Rover but paused when she spied Edison reading a book under a mammoth maple. She walked over to see it was *American Gods*, the book she loaned him.

"How are you finding the book?"

Edison closed the cover, sticking his finger into the section to save his place. "I'm thinking I have a lot in common with Shadow. We both lost an important person. We both feel out of control, that someone else is choosing our path in life." Edison's philosophical statement made him more mature than Bay realized.

She asked a question. "Were you and Talon close?"

He gazed beyond her, toward the horizon. "We were completely different people, but we shared the same fate. Our parents want to control everything in our lives. I'm supposed to take over my father's company. Hell, I couldn't even endure a year working there."

"And what about Talon? Did your parents have plans for him?"

Edison shifted his focus to Bay. "Of course. My grandfather's company. How perfect. Two sons. Two major companies to run. A match made in heaven." His sarcasm was clear.

Edison lowered his gaze to the ground, then picked a few stems of wild clover around him. The simple act calmed him. "And Talon would have done it, too. He followed all of mom's desires: hook, line, and sinker."

"And what about you, Edison? Are you following your parents' plans?" Bay treaded carefully.

He shrugged. "I guess so. I mean, now's not the time to push my parents. They're perched at the edge of the cliff." ❧

CHAPTER 11

If this were played upon a stage now,
I could condemn it as an improbable fiction.
~ TWELFTH NIGHT

Cass texted Bay an invitation for a casual supper at Spirit Gardens with her and Posey at four-thirty. Bay was intrigued.

Marva answered the door and ushered Bay into a lush conservatory filled with tropical palms, olive trees, and plumeria. Orchids snaked around the thicker trees and smiled at visitors with their charming faces.

A tile table held three place settings and glasses of something pinkish orange, while colorful enamel bowls of salads rested in the center.

Posey wore a vivid turquoise and orange sundress to finish off the tropical picnic ensemble. Bay was disappointed that her gray capris and cream buttoned top didn't contribute to the festive air. Even Cass wore a bright floral smock over her navy skort giving her vibrancy. Bay was witnessing a transformation in her sister from weary prison face to renewal. Life returned to her blue eyes, and she changed her hair color back to her natural blond from the stark red noir reminiscent of a horror film.

"Is everything okay?" Cass pulled Bay away from her reverie and into the chair beside her.

"Yes." She recovered. "This room and table are gorgeous, and you both look ready for a beach vacation."

Posey smiled up to her eyebrows, her bronzed cheeks revealing deep dimples communicating her pleasure of dinner company. "It's nice to dine with visitors. Now let me tell you about the offerings and we can help ourselves, yes?"

Cass chewed a forkful of caprese salad and sighed in yearning. "These olives remind me of the Mediterranean. Salty, savory, and smooth. But let me tell you about my delivery at the Devane house, Vanity Ridge."

The mention of Cher's family name made Bay twitch, an involuntary reaction.

Cass shared the argument she witnessed between Cher and Nora, adding the housekeeper's opinion that Cher could be mean and rude. "I guess I don't have to tell you that though, huh Lulu?"

"Maybe I should feel relieved I'm not the only one getting the Cher treatment. It means I should keep an eye on Nora and Cher at rehearsals though. We don't need anything else to go wrong."

"There's more," Cass continued. "After Nora walked away from Cher and didn't react to her bait, Cher ran ahead to catch up with her. I thought Cher would goad her into a meltdown, and I couldn't hear what either one said." Cass crinkled her brows together to conjure the image of the pair.

Bay recognized Cass's concentration and knew she was tapping into something below the surface. "What's bothering you?"

Cass opened her eyes and smacked her lips together. "Cher laid her head against Nora's shoulder, and Nora moved away. There's something between them. Sage said the girls were not close friends. I just wonder…"

Posey cleared her throat. "I believe it's time for some Angel Bluff Bird history. Cass gave me a preview of the playbill for your show, Bay, and here are the facts that might help you with your observations. I've taken the liberty of sorting your actors."

Posey set the playbill on the table and opened it to the cast list before picking up rice crackers with slices of brie and golden pear and arranging them in an arc on her plate adjacent to the dill pickle pasta salad.

Bay's brows were sharp question marks. "Sorting the actors?"

"Nora Stroud's parents work for the Devane family. Matthew is the stable manager. His wife, Krista, is an award-winning equestrian. She works with the horse trainers and coaches the show competitors who represent the stables. Before the Devanes took over the stables, the Strouds worked for the Kingsley family." She paused to sip the agua fresca she'd made special from mangoes and passion fruit.

Bay paused to consider. "Do the Strouds live on the bluff?"

Posey wagged her head. "They live in a fashionable quiet neighborhood in town where the larger original homes were built. I mean, they have plenty of wealth, but they are not part of the Prairie Ridge legacy." Posey spoke without arrogance or entitlement, simply resignation.

"What about the Hunts, Jackson Lange, and Logan Thorne?" Bay was psyched to hear all.

"One at a time, Bay. Every family here has a story, but you can't read an encyclopedia in one sitting." Posey nibbled one of the brie cracker sandwiches and took another drink.

"The Hunts and Langes are historically connected and thick as thieves. Malcolm's parents owned an international shipping company destined to become one of the top money makers in the Midwest, Hunt Advantage Industries. Malcolm was second in line to the throne, behind number one son, Mitchell. Except…," Posey stopped to pick up a rolling cherry tomato that strayed from the vegetable board.

Cass knew Posey enjoyed stringing out a story once she had the listener on the hook. Bay's rapt attention hung on every word.

"Except what? Didn't Mitchell want the company?" Bay stopped to think and munched on a strawberry. "Wait. Mitchell Hunt? Not the senator from Michigan?"

Posey nodded and clapped. "Brava, Bay. There aren't many baubles enticing enough to pull someone away from the family fortune, but political power is near the top of the list. Mitchell started working for our governor as an aide, then rose through the ranks. When he married a Michigan auto company heiress, his political fortune was sealed."

"Which left the door open for Malcolm to take over the shipping company. And from what dynasty does Corrine ascend?" Bay asked.

"Corrine's family is railroad gold from Chicago. She and Malcolm met at a transportation conference in Washington D.C. and the rest is history. Their families made certain of that."

Both sisters detected a hiccup in Posey's tone as she relayed her assessment of the couple and wondered what was left unsaid.

Bay pressed on. "Corrine came from Chicago. How does she find life in Prairie Ridge?"

Posey laughed in derision. "It was like the TV show *Green Acres*. She felt like a prisoner surrounded by a bunch of country bumpkins. You can imagine she was instrumental in bringing upscale social functions and esteemed ideals to the neighborhood."

Cass pounced on the remark. "Oh Posey, I thought you were the one appointed to bring social functions to the community. Everyone in Prairie Ridge talks about your gatherings and volunteer work."

Posey snorted. "I can say with certainty Corrine Hunt doesn't rate my parties as sophisticated, and I can count on one hand the number of charity functions she's attended. No, she leaves those duties to Malcolm." Posey's nostrils flared and cheeks turned scarlet as if she'd said too much.

Before the bluff source dried up, Bay jumped in. "And the Lange family? How are they connected to the Hunts?"

Posey settled back into her seat and crossed her legs. "Billion-dollar companies need million-dollar legal advice. The Lange Group offers just that. The Langes and Hunts moved to Prairie Ridge the same year. Grandfather Lange worked with Wall Street investors in the city but saw an opportunity to move up the ladder and started over here. He grew his company by landing Hunt Industries as a client. They've been inseparable ever since."

"So, Jackson and Talon were as close as Jackson insists?" Bay asked.

"As far as I know. I've seen them linked like Siamese twins from the time they could walk. They're a lot alike, those two. Both know how to make trouble; then charm their way out of it."

Posey's face clouded over. "I guess Talon couldn't charm his way out of this." Her eyes welled with tears.

Bay checked the time. She needed to leave for rehearsal soon, and Posey had made a tiny dent on the cast list. "What can you tell me about Logan Thorne?"

Posey sniffed and wiped her eyes on a napkin while Cass reached over and placed her hand on Posey's shoulder to comfort her. "Sorry about that. There's not a lot to say about Logan. The Thornes are a family fighting to rise to the middle class. They rent a cramped house on Third Street. Since his father went to prison, it's just Logan, his mother, and a sister."

"How was Logan able to attend Flourish? I remember him being a decent English student, and he graduated so…" Bay internally jabbed herself for judging a student's success based on their economic status. "I didn't mean that…" she trailed off.

"If you're not aware, Flourish operates on three levels. There are those students who qualify for full scholarships and aid based on their need and academic potential. A second tier of students are granted some financial aid but have to fund the rest of their tuition. Some will have work study options. The top tier enters through the golden passage of legacy. Their parents or grandparents are Flourish graduates, the single requirement that matters. They skip to the front of the line—no SAT scores, no grade reports, no recommendations necessary."

Bay wasn't surprised to hear about the Flourish policy, but it still smacked of injustice. "How is the college able to function at such a prominent level without all that tuition to support it?"

Posey scowled. "The Birds fund the lion's share of the college operations with charitable contributions. The money stays in a pot and Flourish can operate just on its interest."

She knew the term *quid pro quo* and here it was, staring her in the face.

"Logan must have been a hardship case. I'm glad he graduated, and I hope he leaves here for a fresh start." Posey tapped an electronic button on the tile table.

Bay didn't accept that Logan should leave town just because his father went to prison. "Is Prairie Ridge so prejudiced that people can't give Logan a chance to prove himself?" Her words stung in her throat as she recalled how harshly she'd treated Cass when she got out of prison.

Posey reddened. "You have to understand. Logan's father stole a large amount of money from Hunt Industries."

"Oh my. How was he able to do that?"

"He worked in the warehouse where he skimmed high-end products and fenced them," Posey explained.

Marva entered the room with dessert plates bearing towering slices of chocolate icebox cake and a carafe of milky cinnamon tea.

Cass poured tea into the delicate china cups decorated with lily of the valley. Posey clanged a tiny spoon against her saucer. "I know you need to leave soon Bay. Let's change the subject and enjoy dessert. I've taken the liberty of marking the cast members that are legacy students, and I'll send it along. There are still a few stories to tell. Perhaps we can arrange another visit soon?"

Bay raised her teacup to Posey. "You can count on it."

Bay's overindulgence at supper made it hard to focus on the detectives' briefing prior to rehearsal. She was still grappling with her newfound knowledge about some cast members and figuring out how any of it related to Talon's death.

Downing and Harris brought Narcan kits to the meeting and showed the directors how to administer the rescue drug, if necessary.

Jen raised her hand. "How do we recognize an overdose?"

Harris, who had worked the streets up until six months ago, fielded the question. "Look for grogginess or loss of consciousness, limp body, and shallow or lack of breathing. The person will probably have dilated pupils and may have clammy skin or even make choking or gurgling noises."

Desmond, looking stressed, wanted to know about the case. "What can you tell us? Are you close to finding out what happened to Talon, and who did it?" His words sprung forth like sharp rivets.

Harris pushed around the air with both hands. "Just calm down, Mr. Carver. I know you're under pressure here, but we're on top of this, I promise."

Bay and Jen exchanged knowing glances. Harris was a decent man, but his words sounded hollow.

Downing stepped forward, grim determination etched on his face. "We're looking into several leads and people, with a large cast and crew to investigate. We also can't rule out that someone who's not in the play may be involved."

Downing's idea the killer might be someone outside the show raised the tension.

"Wait a minute. If someone outside the show is involved, how did the prop sword, which was locked up until rehearsal, end up with fentanyl on it?"

Downing gave Bay a quizzical look. "You're sure nobody outside the show had access to the props? This huge cast, along with high schoolers running around to volunteer, not to mention the park is a public space."

Heat rose from Bay's neck up her face. The detective was right; the first rehearsal was disorganized, with the directors crafting the set, arranging the schedule, and trying to practice at once. If someone wanted to, they could just wait for the perfect moment to taint the prop sword. Except…did she dare share her thoughts with the others, or wait until she could talk to Downing alone?

"I don't suppose you can shed any light on Cher and Logan as suspects?" Bay asked the question quietly.

Harris gulped air and linked his hands behind his back. Bay knew this was a tell that they knew details they didn't plan to reveal. Downing shot him a warning look.

"You know the drill. It's an ongoing investigation." But his eyes challenged Bay to reframe her question.

Thoughtful and serious, she tried again. "Should we be keeping our eyes on Logan and Cher?"

The question evoked a lopsided smile from Downing. "You should all be vigilant where everyone is concerned. The most important things are to follow protocols and routines. Watch what people are doing in plain sight. Don't let anyone near the props except for the actors who are supposed to be handling them. We've talked to Maya and Aria, and I think they get it."

Bay determined that Cher and Logan were not off the hook, but maybe nobody else was either. It made her wonder if the directors were being investigated too. She also noticed Edison Hunt wasn't at the meeting.

Demond popped his hand into the air. "Can you confirm there was a K-9 unit searching here?" Desmond heard the report from a couple Flourish personnel.

Downing pursed his lips and fiddled with his notes. "Standard protocol in a drug death such as this. The K-9 unit was ordered after the tox screen report came back on Talon. As soon as the chief heard, he wanted the dogs to sniff around."

"What did they find?" Desmond asked.

"They hit on locations outside the theater, specifically the trash can. They didn't hit on anything in the stage area, the wings, or prep rooms. Hopefully the prop sword was an isolated incident." Downing closed his notebook and jumped off the stage, meaning Q and A was over.

He took Desmond aside to talk. Bay walked over to Nolan Harris.

"Hello officer. Thanks for showing us the Narcan kit. It makes me feel somewhat better, but it's not a solution to the problem."

Harris rocked on his feet. "Dr. Browning, you have to know that we're working our hardest with the help we have."

Bay looked sheepish. "Can the police force spare extra security to hang around the theater?"

Harris stuck out his chest and stared her down. "Look Bay, I like the idea. Now march your suggestion up to that stone castle and tell your college president to shuffle some security guards from the empty campus to the park." Harris jammed his hands in his pockets and walked away.

Downing wove his way to the dumbfounded Bay. "Looks like you pissed off Harris. Congratulations. That's quite the feat."

"Zeus's beard, I feel awful." Bay's emotions were in check as she resumed her habit of replacing swear words with literary expressions. "None of this is your fault."

Bay noticed students began pulling into the parking lot. "I may have helpful information. Can we go for a drink after rehearsal?"

Downing grinned. "I enjoy seeing you contrite. Sure, why not. Call me when you're done."

Desmond directed students to sit in the front two rows of theater seats so he could give them some straight talk.

"Listen up, gang. We're having scads of issues getting this production off the ground. Talon's funeral is Sunday, and I believe a show of unity is in order. We should all attend. Whether you liked Talon or not, it's the decent thing to do. Now, I have one question. Show of hands: do you want to continue with the play?"

The dumbfounded students raised their hands, although a few people were slow to do so and looked around to gauge the group.

Desmond gave a satisfied nod. "Honestly, if anyone wants to walk away, now's the time. Just let one of the directors know so we can fill your part."

Bay raised her brows at Desmond's surly delivery. He tilted his head at Bay and Jen, their cue to hand out the night's rehearsal plan.

"Two more things. One, no screwing around or fighting. If you can't solve a problem with someone, come see me. And two, if you see something, say something. You know what I mean." Desmond rested his eyes on each one.

Bay and Jen ushered students into their stage positions. "We're starting with the first act, and we need the lovers in their positions. Males on one couch, females on the other. Our show host moderator sits here, on the throne. Jackson, you're going to come in from backstage, center."

"Way to show them who's boss." Jen jabbed her elbow playfully into Bay's side. "I'm heading backstage to help organize the makeup room. We'll be prepping the actors next week."

"Fingers crossed," Bay said. "We could use some luck."

She turned to the stage, noticed they were short some actors, and feared the worst— people decided to quit. Logan stood by the throne, chatting with Kitt, the narrator and talk show host. "Who's missing?" Bay asked them.

Kitt answered. "Juliet, Hermia, and Petruchio." The cast was expected to use stage names to authenticate their characters.

Bay calculated and counted. So, Cher, Nora, and Jackson were missing, but so was someone else—ah, Adam. "What about Adam, er Lysander?"

"He volunteered to find them." Logan said.

Bay frowned and moaned. *Can't we even get one frickety snert rehearsal off on the right foot?* She offered an encouraging smile to the actors in position. "Hang tight. We're going to start in two minutes."

She whirled around, leapt off the stage, and strode to the

tech booth to find Desmond. He was looking at notes with Evan when Bay cut in. "Sorry. We have some missing actors. Did Jackson, Cher, and Nora quit by chance?"

Desmond scowled and emitted a stream of swear words. "No. What do you mean, they're missing?"

Bay explained. "Adam is looking for them. I'll go look, too." She twirled around, wove through the rows, and darted behind the stage to the actors' waiting area. She nearly mowed over Cher and Nora in the process as the two were heading toward the outside stage entrance.

"Cher and Nora, where have you been? We're ready to start act one, and you're both in it." Bay hoped her seething look left them unsettled, but the two shrugged.

"Had to use the bathroom," Cher said, an offhand explanation.

Bay took a deep breath. "Any chance Jackson needed the facilities, too? He's not on stage either."

"We haven't seen him," Nora said, more politely. "We're on our way to the stage now."

Bay followed on their heels. No way was she losing sight of the two. A set of steps led upward to the costume and makeup room and the right wing of the stage. When they passed through the makeup room, Jen's eyes widened as she saw Bay's scowl at the backs of Cher and Nora.

"MIA actors located, Professor Yoo. It won't happen again," Bay stated her point.

Jackson and Adam were already in their places. Bay confronted Jackson, standing toe-to-toe with him. "Where did you disappear to? Didn't you hear the call for places?" Bay was not a fan of rule breakers or even rule stretchers, for that matter.

Jackson stared abashed. "Well, I um, was looking for Adam to tell him it was time for the prologue." Jackson cleared his throat and gave Adam a sideways glance.

"Yes. We bumped into each other while I was looking for Nora and Cher. I see you found them," Adam said.

Bay glared from actor to actor. "Adam's prologue is in act three," she said calmly. "Let's get going."

Bay sat near Edison, who had limited prompting to do, one minor bonus at least. Bay couldn't help noticing that Jackson gave Edison the evil eye from time to time, something that must stop.

The actors rounded up for feedback while the stage was reset for the second act. Desmond began with notes.

"Juliet, you need to act desperate about your love for Romeo. Convince me you want Shakespeare to rewrite the play with a happy ending, which means we must believe you're pleading with The Bard."

"Petruchio, excellent arrogance and confidence on your part. I love how you're willing to toss aside Katherine and have a go at Hermia. Good job."

"Katherine, I love it that you don't give a damn Petruchio wants to throw you away for another woman. Well done. And well done to The Bard for coming unglued when his characters all start to revolt."

Notes went on a little longer, then Bay was asked for her feedback. Desmond had covered the good, bad, and ugly, but Bay asked for a private word with Jackson.

"It appears you have an issue with Edison?"

It was the second time in an hour Jackson messed up, and

he hung his head, which surprised Bay. "It's no secret Edison and I don't like each other. As Talon's best friend, I saw a lot."

"I imagine you did, but you need to put it aside for the show. Can you do that?" In the short time she'd been at the Hunt house, she'd witnessed a few things herself, things that made her feel sympathy for Edison. She wondered about the image on the opposite side of the coin.

Jackson nodded but a tick pulsed along his jawline and tears welled in his eyes. He couldn't speak and walked away toward the restrooms.

Bay strolled over to sit beside Edison. "Hey, what's with you and Jackson?"

Edison chuckled, low and nonchalant. "The great Jackson Lange from the big Lange law firm. He is so much bullshit," Edison laughed again, but sobered when he saw Bay's face.

"Jackson loved sucking up to my parents and making me look bad. Not that I needed any help in that department. He's just an outsider who reminds me I'll never measure up to Talon." Edison pretended to study the script binder.

"Look Edison, we can't afford to have turmoil around here. Your parents requested the college give you a position on the show. Can you handle it?" Bay decided teaching high schoolers must be a lot like this.

"Yeah. Consider it handled, Professor Browning."

Dousing one fire only fanned a new ember elsewhere. Bay saw Nora on stage, sitting on the couch holding something and crying. Kitt attempted to console her while Cher chattered dramatically with Logan, who looked like he might take off her head. Cher stormed off.

Desmond vaulted onto the stage just ahead of Bay. "Now

what?" His head swiveled to and fro.

Bay found Nora and Kitt on the stage couch and headed there. "What's that, Nora?" She indicated the piece of paper Nora was stuffing into her pocket. "May I see it?" Bay was running low on patience.

Nora handed her the crumpled paper. The all-caps warning was written in blood-red marker: *STAY AWAY FROM HER!*

"Are you sure this is meant for you?" Bay asked.

Nora nodded. "It was in my cubby." All the actors were assigned a labeled shelf in the costume area, for convenience.

"What does it mean?" Bay asked.

Nora's face went from distraught to helpless in an instant. "I have no idea," she murmured.

What it meant to Bay was obvious. It was time to get extra security at rehearsals. There were too many shenanigans happening, murder included. Just then, a car peeled out of the parking lot. Cher Devane had left the building. ✿

CHAPTER 12

Good company, good wine, good welcome
can make good people.
~ HENRY VIII

The drama queen's absence proved a catalyst for progress and decorum. The rest of rehearsal was a stroll in the park. Even Nora calmed down after Desmond, Jen, and Bay smoothed things over and promised to investigate the source of the demanding note.

The hitch was substituting someone to play Cher's roles— she was in every act. But Maya, props master, pinch hit with finesse, while Aria got better acquainted with handling props.

After dismissing the cast and crew, the directors lingered to debrief.

"What's going to happen to Cher with her abrupt departure?" Bay asked Desmond, who cringed.

"I'm calling her after we wrap up. As far as I'm concerned, she gets one more strike, then we find a replacement. What do the rest of you say?"

Jen and Evan agreed without comment. Bay played devil's advocate.

"Brave words, my friend. Do you have someone in mind, because Cher may push you to the edge of that cliff. I agree with your plan, though."

"We had a list of back-up actors until Talon died and a slew of them bowed out. I thought Maya proved herself tonight. She's capable and spirited. She could pull it off. It's easier to replace a props master than a lead actor." Desmond looked hopeful.

When Jen and Bay strolled to the parking lot together, Jen continued past her ancient compact car. Bay could tell Jen was bursting to tell her something since rehearsal began.

"That note to Nora. It's from someone who has a thing for Cher." Jen's eyebrows hiked up and down like pogo sticks.

Bay accepted the bait. "What else do you know?"

Jen shushed Bay's sharp retort that echoed in the dark, but she saw they were alone in the lot. "I walked in on Nora and Cher in the costume room. They were beyond friendly."

Jen's report seemed to confirm what Cassandra suggested earlier, that there was something going on between the two. "When was this?"

"Between acts one and two, after Desmond gave notes."

Bay produced a curious smile. "Who else was there that might have seen them?"

Jen frowned. "Just me, I think. I backed out of the room fast and didn't see anyone. I know they saw me or at least they saw something. I heard one of them gasp and the other giggle."

Bay folded her arms across her chest. "That doesn't track. Someone must have seen or at least suspected, otherwise why send the note to Nora?"

Jen shrugged. "That makes sense. Maybe someone saw them earlier. Didn't you follow them from outside before rehearsal? I heard they were missing."

Bay pressed her lips together. "Yes. I found them behind the stage where the actors gather to wait for their cues. They claimed to be returning from the bathrooms, but that wouldn't be the logical path to take. Hm. Anything else?"

"No, I thought that was substantial, Detective Browning." Jen mocked a pout.

"Speaking of which, I'm heading to the Pig Squeal to meet the detective for drinks. I'll fill him in on tonight's rehearsal." Bay opened the SUV door. "Hey Jen, should we tap Stasia or Dean Pamela for some campus security down here?"

Jen gave two thumbs-up.

The Pig Squeal, a cops-only hangout that looked like a mechanic's garage, lit up the dead end of the road. The site was secluded, self-sustaining, and run by volunteer rookies, police cadets, and retired cops. The former owner of the property had two brothers on the force, so the department pooled their money and sponsored fundraisers to buy the place at a steep discount.

Bay had learned self-defense in the basement from cadet Mandy Harris, Nolan Harris's sister. She'd also met Downing for dinner on a few occasions while consulting on the Medusa case.

She strode to the entrance with confidence as she recognized the bouncer, who also was a top chef there in the mornings, roasting pork in a pit. The place smelled delicious as usual.

Smoky grilled meats ruled the menu, but the country music was summertime loud tonight.

The bouncer gave her a half smile. "Hello Professor. Downing said to expect you." The man pointed his thumb beyond the building. "He's outside where it's quieter."

Bay walked around one side, surprised to see a paving stone patio where a hodgepodge of round and square tables with umbrellas sat amid longer wooden picnic tables. She decided the mismatched furniture was picked from rummage sales or donated. Downing sat alone on the patio underneath a solar lantern.

"The music in there must be decent, or else you haven't showered today." Bay delivered a playful jab.

"I chased them all inside, so here's hoping they like the band. And hey, I thought this was a friendly meeting," he said.

"I ordered us beer and pig-out nachos." Downing pointed to a metal bucket with four Coronas and a giant platter mounded with chips, gooey cheese, meat, onions, tomatoes, and cilantro. Bowls of guacamole and fresh salsa sat waiting for dunking. "The nachos arrived just before you."

"If you want something else, Watts will be back in a minute."

Bay lowered her eyes, thankful for the darkness that hid her blush. She noticed the detective had asked for a bowl of lime wedges, which is how she drank her beer. "It looks like a hot mess. Let's dive in."

The Detective pulled out a bottle, uncapped it, and handed it to Bay. He opened one for himself and held it up to toast. "What should we drink to, Professor?"

"To getting reacquainted." She clanked her bottle against his, after squeezing a lime wedge into it.

The nachos were smothered in a mixture of queso fresco and sharp cheddar, but the star of the platter was the pork carnitas that were slow-cooked and spiced to perfection. Neither of them spoke until they were onto a second beer, and more than half the platter was empty.

Bay enjoyed watching the fireflies in the nearby grass, listening to the muffled music that seeped into the night, and soaking in the cool late spring evening with the company of Bryce Downing.

Watts, a new academy cadet, stopped over. "Can I get you something else to drink?"

The two were well into their second beers, but Bay asked for iced tea and Downing ordered a cola.

"Did you want a box for the nachos?" Watts asked.

Bay and Downing put on their game faces. "Sounds like a challenge to me, Professor. I think we can take down this platter. What about you?"

"You're on."

Watts winked. "So, taking no prisoners I see. I get you." The cadet performed a bob and weave move, his attempt to act cool in front of his superior. "I'll be back with those drinks."

Bay and Downing burst out laughing.

"We'll need time to tackle this platter, so let's get down to business," Bay suggested, a bit reluctant to break the relaxed mood.

"Take it away, Professor. Teach me." Downing sat back in his seat, legs extended, a mellow smile on his face.

Bay thought he would direct the conversation, so she chose to share the details from rehearsal about Cher and Nora, what

Cass observed about the two, and how Jen walked in on the pair in an intimate moment. "The real capper though is this note Nora found in the costume room." She held up her phone to show him the photo she'd snapped of the note.

He leaned forward, alert and animated. "Where's the note now? Why didn't Desmond call me?"

Bay faltered. "Desmond has it. I think he's going to try to find out who wrote it."

Downing backed down. "I suppose there's no specific threat stated. Still, we've had one murder. I don't want Desmond trying to play detective."

Bay's stomach flipped. Wasn't she playing detective?

"How did Cher react to the note? And did you notice the others' reactions?" In the dim light, Downing scrawled notes on a pad of paper.

"I didn't see any notable reactions, just Kitt sitting beside Nora to calm her down. But get this: Cher left the stage and peeled out of the parking lot."

Downing knew the type. "A real dramatic exit, huh? Any ideas about who the writer might be?"

The question was twirling through Bay's mind ever since the note showed up. "Logan Thorne, maybe. It sometimes looks like those two are involved."

"Ah huh. Anything look familiar about the note?"

Bay brightened. "The tech crew uses red markers to put stars on the script for lighting changes. That's five people plus Evan, the tech director. I haven't observed interactions between the cast and crew, though." Then she recalled her encounter with Henry Knight, the person who engineered the trap door.

"I just thought of something. There's a trap door on stage behind the couch for characters to come and go. Shakespeare will use it often to appear out of nowhere at times, like a spirit. In fact, there are spirits in the show who will use it, too."

"And your point is?" Downing paused his pen.

"The trap door leads below stage to an outside exit behind the theater. There will be a tent set up there once we start dress rehearsals for actors to await their cues. I wonder if Cher and Nora were below stage when they went missing. I ran into them outside in the actors' waiting area." Bay frowned.

"What is it? Something's buzzing around up there." Downing pointed to her head.

"Henry Knight designed the trap door and the lighted pathway below stage. But he's just nineteen. I don't think he's interested in Cher. She's not his type." Bay realized her thoughts lacked logic. She couldn't guess what kind of person Henry's type was.

"I'll pay Henry a visit, just in case. The interviews with Cher and Logan didn't yield much. Each one points the finger at the other as having motive to hurt Talon. Both call Talon's death an accident, even as they suggest each one might have been involved," he said.

Bay nodded along. "That's what rehearsal looked like, too. Logan and Cher making public accusations and insinuations that each was the prime suspect."

Downing jotted that tidbit in his notes.

"I get Logan's motive is personal. Not about wanting the lead either. I mean because the Hunts are responsible for his father being in prison. But what is Cher's motive?" Bay asked.

"Cher wanted to hitch her star to the Hunt fortune. What

better way than getting her hooks into Talon? They dated, but Mother Dear stepped all over that," Downing said.

"And your other suspects?" Bay asked, her voice creamy and nonchalant.

"Okay, eager beaver, let me ask you the same question. Who's on your list?

Bay pushed back into her seat, hands in defense mode. "I'm still trying to get to know the players." She smiled slyly. "But I'm taking lessons from Posey Hollingsworth. She knows everyone in Prairie Ridge."

Downing balked. "I suppose she does. You're forgetting that I probably do, too."

Bay didn't think that was an accurate statement. Posey knew Angel Bluff history. The detective was a transplant.

Their drinks were delivered, so Bay swigged the remaining Corona and exhaled a satisfied sigh. The liquid courage provoked her next question.

"What did the K-9 unit find in the trash?" She gave Downing a sideways glance, and he grinned as he gulped the rest of his beer and put the empty back into the bucket with a loud clink.

"I can guess, I suppose. I'm thinking gloves of course. Someone handling lethal drugs would want to wear gloves. And a carrier for the substance—a baggie maybe." She studied her sparring partner. The amused crinkle around his eyes and one-dimpled smile meant she was on track but not quite there. She waited, hoping he would fill the gaps.

"Sterile gloves—check," he confirmed.

"Not a baggie then. Perhaps a pill bottle?"

His amused smile remained intact.

She shifted in her seat and picked up a naked chip from the platter. "Well, some sort of container that I'm certain the lab is testing for fentanyl residue." She was losing patience with the game, but also aware the detective's ethics dictated he keep her in the dark.

"Yes, the dogs sniffed out a glass vial and the lab has it." He leaned toward Bay like a child with a secret he wanted to share. "You're never going to guess the final item. Never."

Bay took the bait, but surrendered after guessing a makeup case, mask, a note, a shoe, hair, jewelry, and cigarette butt. "You're right. It's something unexpected, so we could be here all night," she complained.

Downing was enjoying matching wits with her. "Like a hint?"

Bay shrugged, nonchalant. She ate a chip in several tiny bites. She waited. She sipped some tea, waited longer. He wanted her to crack, but she wouldn't. It was like an adult game of flinch, and her competitive side showed.

Downing faked a yawn, stretched his arms overhead, and slid his notepad into his satchel. "I think we should call it a night. Tomorrow starts early with a long list of interviews to slog through. Keep your eyes and ears open, Professor. I like hearing from you." He had the audacity to wink at her.

Bay stood up briskly and sent the metal bucket teetering. "Okay, I give up. Let's skip the hint and you can pretend I guessed. What else did the dogs sniff out?"

Downing chuckled. "Sit down, Bay. You give as good as you get, and you're a worthy opponent."

She stayed standing and slid her purse handle off the chair back. A saucy smile played on her face. "No. It's been a long day for both of us. We'll pick this up later."

She turned around and walked away, but Downing was on her heels, then at her side. He reached for her arm and linked his around it. She almost pulled away in surprise but laughed instead.

"What's this?" she asked, indicating their linked arms.

"It's dark. Thought I'd walk you out."

They stopped at her Land Rover.

"Nice wheels. I like the color, too, metallic copper, easy to pick out on the road."

"Thanks. Cass needed a car, and I wanted an upgrade. I see you're still driving the General Lee," she snickered. Over his shoulder, she spied the detective's older model sedan.

"Oh, come on now, it's not even orange. But it is a treasure."

Surprising herself, she leaned in and pecked him on the cheek. "You're a treasure of a different sort, Detective."

"A condom," he murmured. "The dogs found a condom." ✤

CHAPTER 13

Entr'acte

Bay threw wide the drapes and opened the glass doors to the apartment patio. The flowers, herbs, and vegetables were thriving, thanks to a mixture of daytime sun and evening rain showers. *May was such a pleasant month but sadly, today it would breathe its fond farewell.*

Bay laughed at her thoughts. "I'm waxing Shakespeare thanks to this monstrosity of a production." She addressed the sweet turned-up face of a purple pansy.

She sat on a metal chair and sank into its cushions, her face raised to the new day. Then, pen in hand, she pulled out the wrinkled paper that was Edison Hunt's essay. She'd forgotten it existed with each day running rampantly into the next since Talon's death. Today was a hiatus from it all; no rehearsal, no meetings, and a funeral waiting until tomorrow.

Edison's task was to write about his future plans and how

the graduate business program fit into the big picture. Bay read the piece, then reread it. It was short, but well organized and cohesive. Perhaps Edison Hunt had been underestimated in his intelligence, or maybe he just kept it to himself.

The true bombshell in the essay was Edison's professed plan to build his own business, rejecting both of his parents' companies. It turned out the young man loved hard labor and nature and planned to combine the two into a landscape design company. He even confided he would receive a lump sum from a trust fund in three years, and he would use it to bolster his business venture. Bay smiled with optimism for the first time in days.

"You're wearing a Cheshire cat face, Lulu. What's up?" Cass appeared on the patio, yawning and stretching. Saturday was a reprieve for her, too. Posey asked for her company at Talon's memorial service Sunday at noon.

Bay pointed to the paper lying on the table. "Edison Hunt's essay." She jabbed the paper for emphasis.

"That bad, huh? Well, I guess it's what you expected." Cass screwed up her face as the winds of change washed over her from Bay's orbit. She had guessed wrong.

"It's decent. There's hope for this kid yet." Bay cheered. "Take a look."

Cass scanned it and blinked. "You approve of his plan, I take it? What about mummy and daddy?" She pouted for effect.

"I imagine his parents will be a hard sell, but there's something here I never expected— determination. His attitude may win the day, and if not, he will eventually have his own money." Bay slapped the table, satisfied.

Cass grimaced. "Too bad it's not so easy for those of us who dwell below the great Angel Bluff."

Bay studied her sister and reached out to touch her arm, but she sidestepped the gesture. "Are you okay, Cass? Everything good at Posey's?"

"It will be, I suppose. I'm thinking about going to the memorial service tomorrow. The Hunts at Fox Hollow," she spoke in an exaggerated British accent.

Bay smiled in understanding. She wasn't thrilled about attending either, but the college made no bones about it. The four directors would be there.

"Let's enjoy today, shall we? How about some breakfast before we pick up Diana?" The sisters planned an excursion to Prairie Greenhouse to finish the patio project.

Bay, Cass, and Diana browsed table after table of flowering plants and fillers, discussing options and combinations for five hanging pots on the Windflower Gardens apartment patio. Bay gravitated to the begonia varieties accompanied by trailing bacopas in pink and blue, but Cass made faces at the color options.

"I like the bright and bold begonias, but those bacopas belong in a baby's nursery. Gag." Cass complained.

Diana laughed. "You know, you two should just look up. The greenhouse is full of hanging pots ready to take home. Pick out the ones you like."

Bay and Cass scoffed. "Nope. We want to make our own concoction," Cass informed her.

The trio started back at the beginning again, scrutinizing their options.

"Tell me how you like working at the library, Diana," Bay said.

"It's a bit too quiet during summer break. And I miss my coworker, Bree. It was nice to make a friend." She brightened. "Bree will be back in September though."

Diana pointed to a row of crimson ivy geraniums as a potential candidate for her sisters.

Cass and Bay shook their heads simultaneously. "Too stinky," Bay said. "Too common," Cass said.

"What about your supervisor? Are they treating you well?" Cass knew plenty about lousy bosses and hoped Diana didn't have to suffer one.

"Joanna's decent. She leaves me alone and trusts me to do my work. She's not around much, always in the stacks finding obscure books or antique first editions for patrons. People consider her an excellent curator."

"That's good to hear. What are your summer duties?" Bay picked up a tray filled with colorful Gerbera daisies and shoved them at Cass for her approval.

"Well, it's a bit boring, but I'm writing descriptions for new acquisitions, pulling books from the shelf to repair them, reviewing circulation stats so we can withdraw books for the fall sale—stuff like that." Diana gave an enthused thumbs up to the daisies, and they were added to the shopping wagon.

Bay sighed. "I'll trade places with you, Diana. I'll hole up in the quiet library and you can direct *Shakespeare's Couch*."

Diana puckered her lips. "I may be caged up in the college library, but I did hear about the drama. Unsolved murder. Cast members fighting. No thanks."

Cass tsked at her sisters. "With all the people using the

library, I'd think you'd meet more potential friends, Di."

Diana's brows drew together. "I think I scare people away. You know. They're afraid I'm about to forecast their doom or something." She made an X with her pointer fingers.

Diana and Cassandra inherited the gift of extrasensory perception from the Charming family on their mother's side. Bay grappled with the knowledge of their abilities, wondering why she had not been duly graced.

Cass frowned. "Diana, you should know by now to keep your talent quiet. Flaunting it will lead to trouble. Believe me, I know."

Bay pushed the two of them along the row. "What about these, Cass?" Bay pointed to lush fuchsias in purple, ruby, and magenta. "The hummingbirds will love them. At least that's what the card says."

Cass laughed. "Yes. And we'll add these and these." She pulled out a tray of striped petunias and lime green sweet potato vine."

Bay added pots of golden money plant, and Diana brought over a trio of dragon wing begonias with startling red-orange blooms.

"I think our work here is finished," Cass said.

"Not so fast. I want to pick up something for your dad's apartment. It could use some sprucing up." Diana held up a hanging basket of verbena in burgundy, white, and neon coral.

"What about the Boston ferns in the living room?" Bay remembered placing the baskets on pedestals near his sofa and recliner.

"Dead. I tossed them out shortly after I moved in. They were drowning in standing water. H2O overdose."

"There's a graceful parlor palm in his office," Cass said.

"Not anymore." Diana made a slicing motion across her throat. "Brown and crispy and hidden away in the hall closet."

Bay frowned. She was beginning to think she'd inherited the poor traits of the Browning side of the family when it came to growing and nurturing things. Cass intuitively sidled up to her and rested her hand on Bay's elbow.

"You have plenty of lovely gifts, Lulu. And there's more to discover."

The intensity of Cass's blue eyes gazing into Bay's was unnerving and so was their physical contact. Overwhelmed with a desire to weep, Bay spun around and placed the shopping wagon between them. She did smile sweetly at Cass, though. ✿

CHAPTER 14

When sorrows come, they come not single spies,
but in battalions.

~ HAMLET

If Talon Hunt's funeral was a New York production, it would be billed as part fashion runway, part mystery, part tragedy.

Corrine Hunt, dressed in a custom black gown trimmed in feathers, delivered a eulogy, if you could call it that. She began speaking about what might have been if Talon had lived: his masterful post as captain of the company her grandfather birthed, an American original, the iron horse in all its glory from sea to shining sea. The rest of the speech centered on bragging rights about her grandfather, her father, and their powerful cronies, links in America's aristocratic chain.

Bay stopped listening and started people watching. It was impossible to believe, but the attendees sat in awe at the feet of Corrine as she held court in the grand hall of Fox Hollow. She failed to recognize Downing at first, dressed in a dark suit and sunglasses, sporting an earpiece. *Is he supposed to be undercover?* She admired the secret service guise, and her heart skipped a beat.

She sat in an aisle seat, so she made herself small and crept back the few rows to stand near Downing against a wall. She wouldn't interrupt the service, but she wanted to be in position to pick the detective's brain as soon as possible. His stern visage did not invite chit chat.

A hired gospel choir belted out numbers after Corrine swished from the stage to her seat. The songs were an odd combination of lively hymns and contemporary tunes from Talon's playlist, including a questionable hip-hop song. Bay couldn't conceive how that number made it into the service without proper vetting. Maybe Corrine's grief was cracking her constrained composure.

The view from the back wall gave Bay perspective on Prairie Ridge's social hierarchy. The rich and locally famous occupied the front three rows of the great hall, dressed in clothing meant for public consumption and envy.

The middle section included Flourish college personnel, the community business class, and civic leaders. Bay noticed many of them rustled in their seats as they dealt with Corrine's unusual speech and curious music mix. Furthermore, where was Malcolm? Of course he sat with the family, but why didn't he speak at his son's service?

The back section incorporated an odd mix of Talon's classmates from high school and college, including the *Shakespeare's Couch* cast and crew, and staff who worked for the Bluff Birds. The staff whispered among themselves, sometimes poked each other in reaction to Corrine's bluster, and gasped during the hip-hop number. The majority of the students didn't pay close attention, too occupied on their phones, snapping pictures, or scrolling through videos. Cher Devane and Logan Thorne were notably absent.

The service closed with Professor Gabriel McNelly offering a prayer for Talon and the Hunt family. Bay, who was perplexed by her colleague, was moved by the prayer, which was sincere and hopeful.

The funeral director invited those assembled to sign the memory book in the viewing room, which is where Talon's closed coffin, surrounded by floral arrangements, was staged. He also pointed toward the grand salon and asked the attendees to enjoy refreshments and conversation there.

Collective murmurs bounced around the hall as people filed out and stood in line outside the mammoth, carved ebony doors leading into the grand salon, where luncheon was laid out on long banquet tables.

Downing and Bay stood apart from the throng.

"That was unlike any funeral I've ever experienced," Bay said. "It's odd having a separate viewing room, as if Talon wasn't even included at his own service. And Corrine seemed to almost forget about her son." She cut herself off. This wasn't the time for a review of the service, nor could she know what Corrine might be feeling.

Downing kept his dark glasses on and perused the guests. "I wish I could say this is a first for me. I've attended services up here over the years. They are nothing if unconventional." His head swiveled toward her for a moment. "Sorry Professor, duty calls. Talk soon."

From the back of the luncheon line, Bay observed the elites occupied all of the seating in the salon, away from the heat and sun. After making her food selection, Bay veered in the direction of the atrium and outdoor patio beyond. Cass waylaid her and pointed to a table near the back corner where she sat with Posey and another woman.

"There's an empty seat we saved for you." Cass said.

A grateful Bay followed her sister's trail, wishing she had time to ask about Posey's company. *Maybe I can't ask questions about some of the guests now.*

Posey imparted a warm smile. "I'm so glad Cass found you so you could sit with us. An occasion like this can be a lot to navigate. Let me introduce you. Professor Bay Browning, this is Joyce Strost, current president of the Prairie Ridge Literary Society."

The two women exchanged pleasantries, and Bay dug into her lunch, trying to take dainty bites. The others were about finished when she arrived, but she didn't think it would be polite to empty her plate in two minutes, despite her growling stomach.

A server brought a crystal platter with enough dessert options for a dozen people and set it in the center of the four women, along with a carafe of coffee.

Joyce Strost wasn't shy about settling three desserts on her plate or pouring coffees around the table. About halfway through the strawberry Schaum Torte, Joyce paused and leaned forward to share a tidbit or two.

The woman cocked her head toward the banquet table where the Prairie Ridge founding families were seated. "Tell me why you're not up front with the other royals, Posey." She cleared her throat on purpose when she said "royals."

Posey hid a knowing smile behind her napkin. "I wasn't

invited, Joyce. Just like you, I've never been one of the upper echelon."

Joyce explained. "You see, I'm an outsider, a descendant of a Milwaukee beer maker. My German heritage and being from out-of-town places me in the lower social tier. But Posey, your grandparents are founders. I don't understand."

"Never mind, Joyce. We both know there are forces at play on the bluff. I've given up caring about it. Now Bay, I see you're interested in some of the guests. Can I fill you and Cassandra in on the who's who?"

Bay couldn't curb her curiosity. "Please do. Who's the fashionista up there wearing the hat the size of a tractor tire?" Bay noticed her from the get-go, dressed in a black on gray paisley skirt with a stand-up ruffle and black blouse with tight sleeves trimmed in flared chiffon ruffles. "How can anyone eat in an outfit like that?"

Posey giggled, then cleared her throat. "Eating is not the point, my dear. She's here to be seen and she's on the prowl." She waved Bay and Cassandra closer to her to be heard.

"Her name is Anya Nova and until last week, she was soon to be engaged to Talon Hunt."

Posey explained the Nova fortune derived from her Italian-American father's luxury boat enterprise and her Albanian mother's interior design corporation that spanned across the United States.

"The families planned to announce the merger of their offspring at a September soiree. Talon planned to relocate to Minneapolis to run the railway company. Anya would be living there too, setting up her own company, Nova Now. The company makes clean beauty products from sustainable sources."

Posey was still in the Birds' circle, even if she occupied the edges. She knows everything, Bay thought.

"I see why she's here. Did her parents come, too?" Bay figured they might show up out of respect for the Hunts.

Posey craned her neck to study the table of distinguished guests. "I imagine her parents were occupied with business of some sort. Anyway, it appears she's auditioning for a new fiancé."

The other women followed Posey's inspection, aware that Anya Nova was on the move, her ruffles seeming to lead her in a waltz to a new partner, Jackson Lange.

"That's Jackson Lange," Bay whispered. "Talon's best friend."

Cass and Joyce gasped, but Posey already knew the players.

"That table is the Lange Group. Next to Jackson is his father, Lincoln. Then the older Lange brother, Monroe, with his newest wife, Bianca."

"Newest wife? I thought she might be his daughter," Cass observed.

Posey snickered and clucked her tongue, as did Joyce.

"Monroe Lange is vying for Henry the Eighth's record in marriages. What's his current tally of exes now, Posey?" Joyce mowed through a chocolate mascarpone cheesecake. Sugar and caffeine loosened her tongue.

Posey held up three fingers. "Monroe must believe in equal opportunity because he has one child per wife. You can see the three of them sitting at the table with Jackson: Taylor is the oldest, then Reagan, then Madison. We're all holding our breath to see if Bianca will be able to produce a male heir."

Bay scrunched up her face. "Am I imagining this, or are

they all named after presidents?"

"Well done, Professor. Indeed, John Quincy Lange founded his legal dynasty after the First World War. He named his son Jefferson, and the tradition continued."

All four gave Anya and Jackson their full attention and perhaps a number of guests noticed them too, because the pair stood and dashed out of the grand salon.

Bay stared after the two young people as her stomach produced an angry lurch. "I'm sorry, but I think it's disgraceful for Anya and Jackson to be so disrespectful at Talon's memorial service."

Posey's face fell as she stared off into space. "Perhaps Talon's past has come full circle," she murmured.

Nobody at the table was certain how to respond to Posey's remark.

Bay left the Schaum Torte unfinished and excused herself. "It was lovely to meet you, Ms. Strost. Thank you both for inviting me to sit with you. I'm going for a walk."

Cass excused herself and followed on her heels, caught up to Bay, and tugged her sleeve.

"What's with the 'it was lovely to meet you' schtick, Lulu?" Cass knew her sister spoke precise language, but was typically straightforward, too.

Bay laughed. "I suppose hobnobbing with the upper crust may result in putting on airs." She elbowed Cass playfully. "Relax, I'm just trying to fit in."

The sisters bypassed the viewing room and trailed through the atrium outdoors into the afternoon sunshine. They could hear a fountain bubbling nearby and followed the trail to a formal rose garden decorated with white statues of nymphs, seahorses, and dolphins.

They admired the rose varietals, which Cass called out by name for Bay's instruction, then sought out the shade of the lower garden closer to the property's edge. The garden offered privacy with its border of emerald privet hedges that sheltered impatiens, ferns, hostas, and irises. Benches dotted the stone pathway, but there were surprises hiding among the plants, too. Cute statues of woodland creatures peeked out while whimsical butterfly and bird houses hung willy-nilly on posts.

"This looks like a children's garden," Cass said, then stopped at a bend in the path and pointed.

A red oak stood around the bend with ladder steps heading into its canopy where the remnants of a treehouse held on. Steppingstones led the way to the trunk, their faded paint worn by age and weather. Bay could see one still bore Talon's name; another bore Edison's.

"This tree must be the cornerstone of the garden."

They stared in wonder, trying to process a time when Corrine and Malcolm were new parents, kind and loving, doting on their sons. Bay heard a noise nearby, a combination of humming and slurred words. She raised her finger to her lips for quiet and pointed.

The two found Edison sitting against the trunk of the tree, obviously drunk or stoned. He didn't even try to stand when he saw Bay and Cass. Instead, he started laughing.

"You found our secret spot. This is where Talon and I used to hide, often when we were in trouble." He jammed a string of words together while others tumbled out in a stream of slobber.

"Come on Edison. Let's see if you can walk." Bay doubted he could, and when they both tried to raise him and failed, she changed tactics. "Can you try to find the detective?"

Cass left and returned in short order with Downing, who was patrolling the grounds nearby.

"Aw geez," he said looking at Edison's state. "It's going to take three of us to lift him, but then what?" Hands on his hips, he reviewed the scene.

"Would you mind staying with him? I'll drive my car down the back path and park, and I'll bring Harris with me."

Harris and Downing were back to find Edison asleep. It took all four of them to carry him and deposit his limp frame into the back seat of the car.

"What will you do with him?" Bay asked.

Harris replied. "I'll drive him to jail and let him sleep it off in the holding room."

"Are you going to tell the Hunts? You're not going to charge him, are you?" Bay's concern was sincere.

Harris looked to Downing for the answer.

"I'll speak to Malcolm privately while Harris takes him. It's the best solution. We can't carry him through the house now and we can't leave him here."

A series of loud bangs and metallic pops sounded off close to the garden, which was near the property line.

"Wait here." Downing raised his service revolver and Harris circled around the left side, his service gun drawn.

Bay and Cass peered around the privet hedges in curiosity.

Metal cans volleyed over the property line from the woods, exploded midair, and landed in smoking thuds on the ground.

One more barrage blasted through the air, then Downing and Harris dragged two individuals from the woods beyond and knocked them to the ground.

Bay recognized Logan Thorne lying under Downing's boot. He didn't struggle.

"Professor Browning?" Logan gazed upward in surprise. He too, sounded drunk.

"Logan Thorne. Are you crazy?" Bay said.

Downing handcuffed Logan and pulled him to his feet. "Who's your friend?" He nodded toward the fellow Harris was cuffing.

"My neighbor. Please don't take him in. He's underage." Logan had regained some of his faculties. "Crashing this fiesta is on me. My idea."

Harris sat the teen on the ground, propped against a bench, and radioed for a squad car to come get the pair. "I'm off to the station to take care of our other issue, but Bronson will be along to pick up these two."

Downing stood between the two firecracker shooters, glaring.

"Bay and Cassandra, I need you both to skedaddle. When the officer arrives, I'll bring Malcolm Hunt here for a one-on-one, and I don't want him to know you two were anywhere near this. Got it?"

They understood and found the nearest path leading back toward the manor.

"We've had about enough of the jet set for one day, Cass."

Cass agreed. "I'm trading this dress for something comfy. Maybe order a giant meat lovers pizza and split a bottle of wine?"

They continued along where the property sloped upward toward the fountain and rose garden but found themselves in a copse of trees with a riding trail visible beyond.

"I guess we took a wrong turn," Bay said. "This property is huge."

They paused in the shady grove to catch their breath when they spotted movement in the trees. Like watching a movie, Bay and Cass saw two people sitting on the ground, entangled.

The man, whose face wasn't visible, cried in sorrow and clutched the woman, who tried to console him.

Bay and Cass gaped at Posey Hollingsworth. If memory served correctly, the man was dressed like Malcolm Hunt. He spoke but his words were carried away in the opposite direction of the sisters. Bay and Cass turned around and retreated, keeping away from the couple's line of sight. ✿

CHAPTER 15

*Our doubts are traitors, and make us lose
the good we oft might win, by fearing to attempt.*
~ MEASURE FOR MEASURE

Bay maneuvered the Land Rover into the police station lot and parked. Monday mornings were bad enough, but this one was worse. She woke up remembering the strange Hunt dramedy of yesterday was not a nightmare, but a memory. She decided to check in on Edison and Logan.

The security entrance was monitored by an officer she didn't recognize, someone who looked young and fresh. She greeted him cordially and passed through the metal detector, then punched the elevator for the jail.

She'd encountered the desk officer before, Sergeant Keene, in the evidence room when her raincoat was being held as part of a murder investigation. She prayed Keene wouldn't remember her impropriety.

"Professor Browning. Are we holding something personal of yours in the jail?" Keene's memory was, well, keen.

"Good morning, Officer. No, nothing like that. I'm checking on Edison Hunt and Logan Thorne. I understand they were brought here yesterday, and I wondered if I could see them." Bay hoped her contrite tone and downcast eyes would help make amends.

Keene was stone-faced. "This isn't a hospital, Ms. Browning." Keene checked the jail roster. "Looks like you're in luck. A two-for-one deal. They're sharing a cell. Sign here as a visitor." She pointed to a page on the roster clipboard.

"You won't have much time. Edison's being picked up this morning, and Logan's public defender will be here anytime." Keene stood and unlocked the door. "Harris will take you from here."

Bay smiled to see Mandy Harris on duty. "It's nice to see a friendly face, Mandy. I didn't know you were a guard."

"Oh, I'm not. We're short-staffed due to illness and vacations, so I'm picking up a few shifts." Mandy turned down a hallway, walked past three empty cells, and stopped at the end one. "Here we are. I'll just be over there."

Bay sat on a stool outside the cell, shocked to see Edison and Logan engaged in a card game. "Good morning."

They were both bleary-eyed, hungover, and did double takes at Bay's presence there. "

Are you here to see me or him?" Logan asked.

"Both of you. I didn't realize you'd be sharing accommodations." Bay treaded carefully, but couldn't resist her trademark sarcasm.

"I'm sorry you had to see me like that yesterday," Edison said. "Thanks for not making a scene. The officers said you didn't make a big deal out of it."

"I think, under the circumstances, you've been through enough lately. I hear you're out this morning."

Edison gave a quick nod. "My dad thought staying overnight would be a valuable lesson. It was his idea to put Logan in the same cell." He grunted.

Her gaze tracked from one man to the other. "And how did that go?"

Logan snorted. "First, we snarled and swore at each other. Then we got sick together. After some sleep, we decided to talk like real men."

"I think we have an understanding," Edison added, grinning.

Bay stood up. "That's surprising, frankly, and it makes me glad I stopped in to see you two. My optimism in the world needs some restoration. See you tonight, Edison? Logan?"

"See you at rehearsal, Professor." Edison said.

"I'm seeing my lawyer and should be out sometime today. I plan to be at rehearsal." Logan gave Bay the peace sign.

Bay wished Mandy well and thanked Keene politely, then waited for the elevator. The doors opened on Detective Downing, and Bay's pulse revved up without her permission.

"Why are you here?" He asked. He didn't get off the elevator even though this floor was the end of its upward progression.

"Top of the morning to you too," she said sharply. "I've just left Edison and Logan. I'm heading down." She stared at Downing, reluctant to push the first-floor button. "Aren't you getting out?"

"No. I'll see you to your car." He tapped the button. "I should have known you were here to check on those two. You sure care about your students."

Bay smiled politely. "As much as you care about your case

victims."

"What's going to happen to Logan?" Bay asked.

"Fortunately for him, the Hunts will not press charges. They're asking him to clean up his mess on their property and perform ten hours of community service. The juvie was given a warning, and he'll be logging community service, too."

Bay scoffed. "You're telling me Corrine was on board about not pressing charges?"

Downing puffed his cheeks, blew out his breath. "You didn't hear this from me. It was Malcolm who insisted on Logan not being charged. Malcolm also insisted he and Edison share a cell. He called it therapy."

Bay was pleasantly surprised. "A marvelous idea. Cass told me Malcolm was decent when Corrine wasn't around."

"This time, Corrine was around, but he put his foot down. I wish I could have captured the look on her face. It could have peeled paint." Downing chuckled at the mental picture.

"I'm glad we ran into each other. There's something bothering me about Talon's death."

"By all means, go on, Professor."

"If he was targeted for murder, the killer relied on plenty of coincidences. How did the killer know Talon would be exposed to the fentanyl on the sword? How did the killer know Talon would be on the balcony, or fall from the balcony, for that matter? Didn't you say the fall killed Talon—the fentanyl was a contributing factor?"

"Hold up a minute, Bay. Those are all valid questions, and I've asked them myself. The fentanyl caused Talon to get dizzy, lose his balance, and fall. He didn't have to fall off the balcony to hit his head hard enough to die. He could fall down the stairs, off the stage, or even just a hard fall to the floor could be enough."

Bay frowned. She was certain she was on to something important.

"Don't look so disappointed. You're right about the fact that someone tainted the prop sword with no idea who might be exposed to it. It could have been Maya or Aria or any of the actors." His intense look made Bay think harder.

She turned the ideas over again in her mind. When they arrived at the Land Rover, she mechanically reached for her keys, then punched Downing's bicep.

"One thing was for certain: we could count on Talon and Jackson goofing around, testing the props, doing the opposite of what they were told."

Downing egged her on. "Which means?"

"Which means the killer knew that, too." Bay enjoyed her deductive victory, until she saw Downing's serious expression. "What is it?"

"It also might mean that Talon wasn't a specific target. Maybe he was just one target."

Bay shuddered. "Maybe there's more coming." Her response was hushed.

Something triggered the detective. "You have a key for the theater, don't you?" She nodded. "Can we go there now?" She nodded again.

When Bay and Downing pulled into the lot at Carillon Tower Park, they saw a car parked on the grass by the backstage entrance. He motioned for Bay's silence as he pulled out his service revolver, and Bay followed behind him.

The two crept up the back stairs and saw Maya, the props

master, going through costumes on a long rack. Downing stowed his weapon and Bay exhaled.

"Maya, what are you doing here?" Bay's voice was friendly, but it startled Maya.

"Hi Professor Browning. I didn't hear you coming. Guess I'm in the zone. Mrs. Knight is meeting me here to pick up costumes that need to be repaired." Maya recognized the detective and was curious. "Is everything okay?"

"I'm glad you're here, Maya. I came to collect the fencing saber prop, and you can save me the trouble of digging through all the weapons."

Maya cringed at the idea of anyone digging through the props. "Actually, we have six fencing props. I'm guessing you want the one Talon Hunt was dueling with before…well, before…" she trailed off.

"Yes. Why are there six fencing sabers? Are there that many dueling scenes in the show?" Downing looked between Maya and Bay.

"Here's my system when it comes to props. Each actor has their own, and they are responsible for keeping track of them and having them in place for their scenes." Maya motioned the detective to follow her. One upright wooden box held the sabers and swords, each one standing in a slot, like bottles in a beverage case.

"Each actor has a tape color assigned to them. Their props are all marked with a piece of colored tape. They're not supposed to touch anyone else's props." Maya's words carried authority.

"Clever. You're quite organized. Which one is the saber Talon used?"

Maya pulled out a black carrying case and passed it to Downing. "I'm sorry to tell you that I cleaned the saber before I returned it to the case." Maya's serious tone was matter-of-fact rather than apologetic.

His eyes narrowed. "And why did you do that?"

Maya carried on with no shift in tone. "I clean the props after every rehearsal. It's an important part of taking care of them."

Downing and Bay exchanged quizzical looks.

"Show me your cleaner, please." He had his notebook and pen out. Maya showed a simple alcohol-based cleaner and box of gloves.

Downing pointed to the box. "Do you always wear gloves when you clean the props?"

"Always, and so does Aria. I have her trained." Maya wore a proud smile.

Downing stuffed his notepad and pen back in his pocket, turned toward Bay, and jabbed his thumb toward the stage. "Thanks for your help, Maya. The lab might have the saber for a while."

Maya shrugged. "We have extra sabers. I'll get one from the college's prop storage."

Bay followed Downing out to the stage. "What is it?" She whispered.

"I'm testing this for fentanyl residue." He held the carrying case aloft.

"The cleaner won't wipe away the evidence?" Bay was curious, anxious to learn.

"It might or might not, but the carrying case wasn't wiped, so if the killer dosed the saber with the drug, then stashed it back in the case…"

Bay sucked in her breath. "And if the killer knew about Maya's tape system, it could mean Talon was the target. If you find drug residue on the saber…" she hiccupped.

"It means the killer has a list," Downing's expression was grim.

"Who else has a key to the theater, besides the directors and Maya?" Downing pulled the notepad back out.

"I don't think anyone else," Bay answered. "But you'd better ask Desmond. I didn't know Maya had a key, but I'm not in charge of the protocol."

"I'll call Desmond. Meanwhile, keep your eyes and ears open, Bay. Watch Maya."

Bay returned to the costume room to wait for Mrs. Knight to arrive, so she could meet her.

Minutes later, a middle-aged woman pulled up in an old-model minivan. She made her way up the back stairs and into the stage rooms.

"Hello, Mrs. Knight. I'm Maya Leary, and I'll show you the costumes."

"Hello, I'm Bay Browning, one of the assistant directors for the show. Thank you for agreeing to work on costumes."

"Hello Maya and Ms. Browning. Please call me Ginny. I can't wait to see the costumes for this show. Henry's told me a lot about the production."

Bay smiled. "Henry is quite the engineer. You'll have to see the trap door and underpass he designed for characters to come and go from the stage."

Ginny's cheeks flushed, and her smile was tentative. "I'm glad Henry is part of the show. He needs involvement. He has difficulty fitting in sometimes."

Bay reassured her. "Henry just finished his freshman year. He will find his place."

Ginny turned her focus to the costume rack. Bay stayed in the background, watching, as Maya expertly pulled out the hanging costumes one by one, indicated possible character matches for each one, and showed Ginny the necessary repairs. Bay assumed Maya must have been involved in theater productions for years.

Ginny nodded along, making notes on her phone after taking a photo of each piece. "I can have these back to you in two or three days. I will want to have each actor try them on for fitting, however." She looked backward toward Bay. "What night works in your rehearsal schedule for me to pull aside the actors?"

Bay didn't have the schedule committed to memory, but the actors would be at all rehearsals, since they played multiple roles. Should she speak for Desmond? "Tomorrow night? We begin at six and take a break around seven-fifteen."

"Perfect," Ginny said. She selected five costumes from those piled across the countertop. "I'll take these with me and return them then. I'll take the rest after I measure the actors." Ginny and Maya would work well together, it seemed.

It was hard to imagine, but Cassandra felt sheepish entering Spirit Gardens House to find Posey. She began whistling, a sign she was out of sorts. Whistling was her tell, and her parents knew it meant she was covering something up. In this case, she felt awkward, wondering what she should say to Posey about seeing her with Malcolm yesterday. Maybe she shouldn't say anything at all.

"Hellooo. Anybody home in there?" Marva rapped the countertop where Cass stood, staring into oblivion.

"Oh, good morning, Marva. Sorry, I didn't see you." Cass muttered.

"I've been standing right here the whole time. What's the matter with you?" Marva tugged her vibrant blue strand of hair, twirling it around her finger, a sign of trouble.

Cass stood up straighter. "What's wrong, Marva? Is Posey okay?"

"Miss Posey's okay, far as I know. It's my sister, Fanta. She's in such a fix about the upset at the Hunt house. I'm not sure she wants to stay. Mrs. Hunt has been extra, is all I'm saying."

Cass shrugged, her voice impatient. "Extra. Meaning?"

Marva sniffed. "I shouldn't say, when people are going through the terrible things like they are. She's such a shrew to Fanta. Her family too. She ought to be careful or she may regret it." Marva spoke in a deliberate staccato.

Cass stared at her. "Her family too. Does that mean the family is being mean to Fanta or Corrine is being mean to her family?" Sometimes a person needed a road map to follow Marva's sentences.

Marva jutted out her chin. "She's the mean one. Mr. Hunt is as kind as they come, and Edison. Well, he's a bit lost is all, but never mean."

"I'm sorry to hear Fanta is having trouble. I hope she can sort it out. I'm off to the study or greenhouse, I guess." Cass pecked Marva on the cheek.

"Oh, Miss Posey has company in there. So be forewarned."

The study was unoccupied, so Cass supposed Marva

meant the greenhouse, a place that always held surprises. Just opening the door delighted Cass, who soaked in the scent of earth, water vapor, and blossoms.

She saw Posey talking with two people in the exotic section. They appeared to be admiring the baneberry and exclaiming over the beauty of the Cattleya trianae orchid, the national flower of Colombia dressed in pure white and royal purple.

Cassandra's trained ear caught their conversation in Spanish, but since she was rusty and they were moving along at a fast pace, she could discern just a smattering of words. Funny, she didn't know Posey spoke Spanish, but then there was a great deal Posey didn't know about her either.

She ducked behind a hutch filled with gardening supplies, knocking loose a pewter plant marker that flew to the floor with a clatter.

"Cassandra, is that you?" Posey's voice rose over blooming camelias. "Come and meet my friends."

Cass recovered from her clumsy attempt at espionage and wondered if she was losing her touch. She smiled at the handsome man and pretty woman.

"This is Dr. Marcel Domingas and Lisa Domingas. Please meet Cassandra Browning, my personal assistant." Posey looked at all three as she would a treasure. Cass beamed and shook their hands, feeling at ease with the man and woman.

"Marcel is a botanist, one of the foremost experts on Central American vegetation. I'm happy to say he is now a full professor at UW–Madison." Posey gushed with pride.

Cass smiled, too. "Dr. Domingas, how do you know Posey?"

"Call me Marcel, please. Posey and I met a long time ago. My father and her father knew each other. She helped me procure my position at the university."

Posey disagreed. "I simply told Marcel about the post. His expertise won over the university. I'm happy he and Lisa are here. They're my greenhouse consultants."

Cass looked at Lisa, a tiny woman with long black hair who seemed ageless. "Are you a botanist, too?"

Lisa produced a quiet smile. "No, I'm a horticulturalist. I'm working at the university part- time, but Marcel and I hope to start a family soon."

Lisa's announcement contained great hope and desire. Cass understood both feelings, but for vastly different reasons. The idea of having a family seemed so normal to Cass, yet foreign and fantastic, too.

Cass reached out to Lisa again, but the woman stepped back slightly away from Cass's touch. Cass's eyes widened in surprise. She nodded her head once at Lisa, hoping to convey sincere wishes for her dreams.

"I'll let you carry on with your tour of the greenhouse. Is there something I can work on, Posey?" Cass felt an urge to be alone.

"I'll meet you in the study shortly." Posey turned to the couple, and they resumed speaking in Spanish. This time Cassandra caught the words "Be careful around her," coming from Lisa.

Cassandra sat at Posey's computer, browsing websites about essential oils and herbal teas beneficial for pregnant women. Another tab opened onto the people of Guatemala, its culture and history. She thought about opening Posey's email but decided she had not yet been given permission. Meanwhile, the rosewood desk's locked middle drawer taunted her with the red file folder.

I could easily open it with a nail file or pair of scissors. Like those, sitting on the corner of the desk. It's like someone left them out on purpose.

Cass continued to stare down the scissors, daring them to come closer. She rattled the middle desk drawer in an angry reaction to its temptation. The drawer, thankfully, held firm. She leapt from the chair and crossed the room to look out the window. The mail carrier was coming up the walkway, a useful excuse to meet him.

She flung the door open and startled the mailman.

"Oh, you must be expecting these." He handed her a stack of postcards banded together. Cass figured they were RSVPs to Posey's upcoming Shakespeare party. She skipped to the study, eager to update the party plans.

Posey was sitting at the desk scrutinizing Cassandra's online searches, but Cass didn't care.

"Look, you're already getting RSVPs to the party," she reported.

Posey reached for the stack of cards and patted the nearby chair. "Is there something you want to share with me, Cassandra?" Posey's face was unreadable.

Cass raised her brows.

"You're searching for teas and oils for pregnant women. I didn't know you were seeing someone." A smile crept onto her face.

"I'm not, not at all," Cass protested. "I was looking for Lisa Domingas." She might have continued, but decided tattling news that isn't yours wasn't a good look.

Posey grunted. "Hmm, and just how did you know Lisa was

pregnant?" She dismissed the question with a wave. "Never mind. I know how it works."

"It's happy news for them though, isn't it?" Cass asked.

"Yes, wonderful news. They've been married ten years, trying and trying. What would you like to know about Guatemala?" Posey pressed the tab where the page on Guatemala's people popped up. Posey suppressed her awe of Cass's ability to know the couple's background.

Cass looked at her fingernails, embarrassed. "Just curious. Marcel is much taller than Lisa and his features are different. I wondered about Guatemala's ethnic background."

"Guatemala is divided evenly between Ladinos and Mayans. The Mayans are native to the country, and the Ladinos are a mixture of Spanish European and indigenous people. Lisa is Mayan; one of their traits is being slight in stature. Marcel is Ladino." Posey would have made a talented teacher.

"Did you learn all that from your father?" Cass asked.

"My father went there often. He loved all of Central America, the people and customs. He shared his experiences with me and anyone else who would listen." She seemed far away in another time.

"Posey." Cass waited for her attention. "Yesterday at the Hunts', Joyce Strost said something about not being one of the Bluff Birds because of her heritage. Can you explain that?"

"Wisconsin was settled by a large percentage of Germans. They came here because it reminded them of home. Prairie Ridge had and still has numerous families of German ethnicity. But during World War I, civic leaders began shunning German Americans, seeing it as patriotic duty. Our Ladies Home Social Club followed suit, banned German books from the library, and stopped associating with their German neighbors. It became ingrained in the minds of the Bluff Birds, to discriminate against anyone with German ethnicity. To treat them as if they were somehow less human, less deserving." Posey choked on the words, alarming Cass.

"That was so long ago. You're saying it's still happening?" Cass was incredulous.

"Old habits die hard, Cassandra. Many of the bluff properties are still owned by founding families. Their prejudices are dyed-in-the-wool." Posey's nostrils flared. She snatched a tissue from the desktop and blew her nose.

Cass's thoughts spun on an axis between pursuing the subject or changing it. "What about you? Are you German, Posey?"

"I am not. Let's open my emails and update the party spreadsheet with yeses and nos.

Can you make a sign-up sheet for them to choose a Shakespeare character for the party? I don't want duplicates because it won't be as much fun."

"Yes, I can create a spreadsheet in a jiff. We'll send out the form to people as they RSVP, so they may choose a character from a suggested list. And I'll make it so you're the only one who sees their answers."

Hours later, Bay was at Carillon Tower again, just as the clock chimed the hour. She'd been crafting a bulletin board with cast photos, each with at least one or two notes tacked beside them. She just started adding strings between actors when her phone alarm sounded. Cass wasn't home to keep their dinner routine, so Bay had forgotten to eat, and now she had to leave.

At the park, she closed the SUV's door and made a beeline for the stage, munching a protein bar en route. Desmond was talking to the cast but motioned for Bay to sit between him and Jen.

"Okay, places everyone. We're starting with the third act. It needs some attention." While the actors found their spots and waited for their cues, Desmond stood between Bay and Jen.

"Ginny Knight will be here at seven o'clock to start fitting the actors in costumes, so Maya can tag them, and we can see what works and what we need."

"Oh, sorry Desmond. I met Ginny this morning, and I told her to come tomorrow night. She asked for a date and wanted to take costumes with her to start sewing." Bay feared she may have overstepped, but Desmond waved her off.

"No problem. I'm glad you were here when she came. But I called Ginny after I talked to Maya to ask her to come tonight. I just want to keep things moving along," Desmond nodded to himself. He was operating in fifth gear.

"I understand. I'm glad she can be here tonight. Wow, that Maya is something, Desmond. She has a system for everything."

Desmond smiled, then frowned. "Yes, I'll miss her. She's a real marvel. I hope she can train someone to take her place. Maybe Aria. She's a quick study."

Bay smiled, thinking Aria would be pleased to hear that.

Ginny arrived early to watch the actors rehearse, so she could gauge costuming needs. Jen and Bay sat with her to answer questions and offer input as needed.

Before the break, Ginny returned to the costume rack and

browsed the hair and jewelry accessories, too. She picked up one of the stiff lace Elizabethan collars and laughed. "Which of the actors has the misfortune of playing Portia? She's going to be wearing this." She twirled the large, ruffed neck collar, which was the circumference of a small pizza.

Bay and Jen giggled, admiring Ginny's wit. "Kitt. The tall blond woman with her hair in a thick braid." Jen pointed to Kitt, who was chatting on stage with Nora, a redheaded curvy female.

"I think I'll fit Kitt now. Check this out: all the makings for the Portia character, who was inspired by Queen Elizabeth herself." Ginny held up a chocolate-brown velvet headband trimmed in pearls against a heavy gold and ivory brocade gown. "Won't this be smashing?"

Kitt, who heard her name, skipped into the costume room and exclaimed at the ensemble Ginny crafted for her. The remaining female cast members couldn't wait for their turns to see what Ginny and Maya had in store for them.

Cher made a sour face when she saw Kitt stepping into the grand brocade gown, fit for a queen. "Which character is wearing that?" She pointed to the gown.

"Portia, from *The Merchant of Venice*, the worthiest hero in your production." Ginny wasn't bothered by Cher's attitude.

"Isn't that in act three? Professor Browning, I'm not in that act. I could play Portia." Cher thrust out her chin like a petulant child.

Bay couldn't decide if she should refer Cher to Desmond or nip the whole idea in the bud herself. "That's amusing, Cher. The cast is set." Her comment hit Cher below the belt. She expected to be taken seriously and was accustomed to getting what she wanted.

Ginny rescued the kettle before it boiled over, took Cher by the hand, and led her to the costume rack. "You're Juliet in act one, yes? What about this gown?" She pulled out a sapphire gown overlaid with silver gossamer and a French hood trimmed in silver spangles.

Cher examined it with skepticism, twisting her lips around, and scrunching her nose.

"It's a perfect match for your blue eyes, and the silver trim will accent your dark hair. Try it on, please." Ginny was kind but firm.

Bay and Jen praised Ginny's choice for Juliet and grudgingly complimented Cher, who stuck her nose in the air and strutted onto the stage.

"Two more years before she graduates," Jen ribbed Bay.

"I'm such a Katherine. I best learn to trim my tongue," Bay said, "lest trouble findeth me in the Devane way." Her reference to the fiery titular character from *Taming of the Shrew* made Jen chuckle.

Ginny dressed the act three heroines, then the lady loves from the first act, but soon ran out of time when Desmond said rehearsal must continue.

"Sorry, we're short on time and must move on. Can you come back another night this week?" Desmond asked Ginny.

"Of course. I have plenty of sewing to do on the costumes we chose tonight. I'm glad we're getting an early start, so I have time to finish before the show."

Desmond ran his hand through his hair twists, a sign of stress. "About that. The sooner I can get the actors into costumes for rehearsals, the better."

"I'll bring back anything that's finished tomorrow and continue trading out costumes until they're all ready. There's just one problem though. There are not enough costumes for every character. Nothing works for Cleopatra, for instance. Then there's the trickster characters. They can't all dress as jesters."

Bay had an idea. "I think I might know where we can get our hands on more costumes. Let me check into it and I'll let you know tomorrow." She remembered Cassandra sharing details about Posey's costume closets. Since Posey invited Bay to attend her literary society meeting tomorrow, she could ask then.

Ginny stayed to watch the next act, which featured Shakespeare's famous tricksters. Bay and Jen were relieved when the act concluded without an argument between Logan and Jackson. In fact, the two were well-behaved. Maybe Talon's funeral helped Jackson to move forward. Maybe Logan's night in jail calmed his beastly side. Maybe both were true.

The two directors helped Ginny load her minivan with costumes to alter and repair while Desmond gave scene notes to the actors. Maya carried one last gown to the van before Ginny shut the hatch.

Maya was fuming. "Cher tore her gown, flouncing around the stage. Show off," Maya said the remark under her breath.

Ginny hoped it was just a torn hem. "I'll take care of it. Thank you for your help. I'll be back tomorrow." ✺

CHAPTER 16

Lady, you know no rules of charity,
which renders good for bad, blessings for curses.
~ RICHARD III

When Bay arrived at Posey's for the literary meeting, she was in for a surprise. Posey introduced Bay as the takeover host for the meeting who would lead them all in a literature-themed game.

After she lifted her face off the floor, she painted on a smile, introduced herself, and asked the seven people attending to do the same. Of course, she already knew Gabriel McNelly, her colleague from Flourish, someone she had not expected to see.

Joyce Strost called the meeting to order and welcomed Bay. "Professor Browning and I met at Talon Hunt's memorial service, you see."

Four were Bluff Birds, according to their introductions, since each mentioned where they resided. *A bit pretentious.* Two women and one married couple rounded off the group for the day, but Joyce pointed out there were over twenty club members at times.

"It's hard to get people together in the summer. Too many competing activities."

To Bay's credit, she was quick on her feet. "Some of you might know that I'm one of the directors for the summer theater production at Flourish. The play is a takeoff on Shakespeare's characters, so I thought we might play a game called "Plot Twist," which is rewriting the ending of a well-known story."

Joyce and Posey clapped with enthusiasm, while the others raised their questioning faces toward Bay. "Let's rewrite an ending for Romeo and Juliet. Each of you can write your own ending on paper. I'll collect them in, let's say six minutes, and someone can read them aloud. For fun, we'll vote on our favorite ending. Be sure to keep them anonymous."

Posey handed out scrap paper and everyone joined in. Even Bay, who wanted to be a role model, crafted an alternate ending in which Friar Lawrence, who marries the lovers, dies drinking the poison meant for Romeo, thereby making the ultimate sacrifice and healing the two families.

The game went better than Bay anticipated and ended with a declaration that all the optional endings were worthy. Bay suspected the ending in which Romeo joins the priesthood and Juliet joins a convent belonged to McNelly, but she couldn't know for sure.

She was just happy to be off the hook for the balance of the meeting. Society members bantered about their upcoming reading choices for the remainder of the year, beginning in September. Ideas for a fall fundraiser enticed a lively discussion, ranging from a book bazaar to book bingo to a moveable book themed feast. Posey suggested the feast.

"Speaking of book themed events, I hope you're all thinking about which Shakespeare character you plan to dress as for my party. If you need ideas, I imagine Professor Browning will be happy to assist you." Posey smiled brightly.

Marva wheeled in a silver cart filled with breakfast pickup foods and two carafes: one with coffee and one with tea. She winked at Bay perhaps to convey she knew about Posey's diabolical plan to make Bay the guest host.

McNelly sat apart from the members in a wingback chair near the arched windows. Bay took her plate and coffee and sat in the opposite chair.

"I'm surprised to see you here, Dr. McNelly. Do you live on the bluff?" It was a casual question, but a baited one.

"I've known Posey and the Bluff Birds my whole life. I live just below the bluff, on Bird Street in my family's farmhouse."

"Ah, between two worlds, I see." Bay didn't mean her words to sound harsh, but McNelly was known to bring out her prickly side. "What I mean is…" she faltered. *What exactly did she mean?*

He chuckled and crossed one leg over the other. "It's okay, L.L., no need to explain."

"It's Bay. I'm not using L.L. any longer," she said without explanation.

"Bully for you," McNelly's congratulatory tone came off as judgmental to her.

"Will you be coming to the Shakespeare party?" She asked him.

"I thought I'd dress as Friar Lawrence," McNelly taunted her.

Bay sputtered mid-drink. "I think that's perfect. You harbor a number of secrets, don't you?"

"Don't paint me the villain, Bay. Consider me the librarian with a catalog of authors and their sins." McNelly's eyes crinkled, making him look wolflike. He was a hairy man who wore a bushy mustache and thick curly beard, often making his face difficult to read.

"What benefit is all that locked-up knowledge, anyway?"

"It has its functions from time to time," he said, draining his cup.

"What do you think happened to Talon Hunt? You must know them well or they wouldn't have asked you to give the closing remarks."

McNelly leaned forward in the chair, staring out the window. "People who live like the Bluff Birds make enemies. Sometimes, because they use their status for ill."

Bay leaned in. "Are you speaking of Talon specifically or the Hunts as a family?"

"The general consensus is that Talon was a punk with a big ego." McNelly appeared poised to reveal more, but stopped.

"How about Jackson Lange?"

"Same pig, different sty." McNelly quipped. "Monroe should have been that lad's father. Lincoln is a decent man."

"And Edison Hunt?" Bay wondered if she was on track thinking the number one son was treated unfairly.

"Edison squandered his station but realized he couldn't get by on just the Hunt name. However, there's more to him than meets the eye. I wouldn't discount the young man just yet."

Bay grinned in agreement. "You mean, like his parents do?"

"Oh Bay, which of his parents do you mean? One is not like the other, that's for certain." McNelly rose, brushed crumbs from his beard onto his plate, and wished Bay a good day.

Bay joined the group situated around the food cart, just in time to hear the latest gossip.

"I hear Monroe Lange's latest flavor has a baby bulge," Melinda Townsend said, a knowing smirk on her blotchy face. "Perhaps he will finally get the son he's always wanted."

Paula Bryant, seated beside her husband, popped a mini quiche into her mouth then tossed out additional scuttlebutt. "Speaking of the Langes, did you see Jackson undressing Talon's fiancée with his eyes? I mean, what nerve. He's supposed to be Talon's best friend."

Melinda pounced on the remark. "She wasn't no slouch either. Practically throwing herself at Jackson. I heard her family needs the money." She spoke in a hush, as if the words might conjure bad luck for all of them.

"Professor Browning, how is the murder investigation going? You must be tuned in to the progress, you know, with your special connection to the detective." Paula's sharp barb hit its mark, and Bay colored crimson.

Posey cleared her throat like she might perform an aria. "All right now, let's adjourn. We have our reading list. Joyce, did we decide on a fall fundraiser?"

Joyce looked over the notes. "No. Lots of inspiring ideas are on the table. Let's finalize one at our July meeting. I'll send them to all the members with a note to come prepared to decide. Meeting adjourned."

Like a shepherd, Posey ushered the members out the front door with her thanks. Bay lingered in the foyer.

"Next time you invite me to a meeting, let me know in advance that I'm the entertainment, would you?" Bay smiled, half annoyed.

Posey looked smug, swaying a little from side to side. "You're a quick study, Bay. Thanks for indulging me. Now, how can I make amends?"

"Funny you should ask. Cassandra tells me you own a surplus of costumes. Our production could use some. Would you be willing to loan them to the college?"

"Of course. What do you need?"

"I'm not certain. Ginny Knight is organizing, altering, and repairing costumes. Would it be okay if we both came over to pick some out?"

"Ginny Knight." Posey's head clouded with memories. "I haven't heard that name in a long time."

Bay folded her arms. "Tell me about the Knights."

"The family used to be my neighbors—that way. She pointed north. I grew up with Henry the third. His parents were nice people, salt of the earth, but then the Knights lost their fortune in bad business deals. They sold the property and scattered. The third Henry started over in Chicago, married, had a son, and died of a heart condition when his son was five. I'm surprised they've relocated here, except…" She tapped one manicured finger against her temple.

"Henry's a student at Flourish, isn't he?"

Bay nodded. "He just completed his freshman year."

"Chances are he was admitted as a legacy student, since many of the Knights went to Flourish. It may be the option for someone less fortunate." Posey turned away from the conversation.

"Just let me know when you and Ginny want to stop over. Cass will be here any moment, and it's time to switch gears. It was good of you to come today, Bay."

Every encounter on the bluff created a tailspin for Bay, as abrupt mood changes appeared to rule the day. Posey, McNelly—who wasn't technically a Bird, Edison Hunt: she wondered how much time each spent playacting, and for what purpose.

She didn't have long to contemplate the idea with the Hunt house nearby, but she wondered which side of Edison she might be tutoring today.

She said a cheery greeting to Fanta, who ushered her into the library. "Coffee, tea, water, something else?" She asked Bay.

"Water would be nice. Thank you."

"And there will be pie later. It just needs to cool a bit longer. Strawberry rhubarb." Fanta whirled around, dismissing herself.

"Hello, Edison. How are you?" Bay dipped one toe in the pond.

"Fine, I suppose. What's today's torture?" He wore boredom well, a look Bay recognized among students who didn't want to be in class.

"Let's change the venue. How about the shady area in the atrium?" Bay suggested.

"Sounds good." Edison gathered his book, notebook, and drink.

"How are things with your parents?" Bay hoped his drunken performance at Talon's service wouldn't create more friction.

"If you mean my mother, I'm happy to report she's leaving this evening for a conference in Atlanta. She won't be back for a few days." Edison's sarcasm mixed with disdain oozed from his pores.

They entered the atrium and sat among the palms and

weeping figs. "How about dear old dad?" Bay meant the offhand remark to be inviting.

"What about dear old dad, Professor Browning?" Malcolm appeared from somewhere close by, coffee mug in one hand, newspaper in the other. A pair of reading glasses perched on his nose, making his amused expression appear comical.

"I'm so sorry, Mr. Hunt. Just making small talk with Edison. We decided a change of scenery might be favorable." Bay hoped her hopscotch chatter would cover her faux pas.

Malcolm chuckled. "Relax, Doctor. I'm not the enemy, but unfortunately, dear old dad has to meet with the board of directors tomorrow in Minneapolis. I'll be gone overnight, Eddy. Okay with you?" He squeezed Edison's shoulder warmly.

"Your sister is skilled with horses. Do you ride, Doctor?" Malcolm asked.

Bay shook her head. "I've always wanted to learn."

"Come by sometime, and I'll show you the stables and choose a safe starter horse for you. Bring your sister along. She's welcome to ride Posey's horses anytime." Malcolm bobbed his glasses as he walked out.

Edison laughed, a robust, cleansing laugh. "The look on your face when you said 'dear old dad'—that was priceless. I'm just glad it was him who heard it and not my mother." He made a slice motion across his throat.

"Let's get to work, shall we?" Bay giggled.

Bay concluded the lesson with Edison writing a summary of the initial five chapters of *American Gods*. "We'll analyze your writing tomorrow, sentence by sentence." It was her turn to make slashing motions across the paper.

Ginny Knight agreed to meet Bay at Spirit Gardens before rehearsal to rummage through Posey's costume collection.

When Bay phoned to ask Posey about the visit, she said yes and insisted that Bay come to tea at four o'clock.

Cass met Bay at the main entrance and ushered her into the salon where the literary society had met that morning.

"How's your day going, Bay?"

"Interesting. Posey tagged me to host the literary society game this morning, so that was something. McNelly is a member of the club. I know, shocking. At the Hunt estate, I lodged my foot in my mouth by asking Edison what his dear old dad was up to. Turned out Malcolm Hunt heard my blunder but was good-natured about it. He invited you and me to ride horses anytime." Bay stood by the blooming plumeria and inhaled its sweet spicy fragrance.

Cass followed her lead, enjoying the plumeria blooms. "Malcolm seems friendly enough. Maybe that's why Posey is attracted to him. But I didn't think you could ride."

"I can't. Malcolm offered to pick a starter horse for me to try out. I think we should take him up on the offer. Where's Posey, and is Ginny coming to tea, too?"

"I don't know about Ginny, but Posey sidelined to the greenhouse to pick some herbs for garnish. She might be in the kitchen surveying Marva's culinary offerings. She's been bouncing around the house all day today. Your buddy McNelly put her behind schedule. He didn't leave until one-thirty."

"McNelly? He was here for the morning meeting, so he must have come back for, what?

"Legal business, I suspect. Attorney McGann was at the meeting. It is curious that Posey would have business dealings with an ex-priest. She associates with all kinds of people, though."

Posey arrived in denim capris and a chambray shirt, a change from her society meeting red and white sundress. Bay felt overdressed in her skirt and floral button down top and wondered if she'd ever figure out a winning fashion choice for a Posey occasion.

Posey beamed at Bay. "You match the plumeria. You'll have to excuse my attire—I've been working in the greenhouse."

Marva wheeled in the familiar silver cart, this time loaded with finger sandwiches, pita wedges with hummus, assorted olives and pickled vegetables, and shortbread cookies. She poured out tea for the ladies and pointed to the creamer and sugar.

"If I'm going to eat here too often, I'll need to take up running or rowing. I can't imagine how my sister manages to stay in shape." Bay exclaimed over the homemade hummus and pita, topped with Kalamata olives and a sprig of Posey's own oregano.

Both women laughed. "The secret is that we don't overeat. We burn some of it off in the hot greenhouse," Posey reported.

Cass added, "It's not like this every day. Just when Posey has company."

"Speaking of company, is Ginny Knight coming for tea?" No matter how Bay said it, she knew it was a forward question, but Posey was unflappable.

"I didn't ask her—this time. I wanted to share more history with you about your cast and crew. Jackson Lange and the Lange family."

"Funny you should mention him. After Melinda brought up

Jackson this morning at the society meeting, I thought there may be blanks to fill in. Oh, and thanks for rescuing me from the hot seat." It seemed like all the Bluff Birds expected the police to wrap up Talon's murder promptly, and Bay did, too.

Posey added cream to her tea and swirled in a dribble of honey. "Have you met the ex-Ladies Lange?"

"You mean Monroe's former wives? I haven't. I also haven't met Jackson's parents. Most parents stay out of their college kids' school life." *Of course, the Bluff Bird parents may be the exception to that rule.* Cher Devane's parents came to mind, as did Talon Hunt's.

"They're an odd trio of compadres, considering each one was partly responsible for the other's divorce." Posey paused for effect. "For starters, they all live in the same condo complex by the Monona Terrace. Ex Number One, Suzanne, hired a shark for a lawyer, a Madison hotshot who salivated at going toe-to-toe with the Lange Group. The lawyer did all the work while Suzanne found a luxury condo to move into with daughter, Taylor. When the next two exes found themselves adrift in Monroe's life, Suzanne retained her divorce lawyer and found condos in her building."

Bay and Cass fist-bumped each other in celebration of the savvy Lange exes. "It's hard to believe they get along together. Kudos to them," Cass commented.

Posey pressed her lips together and shrugged. "Their children share a common father, and the women share common circumstances. There's comfort in the bonds of heartbreak." Posey's eyes misted over. Bay and Cass both wondered what Posey's heartbreak might be.

"I've heard Lincoln Lange is a decent fellow," Bay repeated

what she'd heard from McNelly that morning.

Posey agreed. "The two brothers are like day and night. It's too bad Lincoln's son doesn't quite fit his father's mold. Perhaps he will grow into it."

Bay thought of Jackson's snarly behavior toward Logan and Edison at rehearsals, then remembered he was also grieving his best friend's death. Still, it seemed underhanded if he was making a play for Talon's fiancée.

"I'd love to know what makes Cher Devane tick. She's been a thorn in my side since I've known her." Bay hoped Posey could share some details.

"The Devanes are workaholics with high standards and even higher ambitions. Cher's sister moved away three years ago, and she never visits. I think Cher believes in self-love, since she's not getting it from her family." Posey laid out her evaluation.

"Cher could learn that love is a give and receive proposition. She's self-centered," Bay said.

Posey grunted. "Now Bay, what were you like when you were twenty years old?

"Let's see. I'd just finished my master's degree in English and world literature, and started working on my PH.D. at NYU."

"Cheeky. Well, that doesn't sound normal to me." Posey sniffed.

"Hardly," Bay remarked.

"Did you ever have a serious boyfriend?" Posey volleyed, while Cass enjoyed the ping- pong match between the two.

"No, not me. What about you, Posey? Any romantic lovers in your life?" Bay's sideways glance at Cass was easy to read. They were both wondering about Posey and Malcolm.

Posey sputtered a moment and blinked rapidly. "Yes, there was someone once." Her face drained of color and life.

Without thinking, Cass pounced. "Was it Malcolm Hunt?" She covered her mouth as soon as the words were out, but there was no putting those words back where they came from.

Posey stood up, her eyes flashing. "I believe tea is over. Excuse me. Perhaps Ginny Knight has arrived."

"Oh, hang it all, I overstepped this time." Cass wrung her hands. "I've been trying to think of a subtle way to bring up Malcolm."

"I think you bypassed subtle, Cass. Don't worry too much. I imagine Posey will talk to you when she's ready—or not at all."

Marva told the sisters that Ginny was waiting in the salon by the foyer, so they abandoned the tea party to meet her. Bay saw Cassandra wrap some cookies in a napkin and stuff them in her purse. She wondered if this was a retreat to the past when Cass hoarded food as a runaway or prisoner. A sad gnawing occupied Bay's mind momentarily.

Posey, who looked like her usual self, greeted Ginny with a warm embrace. "Hello Ginny. I'm Posey Hollingsworth and happy to make your acquaintance."

Ginny hugged Posey in return, stood tall, and looked her directly in the eye. "I understand you used to be my husband's playmate."

Posey's smile filled her face. "Henry was a dear friend. We played hide-and-seek all over the neighborhood and had some true adventures. I was sorry to hear of his passing."

"I still miss him. He used to say you two were the park rangers around here, saving animals, putting baby birds back in their nests, and marking trails through the woods. I wish my Henry would have been able to do that." Ginny sighed at what might have been.

"Me, too. And where are you living these days?" Posey's question was basic small talk, not an inquisition, so she was surprised to see Ginny look away.

"We're in one of the old neighborhoods near downtown. I work airport security at Truax."

"Have you always been involved with theater costumes?" Bay asked, as they followed Posey up the grand staircase.

"Yes, for years. My mother was a gifted seamstress, and I learned as much as possible from her. I've volunteered for numerous productions since then."

Ginny beamed when she saw the stash in the upstairs bedroom. "Your production is so fun because of the period costumes. I love putting ensembles together for both the women and the men. Even the men dress fancy, and it's wonderful to watch the transformation."

Posey stood in the middle of the room, arms spread wide. "I think you'll find whatever you're looking for here. Just tell me what you want. I'm here to help." Posey was in her element.

Bay and Cass took their cues from Posey and Ginny, fished out the fool's cap and bells hats in different colors and organized motley coats and tights to pair with the caps. They each searched through piles for woodland fairy tunics, jackets, and boots for Puck and Ariel to wear in act four.

Once Ginny had an ample supply of trickster costumes, the women focused on gowns for the female characters, ranging from wealthy noblewomen and courtiers to peasants and servants.

It took all four women plus Marva to haul the selections to

Ginny's minivan in three trips. She closed the back hatch and leaned against it.

"I can't thank you enough for loaning us these." She glanced at the mound in the back window.

"Yes, thank you both for helping make our production successful. We'd have to borrow costumes from theaters all over the area otherwise." Bay was grateful for the convenience.

"Happy to help," Posey said.

"Hey Maya. What are your plans after we finish the production? Desmond says your place will be difficult to fill."

Maya scanned Bay with suspicion as she tagged the costumes Ginny dropped off earlier. "It's no secret a theater degree's not too useful. I'm starting at UCLA in August for my master's in theater technology and design." She couldn't contain her pleasure in sharing the news.

"Congratulations. That's a big step."

"I can't wait to get out of this town, Dr. Browning. Doing this show reinforces my plans. Actors!" Maya spoke with wisdom beyond her years.

Bay giggled in response. "This hasn't been the greatest send-off for the Flourish grads, for certain. I admire your meticulous system, Maya. I suspect you'll succeed in LA."

"First things first. I have to tell Cher her costume is still out for repairs. I can't wait to see her Oscar-winning reaction." Maya smirked.

"I'll be here in case it doesn't go over well." Bay wasn't about to allow Cher to use Maya as a footstool.

"I have it worked out for this week. Cher can wear Nora's gown from act one. They're about the same build. Nora's reasonable, so it won't matter to her if Cher borrows it for now."

"Good thinking," Bay said aloud, but grimaced inwardly at the idea Cher had so much control.

"Here comes the star now." Maya directed her gaze over Bay's shoulder toward the stage.

"I came early to get into costume," Cher announced as a matter of great importance.

"I'm glad because we have to make a change for now." Maya held out Nora's emerald gown, a fine match for Nora's role as the strong-willed Katherine in *Taming of the Shrew.*

Cher made a face and refused to take the gown. "I'm not wearing that. I hate green. Where's my blue gown?"

"Still out for repairs. The seamstress needs to purchase extra fabric to match with the original, which you tore yesterday waltzing around the stage. Try it on, please." Maya spoke like a parent to a naughty child.

Cher stamped one foot and pouted. "What's Nora supposed to wear?"

"She will wear the act two gown for now."

Cher wasn't convinced. "May I see the act two gown?"

It was obvious she hoped to trade up for something more to her liking, but when Maya held out the dark gray velvet gown made for the married Goneril, Cher stuck out her tongue in disgust.

"Gross. No way I'm wearing that. Nora shouldn't be wearing that either. How is she supposed to feel the part of Katherine in that getup?" Cher paced around in circles as she spoke.

Bay determined this was her cue to intervene. "Look Cher, this is all temporary, so get over it please. Maya's busy."

Cher's hands went to her hips as she huffed and hissed like

an angry alley cat. She grabbed the green gown and stomped behind the tower of cubbies to change. When she came out, Maya and Bay faced Cher and asked her to turn in several directions for them, before pronouncing the gown would be fine.

Cher flounced on stage to sit on one of the couches, ready to perform the role of victim as soon as anyone crossed her path.

Backstage, Maya and Bay shared a satisfied laugh. "I loved it when we paraded around her as if she was a model posing for the camera. I guess my acting skills are better than I thought. Thanks, Professor."

Bay smiled. "Time for round two. I hear Cher talking to Nora."

As Maya had expected, Nora was agreeable about the swap. Bay was happy to see that Cher's attitude wasn't contagious, even around her current flame.

Bay left Maya to dole out the costumes and sought out Desmond and Jen. That's when she spotted the detective, notepad in hand, talking to Desmond by the tech booth. She backtracked down the side aisle and ran into Henry Knight.

"Sorry Professor. I'm running late." Henry was in a panic.

"Settle down. All's well. Everyone's getting into costumes, so we're unlikely to start on time. By the way, your mom is an awesome costumer."

"Thanks. She's been sewing for years and works on shows any chance she gets. She sewed for the Chicago schools and even the community colleges." Henry was a proud son.

He scuttled away, and Bay ducked into the seat by Jen for personal chitchat.

"What's with Mrs. Incredible Hulk?" Jen's description of the sulking Cher, clad in green, made Bay stifle a chuckle.

"Temporary costume substitution until Juliet's gown is repaired."

Downing sidestepped in their row and sat beside Bay. "Hello ladies. I hope you don't mind me observing some rehearsals." He held up the notepad.

"I think it's a great idea, Detective. Especially since the dean hasn't assigned extra security here yet."

"You asked her?" Jen and Downing inquired together.

"I did, and she agreed. Who knows when it will happen, though. I haven't seen campus security so far this week, unless they patrol after rehearsals."

Desmond strolled on stage to check costume progress and hurry along the performers. "Let's go, people."

———————————————

The first act included a few stumbles as the actors became accustomed to moving around in their costumes, but soon found their rhythm. However, things suddenly went off-kilter.

Cher, as Juliet, held the bottle of sleeping potion to her lips. "Upon my word, this vial must certainly be vile indeed."

The line was supposed to be a humorous play on words, but Cher launched into a bout of twittering giggles like a child or someone under the influence. While the directors wore puzzled expressions, Cher tipped the pretend liquid down her throat and fell onto the stage in a lump.

At the same time, Jackson began sweating and his eyes bulged. With an abrupt clatter, the goblet he'd been holding crashed onto the stage and he thrashed around as if on fire.

The actors gazed from Cher to Jackson, then back to Cher

again, who had not moved despite lying inches from where the goblet landed.

Downing and Desmond dove onto the stage and the detective called for the Narcan kit.

"I think it's an overdose," Downing swore out loud while administering the Narcan.

A hysterical Henry Knight launched himself onto the stage to kneel over Cher. He was sobbing, shaking his head, and speaking incoherently. Nora knelt alongside Cher and grabbed her hand. Bay pulled Henry away from the scene and whispered to Nora to back up so Downing had room to work. Desmond called an ambulance.

The rescue drug seemed to serve its purpose, but the detective urged Cher to sit quietly on the floor propped by the couch until the ambulance arrived. It was clear she was still fighting the effects of something.

Bay went backstage for Cher's bathrobe so she and Jen could help her remove the costume. Jen handed the costume to Maya, but Downing's arm cut off the transaction.

"That gown is evidence. In fact, anything Cher is wearing is evidence."

When the medical technicians arrived, they tended to Cher, talked to Downing, and loaded her into the ambulance. One tech stayed behind to look at Jackson's hand, which had a burn blister on it.

"I was holding the goblet, and it started heating up. It felt hotter and hotter until I couldn't hold onto it." Jackson stared at his hand as if it was a foreign object.

Bay pulled Downing aside. "I'm not positive, but I think I saw a red light on the goblet and Jackson's hand. It seemed to flicker back and forth between them."

He looked outward from the stage in all directions. "Laser pointer?" He dashed to the tech booth and started poking around.

Daniel, who ran lights, spoke up. "Right before Jackson dropped the goblet, I noticed a red dot shining on him from over there." He pointed toward the Carillon Tower.

Downing beat it to his car and drove to the tower. He returned a short time later, just as Detective Harris pulled into the parking area in a squad, and Ginny Knight pulled in behind him.

Harris carried large evidence bags to the stage, donned gloves, and began placing Cher's costume and accessories into different bags as Jen pointed them out. Along with the goblet, Jackson's costume was bagged, too, just in case.

Ginny watched the spectacle from the edge of the stage, her mouth agape. "Professor Browning, what's happened?"

"I'll tell you as soon as I can. Cher Devane had some kind of accident. They're taking her to the hospital."

Bay was cut off when Downing arrived and hemmed in the seamstress.

"Ms. Knight, I need you to answer some questions." He escorted her to the makeup room, dismissing a shocked Aria and Maya.

Henry Knight was sitting with a patrol officer in one stage wing, opposite the makeup room. Bay wished she could talk to the distraught young man. Something was wrong, and she suspected Henry was involved. She turned away, feeling sorry for Ginny. She was certain Ginny was not involved, but how would she handle it if her son was?

Jen sidled up to Bay. "This show is cursed," Jen announced. "Dang, I sounded just like my mother for a tick."

"Did you see the red dot, maybe from a laser pointer, on Jackson's hand?" Bay thought Jen of all people would notice.

"I didn't until Jackson started acting strange, then I saw the red light shining on the goblet, so I looked at the stage lights to see if the red one was on. By then, all hell broke loose. What's up with Henry Knight? Do you think he's behind Cher's collapse?"

"Henry knows something. He's part of this. I'm sure of it." Bay tapped her fingers together. "I wonder if the detective will tell me anything."

"You'll get answers out of him, I bet. But Henry can't be the only one involved. If somebody had a laser pointer, it would have to be behind us, and we were in the back." Jen spun around to look beyond the audience seats and technical booth. "The person could have been somewhere in the trees."

Harris returned from placing evidence in the squad and hesitated in the middle, looking around, trying to choose a course of action. Bay walked over to the befuddled officer.

"Hey Detective Harris. I want you to know that I did ask the dean to send campus security over here to patrol until the show wraps up, and she agreed, but I haven't seen anyone yet."

"What we have here is another mess. Too many people to secure the scene and keep the evidence from contamination. I don't even know what all went on, to be honest with you. I could talk to that frightened young man over there, but I think Downing knows precisely what questions to ask."

Bay agreed. "I'm sorry this is happening, Harris. I hope it resolves soon. Maybe we should shut down the show." Bay figured this would be the logical conclusion after tonight's incidents.

Harris shrugged. He wasn't paying much attention to Bay. "Can you look at the scene and tell me if there's anything else I should bag up?"

Bay paused to consider. "On second thought, maybe you should take all the costumes labeled for Nora Stroud. I think she was the intended target, not Cher." Bay knew she was right because she heard Henry murmuring "it wasn't supposed to be you." ✻

CHAPTER 17

At Christmas I no more desire a rose than wish a snow in May's new-fangled mirth; But like of each thing that in season grows.
~ LOVE'S LABOURS LOST

Cass rolled an ice cube around her tongue, contemplating the details Bay just shared from the disastrous rehearsal. The sisters enjoyed fresh strawberry, pineapple, and lime infused water as they sat on their garden balcony to watch the sunset.

"It sounds like at least two people are behind these acts. Your Shakespeare production seems to be life imitating art. My question is: what's your plan? I see you squirming on the inside, Lulu."

"There's a huge cast of characters in this real-life tragedy, and I'm trying to learn who they all are. Seems like the Bluff Bird families have more skeletons than a graveyard, and they're selective about which bones they're willing to rattle. It's easy to see why being a detective is so challenging. Before you push that button, I can't take advantage of Downing."

"Oh, come on now..."

Bay's lips curved into a sly smile. "Well, I can only go so far."

Bay's cell sounded off, cutting into the peaceful scenery. Ginny Knight's voice came through on the other end.

"I'm sorry to bother you, but I don't know who else to talk to. The police are holding Henry for at least twenty-four hours. Tomorrow, they'll be going over my house with a fine-tooth comb."

"I'm sorry you're going through this. Can you tell me what the police said? And did you hire an attorney?"

"I'm going to hire an attorney tomorrow. I have names from when my husband lived here, but that's a long time ago. I didn't tell the police this, but I think Henry is hiding something. There's no way he would hurt anyone, but he may know who's behind these things."

"I see. Who are Henry's friends? How does he spend his free time?" Bay believed that teens were often persuaded by bad influences.

"He doesn't have friends. That's why we moved here. He was bullied in Chicago. I brought him here because his father went to school at Flourish, and I knew the college would let in Henry. I hoped a fresh start in a smaller town would help him make friends. So far, that hasn't happened." Ginny's voice broke.

"He doesn't hang out with anyone at school?" Bay pushed.

"He plays online games with some regulars, but they don't meet in person." Her voice was strained.

"Did Henry tell you he has feelings for Cher Devane, the student taken by ambulance?"

Ginny groaned. "What teenage kid is going to share that with his mother? She doesn't seem like Henry's type. Just from what I saw yesterday…"

"Make sure you hire a competent attorney. You both need one, Ginny. Meanwhile, I'll keep my eyes and ears open." Bay wished her well.

"I heard you worked with the police on a recent case, so I was hoping maybe you could find out what the police are planning." Ginny was grasping for any foothold she could.

Bay drew in a breath. "I can't make any promises, Ginny. I'll try."

She crept once again to the comfy chair beckoning on the balcony. In the sky, stars popped out to join the sisters along with a thumbnail moon. Bay waved her pointer finger in a dizzy arc. "You knew that call was coming, didn't you Cass?"

Sunrise Café was a Wednesday hot spot for the elderly and church crowd. Regulars clustered together in the back after morning Mass at Saint Mary's, while a ladies Bible study group met in the opposite corner. The New Walk Christian men's prayer group occupied the front corner on one side, leaving the local farmers to gather in the other corner.

Bay waited behind two couples with walkers and watched them follow the waitress to a nearby table. She bounced impatiently from heel to toe, grateful all of her limbs were in working order. She looked around for Downing. He'd agreed to meet for breakfast. She didn't see him.

"Table for one today?" Annie was a full-timer at Sunrise and knew Bay as a customer. "Or are you waiting for someone?"

"Waiting, yes. You look busy though." Bay heard the door chime and turned to see Downing, hunkering into himself as if hiding.

"Hey, Annie. The professor and I will order at the counter and take it to go," he said.

Annie handed them menus and seated the waiting customers.

"Good morning, Detective. Are you working undercover? What did I miss?" Bay's irritation was good-natured.

"This place is too busy. An excess of enquiring minds, if you know what I mean." He surveyed the restaurant, mentally noting the locals by name and penchant for spreading gossip.

"Looks like a lot of hardcore criminal types to me, too." Bay chortled. "You're serious, aren't you?"

"Nothing worse in a small town than a network like this. You know the elderly have nothing better to do than tell stories, and some of the churchy types love to spread around bad news." Downing scanned the menu in haste.

Annie must have seen the detective's show before because she was back with a pen and pad in no time. "What'll it be?"

Downing eyed Bay, then ordered for both of them. "Two coffees to go. Two breakfast sandwich specials." He dared a sideways glance at Bay. "That okay with you?"

"Sure. Extra cream for my coffee, please. No sugar. Can I get the breakfast scramble bowl instead of the sandwich, please?" Bay elbowed him after Annie walked away. "Why are you being such a cave-cop today?"

Downing sneered, dropping his head. "Sorry. I'm not a fan of the public. I mean, I want to protect them, but in general, I don't like them. Hey, thanks."

"For what?"

"Changing your order instead of settling for something you didn't want."

Bay stared into his eyes, igniting an ember. "I never settle."

Annie served their order in record time. The two walked into the June sunshine where Bay followed Downing behind the café to his car parked in a shady spot. He set the coffee carrier on the hood, opened the door and pulled back the seat.

"Not too bad, huh?"

"It'll do. Okay, secret agent, I have questions maybe you can answer." Bay sipped the coffee, grimaced at its heat, and set it back in the cup holder.

His lack of response made her proceed. "Ginny Knight called me at home. Are you still holding Henry?"

"We are, and we can for another forty-eight hours. The department sent people over this morning with a warrant to go through the Knight's house. I doubt Henry's mother is involved, but Henry knows more than he's saying."

Bay didn't say that Ginny agreed on that point. "It seems like Henry has a crush on Cher. He could be the writer of that note warning Nora to stay away from her."

Downing nodded. "Did you hear Henry say anything when he rushed on stage?" His eyes bore into Bay. Now was not the time to withhold information.

"Henry was incoherent and emotional. But I thought I heard him say 'it wasn't supposed to be you.'" Somehow, sharing this with Downing made her feel worse.

He nodded. "I heard it. Henry says he can't remember saying it. Besides Henry and his mother, who else had access to Nora's costume?"

"Maya. Aria. Jen. Me. I guess anyone else in the show, too. The costumes are not under lock and key. Did you find something in the costume?" Bay nibbled on the scrambled eggs, bacon, cheese, and hash brown combination.

Downing swallowed a large chunk of the sandwich, barely chewing. "Logically, though. The people with extensive access would be Ginny, Henry, and Maya."

Bay grunted. "Right. What you're not saying is that you did find something in that costume. How do you plant fentanyl on a costume?" Bay's brain was imagining methods and follow-up questions. She moved on.

"Ginny says Henry spends time with online gaming friends, so that's worth a look. What about Jackson's burnt hand?" *So much happened in a matter of minutes last night.*

Downing leaned back a moment and set down the remainder of the sandwich. "Yeah. Someone was in the Carillon Tower and they left in a hurry. We found a shoeprint near the north window, a lens cap possibly from a pair of binoculars, and some fabric fibers embedded in the casement. No fingerprints, though. I'm meeting Harris there in a bit."

"Was the burn caused by a laser pointer?"

"Likely. The person was positioned on the middle floor, close enough to cause damage. Still, they'd need a high-powered laser."

"It confirms Jackson as a target, though." Bay was certain of it.

"Yep, along with the fentanyl residue the lab found inside the prop saber case. The tests were inconclusive on the saber itself since it was cleaned, but the case was tainted."

"How's Cher Devane?"

"I haven't checked this morning. It's on my list." Downing was drinking, not sipping, his coffee. He crumpled the sandwich wrapper into a ball and stuffed it inside the take-out bag.

"Is the college shutting us down?" Bay was conflicted. Part of her wanted the show to close, but she didn't think that was the solution.

"Depends on your dean and the parents. I imagine you'll be hearing something today. The dean's been briefed on the investigation." Downing pulled a bottle of antacids from the glove box and chewed a handful.

"Hey, slow down on those things. Do you need more calming tea?" Bay had given him a supply of the specialty blend crafted by her aunt Venus last winter.

Downing made a sour face. "This case is hazardous to my health."

After breakfast, Bay went to the hospital to check on Cher. She decided it was the decent thing to do, even if she may not be a welcome visitor.

She signed in with the floor nurse, who said it was okay for Cher to have a short visit.

Cher's mother was sitting in the room with her, reading a magazine.

"Hello, do I know you? You look familiar." Mrs. Devane scrutinized Bay, who began perspiring. The previous encounter she'd had with the Devanes was due to Cher's antics during an exam, resulting in Bay awarding Cher a failing grade.

Cher looked at Bay in wonder and alarm. "Mother, this is Professor Browning. One of the show's directors." It didn't appear Cher wanted her mother to recall the exam incident either.

Mrs. Devane screwed her face into thinking mode. Cher's

introduction didn't sync with her mother, but the stress of current events subverted her memory.

"Hello. I wanted to check on Cher. How are you feeling?" Bay stood closer to Cher, avoiding Mrs. Devane's eyes.

"I'm tired and weak, nauseous, too. But the doctors say I'll be fine. They might release me today. I might even be able to rehearse tonight." Cher tilted her head toward her mother, hoping for support.

"We'll see, Cher. What would be nice, Dr. Browning, is to find out who did this. Obviously, someone is out to hurt Nora Stroud, and Cher was the unfortunate victim instead."

Bay wanted to pretend she knew more than she did but couldn't decide how to respond to Cher's mother.

"Look at these marks on my daughter." Mrs. Devane's emotions surfaced. She came over to Cher's bedside, and pulled aside the top of Cher's hospital gown, revealing a row of raised red lines below her neck from shoulder to shoulder, like a necklace. "Pins left inside the costume. They should arrest the seamstress."

Pins? Bay wondered if pins could be dosed with fentanyl. Someone knowledgeable was the perpetrator. She still didn't think it was Henry Knight or his mother. "The police department here is capable. They will put the pieces together, Mrs. Devane. I'm just thankful we had Narcan, and that Cher will be okay."

Mrs. Devane sniffed. "The doctor said Narcan wasn't necessary. The pins were coated in some kind of chemical acid, not a drug."

Bay tried not to react to the news and turned her attention back to Cher. "Let me know if you need anything and keep us posted about your release. Mrs. Devane, it's nice to meet you. I hope the police find out how this happened soon."

Cass was in her glory, standing side by side with Posey like two of the *Macbeth* witches in the thick of brewing a potion. Posey's screenhouse acted as a breezeway between her two greenhouses, and its ventilation made it the perfect location for a summer kitchen. A giant outdoor stove with six burners was installed. Overhead LED lighting, a double stainless steel farmhouse sink, countertop, cupboards, and an island for extra prep work completed the area Posey nicknamed *the firehouse*.

The season for concocting tinctures, infusions, and teas would peak all summer in Wisconsin as gardens produced in abundance, but Posey was one of the fortunate souls to have fresh flowers and herbs year-round. Today's new moon was a good omen for kitchen crafting.

"Would you mind clipping the reishi fungi from the bags on the island? They'll go straight to the dehydrator except for what we're using fresh today." Posey pointed to the heaping container on the counter.

Posey had been growing mushroom varieties for years in bags of sawdust, coffee grounds, and even empty cardboard paper rolls. In addition to using mushrooms in her health blends, she loved offering them to Marva for stuffing and stir-frying.

"Cassandra, why so quiet this morning?"

"Hmm. Better not taint the air with negative words while we're making healing remedies." Cass was half-serious. Part of her wanted to pique Posey's curiosity, but she could hear her mother and Aunt Venus instructing her to surround herself with positivity in her craft.

"Nonsense. We're outdoors. Feel that marvelous June breeze—fresh energy that will blow away any bad omens. So, tell me." Posey snipped honeysuckle blossoms from branches she'd cut that morning into a large colander.

"Some things went on last night at the Shakespeare rehearsal. Cher Devane was sent to the hospital and Jackson Lange was injured." Cass left out words and adjectives with violent connotations on purpose, leaving Posey confused.

"I'm afraid I don't follow. What happened to Cher and Jackson?"

Cass wasn't about to use the name of the drug, fearing the repercussions on their tinctures. "Well, someone did something to Cher's costume and she had a reaction. The ambulance came. Detective Downing saved her with…a remedy. Jackson was—ah, burned." No sooner did the word *burned* leave her lips, when she saw a curl of smoke rising from the dehydrator.

Posey dashed to the appliance and unplugged it. She pulled open the top tray where nettles were drying and sniffed. "No harm done. How weird was that?" She opened the next tray and determined the nettles there were also undamaged. The remaining trays were empty.

"Not weird at all, Posey. I'm telling you, we can't bring shadows into our process." Cass gritted her teeth.

"Very well. Let's take a break outside. Come to the garden and help me gather some willow and cherry bark. Grab a pair of snips." Posey tucked tools in her apron pocket and led the way to the garden grove.

"I know how to harvest willow bark," Cass said. She remembered the process she learned from Aunt Venus as she peeled the curled strips and placed them in her apron pouch.

"Cher's costume was tainted with fentanyl or something. Since it was Nora Stroud's costume, Nora was the suspected target. Detective Downing administered Narcan for recovery. At the same time, Jackson burned his hand on the prop goblet he was holding. It somehow heated up, under the lights or something."

Posey frowned, visibly upset. "This is terrible, Cassandra."

"Tell me about it. What's worse, the last people with access to that costume were Ginny and Henry Knight. The police have Henry in custody, after he jumped onto the stage and acted like he knew it was going to happen."

Posey gasped and plunked herself onto the garden bench. "Poor Ginny. As if she needs any more bad luck." She traded snips with Cassandra and the two moved silently to the cherry trees.

Peeling cherry bark required strength and finesse to keep the tree safe and the bark in premium condition, so Cass concentrated on the task, while Posey fretted next to her.

"Talon, Jackson, Nora. I don't see how Henry Knight could be involved." Posey's face was dark and troubled as she turned over ideas and memories in her mind.

Cass kept an eye on Posey each time she placed one of the pithy strips of cherry bark into the bucket beside her. The aroma of sweet almond reminded her of the birthday cake her grandmother made each year of her childhood. Every time she whittled another slice from the cherry tree, the scent overwhelmed her with the memory of the charmed life she once led.

What was Posey's childhood like? "She never talks much about it." Cass was mumbling aloud, when the cherry bark assaulted her with a bitter aroma.

"I think we have enough cherry for today." Posey looked recovered as if she'd turned the page in a book.

Cass was determined to find out more about the woman who was her boss and her friend. She just had to find a willing source.

"Yoo-hoo, Mary Ellen!" Someone called from the summer kitchen.

Posey stood up straight and marched toward the voice. Cass followed behind at a quick pace, too.

"Suzanne. What a surprise? Let me guess. Your headaches are back." Posey greeted the woman, who was about her age.

"Hello. You must be Cassandra. I've heard about you. How nice for Posey to keep a trusted assistant."

Cass noticed Suzanne stumbled over Posey's name, but otherwise was a picture of elegant poise, a woman well-constructed from head to toe.

"Cassandra, this is Suzanne Lange. We grew up together on the bluff." Posey's smile was tight, making Cass consider they may not have been childhood friends.

"I'm sorry for barging in. Marva said you were making teas and whatnot today, so she pointed the way and left me to it. Yes, I'm having headaches again and spring allergies are still wreaking havoc on my body. Can I procure something useful?"

Suzanne had genuine trust in Posey's medicines, but she sounded like a spokeswoman filming an infomercial. Too polished. Cass received a mixed read on the woman.

"Of course I have just the thing." Posey reached into the firehouse cupboard where tinctures were shelved in neat rows, alphabetically. She pulled out one. "This should help your allergies and headaches. The two are probably related. Use a dropper full twice a day. And follow up at bedtime with this." Another cupboard held baskets of teas organized by alphabet as well. Posey pulled out a packet and handed it to Suzanne.

"You're a saint. Thank you. Well, I'll leave you to it." Suzanne perused the array of clippings, cuttings, and bark, partly bewildered, partly… Cass caught a whiff of disgust wafting her way.

"I'll just walk you out," Cass found herself speaking without realizing it, as she caught up to Suzanne, clicking her way over the terracotta tiles.

"Ms. Lange, may I ask you something? Who were you talking to when you called from the summer kitchen?"

Suzanne's head made a slight turn to answer. "I have no idea what you're talking about."

Cass gave herself permission to be frank. "You called out for Mary Ellen? Who's that?"

"Ms. Browning, I misspoke. Is there anything else?" Suzanne towered over Cass like an iron statue.

"I don't believe you. Posey said you grew up together on the bluff. Were you friends?" Cass knew how to stare into someone's face, compelling them to tell the truth. It was one reason she'd been a successful grifter for so long.

Suzanne faltered, sucked in a deep breath, and looked for somewhere to sit. The women stood in the greenhouse, and Cass directed Suzanne to a bench.

"We went to school together. I lived on Lupine Pond, just

down the road, but I wasn't allowed to play with Posey. My mother thought I could do better." Suzanne was embarrassed, saying it out loud.

"Mary Ellen?" Cassandra's voice was a calm hum.

"Posey's mother called her that. Mary Ellen is Posey's real name. Her father never used it. The teachers and kids at school called her Mary Ellen except her close friends."

"Who were Posey's close friends?" Cass wondered why Posey had acquaintances galore but no single confidante.

"She and Henry Knight were buddies. He lived in the estate on the left, but the real trio were Posey, Malcolm Hunt, and Louisa Findley. They were thick as thieves, as the saying goes. They rode horses all over the bluff, hung out in the woods, fished, hunted." There was the whiff of disgust again.

"I take it you didn't care for those activities?" Cass pressed.

"Not particularly ladylike, but to each their own. They often smelled of the outdoors, maybe a smidge too much. Their parents were never pleased about it either."

"Where can I find Louisa Findley?"

Suzanne deflated and momentary shame replaced disgust. "I'm afraid you can't find her. She was thrown from a horse when she was sixteen and never recovered. It was terrible. Posey and Malcolm were inconsolable for weeks. Louisa was in a coma for several days, then passed away."

"How terrible. Were the three of them riding together when it happened?"

"No. Louisa was alone, out for a morning ride when her horse was spooked by thunder. At least, that's what people think must have happened." Suzanne wasn't used to her composure being ruffled and she didn't like it.

"I need to leave now Ms. Browning. Interesting conversation. I look forward to future exchanges."

Cass watched Suzanne exit the greenhouse, certain the two had a great deal to discuss. 🌿

CHAPTER 18

The labor we delight in physics pain.
~ MACBETH

Bay enjoyed the secluded private driveway to the Hunt estate. The June sun shone in patches through the colossal pines mixed with fir and hemlock, a perfect sanctuary for area wildlife. Her tires made a pleasant crunching sound along the gravel, almost lulling her into a relaxed stupor away from the stress of a production gone wrong.

She rounded the final bend and hit the brakes hard. A backhoe was digging up a chunk of the children's garden on the back end where the old red oak stood. Bay steered the Land Rover down the fire lane and parked a safe distance from the digging.

When Edison Hunt climbed off of the backhoe, Bay's shock was complete.

"Hey Professor Browning, I meant to call. Can I get a pass on lessons today?" He stuffed his hands in his pockets like a naughty schoolboy.

"Maybe, but you have to let me in on your secret. What's going on here?"

"I figured with both parents out of town, I could show them I'm serious about landscaping. I'll present my project to them when my mother returns." He stuck out his chin. "Do you want to see the plan?"

Bay saw a pickup pull up on the back end of the fire lane with a load of lumber. Her mouth dropped open when she saw Logan Thorne get out of the truck and dash toward Edison. The two exchanged a few words and Logan waved at Bay, who waved back.

"Here's the plan." He unrolled a drawing showing a raised deck built around the tree. "I don't want to destroy our old garden, not yet anyhow. But I want a new space where people can relax."

Bay marveled at Edison's ideas which incorporated old railroad lanterns hanging from the tree's branches and two sky swings. Old watering troughs would serve as flower planters, and a western design fence would border the deck on three sides.

"This is a fitting design for your family. I love it. Can you really finish it this week?"

"I hope so. Logan's going to help and so is Reetz." Edison pointed to a young man unloading the lumber with Logan. Bay recognized the minor who was arrested with Logan for tossing cherry bombs onto the Hunt property.

She grinned. "You think three is a big enough crew?"

"I told them they could count this as community service hours, and then I'd pay them after that." Edison looked pleased with himself.

"The thing is, Dr. Browning, you don't need me at play rehearsals. I'd like to work until dusk."

Bay folded her arms. "Is that why you missed last night?"

Edison affirmed.

"Did you hear what happened there?" Bay asked.

"Logan told me. I'm sure I couldn't have helped with…what is it?"

Bay's eyes flashed in anger. "Edison, does anyone know you were here last night? You could be a suspect." She stopped herself from mentioning the Carillon Tower.

"Reetz was here. I took some photos before we started, then more photos before dark to show our progress. Why would the cops suspect me?"

"You're not on great terms with Jackson Lange. Somebody has it out for him and Nora Stroud. Edison, you know this community. Can you think of a reason someone has it out for them? Maybe something the three of them have in common."

Edison's face fell, then he looked away and shook off whatever crossed his mind. "I'll think about it. Can we meet extra days after my mother returns?"

Bay frowned. She'd been hired by Corrine, not Edison, with the sole purpose of preparing him to pass the graduate entrance exam. "I'll tell you what. I'll stop by the house and leave your book summary with my comments. You'll need to revise it, and I'll pick it up tomorrow. I'll leave a practice exam for you to complete. I want that on Friday, so we can review it next week. You'll be burning the midnight oil, young man."

Edison beamed. He only had eyes for the lumber and the backhoe.

Diana was right. The Flourish College library was like a crypt, especially in the windowless back side where the reference section and offices were located. Bay smiled and waved at Diana as she padded across the thick carpeted expanse leading to her desk.

"It's too quiet here," Bay spoke in a half whisper, which echoed around the reception area.

Diana giggled. "You can speak in your normal voice. It's good to see you. Breaks up the monotony of the day."

Bay set down her book bag and retrieved the Shakespeare reference materials she'd borrowed for the script. She set them on the desk with a glossy pink bag on top of the stack, a gift for Diana.

"Oh, you stopped by Sweet Cheeks! Are there macarons in there?" Sweet Cheeks was the local favorite bakery in Prairie Ridge, known for macarons and delightful delectables.

"Something else to make the day go faster," Bay said.

"Palmiers, meringue kisses, and macarons!" Diana squealed in delight.

"I know how much you love them." Bay was pleased. Diana's grandmother made French cookies during her childhood, but her grandmother had passed on.

"Thank you, and I'll take these books over to Joanna. She personally shelves items from collections." Diana looked toward Joanna's desk and frowned. A shadow passed over her face.

"Is something wrong?" Bay followed Diana's gaze and noticed two women, one older, one maybe a college student, talking with their heads together. They both raised their heads toward Bay, as if aware they were being studied. The older woman ushered the younger one out of view.

"It's the young woman. She's been coming in weekly like clockwork, at least since I've been working here," Diana said.

Bay wasn't sure why that would be unusual or a source of irritation. "Who is she?"

"I don't know her name. She came to my desk with a book from collections the first time I saw her. I asked for her student ID. Some of the materials must be used in the library. They're not for check out. The item she had was one of those. Students are supposed to leave their ID at the reference desk and the ID is returned when they finish using the item."

"Okay." Bay hoped Diana would start to make sense.

"She's not a Flourish student. She told me so herself."

"What do you do in a case like that?" Bay asked.

"I sent her to see Joanna. Joanna decides. This woman left with a collection item, and she's been back every week to check out more."

"Why does this bother you so much, Di?"

"It's not like Joanna to bend the rules, and definitely not with someone who isn't a Flourish student. You saw for yourself. They look like they're up to something. If Joanna sees anyone watching, she whisks her away to the back room. It's weird, Bay." Diana's arms sprouted goose bumps, which she rubbed with vigor.

"There's more, isn't there? You're getting some kind of vibe from them?"

Diana shrugged. "I never get close enough to get anything specific, just creepy energy."

Bay reached over and gave her a quick hug, in case the two

women were watching.

"Keep your eyes open but watch your back. And enjoy the cookies. I'll see you next week with the rest of the Shakespeare reference materials."

Bay tucked away Diana's strange vibes for another time and thought about the fate of the show. She figured she would be summoned to a meeting with the dean and directors at any moment. She was deep in thought and almost ran head-on into a figure coming up the library steps. It was Officer Kelly Weber, dressed in plain clothes.

"Dr. Browning, you look like a woman on a mission."

"I'm sorry. I didn't see you. Come to think of it, I've never seen you out of uniform." The parole officer normally wore her hair pulled back into an all-business tight bun, so seeing it hanging loose over her shoulders was a stark change, except Bay decided, she still looked official.

Kelly Weber wore her poker face. "Well, I'm on a mission, too, so I'll leave you to it."

"At the college library?" Bay found it an odd location for a county parole officer.

The unflappable officer kept walking. "I like to read."

The summons to Dean Pamela's office arrived with a thirty-minute notice attached. Bay was already on campus, so she went to her office in the gray lady, her term of affection for the stone humanities building. She took the stairs since she wasn't weighed down by her usual school-in-session bags and realized three floors might have been enough of a workout. Many people lose weight in the summer months, but Bay found she trekked extra steps during the school year dashing between campus buildings.

Finally, the fifth-floor door beckoned. She huffed and puffed past Stasia's office, which was in the corner by the exit, saw it was dark and moved on to her own. The whole floor was dark so maybe Trevor, the receptionist, was on vacation. She stopped by his desk where he'd posted a sign to that effect but would return Monday.

Bay stopped in the break room to retrieve her mail which was both minimal and trivial.

Most of it went straight to the trash. She turned to leave and bumped into Jen Yoo.

"Ahh, good morning. Looks like we have the same idea, killing time until the meeting." Jen's mailbox was stuffed, and it took a lot of yanking to free it.

"Do you always get that much mail?"

"Nope. I haven't checked it in ages. A lot of touring companies offering art sabbaticals and workshops and of course this stuff." She held up flyers for the latest and greatest art textbooks, each more enticing than the last.

Bay sighed. "I wish I could purchase illustrated literature and poetry. What fun would that be. As for our show, I can't guess what the dean will say. I stopped by the hospital to see Cher. She was adamant the show must go on and said so to her mother."

Jen whistled. "How did that reunion go?"

"Interesting. Cher introduced me as one of the directors and her mother seemed puzzled. I'm sure she remembered me from somewhere, but Cher didn't want to relive that experience any more than I did. At least we were on the same team for once."

Jen chuckled. "Yeah, team deception." She tossed half of the mail away without looking at it and crammed the rest into her satchel. "Well, shall we walk over the hot coals together?"

"Lead on, Dr. Yoo."

Downstairs, the two rapped on the door to Pamela's office and were told to come in. Desmond was seated, playing with his hair twists. Bay recalled the habit so much the past weeks, she wondered if he'd lost any hair in the pulling.

Stasia stood near the seated Pamela, who looked relaxed—an auspicious sign, perhaps.

"Let's get started. This isn't going to take much time, directors." Pamela smiled, a formal all business smile.

"Are we waiting for Evan?" Bay asked.

"He's unavailable. Desmond will brief him later. I thought about closing the show the instant I heard about Ms. Devane and Mr. Lange. It appears we're fighting multiple villains, and I hope the police will add personnel to the case." Pamela stepped forward and stared directly at Bay.

"To that end, I have called back all of our campus security officers to cover the park. Normally, we operate with a skeleton staff, but several agreed to return. The seasoned officers will be posted at the park. I think our campus buildings will be safely monitored by the others. Dr. Browning asked for extra security earlier and I apologize that it took time to make that happen." Pamela walked backward and faced the three.

"Flourish has an independent and determined nature as a college. We are not going to cave in to someone with a vendetta. I want all four directors to stay vigilant and report any unusual detail to the police. I'm relieved Detective Downing was there and that our students are okay." She clasped her hands together as if in prayer.

Desmond cleared his throat. "You didn't receive any demands from the Langes or Devanes?" He swallowed a hard lump, expecting the worst.

Pamela cocked her head. "I spoke with both families. Mr. Devane is away on business. Mrs. Devane said it would break Cher's heart for the production to be canceled. Rather dramatic if you ask me. Mr. Lange spoke to the police about offering a reward for information about the criminal. He was skeptical about the production continuing, called it frivolous, but he didn't push to end it."

"As I said before, be vigilant. Our reputation's at stake. Make this a remarkable summer production, one that will speak to the hearts of the donors." Pamela returned to her chair and began rifling through papers.

The three directors left the office side by side.

"Des, why did Cher make such a production about continuing the show? I mean, we know she's a stage hog..." Bay walked between him and Jen.

"Remember, she still has two years of college left. She's building a résumé. The show means a great deal to her. I thought she tried out to keep tabs on Talon Hunt or make him jealous, but that doesn't fit anymore." Desmond shrugged, nonchalant about the matter.

"Is anyone besides me surprised the show wasn't canceled? Does the college need donors that badly?" Bay felt she had a great deal to learn about her workplace.

"The music and theater departments bring in large donations. People like to see concerts and shows. Puts them in the giving mood," Desmond said.

"The college always needs money. They want to build a combination dormitory and student union in the library area . Plans are being tossed about, and they're going to need at least thirty million dollars to make it happen." Jen added.

Desmond stopped, so Bay did, too. "How do you know this, Jen?"

"I'm on the planning committee. That's the perk of being head of the art department, I guess." She sniffed, pretending arrogance.

"Changing topics. You two have been here much longer than I have. Is there anyone who has a grudge against Talon, Jackson, and Nora? Or anyone else, for that matter?" Bay knew enough about criminals to know there must be a connection.

"Those three and most of the cast have been in theater productions since their freshmen year. I can't think of any hardcore enemies they made. If someone's holding a grudge, why act on it now? Graduation is over. These three are in their last show here," Desmond said.

"Maybe that is the point. Someone wants to ruin their last show, their last memories of Flourish College. Are there any graduates that were kicked out of the theater program?" Something was itching under Bay's skin.

"No. I can't think of anyone," Desmond said. "But I'll think about it some more."

Lost in thought, Bay turned on her heel and headed back inside the humanities building. Desmond shrugged and continued to his car, but Jen turned around to follow her friend. She met Bay at the elevator.

"What's up? You've thought of something." Jen was excited.

"There must be a connection. I'm going to look at their

student records. At least the ones I can see." Privately, Bay wished she could enlist Cassandra to hack into the college system.

Jen's eyes lit up. "We could break into the student records room. Bird Hall is the oldest building on campus, easy to break into. Plus, there's limited security around."

"You're kidding. We're not breaking into the records room. Let's see what we can find with the faculty access. You might be surprised."

Bay unlocked her office door and fired up her computer before turning on the lights.

"I'll be back with my laptop," Jen said. "We can get this done faster with two."

Bay showed Jen how she accessed information about Edison Hunt before she started tutoring him. "If you click into this folder, you'll find a list of courses and grades for each student. Maybe they've all been in the same courses together. And maybe we can find the class roster for a course they all took together."

"Great plan. I'll look at Talon."

"I'll check Nora. There's a fair chance that the besties would have similar schedules, but not Nora. If I can find a match with Talon, we can look at Jackson's. Let's work our way backward from their senior years, since the crimes are happening now. You read Talon's spring schedule and I'll check it against Nora's."

The two continued but didn't find a common course until their first semester of sophomore year. "They both took criminal justice with Professor Adams, same section. But that's at least two years ago."

Jen tapped keys; she'd moved on to Jackson. "Just pulled up

Jackson's sophomore schedule. He didn't take criminal justice."

Bay stopped Jen from exiting out of Jackson's folder. "Wait a minute. Jackson is going to law school. He must have taken that course. Keep looking."

"Yes. Here it is. Freshman year, fall semester, with Adams. Bet he was able to make that class easy for Talon." Jen scoffed. "Maybe this is about cheating. Maybe these three were cheaters, and someone knew about it."

"But why wait for them to get their diploma, when you could turn them in, prevent them from graduating, and look like a hero in the process?" Bay protested.

Jen deflated. "I suppose you're right."

She tried closing her laptop again, but Bay put her hand in the way. "Wait. I found out a lot about Edison in the essay I asked him to write. Maybe the admission essays are still on file."

Jen started clicking into the student records when a huge smile radiated from chin to eyeballs. "Jackpot! Look at this."

"How did you get in? I couldn't." Bay complained.

"I served on the admissions committee maybe four years ago. Apparently, nobody bothered to reset passwords or restrict access. I've got Talon's essay. I'm copying it to a doc and sending it to you. Just delete it when you're done. I'll find Jackson's now."

Bay and Jen read quietly. Typical of admission essays, the candidates bragged about their high school accomplishments, listed their awards, and stated their program goals. Nora Stroud's was similar, but at least she outlined her program goals with authentic passion.

"Boilerplate admission essays. Tell me what you're looking

for when you read these, Jen." Bay was curious.

"We watch for essays that stand out for discussion of the student's story about where they're coming from and where they plan to go in the future. Like your, half sister Diana. She has a memorable story. A foreign student raised by her grandmother, her unfortunate family situation, and a passion to serve the public through social work. That's why she won a scholarship to come here."

Bay batted her eyelashes and pointed to Talon's essay on her screen. "Then explain how this mundane drivel passed muster?"

"Oh, it didn't have to, Bay. Remember, Talon, Jackson, and Nora are legacy students. The admission essay is merely a formality."

Bay smacked the desk. "Maybe that's it. Legacy students. Somebody has it out for legacy students. Somebody who knows them but didn't get into Flourish. Maybe someone who went to Prairie Ridge high school." Bay smiled smugly. "It's something, Jen."

"Okay, it's not nothing. It means more work. We have to find which students in the show are legacy ones." Jen stretched her arms and rolled her wrists.

"That's the easy part. How are we going to find the student who didn't get into Flourish?" Bay asked. ✂

CHAPTER 19

Entr'acte II

The sisters, dressed in summer frocks, ascended ten floors to Suzanne Lange's condominium in The O'Keefe overlooking Lake Monona. An attendant parked Bay's SUV and called Suzanne to approve their arrival.

Cass fidgeted with her handbag, earning a sharp stare from Bay.

"Stop it. You're not the nervous type. It's just breakfast." Bay patted her sister's arm.

The two received the invitation the previous evening, before Shakespeare rehearsal, and couldn't guess why. Rather than ask questions, curiosity won out and they accepted. Cass phoned Posey to say she would be late for work without explanation. Bay wasn't under time constraints since Edison was busy landscaping.

"I wonder what they want," Bay said.

Cass squirmed and smoothed out her dress. "I've just met Suzanne yesterday at Posey's. She's a hawk. We traded barbs, and she did tell me a little about Posey growing up on the bluff. Suzanne was raised there, too."

Bay's eyes widened in surprise. "Wish you would have told me that earlier."

The elevator doors opened into the plush airy condo, decorated in white with muted greens and blues. Suzanne greeted them personally and led them to a long curving room that overlooked the glassy surface of the lake.

"Cassandra, nice to see you again." She nodded. "And this must be Professor Browning."

"Just Bay, please. A pleasure to meet you, Ms. Lange." Bay gave a demure nod.

"Suzanne. There are too many Ms. Langes to count. First names will be fine. Please be seated and let me make introductions."

Bay and Cass sat together on a tufted settee facing a long sofa ensemble where two women posed, legs crossed, in relaxed expectation. Suzanne indicated the brunette woman on the left.

"Please meet my sister-in-law, Gretchen." Gretchen said hello, her voice pleasant but formal. Suzanne indicated the petite woman, the youngest of the three, with burgundy hair that hung just above her waist. "Please meet my other sister-in-law, Heather." Heather's hello was lighthearted and friendly.

Suzanne directed them to the side table laden with breakfast pastries, fresh fruit, and mini quiches. "Sylvia is making coffees to your liking." Suzanne waved a hand as if magically making the coffee station appear across the room against a wall adorned with framed art of Parisian advertisements.

Bay and Cass selected a coffee flavor, thanking Sylvia to the point of embarrassment. They were grateful to sit down again with their plates, until they realized the settee wasn't designed for dining. They stationed their plates on a nearby side table and sipped their coffees.

"I suppose you're curious about our invitation." Suzanne's lips twitched when she spoke, even as she nibbled a bite from a chocolate croissant.

Bay settled her cup and brushed her hand against Cassandra's jiggling knee. It was time to break the ice and maybe get Cass to relax. "I'd like to know why you introduced Monroe's exes as your sisters-in-law."

Suzanne threw her head back and laughed out loud. "You don't mince words, Bay. Attagirl. Two reasons. One, Gretchen and Heather are both attorneys, so it's a lovely play on words, don't you agree?"

Bay admitted using the word law to describe the two women was clever.

"Two, it's hard to explain to people what our relationship is. I mean, we're family to one another, so why not sisters. I've become accustomed to introducing them this way. It appears you know about our situation then?"

"I was at Talon Hunt's service. The Lange group had its own table. Jackson is one of my students and he's in the production I'm directing, so someone pointed out those seated at the table." Bay wouldn't throw Posey or her friend, Joyce, to the wolves for telling the Lange history.

"Yes, of course. Monroe Lange paraded his family out in

public. Typical political stunt.

Unfortunately, he is allowed to bring the children to these types of affairs." Suzanne sniffed as if the distaste of Monroe still lingered.

"The three of us applaud independent women, Bay. So, we're wondering, how can we help the investigation into the troubles your production is experiencing?" Suzanne's expression was earnest and eager. Moreover, it was unexpected.

Bay and Cass exchanged stunned looks. Cass picked up her plate, glad she wasn't on the hot seat. She nibbled her selections.

"That's kind of you, but I wonder how you can help. Did you all grow up on the bluff? Did you attend Flourish College?" Answers to those questions would be useful.

Suzanne was the spokesperson for the three. "I grew up on the bluff, and I attended Flourish, but I haven't lived in Prairie Ridge for a long time. Neither Gretchen nor Heather lived on the bluff, but Heather knows the Bluff Birds well."

That was Heather's cue. "Of course, I lived on the bluff while I was married to Monroe, and we divorced two years ago, so I know the recent history there. Plus, I specialize in real estate and tax law, so you can imagine the number of bluff families in my clientele." Heather had the angelic voice of a Sunday school teacher.

Bay tried to formulate questions around this enlightening information but decided to hit the ball head-on. After all, these three invited them here, so they must want to let the canary sing.

"I'm curious about recent bluff history. The three students who were injured in this production are all legacy students who went to high school together. They would have graduated four years ago, and I'm wondering if there's something to that." Bay finished her coffee, and the vigilant Sylvia took the cup away to prepare refills.

Heather's face contorted with sorrow. "That was a terrible summer on the bluff. I remember because we attended Jackson's graduation. The graduating class was a close-knit group. I used to see them together at house parties, hanging around the pool or riding horses." She paused to sip from a mimosa Suzanne had passed around on a tray. "Oh, you made these with pineapple and passionfruit. Nicely done, Suz."

Bay took a drink and found it refreshing. "Terrible summer…" she prompted Heather.

"Oh yes. The week after graduation, the Kingsleys were away, so the grads decided to throw a party at their house. I'm sure there was plenty of drinking and goofing off, and one of the party goers ended up dying." Heather hiccupped on the word *dying*.

"I'm afraid I'm not following," Bay said. "Who died and how did it happen?"

"A boy from town. His name was Brody. He was a friend, maybe a boyfriend, of Ophelia Kingsley. He was thrown from a horse. A dizzying number of injuries." Heather looked away.

Gretchen picked up the tale from the sensitive Heather. "I knew these families, too, from living with Monroe. The kids were just younger when I left. The aftermath of the party destroyed the Kingsleys. They lost everything and had to move away."

Bay was incredulous. "They lost everything because of the party and the boy's death?"

Gretchen nodded. "The liability of course was one thing. There was insurance but a death at an unsponsored party is a catastrophe. I dare say the horses is what put Peter Kingsley out of business."

Bay was still in the dark. "Horses?"

"Of course, you're new to Prairie Ridge, aren't you? The Kingsleys lived on the property now owned by the Devanes. Peter was a master horse breeder and trainer. His stables housed priceless show and racehorses so the party was a paramount breach of trust. All of the owners removed their horses after news of the party and the death got out. Peter had to close the stable, pay off what contracts he could, and place the property up for sale."

Bay's head was spinning from the story. "Talon, Jackson, and Nora: were they at this party?"

Heather took up the story again. "I know Jackson was and where Jackson was, Talon was certain to be, too. Nora was Ophelia's closest friend, so I assume she was there. All the teens on the bluff knew about the party, and these kids were always together."

"What happened to Ophelia? Did she move away with her parents?" Bay asked.

Heather and Gretchen looked at each other, then busied themselves with their plates.

Either they didn't know what happened to Ophelia or wouldn't tell.

"I know the attorney who represented the Kingsleys. Ophelia had not yet turned eighteen, so she wasn't held criminally liable for the boy's death, but the details from the party bounced around all summer, one wild rumor after another. We may never know what happened at that party." Gretchen claimed.

Bay didn't know if the exes were finished delivering the goods, and she didn't want to miss anything. "Gretchen, who was the Kingsleys' attorney?"

"Anthony McGann. He's a local." Gretchen was preoccupied cutting a mini quiche into tiny bits.

Suzanne cleared her throat. "Gretchen worked with Anthony for a time after her divorce. She cut her legal teeth at his law firm."

"What kind of law do you practice, Gretchen?" Bay asked.

"Estate planning, but I've handled cases in civil liability and personal injury, too. Now that I have my own practice, I focus on estate planning. Everyone's dying to lay out plans for their legacy, you know." She chuckled at her own joke.

The tiny hairs on the back of Cassandra's neck stood at attention when Gretchen said she worked for Anthony McGann. She thought of ways she could get Gretchen to tell her what she knew about Posey. None of those ways were aboveboard.

"Why Cassandra, you've been practically invisible this whole time. I must apologize for ignoring you. Do you enjoy working for Posey Hollingsworth?" Suzanne offered Cass a second mimosa, but she waved it away. Now that all eyes were on Cass, she much preferred being invisible.

"I enjoy working for Posey. We have a great deal in common." She hoped the short answer would suffice. It did not.

"Like what? Did you and Bay grow up in the lap of luxury?" Suzanne breezed back to her seat, tossed back half of the mimosa she held, and leaned against the backrest.

Cass bristled, then took a deep meditative breath. The match between the women had resumed.

"Lap of luxury? That's a good one." She performed a tinkling giggle. "Our parents were college professors, so we lived in a variety of places. I've always had a green thumb and made my own tea blends, so Posey and I share that vocation. I admire her greenhouses and exotic fauna." Cass made certain to turn the conversation toward Posey.

"I'm curious, Suzanne. Are you a sister-in-law, too?" Cass was stone-faced but knew she needled the woman.

Suzanne pretended to cough and leaned forward. "No. I thought the Langes had enough lawyers in the family. Like so many young people, I went to college without a plan and finished with a liberal arts degree. Of course, I was engaged to Monroe, so I foolishly thought my life was etched in stone. I'm trying to make amends for tossing away my education, which is why I have my own art studio at Olbrich Gardens. That's the important thing, isn't it Cassandra?"

"What's that?"

"Making amends for the error of one's ways?" Suzanne's eyes bore into Cass, but Cass was resolute and maintained a serene smile.

Bay read the contest going on between her sister and Suzanne. It was time to leave. "We've enjoyed your hospitality, but we both have places to be. Thank you, Gretchen and Heather, for sharing some particulars about my students. I'm hopeful the investigation will wrap up soon without any more victims."

"You can count on the three of us to be at the production, Bay. We all donate to the arts and specifically to Flourish."

Suzanne stood to shake hands with Bay.

"How kind of you, especially since your daughter isn't a Flourish student." Bay remembered Joyce mentioning that at Talon's service.

"Taylor will be a junior this year at Northwestern. I wanted her to have opportunities outside a small college town. No offense, Bay." Suzanne shook Bay's hand. "It was kind of you to come."

Once the elevator began its descent, Bay turned to Cass.

"What's going on between you and Suzanne? It was like watching a chess match," Bay said.

"I think Suzanne knows about my background, and she's toying with me in case I slip and reveal something. I bet she's wondering why Posey hired me. Anyway, did you get anything useful out of that bluff party story?"

"Maybe. I think we've started at the tail of the kite. There's a lot of string left to unwind." ✑

CHAPTER 20

For now, these hot days, is the mad blood stirring.
~ ROMEO AND JULIET

"Did you have an appointment this morning, Cassandra?" Posey asked when Cass arrived in the summer kitchen to resume working on teas and tinctures. Cass always shared her schedule in advance with Posey and now she needed to decide whether to tell her the truth.

"The ex-Ladies Lange invited me and my sister for breakfast at Suzanne's condo." Cass absently pulled herbs from the drying trays and placed them in the labeled jars.

"Isn't that something? I know Suzanne had a motive. What did she want from you?" Posey's nose was bent out of joint, alerting Cass's radar.

"Nothing I can imagine from me, but the three exes wanted to share their knowledge of bluff history for my sister's benefit. Specifically, the history surrounding a high school party four years ago." She paused to see if Posey would take the bait.

"Interesting," Posey stripped the thyme stems faster than usual. "And what did they say about it?"

"Enough that Bay would like to talk to you. You might have useful information and not even realize it." Cass watched Posey bite her bottom lip and tear off thyme stems even faster.

"Come on, Posey. Why are you so reluctant to talk about the past?" She didn't like the idea of Suzanne Lange trotting through her history either.

"You of all people should know the past is not always a safe place to muck about, Cassandra." She popped the spent thyme stems into a waste container for compost.

"Come with me. I want to show you something." Posey removed her apron and walked into the house.

She stopped at the expansive, secluded library and opened its carved doors. Cass followed her inside, overcome with curiosity.

"This room isn't just my favorite room in the house. It means the world to me." Posey walked along each section of bookshelves. "Before his death, my father stocked our collections, including first editions. He spent his free time here and carved out a space for me to share it with him. I've continued to add to his collections."

Posey crossed the windowless room to the back wall. "This is my personal stash. My favorite books are here, including a treasured Jane Austen first edition." She took out the blue leather-bound illustrated edition of Persuasion and handed it to Cass as if it were a bird egg.

Cassandra's eyes widened. "It is okay to touch this without gloves?"

Posey nodded. "Briefly. But should you ever want to

browse anything here, you will find a box of gloves on the desk. The valuable books are noted in the bound catalog next to the gloves."

Cass handed back the weighty book. "I understand what it's like to keep a treasured possession. One day, I'll bring mine to show you. Thank you, Posey."

———————————

Cher was back at rehearsal ready to take advantage of a chance to show some humility.

"Hi Maya. What am I wearing tonight while my Juliet gown is being repaired?" Her toothy smile was forced, but at least she tried.

Maya handed her a simple neutral-tone peasant style dress which was adjustable for most sizes. "Sorry, this is what I have for now. Ms. Knight says your dress will be here on Monday."

"Nora, she's altering another dress for you, since the police have your gowns." Maya looked past Cher where Nora stood browsing the costume rack.

"I'll wear the dress you gave me yesterday." Nora stepped forward to greet Cher. "I'm glad you're back, and I'm glad you're okay." She clasped Cher's hand, but Cher jerked away.

"I'm going to get ready." Cher walked away.

Bay witnessed the exchange and wondered about the dynamics operating in the cast. Henry Knight was still in jail, but time was running out. If the police didn't have something solid, they'd have to release him tonight. She turned over the bluff party conversation with the Lange exes in her mind. What was Henry's connection to a party from four years ago?

The costume area filled up with cast members, so Bay stepped back in the shadows to watch. Aria looked serious holding the clipboard for prop inventory and checking off items as each was located. She was Maya's prize student.

Bay waved to Jen Yoo, who stood at the opposite entrance to the costume, prop, and makeup room. Both women were thankful to see that Dean Pamela kept her word; the place had been crawling with security officers since yesterday. Each park entrance was covered by an officer and an extra guard was posted on a moped at the Carillon Tower.

Bay almost shrieked when a hand reached through the backstage curtain and gripped her shoulder. Then Downing's face emerged full of mischief.

"What's the big idea? We have enough drama going on here, don't you think?" Bay's attempt at a mob boss accent made them both laugh.

"Got a minute?" Downing pointed with his thumb offstage.

Bay waved to Jen and pantomimed she was leaving. She followed Downing behind the theater where a guard was posted.

"The Stroud girl's costume will be cleared tomorrow. The pins that lined the bodice tested positive for the chemical sodium hydroxide and a waxy substance. The rest of the costumes were clean." Bay giggled at the detective's discomfort with the word bodice but appreciated his news.

"Waxy substance?"

"Beeswax, easy to find around here. It works well as a carrier. When the body temp melts the wax, the chemical is absorbed."

"Anything come out of searching Ginny Knight's home?"

"No. Nothing unusual. Nothing in her car either. Definitely nothing at her place of employment."

"Sounds like you didn't expect to find anything at her work."

Downing leaned toward her. "She's a TSA agent at the airport. She'd be foolish to keep drugs or paraphernalia there."

"Where does that leave Henry?" Bay secretly rooted for the boy.

"We have to release him tonight or in the morning. It gnaws at me, Bay. The kid knows something." Downing kicked the grass with the toe of his boot.

Bay was reluctant to confide her thoughts. "I agree with you. Henry knows something. The pieces don't fit. I heard some information this morning that you might…"

Their conversation was cut by a backstage clamor.

"Dammit, now what?" Downing vaulted onto the stage, Bay on his heels. Desmond, megaphone in hand, jumped on behind them.

Aria, hand over her mouth, stared at Nora, who in turn shuddered at a velvet hood she'd flung onto the floor; a piece of her costume. A squeamish Jackson sat on the floor nearby, in danger of vomiting. He was in his stockings and his boots lay several feet apart as if knocked over by a wind. An angry Maya held a mammoth flashlight, inclined to wield it at someone or something.

"What's happened?" Downing demanded. He looked from one to the other in the freeze-frame.

Maya glared at Aria. "I put you in charge of checking the costumes for act one."

Aria whimpered. "I did. I made sure each one was in place, ready for the actor to dress."

"Someone put a rat inside my hood. I was putting it on my head when it, it, it fell out."

Nora held back tears but was shaking and pointed at the

velvet hood on the floor.

Downing took the flashlight from Maya and shined it on the hood. Nothing moved. He kicked the hood with his boot. He could feel the meaty critter in it or under it, he wasn't certain. He kicked it again. Nothing moved, so he lifted the hood. The rat's eyes were glazed over. "I think it's dead," Downing said.

"Mr. Lange, do rats make you nervous, too?" Downing noticed Jackson still looked green and sweaty.

"My boot," Jackson managed to spit out the words. "There's a rat inside." He pointed to the boots lying askew on the floor.

"Dead or alive?" Downing asked, as he approached the boots, flashlight held aloft.

Jackson shrugged.

Downing picked up each boot by the heel and turned them upside down. A dead rat fell out of one.

"Someone's idea of a practical joke. I'll bag up these rodents and take them to the lab. Meanwhile, if you're still getting dressed, I recommend shining lights over and around your costumes." Downing wished the production was over.

Bay was beside Maya, calming her. "Don't be upset with Aria. I wouldn't expect either of you to go through every costume with a fine-tooth comb. From here on out, you two can set up props and costumes as you normally would, and the actors will have to check them."

"But I'm the one in charge of this. The blame falls on me, Professor Browning," Maya said. "I don't know how this could even happen. I've seen security people all over the place. How did dead rats get in here?"

Bay knew the answer was that someone who had a key was

responsible, but who was that someone?

Downing was back with evidence bags, paper sacks that concealed the sad dead rats. "I'm taking these to the lab. Call me after rehearsal and we can finish our talk."

Desmond called places on stage minutes later after checking that nobody else had a costume malfunction. He turned to Bay and Jen.

"Is it wrong to wish this show were over? I considered invoking that Scottish play to seal the deal." Desmond was kidding, but like the Macbeth witches, his cauldron was set to boil over.

One act over, three to go. Rehearsals were progressing to the point that all four acts would be practiced in order, in costume. Desmond hoped makeup would follow by the end of next week.

Maya came on stage at the end of act one to announce she and Aria had gone through the costumes to look for creatures or any strange objects and all was in order. The actors were able to make a brisk change and take their places on stage.

Desmond chugged the remaining death wish coffee drink he'd brought to rehearsal; a triple espresso Americano with an energy shot. Bay and Jen were revolted.

"That stuff will kill you, Desmond. Are you sleeping at all?" Bay asked.

"I agree. That's lethal. You should try meditation or yoga with Bay." Jen ribbed Desmond, who glared in response.

"Okay, places. Let's begin." Desmond called.

Act two included intense, but humorous, exchanges among some of Shakespeare's famous dysfunctional families. The aging King Lear planned to pass on his throne and fortune to the daughter who loved him best. Lear's three daughters include two who deceive him and want him dead, while the youngest is honest and kind, but inadequate for Lear. Another father, Prospero, from *The Tempest*, was stranded on an island with his innocent daughter Miranda.

Prospero uses his magical powers to bring his enemies to the island along with the innocent Ferdinand, who falls in love with Miranda. A confused Miranda has to fend off the advances of an island native, the stranger who desires her for a wife, and her dishonest father. Of course, no family drama would be complete without the feuding Montagues and Capulets from *Romeo and Juliet*.

The act was Bay's favorite to write, coming from her own dysfunctional family. She found ample fodder to unload in the script but added sarcasm and humor in keeping with a parody.

Desmond gave her leeway in guiding the actors about line delivery and exchanges, something she leaned into with relish as therapy of sorts.

She didn't realize she'd disappeared into a memory hole until a shriek that wasn't written in the script rang out. She jolted to the present, her eyes riveted to the stage.

The shriek came from Nora, playing Miranda, who stood to the left of Adam Lee, playing Prospero. Adam stared into a bronze box he'd just opened to retrieve his book of incantations. His mouth formed a perfect oval, and his eyes bulged. Cher Devane moved toward Nora for a better view.

"It's another dead rat, Professor Carver." Cher spoke as if this was a normal occurrence. She took Nora's arm and led her to one of the couches.

"I'll call the detective," Bay said. "Don't touch the box." She turned to Desmond. "Should we continue rehearsal?"

Desmond shook his head in disbelief, then announced: "The show must go on."

Cass stopped at Anthony McGann's office after finishing at Posey's. This time she had an appointment. The office was empty, and the receptionist must have turned off the outer lights.

"Hello? Attorney McGann?" Cass called out. She noticed lights were on in one office. Anthony McGann stepped into the doorway and smiled.

"Cassandra Browning, I presume? You look lovely without the powdered wig." He smiled and gestured for her to come back.

"I forgot that you might not recognize me out of costume."

"Please take a seat and call me Anthony." He took a fresh legal pad from his desk drawer and set a pen on top of it.

Cass giggled. "This isn't a professional consult, Anthony. I doubt you'll need to take notes."

He let out a snort. "Creature of habit, I'm afraid. Almost every meeting in this office requires note-taking. What can I do for you?"

"What can you tell me about a party on the bluff four years ago that resulted in the death of someone named Brody?" Cass sat comfortably, legs crossed, hands clasped around her knee. She hoped her question, launched out of the blue, would catch him off guard.

He blinked and swallowed hard. "Well, let me think. I represented Peter Kingsley and his daughter, since she was a minor. What happened to Brody Lynde was tragic and unnecessary."

"What did happen? I heard he fell off a horse because the partygoers were goofing around." Cass knew there was more to the story, and gauging Anthony's emotional reaction, plenty more.

"Goofing around? That's what you might call a broken window or hole in the wall, but it doesn't describe what happened at that party. Between the alcohol and whatever recreational drugs were in play, these kids were a disaster in the making." Anthony rose from his chair and began pacing as if a judge and jury were present.

"You know what happens when rich kids, fresh from high school graduation, get bored? Stupidity. With Peter Kingsley away, Ophelia's house was the perfect place. Plenty of dad's alcohol to go around. Beautiful swimming pool. Lots of empty rooms for teens to occupy." He paused, folded his arms across his chest and glared at an invisible antagonist.

Cass pondered the information. She'd been to elite parties. In fact, that's where she did her grandest work, hacking into safes and computer systems. She lost track of the number of security systems she'd shut down so people in her entourage could steal art, jewelry, or documents.

She raised her eyes to Anthony, who was still somewhere else, thankfully. She didn't want him to read her. "My guess is these kids had been to an excess of parties just like that one. They wanted some fresh entertainment."

Anthony snapped to attention, impressed by Cassandra's insight. "Why yes, that's exactly right. The Kingsley stables housed many fine racehorses. Some in the graduating class were known for gambling, poker parties and betting that couldn't be traced, or the police chose to look the other way. But an impromptu race featuring the choice horses seemed like a prime idea to teens whose faculties were out of whack."

Cass knew the Devanes, who now owned the Kingsley property, had an informal practice track. She also knew the bluff contained a network of intersecting trails that crisscrossed several properties.

"Whose idea was it to stick Brody Lynde on a horse?" Of all the questions running through her mind, she decided this one could yield the biggest take.

Anthony grunted, unfolded his arms and leaned toward Cass as if she were opposing counsel. "You'd make a smart prosecutor, Ms. Browning. Let me pick apart that question for you. First, you must know that Brody Lynde was from the wrong side of town."

"You mean he wasn't a rich bluff kid?" Cass wanted to encourage Anthony.

"Correct. He'd been Ophelia's friend since middle school when she took him under her wing. Brody had some cognitive issues but functioned at a high level. Of course, he was bullied, and Ophelia had a soft spot for underdogs. She invited him to the party to rub it in the faces of the bluff kids."

Cass immediately judged Ophelia to be one of the good ones. She'd associated with people like Ophelia, people who justified taking from the wealthy to benefit the less fortunate. "Strike one against Brody Lynde."

"Indeed. Someone, and we will never know who they are, plied Brody with alcohol all night, and someone slipped him a roofie. Witnesses at the party said it was Ophelia. They said she hoped to score with Brody."

Cass frowned as the girl she just championed in her mind teetered on an imaginary pedestal. "That doesn't seem to square. What did Ophelia say?"

"Swears she didn't do it, but she couldn't say who did. Anyway, the trashed party animals headed to the stables and lined up bets for three races, four jockeys per race. They finished the first race and set up for a second one. Talon Hunt, Jackson Lange, and Adam Lee would jockey, and lucky Brody was hoisted onto the back of a horse as number four."

"Strike two," Cass whispered. "Where is Ophelia when this is going on?"

"Staggering around, yelling, but nobody will listen to her. The party is out of control. At least, that's what she says." Anthony motions to Cass to take it away.

"Let me guess. There are witnesses who say Ophelia orchestrated the whole thing."

"Yes. Something like that. Well, the race begins and Brody, who has zero riding skills and is inebriated, falls off. He's too wasted to move and is trampled by Talon Hunt's horse. Allegedly."

"Strike three. Wait—allegedly?" Cass lunged off her chair.

"Witnesses say there was no second race. Brody was riding alone. He fell from the horse and was trampled by it. Witnesses say Brody bragged he could beat the winning time from the race and got onto the horse to prove it."

"Looks like it's your client against the rest of the partygoers, and a dead victim who can't testify. Did this go to trial? What happened to Brody's family?"

"You can imagine the Kingsleys didn't want a trial. Both Peter and Ophelia wanted to do the right thing for Brody's family, and that was to settle the suit out of court. The Lyndes moved away afterwards. Peter lost his business when his clients pulled their horses and sued him for damages. He lost everything." Anthony's narration dripped with sympathy. "I couldn't do much except save him and Ophelia from going to prison."

"I can't understand why Posey brought up the party, though," Anthony said.

Cass took a breath. "Posey didn't tell me about the party. Gretchen Lange did. My sister and I had breakfast with the ex-ladies this morning. Gretchen said she used to work for your law firm." Cass dropped in the detail as if it were an afterthought.

Anthony colored crimson. "That explains it. Gretchen: no surprise there. May I ask why you had breakfast with the ladies?"

"We were invited, of course." Cass wanted to torment Anthony, just a little. Why, she wasn't sure, maybe because he had a treasure trove of knowledge about Posey he wouldn't share. "To be honest, Bay is directing the summer production at Flourish, and with all the troubles there, I think the ladies decided they might be able to provide helpful information."

"By talking about a party that happened four years ago. I don't follow."

Cass bit back an explanation and asked, "What happened to Ophelia?"

Anthony grunted. "She lost her college scholarship. I couldn't control that decision either. She moved away with her father. I hope she went to college somewhere else. She was a brilliant student."

"Was she supposed to go to Flourish?" "Yes, she was."

Rehearsal wrapped at nine-thirty without another rat sighting. Bay called Detective Downing from the parking lot to invite him to drop by for a nightcap, even if it was just herbal tea. He said he'd see her in a half hour.

Cassandra pounced on Bay at the door before she had a chance to set down her bag.

"I just made iced blackberry hibiscus tea. Come sit with me. I have so much to tell you." Cass handed Bay a cold glass.

Bay sat at the dining room table where Cass was working on her laptop. She glanced at her phone. "Will it take longer than twenty minutes? Downing's coming over for a nightcap." Bay tried out the phrase aloud, wondering if his visit meant something apart from business.

"A nightcap, you say?" Cass teased. "I'll talk fast, then disappear to my room."

Bay wanted to be defensive but found herself giggling. "Honestly, we're not teenagers, Cass. Tell me your news."

Cass shared her conversation with Anthony McGann, reminding Bay he had represented the Kingsleys following the fiasco at the unauthorized party.

"Wow, that's a lot to absorb. Did the bluff kids band together on one story and throw Ophelia to the wolves?" Bay traced a rivulet of moisture down her glass with one finger.

"That's one scenario. Or else Ophelia was guilty and acted alone, getting everyone drunk, then orchestrating horse races. I vote for the bluff kids saving themselves by making one of their own the goat. It was Ophelia's house, after all." Cass was disgusted.

"Why was Anthony McGann so forthcoming, Cass? Did you bewitch him?" Bay waved her hands as if casting a spell.

"Very funny. Despite the fact I can't get him to tell me things about Posey, I like him. He's a straight shooter and..." she trailed off. There was something a bit naughty about him, Cass decided. She wanted to explore that side of him.

Bay studied Cass. She was impressed how much her sister changed these past months. She'd arrived from prison hardened in places, wounded in others. Her face bore whatever ordeal or lessons prison taught her. Lines, shadows, sallow tones, and a tiny scar on her chin testified to her three-year sentence. Now the lines and shadows were gone, replaced by a radiant rose and cream tone. The scar remained as a symbol of resilience.

The light Bay saw dancing in her sister's sky-blue eyes told her Anthony McGann better be on his toes.

Bay was reluctant to mention the parade of dead rats that interrupted rehearsal. Cass wasn't afraid of much, but rats always made her shudder. Still, she knew the subject would surface once Downing arrived, so she pushed forward, sharing the minimum details from the night.

"Egads. What a strange regression from harmful drugs and laser burns to school pranks. Seems odd. What's your theory?" Cass asked.

"I haven't had time to think it through. I wonder if the extra security has scared the perpetrator, maybe making them cautious. And with Henry Knight in custody until tomorrow, the perp lost their accomplice. Maybe."

A knock on the door ended the conversation. Cass greeted Downing before retreating and suggested the two enjoy the garden deck.

"Your sister seems to be in cheerful spirits. You two getting along?" He followed Bay into the kitchen.

"Her spirits are definitely soaring." Bay thought about both her gift and her well-being. "We're in a good place." She beamed.

"Now, pick your poison." She spread her arm in presentation. "I have hot teas, iced blackberry hibiscus, Summer Shandy, and a stocked liquor cabinet."

"I'll take a hard pass on fruity beer, Professor. How about Jack on the rocks?"

Bay smiled. She pulled a bottle of Jack Daniels from the freezer, where she often kept the hard stuff during summer for refreshing cocktails. She poured a double over ice and handed him the tumbler. She uncapped a bottle of shandy for herself and led the way to the deck.

"Wow, this is nice." Downing's eyes lit up in appreciation of the garden getaway.

"Thanks. Cass gets most of the credit. She chose the plants. I helped plant them. We both arranged the space." She sank into a wide rattan chair. Downing sat across from her.

Bay swigged the beer and felt it course through her. She looked outward to the park at the dark sky of glittering stars above the treetops and inhaled deeply. "What's the news on Henry Knight?"

Downing followed Bay's inspection to appreciate the scene. "There's nothing for us to hold him on besides the note. Flimsy evidence. The rat show tonight points to another perp, since Henry was in jail. I still think he knows something, so we'll release him and keep watch."

"Did you turn up anything useful from Henry's past?"

"Maybe, maybe not. Henry was bullied to the point of a breakdown. We got confirmation on that from his Chicago school records and talking to the guidance counselor. We're trying to find out if he's been bullied at Flourish. That's a motive for getting even."

Bay fumed inside. "I hate bullies. I know Ginny Knight hoped moving back here would help Henry's self-esteem. I hope we're wrong about him."

"Me, too, Bay."

"Cass and I had an interesting morning: breakfast with the ex-Ladies Lange. Are you familiar with them?"

Downing swirled the golden whiskey, an inscrutable expression on his face. "The Lange Group is famous around here. I know Monroe Lange's reputation as a player. So, how did you two come to hobnob with the exes?"

Bay giggled. She loved it when he used unpredictable words, particularly when they were words she enjoyed using, too. "We were invited. I suppose because Cass met Suzanne Lange at Posey's house. You know the rumor mill. The misfortunes of our production traveled like wildfire. Be that as it may, the younger exes shared some useful information."

Bay told Downing about the postgrad party at the Kingsley ranch four years ago. "It looks to me like legacy students who just graduated from Flourish are targets. They were in the same high school class, too. I just don't know how Henry Knight is connected."

Downing raised his eyes to Bay. "Maybe. It's a stone we need to turn over."

"Do you remember the party, Brody Lynde's death, the case

against the Kingsleys?"

"I heard about it, but our department didn't handle the case. Someone asked it to be moved to Dane County, and I recall the county brought Madison on board." He snorted in disgust and took a swig.

"Can someone do that—ask a case to be transferred to a different police force?" Common sense told Bay the local police had jurisdiction.

Downing scowled. "Some people have the power to dictate a transfer. I'll dig into it."

"According to the Lange exes, Attorney Anthony McGann represented the Kingsleys. If you're nice to him, he may share the details." Bay swallowed more of the shandy.

Downing's brow puckered. "I get the feeling you already know the details. Bay, you need to be careful. Campus security isn't foolproof, which is why you had a rat infestation tonight."

"I guess so. I can't understand why the park department doesn't change the lock on the stage door. Wouldn't that be an easy solution?" She stood up. "Can I refill your drink?"

He handed her his glass. "Sure, but switch me over to one of your potions. Something hot if you don't mind." The night ushered in cooler temperatures, typical of June in Wisconsin.

Bay returned with two mugs of tea, a relaxation blend Cassandra crafted with Posey.

"Cheers. Here's to a restful night's sleep." She clinked mugs with Downing.

"You raise a good point about changing the lock. Unfortunately, it takes a committee and council meeting to make it happen. By that time, your production will be over."

"Any news on the Carillon Tower evidence?"

"The evidence is at the lab, but that could turn up nothing. If the person isn't in the DNA database, then we'll just stow it away until we get an arrest. I've talked to everyone with a key to the stage door, but maybe I'll go another round with them, one where my acting skills are on display." He batted his eyes and bowed dramatically.

Bay laughed. The man was such an enigma, and oh, did she love a puzzle. ✿

CHAPTER 21

In Nature's infinite book of secrecy,
a little I can read.

~ ANTONY AND CLEOPATRA

Friday morning was the perfect day for a horseback ride, so the two called Malcolm Hunt and asked permission to come out to Fox Hollow.

Malcolm greeted them at the stable, holding onto Fauna, while a groom stood next to him holding the reins of a sorrel and white paint horse.

"Good morning, ladies. Cassandra, I thought you and Fauna suited each other, so I hope you don't mind." He handed her the reins.

"For you, Professor Browning." He walked over to stand alongside the horse for assistance. "This is Queen Maeve, but she responds to Maeve. She's gentle, an excellent beginner horse. Here's a carrot to make friends with her." He slipped the concealed carrot into Bay's hand.

Maeve took the carrot, bubbled and let out a quiet neigh,

her tail swinging in appreciation. The groom helped Bay into the saddle and handed the reins over to her.

"Cass can ride, so I think the two of you will be fine on your own. Maeve will follow Fauna's lead. You're in charge, Cassandra." Malcolm winked at Cass, while Bay stiffened in the saddle.

"Don't tense up, Bay. Maeve will sense your fear. Just relax and trust me." Cass reassured her.

The two riders started down the trail and into the woods on the Hunt property. Soon they found themselves skirting around several estates on the bluff.

"I see what you mean about the intersecting trails up here. I guess most of the Bluff Birds owned horses, so they wanted the space to ride. What a great way to have clandestine meetings and such." Bay was reminded of regency novels she'd enjoyed where secret trysts took place among the gentry, never considering modern wealthy folks might keep the practice alive. She recalled how she and Cass came upon Posey and Malcolm on the day of Talon's service.

"Bay, are you there?" Cass had been talking, apparently to nobody. "What's on your mind?"

"Just thinking about the secrets these trails could tell us. Generations of Bluff Birds rode around here doing who knows what." Bay laughed.

"You're thinking about that party, aren't you? That makes two of us. I'm not typically a fan of the rich and famous. I can relate to Ophelia Kingsley's adoption of the underdog. That's why I can't believe she would ply Brody Lynde with alcohol and set him on a horse. And Anthony McGann agrees." Cass jutted her chin forward.

Bay understood how Cass felt. Neither of the sisters had a typical childhood. They attended public school sporadically, but were often taught by tutors at the universities where their parents were employed. Bay's precocious behavior trickled over into how she related to people and her preference to spend time with adults rather than kids. Cassandra was labeled weird wherever they went, testimony that others recognized her gifts but misunderstood them.

Yes, the two could relate to underdogs and outcasts. Perhaps that's why Cass gravitated to the wrong side of the law.

"I understand what you mean, Cass, and I trust your instincts. I know Henry Knight was bullied, and I hope that hasn't continued at Flourish."

The trails led back through a wooded area again, this time between Posey's property and the former Knight estate. Cass spotted a cloud of dust on the trail and pulled Fauna to a stop. She held her finger to her lips as she peered down the path. Both Fauna and Maeve flattened their ears back while Fauna tossed her head and snorted to Maeve.

Cass led the horses off trail behind a thicket and quieted them. The sisters listened and turned their heads in all directions. Cass pointed toward the trail where a figure mounted on a walking horse came into view.

Cass snapped a series of photos of the figure without much hope, since the person wore a ball cap and zipped sweatshirt. The rider seemed to sense their presence and kept the horse quiet until the pair rounded the bend where the trail broke open. The rider hawed the horse into a gallop and disappeared deeper into the woods heading away from Posey's property.

Cass pulled up the photos. "Look at this one. I think that's an earring."

Bay studied one photo closely. "And this one. Riding gloves. The person's hands are slender. I think it was a woman." Bay examined a couple photos again that showed facial features, although they were fuzzy. "This reminds me of someone I've seen before." She thought of all the college students she'd crossed paths with.

"Let's get the horses back to the Hunt stables. I need to get to work," Cass said.

After the Hunt's groom took the horses in hand, Bay gave the gentle Maeve a carrot and stroked the paint's velvety face. Bay wished Cass a productive day and walked up the stone path to the back door. She rapped lightly and heard Fanta tell her to come in.

The housekeeper was preoccupied cutting up vegetables to arrange on a charcuterie board around the cold meats and cheese cubes. "Morning, Ms. Browning. Dinner is easy work around here when Mrs. is gone. Mr. Malcolm and Edison are happy to eat a cold spread for lunch and dinner. I usually bake fresh bread and call it a day." She snapped her fingers to emphasize her ease.

"That's a nice break for you. No dinner parties and whatnot to plan." Bay was making small talk. She had no idea how many dinners the Hunts hosted.

Fanta nodded as she peeled a cucumber. "You'll find Mr. Edison in the back forty working on his project. He's just about finished." Fanta beamed. "I haven't seen that young man put his back into anything with that kind of zeal in, well, ever, I dare say."

Bay smiled at Fanta's candor. "I'll just head that way. Enjoy your reprieve, Fanta, while it lasts." They both knew Corrine would be home tomorrow.

Bay drove her car halfway down the driveway toward the outdoor project Edison was creating. She pulled the practice exam from her satchel, along with a new sample exam, and walked toward the sound of lawn equipment, which turned out to be Edison wearing goggles and running a sander along a large slab of wood. He paused when Bay came into view and lifted the goggles.

"Hey, Professor. What do you think?" Edison spread his arms wide, inviting her assessment of the deck circling the red oak, a stunning tri-color combination of golden, honey, and cinnamon Brazilian wood. One wooden water trough planter was varnished and filled with dirt, fit for flowers. Edison was sanding the other trough.

"The deck is beautiful. Such welcoming colors. Will you be planting the troughs today?"

"Yes. Logan and Reetz went to pick up the plants. The lanterns are ready to hang, too." He gestured to one corner of the deck where the railroad lanterns lined up. "That will take all three of us to manage." He raised both arms like a weight lifter. "If you look over the deck railing there, you'll see the furniture."

Spread out behind the tree toward the fence line, Bay spied a rustic couch, love seat, and three chairs, all with barn door style backs and sides and roomy leather cushions. A wet bar, made from hammered metal, and a stone sink completed the ensemble.

"Nice choices. It all fits beautifully together. Are you

running plumbing back here for the wet bar?" Bay wondered just how much could be accomplished under the tight deadline.

"That's the plan, but the plumbing won't be finished before my mother gets home. We'll set it up as a display, though, and keep working on it. Logan knows enough about plumbing to be dangerous, so we might try our hands at it." Edison wore the smile of the victorious.

Bay determined there was no proper time to deep dive into someone's past, so she plunged ahead. "Edison, can I ask you a question about the summer after Talon graduated?"

Edison's expression was blank. "Yep. What is it?"

"There was a party at the Kingsley house. A boy died at the party."

"Brody Lynde. He was outside the bluff circle, but he was Ophelia's friend. God knows she needed some. I didn't hear a question."

Bay stuck a pin in her question to circle back. "She needed friends? Wasn't she friends with the bluff grads?"

Edison snorted. "It's hard to have real friends when you're rich. Your guard is always up, you know. People want to use you. All the time." He spaced out each word like a drumbeat.

"The guys goaded Ophelia into having that party. A big house and no adults. Great recipe for a body binge."

Bay was filing away information as Edison spoke. "Were you at the party?"

He scoffed. "No way. I was of age, already in college. Talon's gang was not my crowd."

"But you heard all about it afterwards, I bet." Bay continued.

"I heard Ophelia pumped Brody full of alcohol. I heard

there were plenty of recreational party candies to go around. I heard somebody thought it would be fun to take bets and race expensive horses. Don't you want to ask me if Talon was involved in any of it?"

Bay gave a quick nod. "Yes, I do."

Edison snorted. "My brother was a rich asshole, and his accomplice Jackson was too. What trouble one didn't invent, the other one did. I think they were involved up to their eyeballs. The party kids banded together and stuck to one story about how that night went down. Ophelia became the villain in their version, and she took the fall."

"Why her?" Bay asked the age-old question of why someone becomes a scapegoat.

Edison shrugged. "I guess because it was easy to sell that story. Simple. Way less complicated than the truth. It was easy on the cops handling the case. I mean, who wants to go up against a passel of snobs and their pricey attorneys?"

Bay let the explanation sink in, along with the pertinent details she'd be revisiting later. "Thanks for your honesty."

"Can I yank you back to academic reality for a minute?" She handed Edison the practice exam. "You can't be too unhappy about your trial run score. It's a hair below average, so you're going to need to raise that up. About ten to twelve points for a solid pass."

Edison frowned. "I imagined I'd do a little better. Okay, Professor. What's next?"

Bay handed him more papers. "Here's a set of sample writing prompts from the graduate entrance exam. Your essay will be a timed prompt, Edison, so let's plan for that Monday morning. This one is an extra sample exam booklet. I want you to take it when you're in top form, but sometime before Monday, because I'll collect it then." Bay knew she delivered a tall order, but with Corrine back to watching from the wings, there was no choice.

Edison groaned and set the stack on the work bench. "Right. I've got one day left to enjoy this project, and then I'll get to it, Professor."

Bay grabbed the stack. "Why don't I take these up to the house, save them from getting dirty or blowing away in the breeze? Best of luck finishing the project. It's awesome." That was a word Bay reserved for special occasions.

When Cass entered Posey's back door, Marva was nowhere to be seen. Cass walked the short distance to the nearest bathroom with her nylon gym bag and changed from her riding clothes into something fresh. She ran her fingers through her rebellious hairdo, which she'd let grow out from the short pixie to a choppy cut that hung halfway to her shoulders in waves. She'd dismissed the dark hair dye and embraced her natural blond again. Cass gave the mirror a satisfied shrug.

After stowing the gym bag in the bathroom, she padded down the wool Turkish runner that ran the length of the great hall to the main doors. She headed by rote to the study situated at the corner facing the main promenade of Spirit Gardens but made an abrupt stop at the sound of lighthearted conversation bubbling from the atrium.

Cass paused outside the entrance to listen, standing back against the wall. She could hear Posey's lilting laugh in response to something said by the gentleman with the rich voice. Malcolm Hunt. Cass couldn't understand their words, but caught the tone, which traveled from light to anxious to secretive and back again.

Her espionage was cut short by Marva, charging through the doorway with a tray of dirty dishes. She never missed a beat in her step as she leaned in toward Cass to whisper loudly. "Are you going to just stand there gawking or are you going in? For the love of Mike, you look like the CIA."

Marva's admonishment made Cass smile. The woman made a good point. Cass walked through the open entryway and greeted Posey and Malcolm, who were putting a period on breakfast with pieces of Danish kringle. An extra dessert plate sat in front of an empty chair.

"We've been expecting you, Cassandra. Malcolm tells me you and your sister went horseback riding this morning. How was it?" Posey's jovial mood couldn't be missed.

"Enjoyable. Such a beautiful morning for a ride." She turned toward Malcolm. "And Queen Maeve treated my sister like a princess."

"Good to hear. You both are welcome to ride again, anytime," Malcolm said. An amused expression bloomed on his face. "I hear you and your sister had brunch with the ex-Ladies Lange. Did you hear any juicy gossip about the Hunt family?"

Cass's skin prickled with electricity. What was Malcolm driving at, she wondered. "Nothing, I'm sorry to report. The conversation centered around a deadly postgraduation party on the Kingsley property." Her voice was sharper than she meant it to be, causing Posey's eyes to widen in surprise.

"I'm sorry to say that wasn't one of the bluff's shining moments. In fact, there were several dark months following that party. It overshadowed graduation celebrations and the students' last free summer together before they all dispersed to college." Malcolm's happy mood dampened at the memory.

"Most of the bluff students went to Flourish though, so there wasn't much disbursement it seems. Except maybe for Ophelia Kingsley." Cass's words cut like a knife.

Posey inhaled sharply. "Honestly, Cassandra. Eat some kringle. It will sweeten your disposition." Posey cut a thick slab of the cherry pastry and slid it across to her.

Malcolm settled his hand over Posey's shaking one, and she immediately relaxed. "It's fine. Cassandra is fact gathering, and that's to be applauded. You should know your working environment, after all. You may have heard that the Kingsleys left the bluff in disgrace. Ophelia was a shining star at Prairie Ridge. She would be successful at any college she chose." Malcolm looked sad as he gave Posey's hand a squeeze before letting go.

Posey frowned, too. "Ophelia Kingsley had a year she would never forget, I imagine. First, her mother. Then the rest of her world fell apart because of a wild party. I think she was quite close to the boy who died, too."

Cass's ears pricked up on one piece of Posey's statement. "What about her mother?"

Tears formed in Posey's eyes, and she reached for Malcolm's hand again. "Cynthia Kingsley was killed in a car accident just weeks before graduation. When they buried her, the whole bluff was there." She wiped her eyes with a napkin.

Cass softened her tone. "Everyone here must have loved and admired Mrs. Kingsley."

Malcolm cut in. "I wouldn't go that far, Cassandra. Ophelia

wasn't part of a fairy tale. I wouldn't describe anyone on the bluff as loved and admired—perhaps of bit of one or the other. I dare say the lot of us are just tolerated; wouldn't you agree Posey?" There was that amused expression again.

Posey giggled and patted his hand affectionately. "Malcolm, you're a rogue. Which reminds me, what Shakespeare characters will you and Corrine dress as?"

The question was Cassandra's signal to eat her kringle and stop probing around the past. She sipped some hibiscus tea and nibbled on the sweet pastry.

Malcolm leaned toward Posey, as if just the two of them were there. "You know Corrine won't be coming. It's too soon after Talon for her. I plan to show up as The Bard himself. Unless you tell me that role is cast."

Posey giggled, sounding carefree again. "It's not been cast, Malcolm, because I asked the guests to choose from a list of characters from the great man's plays."

Malcolm's smile rose all the way to his eyes, which Cass decided were captivating. No wonder Posey was smitten with him. "Suppose you tell me which part you will be playing."

"Shakespeare's only female patron, and the greatest one, I might add. Queen Elizabeth the First." Posey did a mock bow toward Malcolm, her eyes glittering.

Malcolm nodded. "Then it's settled. I'll be The Bard of Avon, and you may be my patron and queen." He tilted his head and brushed his lips against Posey's hand.

Cass was embarrassed and wished she could ascend into the atrium's treetops like water vapor. It was clear Malcolm wasn't bothered by her presence. In fact, the man gave a critically acclaimed performance of someone looking like he was just where he belonged. And maybe that was the bare truth—he was.

Cassandra guzzled her tea and rose to leave. "I'll meet you in the study, Posey. Mr. Hunt, it was kind of you to let me ride at Fox Hollow again. Thank you."

Malcolm excused himself to follow Cass down the hallway. "Cassandra, a minute, please. The funny thing about airports: you never know if you'll bump into someone familiar. Peter Kingsley became an airline pilot after losing the stables. I saw him after landing two days ago in Madison. He was having coffee with Ginny Knight. They looked cozy. Maybe your sister would like to know."

Desmond announced mandatory rehearsals on Fridays until further notice, with performances three weeks away. The four directors had their heads together, sitting in the back of the outdoor seating area when Downing arrived.

"I know I'm early, but nobody told me a rendezvous was happening," he joked.

Bay, for one, was relieved to see him there, since he could emphasize the seriousness of the subject at hand.

"Take a seat, Detective. Maybe you can help shed some light on things." Desmond hoped.

"What's that then?" he asked.

Bay, who was advocating for Henry Knight, proceeded. "Tonight is Henry Knight's first rehearsal back after being detained. I explained that Henry's been bullied in the past, and someone needs to keep close watch over him now."

Desmond weighed in. "I suggested we might want to cut him loose. One less player to worry about in the fray."

"Except we need him. Henry's a gifted techie." Evan argued.

"Cutting him sends the message we lack compassion. I mean, the guy is trying to overcome bullying and needs this," Jen said.

The four swiveled their heads toward Downing.

"Ah, I suppose it's my turn. Henry Knight was severely bullied to the point of a mental break in high school. His mother wanted a fresh start for him here and hoped he'd be able to put the bullying in the past."

Bay cleared her throat and gave Downing a pointed look that directed him to say more.

"Yeah, it looks like he's been bullied at Flourish, too. You might as well know the whole truth. We think he's hiding something, so we'll be watching him twenty-four-seven, from a distance, which means one of you needs to watch him up close," Downing stated.

There was a pregnant pause before Desmond spoke. "Evan, you should keep tabs on Henry and how others are acting around him. You're the tech director."

Evan looked glum. "I suppose. I'm not a Flourish prof, so the tech crew are new to me."

Bay blew a raspberry. "You're a teacher, Evan. You should recognize trouble when you see it. Jen and I don't know all of the cast and crew either. This is on-the-job-training." She hoped to lighten the mood.

"Meeting adjourned," Desmond said.

"Not quite. Since we can't get the city to move on replacing the stage door lock, the police department settled the matter for the time being." Downing held up a combination padlock and two keys. "We're adding this lock to the stage door tonight.

The gizmo came with two keys. You decide who gets them." He handed the keys to Desmond.

Desmond took one key and dangled the other one in front of Jen and Bay. "It's one of you two. You're both always here early running interference backstage with Maya. Evan has a key to the tech booth, so he won't need this."

"You take it, Bay." Jen spoke up before Bay had a chance to, and the matter was settled.

"Now we're adjourned." Desmond placed the key into Bay's palm and smiled.

Before Bay had the chance to scold Jen, Downing pulled her aside.

"Hang back a minute. I have developments," he said.

The two walked away from the seats to a spot along the trees where two benches sat, away from the parking lot.

"I have personal information about the dead rats." His eyes crinkled with amusement.

"They were lab rats. It appears they were not from any Flourish labs. We're looking at the science centers in the area to see if they have missing test subjects. And, there's this. We found a note underneath the rat in the bronze box. It said, 'who's in control now?' Any comment?"

Bay inhaled deeply as she tried to place the information in the correct files in her head. "I'm not sure what to think. Have you checked into the Kingsley party case?"

Downing kicked a clod of dirt near the foot of the park bench and cussed. "Get this. I talked to my contact at Dane County. He called me about an hour later and said the case was sealed and sent to the feds. The feds! What a crock!"

"I don't understand. How did a grad party with the death

of a local end up in the hands of federal agents? What am I missing?" Bay asked.

"That's what I'd like to know. I have a couple contacts up the ladder. I'll see what I can find out. Don't get your hopes up. Federal cases are a black hole. I've got one or two back doors that might work, though."

"Anything you care to share?" Bay batted her eyes in mock flirtation.

"I do declare, Professor. I could have you arrested for bribing an officer of the law." Downing spoke in a cheesy cowboy accent, tipping a make-believe hat.

Bay smiled, brushed up against him, and walked to the stage. She didn't dare turn around, afraid she might either break the spell or give away her desire to be closer to him.

Backstage, Jen and Maya were matching makeup foundations with the actors' skin tones. As colors were assigned, they were placed in labeled bags, one for each actor. Bay jumped in to help Aria sort out blush and lip colors. No matter one's gender, every actor on stage would be in full makeup to heighten facial features that were washed out by theater lights.

Rehearsal was about to begin, running less than thirty minutes behind schedule, and all had designated makeup. The four women high-fived each other in accomplishing the task without difficulty or argument.

Desmond started the play in reverse to give energy and attention to the second half of the show. "When we break, I want you all to get into makeup for act one."

Bay and Jen found themselves staring at Henry Knight in

the tech booth but looked away in shame when he raised his head, startled by their scrutiny. To say Henry was subdued was an understatement. He spent the rehearsal in silence, his face a mask of sobriety.

At break, the actors scrambled backstage and found places among the vanities surrounded by mirrors and stark lighting. They had to share space, so getting ready was slow going, as expected.

Bay and Jen watched, helping the guys with eyeliner and shadow as needed. Aria appeared to enjoy the process immensely and was excited to feel useful around the college set.

As break wrapped up, Maya reminded them to put the makeup away in their labeled bags and leave them on the vanities. "When you come to rehearsal Monday, your makeup bag will be numbered to match the number on your assigned vanity. That will keep everything organized, and you can use a drawer for your bag and personal items in that vanity for the whole show."

Act one began with polish for once. No distractions set the cast on edge. No dead rats appeared in costumes or inside props. The directors started to relax, feeling at ease for the first time since Talon's death. Their ease was short-lived.

Nora Stroud sneezed, which turned into the World Series of sneezes. Her eyes watered and her face resembled a raccoon with running liner and mascara. She excused herself and went backstage to find Maya, some tissues, and makeup remover.

Jackson, Adam, and Logan formed a trio of scratchers. Adam rubbed his eyes, dabbed them with his costume sleeve, then scrubbed with added vigor. Logan and Jackson had itchy noses and cheeks, which didn't subside with rubbing or clawing.

The problem was contagious. Soon everyone on stage suffered a reaction of sorts to the makeup. Cher and Tamara both complained of tingling lips that felt like electric shocks. The others experienced skin irritations or itching eyes. In no time, the actors were all backstage seeking tissues and makeup remover.

Bay, Jen, Maya, and Aria went from feeling helpless to exasperation. Maya passed around the remover and all four helped to assist the actors. Desmond joined them backstage primed to erupt like Vesuvius.

He pointed one dramatic finger at Maya. "Come here."

Maya gulped and followed Desmond into the wings. "Do you know anything about this? It's your department. First the props. Then the costumes. Now this."

"I swear, I don't know anything. Either someone else has a key or knows some way to get in here. You can't believe I would want to sabotage our show when my whole future depends on my theater reputation." Maya held back tears.

Desmond backed away. "Calm down, Maya. I know. But it's your reputation of running a tight ship that makes me wonder what we're all missing. You haven't seen anything strange going on? People where they shouldn't be?"

Maya wagged her head. "Believe me, this show keeps me up nights worrying about what I might have missed. I have to get backstage. The detective will be here any minute to bag the makeup. I'll drop by Saturday to get all new makeup from the department. Can one of the directors meet me there? I'm not comfortable being alone now."

Rehearsal wrapped up then due to the suffering created by the makeup debacle. Desmond told them to get rest and use the cold cream or sensitive skin care items they personally owned, see a doctor if necessary, and he'd see them Monday. "Run your lines with someone during the weekend to stay focused," he yelled after them.

Downing shoved the makeup roughly into evidence bags. "I'm going to have to start paying rent at the lab. I can't wait to see their faces when I walk in again."

"Desmond, let's get that lock on the outer door. Maybe that will put an end to the reign of terror." The two walked to the stage door and waited for everyone to leave.

Bay wished Downing luck at the lab and trotted off. Enroute to her SUV, she noticed movement in the parking lot behind the tech booth and wondered if a stray dog was about. She suddenly felt quite alone but breathed in relief when she saw a campus security officer near a moving figure.

The moonlight provided clear visibility, along with the streetlight, and when the figure came into view, she gasped. Professor McNelly stood shoulder to shoulder with the security officer, and the two of them got into the campus sedan and proceeded along the service road in her direction. She instinctively ducked, squatted behind the driver's side, and waited for them to pass. She was surprised to see them turn down the lane toward the Carillon Tower.

Instead of getting into her vehicle, Bay quick-footed her way along the edge of the road keeping to the tree line and hurried toward the tower. She wished she had binoculars or Wonder Woman's hearing or both. From her vantage point, she saw McNelly and the officer leave the car and turn toward the tower. A third figure emerged from behind the tower, and Bay wondered if it was the guard assigned to the area.

There was something familiar about the stature and movement of the figure, though. In the moonlight, she noticed the figure's baseball cap looked familiar. Bay pulled her phone from her pocket and snapped a burst of photos. *Could this be the person she and Cass saw on the horse trail?*

The figure handed something to the officer. All three of them conversed, then McNelly and the officer returned to the car and drove away. Bay didn't see where the figure in the baseball cap went. She waited five minutes or possibly eternity, before skirting her way backward to the Land Rover. As she pressed the fob to unlock the door, someone grabbed her arm and placed a hand over her mouth to silence her scream.

Bay spun around as her defense know-how kicked in, but she deflated and blew out a loud gasp when she saw Downing staring into her eyes.

"What the Hell, Bay? Are you trying to put yourself in danger on purpose?"

"Where did you come from?" she asked.

Downing pointed to his unmarked car, parked in the shadows. "I waited to make sure you got to your car safely, since you were the last to leave. Imagine my surprise when you started playing some kind of spy versus spy game."

"Did you see McNelly get into the campus security car? They drove over to the tower and met someone else. It all looked sketchy to me." Bay figured she might sound silly. Maybe Downing knew about the meeting, and it was some kind of undercover operation.

"I saw. That's why I followed you. And no, I haven't got a

clue what that was about or even who the players are. You work with McNelly. What's up with that guy?"

"No idea. I'm still trying to find out. Hey, I took pictures of the three culprits. With the moonlight, you might be able to discover something." Bay sent the pictures to his phone.

"That's fine, except it feels like another tangent to me. There are too many stones to turn over and not enough personnel to assign to the case." He groaned. "Send them over and I'll take a look." Downing reached around Bay's frame to open her door, a move that ignited a tiny flame inside of her.

"And Bay," His voice was preacher serious. "Go home. I mean it. No stops." ⚘

CHAPTER 22

*The evil that men do lives after them;
the good is oft interred with their bones.*
~ JULIUS CAESAR

Over Saturday morning coffee on the garden patio, Bay pondered the clandestine tryst of McNelly and the two unknowns. *Did this have anything to do with Talon Hunt's murder and the other crimes at the show rehearsals? What else is McNelly involved in around the community, and more importantly, how could she find out?*

"You've been stirring your cream long enough to make butter in your coffee, Lulu." Cassandra rubbed her eyes and walked over to one of the cushy chairs. She was still in her night shift.

"That's quite observant for someone who, from the looks of it, just woke up," Bay teased. "Bad night?"

"I was going to ask you the same thing. You were preoccupied and quiet when you came home. Something go off-kilter at rehearsal again?" Cass sat down and propped up her feet.

Bay described the makeup debacle. "I hope adding the extra stage door lock will be the end of all this toil and trouble." She wrinkled her nose at the Macbeth witch reference.

"Hold onto your coffee mug, because I've got news the size of a hurricane." Cass's face was a mixture of anticipation and trepidation.

"Wait, don't you want a coffee of your own before you dive in?" Bay started to get up, but Cass motioned for her to sit.

"Afterwards. This can't wait." Cass leaned forward and laid folded arms on the table. "Guess who was at Posey's yesterday morning for breakfast?" Her bottom lip quivered at the memory of feeling like an intruder.

"Malcolm Hunt. He and Posey acted like a couple, I swear it, Bay. It was hard to watch." Cass felt overwhelming longing and emptiness radiating from the pair when they were together. "That's not the news flash, though. Ophelia Kingsley's mother died in a car accident the month before her high school graduation. Posey said the Kingsleys lost their whole world between the mother's death and the party disaster."

"How horrible. I wonder if it connects to the show crimes in some way." Whenever anyone spoke about losing a parent, Bay was rolled backward like a tidal wave to age seven, when she lost her mother to a sudden illness. Until recently, Bay hung onto a fairy tale that her mother was perfect, but that fantasy burned away into a complicated reality.

Cass frowned. "It was odd how emotional Posey was talking about the Kingsleys, as if the party had just happened." She paused to think about that. "There's more. Malcolm followed me out into the hallway and spoke to me privately.

He just returned from business in Minneapolis, and he saw Peter Kingsley at the airport in Madison. He was with Ginny Knight."

"Huh. Well, Ginny is a security agent there. I wonder why Peter Kingsley's in Madison."

Cass burst. "I can answer that. Malcolm said Peter became an airline pilot following his failed horse business. He also said Peter and Ginny looked cozy. His words, not mine."

Bay stood up and took in the view over the treetops of Elfenham Park across the way. "So, Henry Knight is connected to Ophelia Kingsley, if the parents are an item. Maybe that's who Henry is protecting."

She picked up her coffee mug. "Thanks for the information. I'm heading to the office. There's another stone to look under."

On the way to Flourish, Bay called Jen Yoo to meet at her office. "I'll buy you breakfast afterwards and make it worth your while."

Jen clomped into Bay's office about fifteen minutes after Bay arrived. Her hair was in a messy bun that looked like a donut frosted in sunset stripes. All it needed was sprinkles to complete the look. Jen wore spandex capris and a loose T-shirt that she may have worn to bed the night before.

"Did I wake you up?" Bay laughed, taking in her disheveled appearance. "If you were a college kid, I might ask if you tied one on last night."

"Funny. It was sorta like that. I video chatted with my parents. About thirty minutes into the call, I started drinking shots. Well, I had two." Jen made a sour face.

"After rehearsal? Isn't that late for a social call?"

"California time. Two hours earlier. It wasn't late for them." Jen yawned. "Why am I here on a Saturday morning in June?" Jen tucked a loose strand of hair behind one ear.

"Covert operation, sanctioned by Stasia." Bay waggled her eyebrows. She filled in Jen about Ophelia Kingsley, the unauthorized postgraduation party, the death of Brody Lynde via intoxicated horseback riding, and the subsequent ruin of the Kinglsey family. "To top it off, Ophelia was supposed to attend Flourish but lost her scholarship due to the scandal. That's what we're looking for. Her admission papers. An explanation of why she was denied admission. A photo; especially a photo."

"Good thing for you my brain was awake enough that I brought my laptop." Jen sat opposite Bay at the desk and logged in. "I'll look at admissions. I have more access than you do."

"That's great. I'm going to dig around social media for posts and photos from graduation. Those things never get deleted." Bay started by searching for Ophelia's name but came up empty. "Darn. She must go by a different name on her account."

Jen peeked over the top of her screen. "Try Ophelia Janine. That's her first name, middle name. I'm in her file as we speak."

Bay tried and failed. "Nothing. Guess I'll look at Nora Stroud. She was supposedly Ophelia's best friend." Nora's graduation photos showed faces Bay recognized, including Talon, Jackson, and Adam, other named females, but no Ophelia. "Empty. Looking up Brody Lynde."

Brody's social media page contained written memorials and his graduation photo. His parents had posted a message about his death and funeral, and a beautiful poem that made

Bay choke up. She spent time scrolling through the memorials but there was nothing from Ophelia, despite there being many posted by various Bluff Birds. "Gone but never forgotten" from Talon Hunt, and "we do not remember days, we remember moments" from Jackson Lange; both made Bay nauseous at their hollow tone. Then she noticed an anonymous post: "There are no goodbyes for us. Wherever you are, you will always be in my heart.—Gandhi." *Is that you Ophelia?* Tears welled in Bay's eyes.

Jen heard Bay sniff and saw her pick up a tissue.

"Did you find something useful?" Jen asked.

"Only if you know how to hack into an anonymous social media account." Bay inhaled deeply. "I was on Brody Lynde's page. It's filled with memorials. How sad."

"I found Ophelia's admission paperwork. She was a straight A student with a loaded set of extracurriculars. She received several scholarships, almost a free ride to Flourish. That was back in March when she was admitted. Then on June fifth, a formal letter went out to her and her father. Basically, it says she no longer fit the code of conduct required to attend Flourish and retracts her scholarships and admission." Jen turned the screen toward Bay. "Here, you can read it for yourself."

"Did you find any photos of Ophelia in the college files?" Bay asked.

"Nothing. Usually, there's a photo with the admission form, but I can't find one. It's a blank icon."

"Let me help you on social media. I'll poke around on Talon Hunt's page." Jen's stomach alerted her with a gurgle. "I'm getting hungry. Did you bring breakfast?"

"Nope. I thought we'd go out to Sunrise. I wasn't thinking this would take long." Bay shrugged.

"I'm looking on Prairie Ridge's high school page. They post the senior photos from each yearbook, plus the graduation ceremony. Ophelia was near the top of her class. She must be on there." Bay scrolled until she found the correct year. She saw a young, cocky looking Talon Hunt and Jackson Lange, a geeky Adam Lee, and serious Nora Stroud. But the alphabet went from Molly Keene to David Kytel. "Hey, there's no senior photo of Ophelia."

Bay scrolled through the graduation ceremony collage of speakers, singers, awards, and diploma distribution. The speakers and singers were labeled. No Ophelia. The academic awards were captioned. No Ophelia. The diploma distribution was a collection of candid shots, a trail of grainy faces. Maybe a police detective with a photoshop tool could sort them out.

"Any luck?" Bay asked. "I've got nothing."

"Me either. There's plenty of hot shots of Talon with babes and friends, looking cool from teens years through college, but the tags don't mention Ophelia. Same with Jackson. Should I keep looking?"

"Nothing on Nora's or Brody's pages. I couldn't find a page for either of the Kingsley parents. Let's look at the theater page for Prairie Ridge and science club. Two of Ophelia's passions. I'll take theater." Bay started tapping.

Both pages had nothing about Ophelia on them. Not even her name was listed. "It looks like she was scrubbed from existence in the community."

Jen nodded. "Like an Amish shunning. Weird, don't you think?"

"Yes. It's worth mentioning this to Downing. Maybe he can find a way in that we can't.

Zounds, it makes me mad." Bay drummed her fingers in an irritated tattoo on the desk.

Jen pursed her lips. "How about breakfast?"

"Sure." Bay crinkled her brows. "You want to go out in public looking like you just rolled off the slab?"

Jen stuck out her tongue. "I'll be back in five minutes. Time me." She left Bay's office and strolled off to her own.

Bay raised her head, phone in hand when Jen re-emerged. "Four minutes, fifty-seven seconds."

Jen's freshly combed hair hung loosely around her shoulders. A flouncy gauze top replaced the slept-in T-shirt, and she wore white cotton capris instead of spandex. She even applied a smear of lip gloss and dose of mascara.

Bay applauded. "Much better. The hangover look wasn't a good one."

———————————————

Cass worked on weekends for Posey when a special event or specific need in her universe dictated it. She relished the idea of spending time tending the garden patio and catching up with Diana, maybe even playing some online video games to stay sharp. All of that changed when Bay went dashing out the door.

Cass wrapped loving arms around Minerva, the black rescue cat she'd adopted fresh out of prison. "I just know Bay is looking for Ophelia Kingsley, right Minerva? She should have asked me to tag along."

Cass fed the slinky black feline some tuna fish and tossed her a ball of catnip before she left the apartment. After a stop at the Prairie Ridge Bluff cemetery, she drove to Flourish library. Since Diana worked extra hours when she could, Cass found her sitting at the reference desk reading *The Myth of Normal* by Gabor and Daniel Maté, a nonfiction book about trauma and healing in a toxic culture. After what Diana had been through, Cass wasn't surprised.

"Hey, I didn't expect to see you this morning," Diana greeted her half sister.

"I need to do some work on the computer, and I thought a change of scenery would inspire me." Cass hoped the white lie sounded convincing.

"You mean, you don't want to bother Bay or be interrupted?" Diana stood, wearing a knowing smile.

"Right," Cass agreed. "Is there a cubicle where I won't get distracted?"

Diana pointed to an entire wall of empty cubicles. "Take your pick. It's a summer Saturday."

"What time are you done? Can we do something afterwards?" Cass asked.

"We close at noon on Saturdays in the summer. I'm free as a bird."

"Great idea. Let's go to the botanical gardens and aviary, after lunch, of course."

Cass logged into the library computer with a guest password, fiddled around a bit, then logged out again and back in with a phony username and password. She used incognito tabs to begin searching for Ophelia Kingsley. She expected to come up empty, and she did.

She put her hacking skills to work when she found a backdoor into the admissions department and located

Ophelia's application, admission letter, scholarship offer, and retraction, but no photo. She dove deeper into scholarships for the recipients from four years ago, hoping a photo might be posted there. Of course, the scholarship was yanked from Ophelia, so her photo wasn't there, but... *How interesting*, Cass thought. She stared at the page of recipients, her attention drawn to Nora Stroud. After Ophelia lost the scholarship, it was offered to Nora.

Cass pulled a notepad from her purse and started searching for Cynthia Kingsley, Ophelia's deceased mother. Her obituary, articles about the car accident, and numerous social event articles and photographs popped up. She copied a few to a document, including a clear close-up of the woman, then downloaded them to a thumb drive.

After the searches about the Kingsley party and Brody Lynde case produced nothing, Cass smelled a rat, and it wore the insignia of the FBI. Her time spent in the prison system acquainted her with cases that were investigated and sealed by the feds.

Penny Brown was one of Cassandra's favorite aliases when she was grifting. She shortened her mother's first name from Penelope to Penny and last name from Browning to Brown. Penny Brown, a common name, served her well in clandestine instances. She suspected Ophelia Kingsley might want a new identity after being dragged through the Prairie Ridge mud, and that's why Cass stopped at the cemetery to see Cynthia Janine Gillis Kingsley's tombstone.

She scribbled down some obvious aliases: Cindy King, Cindy Gillis, Cindy Gill. Cindy King had too many hits, and Cass had an inkling she'd spend all day on a wild-goose chase. No, Cindy was an old-school name. Ophelia would want to make it hip. She searched for Cinda King and Cinda Gillis, then narrowed her search to Wisconsin. Once she used Ophelia's birth date from the college application and inserted it into the mix, she hit a home run.

Cinda King had just graduated from UW–Madison in May with a Bachelor of Science in chemistry with plans to attend graduate school at Princeton. Information about her was scanty and she couldn't locate a photograph of Cinda anywhere on the university pages, not even an official graduate photo. But she did turn up promising tidbits. Cinda worked in the biotech lab, a natural rat habitat. Cinda was also an assistant to Professor Halsey, the head of the theater department. She scored Cinda's campus address, too.

Cassandra's skin prickled, a signal someone was approaching her cubicle. She clicked off the incognito screen and switched to the search screen with open tabs about astronomy and horticulture. Excellent decoys.

She lifted her head to see a middle-aged, middle-sized woman dressed in a magenta houndstooth skirt and jacket. The woman walked the way a prison warden would, with purpose, and presented an "I dare you to cross me" expression. Although she seemed to be on her way somewhere, she paused to take in Cassandra, who noted her name tag.

"Are you a new student? I know everyone, and I don't know you." Joanna Stengel blinked, her hands on her ample hips. Cass noticed the glasses she wore on a chain around her neck were still bobbing on her chest from her swift pace.

Cassandra painted on a demure smile and held out her hand in greeting. "Penny Brown. I've just enrolled for a summer course in astronomy." She cast her eyes downward in deference to the formidable woman, who did not shake her hand.

"Hmm. I assume Diana checked your student ID. The library closes at noon, which is in five minutes. I suggest you get things wrapped up and log out. The computers shut down on a timer and you will lose all your unsaved searches and materials." With that, Joanna Stengel went back to her mission.

Cass looked up to see a wide-eyed Diana walking her way.

"Oh God, what did Joanna want? She looked peeved." Diana fidgeted with her hands.

"No worries. I told her I was a student. If she asks you, I'm Penny Brown, here for a summer course in astronomy. And you did check my student ID." Cass grasped Diana's hand to stop the nervous fidget. "Look, I'm logging off. Go close up, and I'll meet you in the parking lot."

Cass pulled the thumb drive out and managed to clear her browsing history before the computer screen went dark. The question now was, what should she do with her newfound knowledge?

After spending a pleasant afternoon with Diana, including lunch from one of the food trucks parked at the botanical gardens, Cass made a quick stop at the apartment to see if Bay was home. She breathed a sigh of relief at the empty apartment, still unsure of whether to share her illegal computer activities. She went to her bedroom, selected a soy candle and bag of tea from her stash, and hesitated. She saw the wooden music box on the shelf and impulsively grabbed it, too.

Cass was determined to visit the Sweet sisters and hoped they were done with bluff work for the day. Using her cell phone, she traversed past downtown Prairie Ridge to one of the neighborhoods that now contained a mix of old twentieth century four squares and ranch homes built in the past thirty years.

She pulled up curbside at a two-tone four square on Stone Mill Street, happy to see Marva's midnight blue Crown Victoria parked in the driveway. Marva relished in her power to slow traffic because of the car's resemblance to an unmarked police squad.

Cass dashed up the concrete steps onto the screened porch decorated with potted plants and a wicker swing, along with other seating. Fanta Sweet came to the door and waved her inside. Marva was the only sister who had married, so her last name was Presley, but as a collection, everyone on the bluff referred to them as the Sweet sisters.

They were drinking lemonade in the living room, watching an episode of *Murder, She Wrote*. Marva and Sage were engaged in a lively debate over who the murderer was in this episode. They disregarded Cassandra until Fanta stomped her foot on the hardwood floor.

"Cassandra, come sit with us and watch. I bet you'll agree the old farmer is the murderer." Marva patted the cushion on the linen sofa where dainty blue tulips bloomed on a tan and cream geometric background.

Sage protested from the matching wing chair. "I'm sure you'll agree the murderer is Mrs. Foster, the nosy neighbor. She wanted revenge because her husband died painting the victim's house."

Cass swung her head between the two women and decided to stand in front of the television, making Fanta chortle. "What

I'd like please, is to talk with you, Sage, about the Kingsley family."

As Sage's mouth flew open, the TV went dark thanks to Marva's punch of the remote.

Fanta sat on the sofa next to Marva, all three focused on Cass. Clearly, the subject of the Kingsley family was juicier than Jessica Fletcher.

Marva cleared her throat. "What brought this on, Cassandra? The Kingsley affair was years ago."

"That's a fair question. All of you lived through it. You must know who Brody Lynde was, and that Talon Hunt was at the party, along with many of the Bluff Birds. And Sage knew Ophelia personally. It's such a sad story, but now it might be coming home for a second act." Cass panned from one woman to the next, engaging their reactions. Marva and Fanta deferred to Sage.

"It is personal to me, Cassandra." Sage wore her heart on her sleeve. "I cared so much for the Kingsleys. Ophelia was always a tenderhearted child. She was kind to anyone who was an outcast, and she treated me like family. Peter did, too."

"What about Cynthia Kingsley?" Cass pried.

Sage flinched, turned away, then lifted her head up to the ceiling, perhaps for divine guidance. "I don't like to speak poorly about the dead. Cynthia was a career woman who cared about the limelight. She volunteered for publicity. She collected awards. And boy oh boy, could she spend money."

"The Kingsleys were rich. Living on the bluff and all." Cass assumed all the bluff dwellers had a fortune.

Sage fussed with a decorative pillow, choosing her words. "Mr. Kingsley ran a solid business, but he housed and trained other folks' horses. He made money, but never think he didn't know he was a notch lower on the social ladder. Mrs. Kinglsey was a school administrator, a professional career, yes, but not born into money. There's a difference, you see."

"I see. And Ophelia? Did she have friends among the Bluff Birds? Talon, Jackson Lange, Nora Stroud, Adam Lee…"

Sage sat up straighter. "Nora Stroud wasn't a Bird, still isn't. Her parents are horse experts, but they live on the ground floor, just like us. Nora and Ophelia were real friends. The others, well, fair-weather friends, I'd say."

Cass was beginning to form a clear picture of the Kingsley party. The Bluff Birds goaded Ophelia into having it and let her take the fall when things went south. Even Nora, her so-called real friend. "Sage, do you have any photos of the family?" Cass was mainly interested in seeing Ophelia, but she chose the careful path to get what she wanted.

Sage rose and left the room, then came back with her tablet. "I keep all my photos backed up on this," she tapped the tablet. "Just a minute."

A screen filled with Ophelia's graduation photos, but Sage swiped backward to an earlier date.

"This one is from the senior prom, right before Mrs. Kingsley's death." She pointed to a photo of a teenager with long blond springy curls, blue eyes, and an aristocratic nose. She stood between her parents and favored her father. Peter Kingsley had tight curly hair, blue eyes, and the same prominent nose. Cynthia and Ophelia shared their average height, but Cynthia's hair was red brown and straight, her eyes were brown, and she sported an upturned nose.

"Here are some from graduation. Here's one with me and

Phee. That was what I always called her." Sage was fighting back tears now, and Marva took her hand and led her to the sofa.

"May I look through these photos, please? I'm trying to find out where Ophelia is now." Cass didn't feel like pretending.

Sage handed her the tablet, then sat quietly letting the tears flow, while Cass deftly copied the sharpest photos and texted them to herself. She gave the tablet back to Sage, touching hands. Cass yanked hers back as a sharp burn stung below her skin.

"Do you know where Ophelia is, Sage?" Cass's voice was hoarse.

Sage stared wide-eyed around the trio of women, swallowed gulps of air, and hiccupped. "How would I know?" Something in her voice confirmed she absolutely knew.

Cass recovered from the momentary spell and smiled. "My apologies. I completely forgot that I brought you all something. She handed a gift bag to Marva that contained a candle and tea. I make soy candles with essential oils, and well, Marva knows I make tea blends. I call the candle Midsummer Dream, a blend of almond, rose geranium, and lemon. The tea is a summer blend for iced tea, bright with citrus and rosehips."

The women admired the candle's scent and tea blend, thanked Cass, and stood to say goodbye.

"Thank you for showing me the photos, Sage. I hope Ophelia isn't involved in Talon's death or the incidents at my sister's production." She was cheerful, but Sage recognized the veiled message directed toward her.

When Cass reached the crossroads downtown, she had to choose. One direction led left to Windflower Gardens, the other led to Angel Bluff. She stared at the wooden box with birds and flowers etched on top, as if asking it to make the decision for her. "Right it is."

Cass parked in the circle drive and rang the bell. Posey answered in moments carrying *Remarkably Bright Creatures*, the book Cass just loaned her.

"Cassandra, was I expecting you today?" Posey held the door wide in welcome.

"No, I wanted to show you this." Cass held the wooden box tight against her chest, afraid to let anyone else touch it.

"Of course. Come in. I was just reading in the atrium." Posey ushered Cass into the study, the closest room.

Posey sat on the antique sofa, hands folded in her lap, waiting.

Cass opened the wooden box, which signaled the upbeat tune, *Music Box Dancer*. Posey's quizzical expression spoke volumes. In her mind, the tune did not pair well with its owner.

Cass swallowed a hard lump and addressed the box. "When I got out of prison, I lived in a halfway house for ninety days. Each day was a trial to travel the straight and narrow, twenty-four hours of fear and temptation. It was in Florida—the house. I could walk to the beach."

Cass moved aside a top cloth revealing multiple shiny seashells. She tilted the box, which had stopped its tinkling music, to show Posey. "There are thirty different shells. I walked the beach every day, picking up fragments of shells and sand dollars. It seemed like the prettiest ones were broken."

She bit her top lip. "Eventually, I found ones that were whole. Maybe not always as lovely as the broken ones. I took them home. Someone told me I could soak them clean, then coat them in a sealer."

She handed the box to Posey. "You can look at them. I often do. I admire how fragile they are, yet they're whole. This is my treasure, Posey. Thirty different kinds of shells but all from one ocean."

Posey gasped. "Like people in the world." She held a stark white angel wing in her palm.

"When I get discouraged or afraid, I open this box and remind myself that I was a broken fragment, but now I'm whole again. Maybe not as lovely as I was once, but whole just the same." A tear slid down Cass's cheek.

Cass picked up a pristine sand dollar and a clear baggie. "This is one of my favorites. Did you know if you break open a sand dollar, you will find five tiny doves?" She held the baggie out to Posey. It contained a broken sand dollar and five V-shaped pieces. "It's said the birds represent transformation. I love that."

Bay left Jen in the Sunrise parking lot and drove back to Flourish. She decided to drop in on Diana, but the library was locked, displaying a closed sign. She hadn't realized the library closed at noon.

She returned to her Land Rover just as Dean Stasia Andino whirled into a space beside her. Stasia was in a hurry, barely shoving the car into park before unlatching her seat belt and turning off the engine.

"Ah Bay. Are you doing summer research for your fall courses?" Stasia looked comfortable in a multi-colored angled tunic, capris, and white huaraches, but the size of her shoulder bag caused Bay alarm. Stasia was tiny like a hobbit, and the canvas bag hung from her shoulder to her knees.

"Hello Stasia. No research yet. I'm occupied with the Shakespeare show for now. I'm sorry to tell you that the library's closed, though."

"Ela! I was going to pick up some items for Aria. She's working on her scholarship essays. She will be a senior this year, so I wanted to help her get a jump start, you know?"

"Is Aria applying to Flourish?" Bay imagined Stasia's niece would be a shoo-in.

Stasia looked over her leopard print sunglasses at Bay. "Absolutely, but the girl wants to apply several places. I said to her, Flourish isn't good enough for you, huh?" Stasia rattled off a flurry of Greek words Bay didn't understand.

"Well, that's teenagers for you. She wants to spread her wings." Bay smiled with empathy.

"I can help her better here." Stasia pointed to the pavement and stamped her foot for emphasis. "I can keep an eye on her. Aria's a good girl, but so naive. Your production has her tied up in knots, Bay. What have you and Jen discovered, eh?"

Bay dreaded that question. What could she tell Stasia that was definitive? "I'm afraid there are a lot more questions than answers, and an excess of suspects." She heaved a sigh. "The police are working on it."

"Yes, I know. The department keeps me informed. You know what they found in the stage makeup? Added chemicals, way above normal amounts. That's why everyone had a reaction." Stasia huffed in disgust. "Now the college has to buy new makeup. This show better make money, that's all I'm saying."

Bay frowned. "Maya Leary is top-notch in the costume and makeup department, don't you think?" If anyone knew any dirt about Maya, it would be Stasia.

"Of course she is. She's been in every production here since high school. If I didn't trust Maya, I would never allow Aria anywhere near her."

That was satisfactory for Bay. "I just can't fathom who's behind this. In the beginning, it seemed personal against Talon, then a few others. Now it seems like someone wants to ruin the whole show."

Stasia grunted. "Couldn't it be both? If someone has it in for certain cast members, why not wreck the whole show? Bah. I trust you and Jen will keep investigating. Many hands make light work, you know," Stasia said, opening her car door to leave.

"Too many detectives spoil the case," Bay muttered.

Bay treated herself to a solitary swim at the college indoor pool after noticing her forgotten gym bag behind the passenger seat, which was last opened sometime in May. She decided the eighty-degree afternoon called for a refreshing swim.

Her skin still tingled when she entered the apartment, where a scent of something delicious wafted from the kitchen in greeting.

She swung open the two-way door and saw Cass, wearing a black apron with the expression "if you think I'm a witch, you should meet my sister." She was scrubbing a mixing bowl and utensils.

"Nice apron. I see either of us can wear it." Bay chuckled.

"It's interchangeable. How's your day going? Wait, your hair's wet!" Cass remarked.

"Don't fall over, but I decided to go for a swim at the college pool. Had the whole place to myself. My day has been loaded with dead-ends. The swim washed away the stench of defeat." Bay produced a half-hearted giggle.

Cass, however, gave her sister a hundred-watt smile. "Here, try one of these. They'll knock the doldrums away." She handed Bay a chai lavender cookie. "Aren't you going to ask me how my day's going?"

Bay savored a large bite of the complex cookie and rolled her eyes like a puppy. "Forsooth, these are magical!" She reached over to the cookie rack and snatched a second one. "I love the white chocolate chunks in here, and is that sea salt sprinkled on top?"

"It's Balinese flake salt, made by dripping seawater through a filter. It tastes better than traditional sea salt. Ahem. You still haven't asked me about my day." Cass waved the cookie spatula in Bay's direction like a baton.

"Sorry," she said between bites. "Do tell. How was your day?"

"Let's start with your day. Let me guess: you couldn't find anything useful about Ophelia Kingsley." Cass paused, spooned cookie dough onto a sheet, and slid it into the oven.

Bay's eyes narrowed. "I would ask how you know that, but never mind. Jen can access some college records, so she poked around there while I browsed social media for graduation photos. No luck. It's like Ophelia doesn't exist."

Cass nodded and leaned against the counter near the stove. "I know, right? You found the admission letter and retraction. Did you look at the scholarship page?"

Bay's puzzled expression told the tale. "Missed that one. Somehow, I'm guessing you did, though."

"The scholarship Ophelia lost was awarded to Nora Stroud.

Someone's loss is another's gain." Cass wore a lopsided grin, and her cheeks resembled rosy apples.

"There's obviously more to tell. Let's have it." Bay helped herself to iced water with mint and lime, which made her pucker after eating the sweet cookies.

"Here's a photo of Ophelia." Cass passed her cell phone to Bay. The picture showed a close-up of the girl in her graduation gown.

"We looked through social media and the Prairie Ridge school sites. Where did you find this?" Bay stared at the photo, disappointed the girl didn't look familiar.

"After my browsing session at the college library, I paid a visit to the Sweet sisters. I asked Sage if she had photos. I helped myself to copies of them." Cass showed Bay the pictures. *I doubt Cinda looks like Ophelia, though.* Cass pulled the sheet from the oven, then scooted the next pan in.

"Smart cookie," Bay said, helping herself.

"Hey, steady there. Don't ruin dinner. Do you want to hear the rest of it?" Cass teased.

"Of course. The college library, huh? Diana won't get in trouble, I hope." Bay's response sounded a bit snappy, and she instantly regretted it. "I'm sorry. I wish I'd asked you to come with me this morning."

Cass turned away a moment as she blinked back a tear. Bay's response was what she'd wished for, a sign that she mattered and could be included. Gads, she was getting soft. "Yes, you should have invited me. I have great search skills." She stumbled over the word search, when she really meant *hacking*.

"I think I know why Ophelia is missing from social media and the school website. She changed her identity. She's using the alias Cinda King, and Cinda just graduated from UW–Madison with a chemistry degree." Cass said.

"One; how did you figure that out? Two; how does using an alias make your other self disappear?" Bay internally marveled at her sister's skills. Little did she know that many of those skills were fine-tuned in prison computer courses.

Cass slid cookies onto a drying rack, while Bay packed a plastic container with the cooled ones, so she'd stop eating them.

"My first stop was the cemetery to find Mrs. Kingsley's grave. Her full name was Cynthia Janine Gillis Kingsley. My favorite alias was Penny Brown. I think you know how I came by that. So, I thought maybe Ophelia used pieces of a familiar name to make an alias. I tried three different ones and lucked out with Cinda King."

"You and your hunches. I doubt it was all luck, Cass. You didn't find a photo of Cinda King, huh?"

"No, and I'm not surprised if she's trying to stay underground. I think the feds are somehow involved with Ophelia's case from the party. It could be drug related. Maybe Ophelia can identify some bad actors. It's one explanation as to why she's all but disappeared from online searches."

A light bulb went on. "Downing said the party case was sealed. Originally, his department lost jurisdiction to Dane County, but then it went to the feds. He's trying to get his hands on useful pieces of the old case, if he can."

Cass beamed. "Let's get him over here for dinner and exchange intel."

Bay faltered. "Oh, Cass. If he hears how you found the information, you could get into trouble. He's a cop, remember?"

At six o'clock, Cass and Bay served up a platter of grilled chicken and shrimp fajitas, atop a mound of peppers, onions, and mushrooms. Bay ushered Downing to the patio table that was set up with sour cream, salsa, sliced avocado, and a warmer of flour and corn tortillas. Nonalcoholic margaritas stood pretty in a pitcher adorned with watermelon slices, lemons, and limes.

"This smells delicious and looks good enough to eat," Downing said.

"Let's dig in. We can talk and eat at the same time. Here, let me fill your glass." Cass picked up a wide-mouthed margarita glass and filled it to the brim, then filled two more glasses.

"I suspected you had an ulterior motive, ladies. After the week I had, your invitation sounded too good to pass up. Fire away. You must have questions, Professor." There was no malice in Downing's voice, just an edge of flirtation.

"It might confound you to know that Cassandra and I are offering our new information to you, and that's why we asked you to dinner." Bay's voice lifted with anticipation.

"Go on, Bay."

"I heard the makeup was tainted with chemicals that assured allergic reactions." Bay was aware this wasn't news to Downing.

"You're not telling me something I don't know, so I'm betting there's more."

Cass tagged in. "We think we know who placed the chemicals there. Ophelia Kingsley."

Downing's eyes narrowed as he tried to look skeptical. "Huh. Why her?"

Bay tried to look serious but was thrilled he'd ask the question they wanted to hear. "She has a degree in chemistry, after all. At least, Cinda King does. Fresh out of UW-Madison, no less. Just down the road from Flourish." Bay waited to pass the ball to Cass.

Downing's lips twitched, but his poker face held. "Cinda King. How did you come up with that one?"

"I'm familiar with aliases Detective. It wasn't difficult to find her. There's a lot to be uncovered just with the correct birthdate. Would you like her address?" Cass slid a piece of paper across the table to Downing.

"Wait a minute. I hope you have more than this. Pretty thin evidence, you two." Downing protested, but he looked at the address scribbled on the paper.

Bay used tongs to pass a second tortilla to the detective. "Cinda volunteered in the theater department, so it's easy to conclude she could get a key to the park stage. Then there's the connection to Henry Knight." Bay passed the platter and sour cream to Downing, then sat in silence.

"What connection would that be?" Downing made a careful design with the platter ingredients, salsa, and sour cream.

"Ginny Knight is involved with Cinda's father, Peter Kingsley. We're thinking Henry didn't want to mess up the family relationship or something like that." Bay answered.

Downing folded the tortilla into a sealed wrap, then sat back, relaxed, and laughed.

A startled look passed between the two sisters. What was going on?

"What's so funny, Detective? Are you stunned at our investigative chops or is it funny to be bested by two civilians?"

Cass taunted.

Downing drank back the margarita and refilled his glass.

"You're both smart enough to be dangerous. Let's assume you're right on all counts. We've been to this address." He held up the paper Cass gave him. "Nobody's home. On the third try, we got the landlord to open the door in the guise of a welfare check. The closet is all but empty. The fridge is empty. The place is clean. We think Cinda moved out."

Bay and Cass deflated. "The feds," Cass murmured.

"Did you talk with Henry, Ginny, and Peter Kingsley?" Bay asked.

"Here's the weird part. Henry has never met Cinda. They've played D and D together online, got acquainted, and became close. She knew about his bullies, and he knew she got screwed over by her friends. He protected her."

"That seems to fit, doesn't it? Henry could suspect Cinda was behind the incidents without aiding her." Bay hoped so.

"That doesn't explain how Cinda had access to the costumes when they were with Ginny Knight." Downing turned his glass in a slow circle.

"What did Ginny have to say?" Bay asked.

"Ginny admitted to dating Peter Kingsley. She said it was a new relationship, and she'd never met Cinda. Peter told her his daughter was out East attending college. She said she didn't know Henry was friends with the person that turned out to be Peter's daughter. I think she was telling the truth."

"And Peter Kingsley? He must know his daughter graduated from UW–Madison." Cass was unimpressed with the cover-up.

"We haven't been able to talk to Peter yet. He's due back tomorrow morning from an overseas flight. If Cinda's alias is part of a federal investigation, Peter wouldn't tell Ginny the truth about his daughter." Downing said flatly.

"What's your gut telling you on this?" Bay trusted the detective's instincts and was done playing the cat and mouse game for now.

"I think Ophelia, aka Cinda, tipped the props with fentanyl, placed tainted pins in Nora's costume, burned Jackson Lange with a laser pointer from the tower, planted dead lab rats backstage, and added chemicals to the stage makeup. She had motive and opportunity." Downing scowled, his face a dark mask of disgust.

"Looks like you solved the case. Why are you angry?" Cass asked.

"We can't find Cinda, for starters. If the feds are involved, the pieces don't fit. Henry Knight knew about the costume. Maybe not the rest of the plan, but he couldn't disguise his fear for Cher and knowledge that it was supposed to be Nora in that gown. Henry's suffered at the hands of bullies and is so young. This isn't a happy ending for him."

"Not to mention the fallout around Peter Kingsley, who already lost so much because of his daughter's party. And maybe there wasn't justice in the party case. Maybe Ophelia has a reason to burn down the lives of the people who destroyed hers. Maybe she never meant to kill anyone." Bay wanted to believe a fair outcome existed.

Downing grunted and held out his empty glass. "Don't you have something stronger than this fruit punch?"

"I'm on it. You two keep talking." Cass stood up and went inside.

"Bay, you know how this works. The police follow the laws.

A jury considers the circumstances. If Cinda and Henry broke laws, there are consequences. I don't always like the way it is, but I have to act in accordance with the laws."

Bay reached over to take one of Downing's hands and gripped it. "Of course. I didn't mean to suggest otherwise. Can you tell me what you're going to do now?"

"Talk to Peter Kingsley tomorrow and keep looking for Cinda. I wish we had a photo to go on. The worst part is that somebody in the department is going to have to shake down Henry Knight. We'll bring in a shrink who will handle the situation a hell of a lot better."

Cass arrived with a whiskey on ice and heard the detective. "Did you say you don't have a photo of Cinda? I can help you with that. I'll text you these." She picked up her phone and showed it to Downing.

"That would help. Thanks. Should I ask how you found these?"

"Of course. I asked Sage Sweet. She was the Kingsleys' housekeeper for years. I figured she must have photos. You know what they say about household staff being invisible? If the feds wanted to erase Ophelia, they screwed up by forgetting about Sage." Cass jutted out her chin as she made her point. She loved it when she pulled off something the authorities missed.

Downing sipped the whiskey while Bay and Cass chose the chai cookies for comfort and drank warm chocolate coffees. The stillness was punctuated with a slight rustling of leaves across the way and the final calls of birds heading home for the evening.

Cass excused herself and headed to the kitchen routine of

cleaning dishes and restoring the space. She'd orchestrated a completely different evening in her mind where she would school the police, but now she felt cheated that they knew what she knew, likely even more than that. Still, she was coming around to respecting the detective as someone who wasn't a poster boy for the department, and she sensed an intimacy forming between him and her sister. She didn't disapprove—not yet.

Bay and Downing sat in silence until their glasses were empty and he'd enjoyed some cookies. He broke the ice.

"You and I have to stop meeting like this." He grinned at the use of the cliché. So did Bay.

"And by that you mean we should do something that isn't related to a police matter?"

"Exactly. Do you like boats?"

Bay's experience with boats was minimal. Did she like them? "What kind of boat are we talking about?"

"Fishing boat, with a motor."

Bay blinked and tried not to grimace. "I don't fish."

"You like to read, right?"

She nodded. "Love to read."

"Bring a book. I'll fish. You can read." Downing suggested.

Bay smiled. "It's worth a shot. My turn for a suggestion. Can we start with using our first names?" She giggled.

Downing frowned. "Not if it's police business, Bay. I'm just Downing when I'm doing my job, that or detective."

"It's a deal, Bryce." Bay held out her hand to shake his, but he lifted it to his lips and planted a warm kiss in her palm.

"Okay, so boat ride on a date to be determined. After your show?"

Bay nodded. "And Detective? I plan to tell Ginny Knight to hire a criminal attorney ASAP. Just wanted you to know."

Downing understood. If he wasn't assigned to the case, he'd do the same. "Okay, Professor. While we're back to formalities, your sister is a whiz. She has skills any police department would welcome. It took our computer hackers three days to accomplish what Cassandra did in one morning."

"I'd be in your debt if you promise me you won't report Cassandra's activities to her parole officer." Bay was asking out of friendship and hoped she hadn't crossed a line.

He smiled and traced one finger over her palm. "I'm sorry, the detective is off duty." ✣

CHAPTER 23

Interlude before the Final Act

The next two weeks passed with little development on the Shakespeare incidents but the simple act of adding a combination padlock to the stage door seemed to do the trick. No more pranks or acts of terror had occurred, and the four directors agreed in frustration that if the locks had been changed after Talon's murder in the first place, there wouldn't have been more incidents.

Whatever the alteration, the moon phase, change in weather, or dumb luck, *Shakespeare's Couch* was knitting itself into a well-woven production and would be fine-tuned for the audience on schedule.

Downing appeared at a few rehearsals but chose to allow the campus security team to handle patrolling and guarding the park and stage. On a couple visits to Bay's apartment, he divulged minimal information aside from his frustration.

Peter Kingsley wouldn't volunteer anything about his daughter, not even whether she went by Cinda King instead of Ophelia. Instead, he handed the detective the business card of his A-listed Chicago attorney.

"Chicago?" Bay asked. "Isn't that out of jurisdiction in a Wisconsin case?"

Downing swore under his breath and pulverized several antacids with his teeth. "Another sign this is a federal case. God only knows why."

The psychiatrist working with the police had reached a stalemate with Henry Knight. Henry insisted he knew Cinda from online gaming. When pressed, he admitted to knowing about her trauma after the graduation party and that Cinda offered to help Henry handle his bullies. One possible conclusion is that Henry confused his trauma with hers and felt compelled to protect her.

The dead end with the Knights didn't sit well with Downing, but he couldn't apply any extra pressure since Ginny hired an attorney, thanks to Bay and to Anthony McGann, who reached out to Ginny urging her to seek representation. Anthony's firm declined, citing a conflict of interest since he'd been immersed in the Kingsley case.

The one piece of fresh information Bay produced was a somewhat fuzzy photograph of Cinda King from an end-of-year party for theater department volunteers at UW–Madison, courtesy of tech director, Evan Barnes.

When Bay questioned Evan, he admitted he crossed paths with Cinda on and off during the past two years, but he couldn't describe any detailed encounters. However, as she grilled him, Evan recalled that Cinda was at the party celebrating the graduates, and he had photos. He showed her some with pieces of Cinda in them, but she never looked at the camera and didn't pose with the group. The best shot showed a profile of her face, with short, wavy red brown hair, wearing a Wisconsin Badgers ballcap.

Bay sent it to herself and to Downing with a note. "I'm sure this is the person I saw by the Carillon Tower with McNelly and the security guard, and the person Cass and I saw riding around the bluff trails. Same hat anyway. Same stature."

When Bay showed the photo to Cass, she raised her eyebrows in disbelief.

"This looks nothing like Ophelia Kingsley." Then Cass smiled like a cat with a mouthful of canary. "She's amazing at disguising herself." She couldn't help but admire the woman.

"Maybe you can't give her all the credit. If this is a federal case, I imagine she's getting plenty of help."

Cass tapped one finger against her cheek. "Why is she here though? If you're Cinda King, with a college diploma, all set to move to a prestigious graduate school—what hold does Prairie Ridge have on your life?"

"Revenge. One last chance to get back at the people who burned your life down. Then you're ready to move on." Bay understood hurt at the hands of people you love, but she didn't have the heart for revenge.

Cass raised curious eyes at her sister. "Sometimes, I underestimate you, Lulu."

The one thing Bay dreaded during the past two weeks was dealing with Corrine Hunt. The Monday after Corrine's business trip, she confronted Bay as soon as she entered Fox

Hollow House.

"Follow me, Professor Browning. I'd like a word." Corrine led the way to her business office on the upper floor.

"It is my understanding you knew about my son's outdoor project." Corrine used the word *outdoor* as a vulgarity, and Bay fought to keep a smile from forming.

"Yes, that's true." Better use as few words as possible, she decided.

Corrine blinked, smoothed her gray slacks, blinked again. Her porcelain features were rigid, revealing nothing by calm. "I hired you to tutor Edison. I explained the urgency of the matter with the graduate school entrance exam in July. Was there something you misunderstood in our contract?" Corrine stood like a statue. There was nothing threatening in her posture, yet Bay could feel the attempted intimidation.

"No, I understood perfectly."

"Then, Professor, explain to me," Corrine said.

Bay interrupted. She could play it cool, too. "If I may. Edison continued to finish lessons, improved his writing, and completed two practice exams while he worked on the project. That was the deal we made, so he could manage both tasks."

"The deal you made. You and my son. I didn't hire you to make deals with my son. You and I had a deal. That's the only deal that matters to me, Professor." Corrine's calm exterior cracked a hair.

"With all due respect, your son showed he can successfully multitask. The landscape project is quite an accomplishment in a short time. Better yet, in just one week, Edison raised his score by five points on the practice exam." Bay wanted to go on but bit her tongue.

"Please don't patronize me. Are you a landscape expert? Stay in your own lane. The fact you encouraged him in this endeavor is out of line." Corrine paused.

Bay's cheeks reddened. Of course she wasn't a landscape expert. She wished Malcolm was part of this meeting. "I understand. I apologize for violating my contract and will see myself out." That was the Bay Browning she needed to be in the moment, proud and stubborn.

Corrine's mouth opened in surprise. "You're not fired, Dr. Browning. Please just do what you were hired to do, and nothing else."

Bay faltered and bit back a snarly reply. "Is Edison in the library?"

Corrine nodded slightly. "You're here for two more weeks. Make it happen."

Edison was sullen for a couple of days during the routine tutoring sessions. "My mother couldn't muster one decent comment about the landscape project. She just badgered me about shirking my academic responsibility to play outside. Play outside? She actually said that."

Bay took a deep breath. She'd found a rapport with Edison built from mutual respect no matter what Corrine insisted upon, and Bay meant to continue supporting his goals. "What did your father say, Edison?"

Edison's smile lit up his face. "He thought it was excellent. He said he could see, in time, I could maybe make a career in the landscape business."

"There you go. Focus on that and on what you need to do to achieve that goal. Business school will help you with the management and accounting end of landscaping. Even if you eventually hire people in those positions, you're still going to need to comprehend how it all works. Correct?"

Edison drummed a pencil against the library table and huffed. "Yep. Suppose so."

"We have two weeks to get you prepped for that entrance exam. Let's give it our all." Bay always felt fake with the cheerleader speech, when she knew it was up to the student to choose success. Part of her knew it mattered to the students that she was in their corner, though.

By the end of two weeks, Edison could craft an academic essay that was above average, and he'd raised his practice exam scores between eight and ten points. Bay wished him luck for the real exam and essay in the upcoming week. Edison surprised her with a quick, tight hug and thank you.

"If you ever need any landscaping done, Professor, I hope you'll give me first dibs."

Bay said she would. On her way out, she stopped in the kitchen to ask Fanta where she might find Mrs. Hunt.

"I expect she's in her office. There's been a lot of business going on since she took that trip to Atlanta," Fanta said amid chopping carrots and celery. "You can just go up and knock on the door."

Bay knew the way. She'd been in the office two weeks earlier getting dressed down by Corrine. She knocked lightly on the door, which was partly open.

Corrine looked over from her computer screen and waved Bay inside, then she removed her reading glasses and put them on the desk.

"Dr. Browning, I'll send your payment to you after Edison gets his test results. That won't be until mid-July, at least."

Corrine's face was pinched and the worry lines on her forehead stood out.

Bay fumed inwardly at the insult. As if she was here for money. "That's not why I stopped in. I wanted to say something if I may." She thought asking permission to address Corrine might be a mistake; the woman could dismiss her on the spot.

"Yes?"

"Here it is. Edison is thirty years old, and he has a decent head on his shoulders. He's passionate about landscape design and could be both successful and happy. There's something to be said for that." Bay couldn't decide if she should wait for a response or leave. She went with the less rude option.

Corrine cleared her throat. "Yes, there is something to be said about happiness, I suppose. Thank you for your patience in tutoring Edison. Teachers have given up in the past. I'll be in touch." She turned her office chair sideways toward the computer screen and slid the reading glasses back in place. Bay was dismissed.

The week before the Shakespeare party, Posey gave Cassandra two assignments. She would oversee tallying the scoresheets the party goers used to guess the character roles. Cass alone would have the master list of who's who in Shakespeare's world. And, Posey assigned Cass to deliver costume masks to those attending.

"Would you like to go by horseback, as you did with the invitations, or by car? Riding horse could pose a challenge with a box full of masks." Posey giggled.

Cass frowned. Posey was right, but she wanted to continue

the authenticity around the party. Delivering masks in a Subaru sounded lame.

Posey clapped her hands like a child. "I know what you're thinking, Cassandra. Luckily, I thought of a third option. Look out the front window."

Cass peered out the wide picture window overlooking the circular drive. A white carriage was parked in the porte cochere, pulled by a horse Cass recognized. "Why is Fauna pulling a carriage and where did it come from?"

"I rented the carriage and asked Malcolm if I could borrow Fauna for the day. That seems like a fitting way to deliver masks. Malcolm loaned us Gary, one of his stable workers, to drive you around."

Cass went upstairs to the costume storage area and browsed the remaining items. The party guests had claimed the bulk of the costumes and accessories, but Cass found a gown from the Regency era suitable for her task, and grabbed an elegant mask trimmed in feathers and jewels to use at each stop.

Going by carriage took plenty of time, but Cass enjoyed the attention and gaping expressions all around town, even from certain stodgy Bluff Birds. Fanta and Sage both posed for photos with Cass, and Malcolm Hunt enjoyed her reaction to his surprise. She was certain Malcolm's pleasure was derived from making Posey happy.

She saved her final stop for Anthony McGann's office. When she stepped from the carriage, she beamed at the man who held out his hand to assist her. Anthony bowed deeply and took her arm.

"To what do I owe the pleasure, Milady?"

Cass stifled a girlish giggle and opened the wooden box

perched on the back of the carriage. Posey ordered extra masks to accommodate everyone's choices and costumes, so there were still plenty in the box.

"I'm delivering masks for the party so the characters may remain incognito. Make your choice, Dear Sir."

Anthony rummaged through the masks, holding up a couple, trying on a few. "How about this one?" He donned a black faux-leather mask.

"Ooh, mysterious. It reminds me of Zorro. Who is your character?"

"Ah, that I cannot tell you, or how will you play the guessing game?" Anthony teased.

"I hate to disappoint you, kind sir, but I have the master list. I will be the keeper of the secrets at the party." Cass whispered.

"In that case, I'm coming as Marc Antony. You know, Anthony, Antony." He smirked.

"How typically lawyerish of you." Cass smirked in return. "Are you wearing a Roman helmet?"

"No, I opted for the comfort of a laurel wreath."

Cass laughed. "Good choice. I think you should wear the black leather one. Perfectly dashing, Marc Antony."

Anthony kissed her hand, making her tingle. Cass couldn't help but notice that the man had touched her several times, and she never experienced any dark vibes, yet she knew he was keeping secrets. Of course, that is quite literally part of his profession, she reminded herself.

"I look forward to seeing you again next weekend at the party, Milady," Anthony said.

"Wait a minute. Don't you need a mask for the mysterious J.S.?" Cass remembered Anthony acted as the go-between for the unknown J.S.

"No. J.S. will not be attending."

Cass couldn't hide her disappointment. "What a shame. I should so like to unmask that one." Cass swished her skirt with a flourish and curtseyed. "Good day, sir."

As soon as she returned to Posey's, Cass pulled up the guest list on the computer. Sure enough, J.S. had not responded to the invitation and missed the RSVP date. A few other invitees had not responded either, but Posey said that was the norm. Not every Bird attended her affairs, but Posey dared not invite them just the same.

With the party less than a week away, Cass decided to check in with the catering service and decorators. She felt an inkling, that is.

Posey's usual choice for party food was Cozy Catering in Prairie Ridge, a local business who indulged her sometimes quirky orders. Being booked for a bluff party gave a local business bragging rights. When Cass checked in with Delia, she confirmed that everything was ordered, and some had already arrived. Delia and a crew of seven would be on hand the entire party: setting up, serving, and cleaning up.

Cass tapped in the number of Fancy Florals and knew immediately something was amiss. When Dawn answered the phone, Cass could hear Barbie, the owner, taking a call on the edge of hysteria.

"Fancy Florals, may I help you?" Dawn's voice was uncertain.

"Hi Dawn, it's Cassandra Browning calling about Posey Hollingsworth's upcoming Shakespeare party on Sunday." Cass paused to allow Dawn to take in the nature of the call.

"Oh dear." Dawn's shaky voice didn't bode glad tidings, and Cass knew the party order was in jeopardy.

"What's going on there? Sounds like you've got an ordeal on your hands."

Deep audible sigh on the other end signaled that was the case. "You nailed it, Cassandra. I know Barbie hasn't been able to call you yet, but there's a big problem here. We're hired for a huge wedding on Saturday, and our main shipment was lost. Barbie just found out, so she's trying to sort things out."

In moments, Barbie was on the line with Cass. "Ms. Hollingsworth?"

"This is her assistant, Cassandra. What's the status on the decorations for Sunday?"

Barbie began to cry. "I'm sorry. The shipment that we need for your party is delayed due to storms in Texas. We're not going to be able to fulfill Ms. Hollingsworth's order."

"I see," Cass said. "We can work something out. I can come down there today and see what's available."

"You don't understand, Ms. Browning. What we have is going to be used for the Saturday wedding. We won't even have enough to cover that. I'm calling around to area florists to see if I can purchase extra flowers from them. This is a nightmare." Barbie's voice wavered again.

"I'm sorry about your dilemma. I'll let Ms. Hollingsworth know. We'll figure out something. Good luck to you." Cass signed off, wondering how to inform Posey about the decorations.

Instead, she called Bay and explained the situation. "I thought maybe the horticulture department at the college could help? I'm grasping here."

Bay was sitting in the Hunts' driveway when the call came, a lucky happenstance. "I doubt the horticulture department can help, but here's a shot in the dark: hire Edison Hunt to do the décor."

"You're kidding." Cass decided Bay was wasting her time.

"Nope. He's gifted, he's hungry, and he's out to prove himself. I'm at Fox Hollow now, about to leave. Want me to grab Edison and bring him over there?"

Cass held her head in her hands in misery. "What have we got to lose?"

Minutes later, Cass met Bay and Edison at the main door and pushed them toward the study.

"Here's the original sketch of the upstairs grand salon and list of greenery and flowers."

Cass shoved the plan toward Edison, who examined the details.

"Professor Browning explained that the local florist is calling around to buy flowers. That means I need a supplier from outside the area. Lucky for you, Ms. Browning, I have different contacts. I can come close to making this exactly as you planned."

"Are you sure?" Edison didn't miss the skeptical expression on Cass's face. "How much will it cost us? It's six days away."

Edison picked up the plan. "Let me take this and get started. I'll get you an update and price by tomorrow. No obligation to hire me."

Edison held out his hand to Cass and she shook it, still uncertain about what to tell Posey. ✤

CHAPTER 24

And thence from Athens turn away our eyes,
to seek new friends and stranger companies.
~ MIDSUMMER NIGHT'S DREAM

Cass, wound like an alarm clock, arrived hours before the Midsummer Shakespeare role play party to check on details and help Posey with her costume and accessories.

She bypassed a conversation with Marva, who was muttering something about her kitchen being taken over by the catering company and made a beeline upstairs to the grand salon.

She was impressed with Edison Hunt's handiwork. In five days, the salon was transformed into a fantasy garden. Every corner was decked out with bowers covered in greenery and roses. Fairy lights cascaded down the walls, and celestial starbursts hung from the ceiling. Crisscrossing the plush carpeting were pathways made from wooden tiles that led to surprising finds: a miniature pond with glowing lights, a waterfall, and a weeping willow tree with a swing. The banquet tables were covered in white damask and laden with garlands of purple stocks, blue iris, cream roses, yellow statice, blue and white bellflowers, feather ferns, and Irish moss. She couldn't wait for Bay to see the result, or Malcolm Hunt, for that matter.

The food tables occupied one wall in traditional banquet fashion, but the dessert area featured a white flower cart decorated with ivy and star lights with tiered shelves to display the sweet offerings. Two of the walls were interrupted by massive double door entrances that led to the four guest bathrooms outside the salon. Behind the back entrance, servers could come and go from the storage room where the wet bar and chafing dishes would be staged when the caterer arrived.

After checking on Cozy Caterers and showing them the grand salon and storage area behind it, Cass left Delia and her crew to set up. She readied the round table at the entrance with sample questions for guests to ask the characters, a master list of all possible characters to choose from, and a numbered sheet for their guesses. Party favors included fans and card games inspired by Shakespeare's plays.

Cass found Posey in the costume room that had once been her mother's bedroom, sitting at the princess style vanity applying eye shadow and blush. Her hair was pinned under a wig cap, but she would need assistance with the towering red-gold mass of Queen Elizabeth curls.

"Have you seen the grand salon, Posey?" Cass couldn't contain her excitement.

"I have. It's magical. Who would have thought Edison Hunt was capable of that?" Posey beamed.

"Are you concerned about Detective Downing being at the

310 | Joy Ann Ribar

party?" Cass wondered. Posey had said next to nothing after the police chief called to insist the detective be present.

"I suppose he has his duty, but I doubt anyone will say anything useful in finding Talon Hunt's killer." Posey added tiny jewels to her fingernails as she spoke.

"Well, many of the guests are connected to Flourish College and the victims. Merrymaking often loosens the tongue." Cass used an exaggerated British accent. She realized she knew more about the case than most and she had to be cautious, even around Posey.

Before changing into her own costume, Cass applied dark eye makeup outlining her entire eye into a catlike design. She tucked her blond hair underneath a wig cap. Dressed in her undergarments, she planned to help Posey step into the wide brocade gown trimmed in pearls, made for a queen.

At least the gown had a modern zipper concealed with braids and pearls. Still, Cass wondered how she'd be able to use the facilities alone. Posey sat down again so Cass could attach the fancy round lace collar.

Both women laughed at the spectacle of Posey appearing to be a bald woman with the collar and makeup suggesting a circus clown. Then Cass lifted the curly wig over Posey's cap and the transformation to Queen Elizabeth was nearly complete. A crescent shaped velvet bonnet trimmed in pearls, spangles, and feathers topped the ensemble.

Posey smiled in the mirror and thanked Cass for her help, but her absent expression showed that something or someone preoccupied her. Cass went into the closet and donned her own costume with ease, then attached the black swingy wig to her cap and slinked from the closet in a grand entrance.

Posey didn't notice. The woman held a linen handkerchief embroidered with a cluster of strawberries. She turned it over and over in her hands as she hummed a melancholy tune.

Cass appeared over her shoulder in the mirror and stroked her sleeve. "What is it?"

"Perhaps I should have played heartsick Desdemona, unlucky at love, seeking justice for the mistreated…" she trailed off as a single tear ran down her cheek.

Cass placed a hand over Posey's trembling one to ask for an explanation, but their contact transmitted images and something powerful that traveled through Cassandra's being: fear. While Cass wilted and slumped to the floor, Posey struggled to breathe and pried her hand away.

Posey gasped, drank in breath, and stared at her assistant, who sat propped against the vanity leg, her face wild with worried eyes that had changed from sky blue to stormy gray. Time stood still.

Cass returned to herself and looked up at Posey. "Who are you afraid of? Tell me."

Posey shook off the look and the question. "This isn't the time. We're needed downstairs in our places. The guests are arriving." Posey blew her nose and fixed her face. She held out her hand to help Cass off the floor; then pulled it away again.

Cass understood. Their connection was too strong. She gripped the vanity seat and pulled herself up, checked her face in the mirror, and followed Posey down the grand staircase.

Cassandra stayed in the background as much as possible when Posey, her majesty Queen Elizabeth, greeted guests in the formal foyer of Spirit Gardens and told them to follow the path upstairs to Midsummer Terrace, the temporary name given to the grand salon. Cass, as the powerful and sexy Cleopatra, checked off guests on her well-guarded list and handed each one a sealed envelope. The envelope contained details about their identity to help act out their role and their assigned number corresponding to the game sheet each guest received.

As arrivals continued to enter, resplendent in their costumes, Cassandra's feeling of doom and worry melted away. When Marc Antony processed through the double doors, her heart skipped a beat.

"Here you are, my dear Antony. Keep what is sealed within a secret." Cassandra's eyes fluttered provocatively.

"My Egyptian queen." Antony bowed and kissed Cass's hand from palm to elbow, making them both stir.

"Perhaps a dance later?" Cass whispered.

Anthony leaned in to whisper in her ear. "Methinks Cupid has slung his arrow and struck me head-on."

Someone behind Anthony cleared their voice loudly again. Anthony bowed and proceeded to the grand staircase.

Lord and Lady Macbeth shoved forward, played by the gossipy literary society couple, Joe and Paula Bryant. Cass checked them off and sent them on their way, anxious to greet the trio of women behind the Macbeths.

The ex-ladies Lange were plenty boisterous, perhaps from starting the party before their arrival. Suzanne and Gretchen were the Merry Wives of Windsor, Mistress Alice Ford and Mistress Margaret Page, respectively, forceful characters created to put men in their place. Heather stood a half-step behind, appearing innocent in a flowing white gown with a sweetheart neckline: Except that Beatrice is one of The Bard's renowned heroic female characters, a feminist before such labels existed.

Cass couldn't wait to discuss the Lange ladies with Bay, but a long line of arrivals trailed out the door into the courtyard, and she needed to finish her greeting duties before enjoying any conversation. Besides, her sister had not yet checked in.

After her initial anxiety, Cass relished the role of keeper of the character list, admiring the costume choices the guests selected. She snickered at the comical characters of Nick Bottom, the weaver transformed by the *Midsummer* fairies to have a donkey's head, and Dogberry, the bungling watchman known for malapropisms in *Much Ado About Nothing*.

Cass raised her brows at a few couples. What kind of relationship did Cher Devane's parents have, dressing as Othello and Desdemona, a tumultuous pair indeed. Compare that to Jackson Lange's parents, looking comfortable as the lovers Lysander and Hermia in *Midsummer Night's Dream*. She couldn't hold back her sarcastic smile for Monroe Lange and his fourth wife, Bianca, arriving as Romeo and Juliet.

Behind the star-crossed lovers, Detective Downing stood in the guise of Hamlet, and Bay, who assumed the role of Rosalind, the witty heroine of *As You Like It*, greeted Cassandra.

Cass pulled on her sister's sleeve and cast her eyes toward Romeo and Juliet. "Did you see those two? How nervy, oops." Cass cut off the rest of her comment, remembering she wasn't supposed to expose their real identities.

Bay giggled. "Here I thought you'd be the best person in charge of secrets. Anyway, I'll figure out who they are, but thanks for the hint."

Cass elbowed Bay, then turned to Downing and handed him two envelopes. " The game sheet and a copy of the master list, so you know which people you want to interrogate." She winked dramatically.

"Thank you, Cassandra. This isn't entertaining for me. I'm working, remember?" Downing headed for the stairs at a brisk pace, a dead giveaway he wasn't there for leisure.

Cass shrugged as she handed Bay her envelope. "Hamlet, huh? Talk about type casting. Moody and brooding."

Bay shrugged in return. "I'll see you later upstairs."

The catering crew met each guest at the entrance to the converted grand salon, handing them their first cocktails for the evening, a Midsummer Punch made from rum, bourbon, fruit juices, and ginger ale, a sneaky drink where the spirits were disguised. Downing asked for a nonalcoholic beverage and selected a cola from the cooler sitting next to the entryway.

Bay had to hand it to Cozy Catering for going the extra mile. Each server was dressed in Elizabethan garb, matching tunics, breeches, and Tudor flat caps, recognizable to anyone needing a refill or directions to the bathroom.

Bay was stunned to see Posey as Queen Elizabeth, escorted by Malcolm as Shakespeare, take the center of the room together to deliver the welcome speech, a charming prologue written in iambic pentameter, and borrowing from The Bard's own verses.

> *Gentles gather 'round where we lay this scene*
> *O' beautiful sight and sound*
> *Where princes and monarchs do strut so proud*
> *Heros and villains of noble deeds and dark*

> *Merchants, soldiers and madmen from abroad*
> *Lovers and fools lit from the same spark*
> *In the guise of clever revels, we spy*
> *Under the moon of the midsummer sky*
> *To dance, to eat and drink, perchance to dream*
> *With the aim to uncover each one's scheme*
> *To beguile, to foil, to rattle the brain*
> *Then fear not the Muse who will lead astray*
> *Shall we then their pageant see?*
> *Lord, what fools these mortals be!*

The guests clapped with delight, some with propriety, then made their way for more punch or to survey the food table. Background music played, quiet Elizabethan tunes featuring string instruments and the spinet.

Once the partygoers finished helpings from the assorted cheeses, skewers of lamb, miniature meat pies, breads, sandwich squares, sugared fruits, and rustic potatoes, a quartet materialized holding period instruments: a lute, hurdy-gurdy, cornett, and recorder. Lively dance music began with Shakespeare and Her Majesty leading a couple's circle dance. Party guests made their own circles and followed the easy steps.

Dancing, drinking, and eating continued as guests mingled, questioned one another, and made notes. In the middle, dessert was announced, and people who were hungry from dancing or hoped to coat their stomachs with something that wasn't alcohol, flocked to the bountiful flower cart laden with desserts on all five levels.

Cassandra nabbed a piece of marchpane, a cake similar to marzipan, and strode to one corner of the room occupied by

Bay and Downing.

"Have you tried these desserts? No wonder Posey always hires Cozy Caterers. These are amazing." Cass was giddy, something Bay couldn't recall witnessing in years.

"Yes, I had the lemon syllabub with one of those cookies, and I'm thinking of going for seconds." Bay smiled. "Jumbal; that's the name of the cookies. Almond and rose water flavored, of all things."

"What about you Detective? What did you have?" Cass gave him a teasing poke.

"Indigestion." His tone was flat, and he continued scanning the room. Having found his target, he excused himself to talk to that person of interest on his list.

"He must be loads of fun," Cass said.

"A regular party animal," Bay replied. "Remember, he's working, Cass. You seem to be enjoying the company of Marc Antony. I take it you chose Cleopatra on purpose?"

"If you mean, have I set my cap for the man, you know me better. He is charming and smart, though." Cass scanned the room and saw Anthony staring at her across the room. Her face warmed, and she looked away.

Bay noticed. "He does appear to affect you. So, charming and smart. What else is there?"

"Trust. There's always trust." Cass nodded and Bay agreed.

"How are you progressing on your character guess sheet?" Cass changed the topic.

Bay pulled the list from the ornate pouch attached to her waist sash. "Hmm, about half. I've talked to more people than I normally do at social functions." She defended herself from Cass's disapproval.

"Let me see your sheet. Ha, just as I thought. You've checked off all the Flourish people. You already know them. You should mingle, Bay."

Indeed, Bay admitted to herself she wasn't even all that comfortable talking to her colleagues, even Vivian Rossi and Simon Devane from her own department.

She was about to say so when a skirmish around the dessert cart caught their attention. They could see the Lange exes circling Monroe Lange and wife number four, Bianca. Suzanne made a remark inches away from Monroe's face, then stepped back to gloat about it. Monroe reached over to grab Suzanne's arm when Gretchen intercepted his move, waving a warning finger in his face.

Cass wasted no time striding across the room toward the clashing Lange clan, just in time to see Gretchen reach over to a cowering Bianca, handing her a business card. "Here you go, Juliet. Before you swallow all the poison, call us if you need anything. Anytime."

Gretchen turned, lost her balance, then staggered toward an exit. Suzanne lifted her head like a runway model and glared at her ex-husband.

"Okay, you all need to head to neutral corners. Romeo, it looks like Juliet isn't feeling well. Would you please see to her?" Cass was calm but firm.

Monroe placed his arm around his wife and led her to a bench near one of the rose bowers.

"Okay ladies, what was that all about?" Cass should have taken matters into hand earlier after she noticed the inebriated women.

Suzanne drooped a tad. "I simply complimented Bianca's

choice of character. After all, I believe Juliet was fourteen in the play, the perfect age for marriage." She stared directly into Cass's eyes, daring her to say something.

"Now that you know who Romeo and Juliet are, why don't you move on to question other characters? We're going to end the game soon." Diplomacy had never been Cassandra's strong suit, and she wondered how she mustered it now.

Suzanne puffed her chest out. "Perhaps, but I'm afraid my glass is empty, so I'm off to find a serving wench." She hiccupped and swayed toward the food table.

"Heather, would you please go with her? Maybe find her something to drink without alcohol."

Cass peered around the room, trying to locate Posey. With so many tipsy guests, maybe it was time to take away the punch and offer coffee. Furthermore, it was past time for Posey to announce the final hour of character guessing.

Cass was waylaid by one of the college library board professors dressed as Puck, the trickster from *Midsummer*. "Excuse me, darling Cleopatra, but might you tell me what to do with my guess sheet. You see, I've finished it." Puck was in his cups, too.

"I'll just take that, thank you. Excuse me, I need to find someone."

Cass chose one of the wooden pathways that led to a bench and pond behind a set of yew hedges. She stifled a gasp as she gawked at Queen Elizabeth in a compromising position.

There was so much dress, Cass couldn't tell what was happening, except that kissing was involved. When the face of Shakespeare emerged over Posey's shoulder, obviously to catch his breath, Cass was both relieved and sad to see Malcolm

Hunt. What was she supposed to do now?

She was rooted to the spot for a moment, maybe longer, when a crash and cry volleyed beyond the hedges. Posey and Malcolm didn't even flinch, but Cass scooted away to investigate. It seemed the party was now in her hands.

As she rounded the hedges, she slid them over the pathway to obscure the entrance to the pond, then walked toward the commotion. One of the topiaries, a rearing horse, had toppled over Falstaff, a popular character known for his bawdy ways. Professor McNelly dressed the part and took the role seriously, flirting with men and women alike and drinking like a sieve.

Lincoln Lange and Anthony McGann each grabbed an arm to hoist the man upward, while a couple of the fools mimed a comic scene of righting the topiary, which included one of them pretending to board the horse for a ride. The distraction proved helpful, as Cass tried to sort out what occurred.

"Our man here was dancing a little too wildly, I'm afraid. He spun in the wrong direction and knocked over the horse, somehow landing under it." Lincoln Lange explained.

"I think we'll take him for some fresh air," Anthony added.

Cass marched to the staging area and told Delia coffee was needed. "Cease and desist on the alcohol, please. We've had enough issues for one party."

She almost collided with Bay as she trotted back to the salon to address the guests. "Hey, is everything okay? Anything I can help with?" Bay asked.

"This is my shindig now, so I'm going to call thirty minutes until guesses are due. Can you help me watch some of the troublesome people?"

Bay looked around. "That's at least half the room. Where's

Posey?"

"Incapacitated." Cass proceeded to the center of the salon and whistled like she was at a baseball game. The music and chatter stopped.

"Hello everyone. I'm glad to see all of you revelers are enjoying the evening. This is your thirty-minute notice. All guess sheets are due to me by then, or you can place them in the box by the double doors. Our servers will be passing around coffee and lemon water. Please stay hydrated and look after each other."

Bay studied the guests' reactions, which ranged from glum to surly to slap-happy. Downing was standing near one entrance in conversation with Amazon Queen Hippolyta, also known as Melinda Townsend, whom Bay remembered as a sharp-tongued gossip from the literary society.

"Guess I'm a killjoy. Just like dad and Aunt Venus used to be when I was a teenager." Cass was despondent. "I wonder if anyone will be left when I announce the winners."

"Hey, this isn't your fault, you know. People under the influence aren't pretty. It's easy to see how that Kingsley party went south."

"Right. Just look at their parents." Cass folded her arms across her chest.

"I've been meaning to ask you all night. Who is the purple fool supposed to be? I mean which play?" Bay taught Shakespeare at the college and assumed she would recognize the characters.

"Purple fool?" Cass was dumbfounded. "There's no purple fool on my roster. Show me."

Bay gazed around the room but couldn't spot the jester in

the shiny silk costume complete with jingle-bell cap. "Maybe they went to the bathroom. Anyway, the person isn't wearing a mask. Their face is painted white with wide black bows, black clownish lips, and a string of black tears down one cheek."

"I'm clueless, but I'll check the bathrooms over here. Will you look in the bathrooms on that side?" Cass pointed.

"I'm on it."

The two went in opposite directions, waited in the bathroom for guests to exit their stalls, then reconvened by the entrance.

"Nothing."

"Same."

Cass shrugged. "We'll keep our eyes open. I suppose a party crasher isn't that unusual, or just someone who doesn't follow protocol."

Soon guests were sipping water or coffee, making final guesses on their sheets, and turning them in. The revelers were mellowing to quieter background music combined with the late hour.

Posey and Malcolm had returned from whatever magical realm they'd occupied, managing to look refreshed and composed. Cass toyed with asking Posey if she'd like to resume the role of hostess but was still fuming inside at her indiscretion.

Cass left the salon and walked down the hallway to the open windows. She counted as she inhaled and exhaled the fresh night air and recentered her emotions. This was Posey, a woman who deserved happiness. A generous, charitable woman to everyone, especially to Cass. *She overlooked my prison time, like it didn't matter at all. We're kindred spirits.*

Cass peered out the casement at the crescent moon, grateful to have Posey in her life. She vowed to share more personal details with her, and hoped Posey would, too.

When Cass entered the salon again, she had the results of the character guessing game, and found Posey enjoying one of the violet cakes from the dessert cart, tapping her toes to the Elizabethan tune.

"Cassandra, you've managed to accomplish quite the party for your first go-round. Brava to you." Posey beamed.

"Thank you. I have the winner of the character game." She handed the paper to Posey. "Should we gather all the characters around for the unmasking?"

Posey stood and clasped Cassandra's hand, as they walked to the center of the salon. She clapped and everyone snapped to attention. "Gather around, my Elizabethans. It's time to end our masquerade. Unmask yourselves and tell us who you've been pretending to be."

As the guests took turns, Cass noticed there was no purple fool in sight. ✤

CHAPTER 25

Hell is empty and all the devils are here.
~ THE TEMPEST

The party goers dispersed with good nights, party favors, and extra desserts. Cass made certain there were ample Uber drivers on hand to get the revelers home safely. Bay stayed behind to help her with cleaning details. Cass oversaw the catering crew, while retrieving empty punch cups hidden behind the bowers and topiaries. Detective Downing sat outside the salon at an antique side table to read his party notes, looking for connections in the details.

Anthony McGann lingered in the salon, talked to Posey and Malcolm, then wandered aimlessly about.

Bay nudged Cass as she came through the entrance holding a trash bag for wayward greenery and fallen flowers.

"I think Marc Antony is bewitched, Cassandra. I believe you might own that man now." Bay giggled.

Cass smiled. "I'm not sure why he's still here, but you know me, I'll go find out."

She crossed the room and Anthony's eyes lit up like fireworks. "Cassandra, what a great party. I mean, even with the miniscule mishaps. You're adept at handling trouble when it comes along."

"It comes with lots of practice. Thank you for saying that. Does Posey need you for something else tonight?"

"Posey, ah no. I wanted to ask you if you're free for dinner on Friday? There's a new restaurant in Madison people are raving about, if you'd like to go."

"Love to." Cass turned away, a smile planted on her face. Anthony floated all the way to his car.

Posey walked with Malcolm, arm in arm, down the grand staircase to the circular driveway.

The catering crew was fast and efficient at packing and loading food and tubs of dirty serving ware into the van behind the house. Cassandra praised and thanked them, gushing over the authentic fare.

"I can share a few of the recipes with you if you like," Delia said and handed Cass her card. "Get in touch with me."

"So did Anthony ask you for a date?" Bay asked. She sat on one of the garden benches in the salon, mesmerized by the fairy lights and the quiet.

Cass sat with her to enjoy the moment. "Yes, he did. We're going to dinner on Friday. What about you and Downing?"

Bay said no. "Too busy with the case, but we have tentative plans after the college production."

"I guess that'll do."

"Let's call it a night. I imagine the rest of this is Edison's to tear down." Bay rose and headed out the door with Cass. The detective had disappeared, and Bay wondered why he would leave without saying good night. Then they saw him at the bottom of the stairs looking grim.

"I just heard someone call out, so I ran down. It may have been Posey. Let's spread out and find her."

Bay went toward the atrium and kitchen while Downing headed out the front door and Cass ran to the study. She passed the library and opened the doors to look inside. Darkness enveloped the room, but she located the light switch.

"Posey, are you in here?" No answer. Cass continued to the study, which was dark as well. She knew that room and flipped on the lights. "Posey, are you here?"

The room was silent, but Cass could hear a muffled moan coming through the far wall.

"The greenhouse," Cass said, and ran out the back end of the study where a second passageway led through the summer kitchen.

Cass faltered in the darkness and called out to Posey as she waited for her eyes to adjust. Red, yellow, and green monitoring lights blinked on the consoles that controlled the climate in the greenhouse. Cass kept calling anyone who might hear her, but only the hum of the overhead fans answered.

She went deeper into the section where Posey's favorite exotics made a thick forest. She thought she saw a mound on the floor and waited for her eyes to adjust again. She wished she had her cell phone, but she dropped everything she was carrying before going to look for Posey.

She was almost upon the mound when it moved, grew taller, and something or someone lunged at her, knocking her down. She recovered from the jolt to see someone lying on the floor. She knew the tall wig and the lacy collar. It was Posey. She felt her neck for a pulse. Maybe there was a tiny beat, maybe not. Cass tore off the Cleopatra wig and collar, both encumbrances to saving Posey's life. She administered CPR and rescue breaths, pausing between each regimen to listen for a heartbeat. Her metal bangles clanged as Cass pumped Posey's chest over and over again. Sweating and breathless, Cass paused and laid her ear against Posey's chest. A puff of air escaped from her lips. A tiny wisp crackled in the darkness. Nothing. A scream caught in Cass's throat and then she let loose a series of loud sharp whistles, before going back to chest compressions and breaths.

Downing and Bay held their phones aloft for light and found Cass kneeling over Posey. In the beams, he saw a vial in Posey's hand. "Stay here. I have to go to my car. Which way is faster, Cass?"

"Go out the side door over there. Turn right. It will take you to the front courtyard."

Cass continued rescue breaths and CPR until Downing returned. Bay tried to step in, but Cass pushed her away. The detective pulled Cass away from Posey and injected her with a syringe of Narcan.

"The ambulance should be here any minute," Bay said. She'd made the call as soon as they found Cass and Posey on the greenhouse floor.

The three waited for Posey to respond to the rescue injection, but she remained still. Downing could see her lips were blue, not a hopeful sign. When the paramedics arrived, it took both Bay and Downing to remove Cass from the scene.

They pushed Cass to the kitchen where Bay made tea, and

Downing returned to the greenhouse.

"Someone killed her. I saw them," Cass's words scraped her mouth like gravel.

"What, Cassandra?" Bay took her sister's hand. "Who killed her?"

"It was too dark. I couldn't see. Someone crouched over Posey and waited until I was close enough. They stood up and knocked me over, then ran away. Did you see anyone?"

Bay shook her head. "I don't think Downing did either. We heard you call out and met in the hallway. I saw some things on the floor leading to the greenhouse. I think someone pursued Posey and she left a trail."

Cass curled into a ball like a child huddled against the kitchen cabinets. She drank two cups of tea with Bay sitting beside her. An hour later, Downing walked into the kitchen like a condemned man. He cleared his throat.

"They tried to help Posey, but it was too late. I'm sorry." He stared at his feet and blew out several breaths.

Cass went deeper into herself and sobbed. Bay let her be, stood up, and hugged Downing. "I know you did all you could." She whispered in his ear.

He held her against him. "I did, but it didn't matter this time." He wanted to punch the wall but restrained himself.

He let go of Bay and held her at arm's length. "I have to secure the scene. Detective Harris is on his way. The paramedics are taking Posey."

"Where are they taking her?" Cassandra's voice was hollow.

Nobody answered. Bay squatted to lift Cass to her feet. "Come on, Cass. We're going home. We'll take care of things tomorrow."

Downing rapped on Bay's apartment door before the first fingers of light waved to the horizon.

Bay, still wearing pajamas, invited the detective to sit in the living room, where electric candles flickered. He could smell something enjoyable wafting through the air.

Bay pressed a coffee pod in the machine and returned with a steaming mug for Downing. "I can't remember how you take your coffee, Bryce." She held out a carton of cream and a spoon.

"Thanks. It's hard to keep up with my coffee habits. They change depending on the time of day and case stress. Cream would be nice." Downing stirred a generous helping of half-and- half into the mug.

"How's your sister?" His disheveled appearance suggested he'd had a long night.

Bay leaned on Bryce and gestured toward the back bedroom. "We haven't slept much either. I just drew a hot scented bath for her. She's soaking."

Downing bowed his head and took a long drink. "Good coffee. I'm used to tar and oil." Returning to the purpose of his visit, he grimaced and took one of Bay's hands in his.

"I have some news for both of you. You might not like some of it."

Bay squeezed his hand. "You must be exhausted."

"I spent most of the night with federal agents. Kind of like being in a viper pit."

"So, the feds are involved in Posey's murder, too?" Bay was confused. "Was she dosed with fentanyl? I saw you give her Narcan." Bay realized there may be a connection between her death and Talon's.

"Yeah. Let's wait for Cassandra."

The two sat in silence for some time, then dozed off. Cassandra entered the room and smiled wanly when she saw Bay and Downing slumped together on the sofa, asleep. Cass went to the kitchen to make tea then collapsed into an oversized chair, hoping it would swallow her.

Bay stirred, sensing her sister's presence. She sat up and nudged the detective.

"Sorry, Cass. We were waiting for you and must have dozed off." Bay reached over and patted her sister's knee.

"I understand. I fell asleep in the tub myself. I take it you brought some news on the case." Cass couldn't bring herself to say Posey's name.

Downing excused himself to use the bathroom and splashed some cold water on his face to wake up. Meanwhile, Bay brought him a coffee refill.

The women waited while Downing composed his thoughts and reread the notes from his pocket notepad. "I'm sorry, you two. My hands are tied tightly on this one, but you deserve to know the truth."

Bay moved closer to Cass and they held hands, poised for whatever they were about to hear.

"Posey's killer is in custody. Federal agents apprehended her within minutes."

Cass's eyes flew open, and she jumped up. "How could that be? Unless someone knew the killer was coming for Posey." She buried her face in her hands in contemplation of such a terrible possibility.

Downing cleared his throat and stared at the coffee mug. "Federal agents have been monitoring Ophelia Kingsley, aka Cinda King, for almost a year. Ophelia is a federal asset working undercover."

"You're saying Ophelia killed Posey? Why?" Bay asked.

Downing ran his finger along the mug handle. "No, she didn't." He raised stern eyes to the women filled with warning. "Look you two. I think you deserve to know this much, but my job is on the line, so you need to swear you won't talk about this to anyone, not even a hint. Not to Jen Yoo. Not to Diana. Nobody."

"I promise," Bay said. "I promise, too." Cass mumbled.

"The feds were after Joanna Stengel. That's who killed Posey." Downing waited.

For Bay, the name triggered the hint of a memory, but Cass stood up and began pacing the length of the room like a caged tiger.

"Joanna Stengel is Diana's boss, Bay. She's the Flourish librarian." Cass was angry at herself for being within arm's length of Posey's killer just days ago when she might have stopped her.

Bay remembered now seeing Joanna when she returned Shakespeare materials. "I saw her once a couple of weeks ago. She was meeting with a young woman, and it looked secretive. Diana said the woman had been coming around weekly even though she wasn't a Flourish student. I bet it was Cinda King."

Cass sat down again and twisted a napkin left on the coffee table. "Go on, Downing. What else can you tell us?"

"Stengel is also known as The Pharmacist. The feds have been after her for a while." He paused again.

"The Pharmacist? You mean, she's been dealing illegal drugs on campus? That's where the fentanyl that killed Talon and

Posey came from?" Bay had read about the infamous drug leader connected to an uptick in trafficking and overdoses the past year, but like many, she thought The Pharmacist operated out of Chicago or Milwaukee.

Downing chewed his upper lip and drew in a deep breath, then looked at his notepad again. "Yep."

Cassandra started tearing the napkin into pieces and littered the table with them. "Why would this person want to kill Posey?"

"Honestly, I don't know. Neither do the feds—yet. What I know is that Ophelia tipped them off. She's been working for Stengel the past year and got close to her. Something The Pharmacist said made Ophelia concerned about Posey Hollingsworth."

Cass jumped from her seat and punched the air like a child throwing a tantrum. "Then why wasn't someone there to protect Posey?"

Downing shrugged and shook his head. "I'm sorry. I was at the party all night, Cass. I could have protected Posey if I'd known." A kernel of anger burned in Downing, too.

Bay's mind zig-zagged another trail. "Does any of this connect to the crimes happening at the rehearsals?"

Downing was relieved to pivot the conversation. "Yes. You both know about the history of the party at the Kingsley's where Brody Lynde was trampled to death. After Flourish College rejected Ophelia, she enrolled at UW–Madison and changed her name, but she never got over the betrayal of her so-called friends. Working with Stengel gave her one last chance for revenge and she took it. She claims she never meant for anyone to die, but she admits she wanted to hurt them."

Bay threw her hands up in the air. "I don't get it. Why would Ophelia want to go through another trial, have her life burned down a second time after moving on and getting a degree. It doesn't add up, Downing."

"Now comes the part you're not going to like, Bay." Downing's jaw clenched. "Ophelia won't be prosecuted. She's a federal asset who went undercover to nab a high roller in the drug trade. She got sidetracked on her own personal vendetta, but she came through for the feds in the end. That's what matters." Downing recited the words like he was reading from a script.

Bay stood up and backed away from him, nostrils flared. "And you accept this? You think this is okay?" Inside, she wanted to slap his face.

"Whoa, Professor Browning. None of this is okay. It stinks. In a perfect world, the people responsible for Brody Lynde's death would be serving time. In a perfect world, Ophelia would be held accountable for Talon's death, Cher's and Jackson's injuries, and the terror she orchestrated at rehearsals. The feds operate by different rules, and my department can't do a damn thing about it." He choked back a growl and closed his eyes.

Cassandra concentrated on reigning in her emotions. She was arranging the tiny napkin pieces into hex designs on the table. When she spoke, her voice was flat and childlike. "Where did the feds find Joanna Stengel?"

"I'm sorry. I can't answer that." Downing said.

"Was she at the party? Is that why it was easy for her to make her way around the house?" Cass probed.

Downing nodded. "I think so. There was a trail of evidence

that Posey was running away from someone. The feds bagged a handkerchief, a hair clip, a glove, a jingle bell, and a piece of purple cloth, all leading to the greenhouse entrance. More purple cloth was found snagged on a post and caught in a tree trunk in the area where we found Posey."

"The purple fool," Cass said matter-of-factly and stared at Bay. They'd both wondered who the unknown guest was. "Oh God, Bay, JS." Cass would be confronting Anthony McGann as soon as possible.

"JS?" Bay didn't comprehend.

"An invited guest, after all." Cass whispered.

After Downing left, Bay showered and said she needed sleep. "You too, Cass. You should rest. Maybe take one of your tinctures?"

Cassandra was adamant. "I'm going to see Anthony McGann. I'm still Posey's assistant."

Cassandra asked Anthony to meet at Posey's house, and he was happy to oblige. The attorney preferred to discuss matters about Posey outside the office, rather than chance being overhead.

Cass arrived to console a distraught Marva, who was in the company of both sisters. Fanta and Sage told their employees they'd be keeping tabs on their sister.

The three women were drowning their sorrows in doctored lemonade and assorted pastries Sage had purchased at the local bakery. Cass found them sitting in the atrium regaling each other with stories from the past.

"I'm glad to see all three of you are here together today," Cass said, embracing Marva.

Marva blew her nose in a tissue as fresh tears rolled down her face. "I'm glad to see you too, Cassandra. Those horrible men in the black suits are poking around here like they own the place. I'll be happy when they leave."

Cass wasn't surprised to hear that the feds were still up to their necks in Posey's house. There was so much territory to cover. "I'm meeting Attorney McGann here shortly. We'll be in Posey's study if the suits allow it."

"Here, take a pastry or two with you," Marva held out a plate to Cass, but she declined.

"Sorry, no appetite, but thank you," Cass said.

"I'd offer you some of our tonic, but I suspect you need to keep your head about you," Fanta said with a little hiccup at the end. "Marva says the caterers left behind two gallons of punch. Somebody has to drink it."

Great. Now I have these three to worry about. "I'll check on you all after my meeting. Please be careful. Maybe take a nap."

Before Anthony arrived, Cass made a beeline for the greenhouse where she guessed the feds would be but was cut off by a man posted in the hallway at the greenhouse doors.

"Excuse me, I'd like to speak to someone in charge." Cass was impatient.

The man eyed Cass with suspicion and looked at his electronic tablet. "State your name."

"Cassandra Browning. I'm Posey Hollingsworth's personal assistant." Cass stood up straight when she spoke.

"Wait here." The man crossed the barrier into the greenhouse and returned with a second man.

"I'm Agent Madrid, Ms. Browning." He was shorter than the guard, well-groomed with slick-backed black hair and a scar on his forehead.

"Yes. How long do you plan to be in Posey's house?" Cass lacked propriety at times. This was one of those times.

Madrid was taken aback and chortled. "Until we finish collecting all the necessary evidence."

"I'm meeting Posey's attorney shortly. Are there any rooms I'm not allowed in?"

"Just the greenhouse. We've combed the rest of the interior. Oh, and stay off the grounds." Madrid pivoted with military precision and disappeared.

Cass went to the study and peeked out the long windows overlooking the apothecary gardens. As she suspected, there were black suits posted along the perimeter as far as she could see.

She waited by the main entrance for Anthony, who was allowed passage by yet another black suit, Agent Morse. Cass noticed something pass between Anthony and Morse, some sort of familiarity that she dismissed when the attorney pulled her into his arms in a warm embrace.

The two stood together in the foyer, hugging and crying. Cass didn't realize how much Posey meant to him.

"Let's go into the study where we can talk privately," Cass said, aware that Agent Morse was watching. "I cleared it with Agent Madrid. He must be the head honcho."

With the door closed, Cass tried to recall the anger and hostility she intended to attack Anthony with before he'd embraced her. After sharing tears together, it was difficult to know where to begin.

"Dammit Anthony, I wish you hadn't hugged me." Cass's face contorted. She turned to face the wall and stared at the portrait of Ramona Hollingsworth, haughty and unsmiling. Cass knew Posey had a complicated relationship with her mother, and now she would never know why. She found that indignant emotion again.

"Are you going to tell me who JS is or do I have to tell you?" Cass waltzed over to stand toe to toe with the attorney.

Caught off guard, Anthony retreated backward and sat down in one of the wing chairs. "You must understand that I couldn't tell you her identity. Posey insisted and…" he trailed off.

"Joanna Stengel. The person who murdered our beloved Posey. Why were you protecting Joanna Stengel? Can you answer that?"

"I wasn't protecting her, Cassandra. She was blackmailing me and Posey." Anthony made a fist and punched it into his other hand. "I never saw this coming." He shook his head, still trying to comprehend it.

Cass folded her arms over her chest and scrutinized the attorney. She wasn't about to be duped by anyone and intended to use her uncommon intuitive skills until she was satisfied. "You won the character guessing game. You didn't question Joanna Stengel? You didn't recognize her?"

Anthony flinched. "Man, you'd make one hell of a prosecutor. I noticed the purple fool and wondered if it was an omission on the character sheet. Every time I made my way to their vicinity, I was waylaid by someone or distracted by the extremely fetching Cleopatra."

Cassandra blushed. She'd chastised herself for dallying with Anthony instead of paying attention to the party guests. "So, you never questioned her?"

Anthony hung his head. "God, if I had. At least I could have asked why she was there. Posey always invited her out of common courtesy, but she never attended any of the parties."

Cass scoffed and stepped forward to lean in. "Why in the world would Posey invite a blackmailer to her home?"

Anthony raised his eyes. "Because Joanna was Posey's distant cousin. Posey recommended Joanna for the college librarian position. No matter what Posey did for Joanna, she always demanded more."

Cass remembered overhearing Posey and Anthony in the library. "The stables?"

Anthony was alarmed, his eyes fearful. "What about them?" He tried to cool his reaction, but Cassandra's intuition was spot on.

"Why would Joanna want the stables?" Cass turned to work out the problem. "A hostile takeover? She wanted the whole estate, one piece at a time. If she acquired enough pieces, she could stake a legal claim at some point. Like after Posey's death."

Anthony was stunned. "Who are you, anyway? Did you go to law school?" There was admiration in his voice.

Cassandra backed up and turned her face away, unwilling to answer either question. She needed to keep her wits, and Anthony was too gifted at disarming her.

"You're working with the feds," Cass proclaimed. "What about Posey? Was she a federal asset, too?"

Anthony laughed. "You watch too many spy movies. You can cooperate with the feds without being an asset. And yes, we were both cooperating."

"Did Joanna suspect that? Is that why she killed Posey, or

does she own enough pieces of Spirit Gardens to make a legal claim on it?"

Anthony's shoulders sagged. "She didn't own enough pieces, and I doubt she had any idea the feds were on to her. She was careful, but not careful enough for a town this size. Maybe she let her hatred of Posey overcome her logic."

"Just like Cinda King or should I say, Ophelia Kingsley? Since Posey was working with the feds, I guess they won't need to interview me." Cass had feared the federal agents would tear her life apart and that would be the end of her parole.

"You know about Ophelia? I'm not surprised. I imagine your sister was informed because of the crimes connected to her show," Anthony concluded, which relieved Cass since she didn't want to make any trouble for Detective Downing.

Bay was right earlier though when she said the pieces didn't quite add up. "I don't understand why Ophelia became an asset. The Kingsley party wasn't a federal crime. Unless Brody Lynde was slipped drugs connected to Joanna. But that was four years ago."

Anthony shifted in his seat, nervous about Cass's comments. "Maybe something hit closer to home for Ophelia."

Cass caught Anthony's drift, set aside her interrogation, and changed the subject. "How long would you say I can remain working here?"

Anthony smiled and patted her arm. "Indefinitely. The house and all of Posey's holdings will be tied up for some time in probate. There is much to sort out and the court calendar always seems to be full. I think you may continue to act on her behalf with correspondence and your normal duties here. You'll be hearing from her estate attorney soon."

"Aren't you Posey's estate attorney?"

"I'm her personal attorney. It could be a conflict of interest to be her estate attorney, too. So, no. You'll be hearing from Gretchen Lange." His tight smile was revealing.

"Hmm, interesting. What about her funeral? As her personal attorney and friend, I think Posey's service should be planned by me, you, Marva, and Joyce Strost."

"I agree with you, but we will wait to hear from Gretchen. Posey may have her own plans." ✤

CHAPTER 26

Queen, King, Knight, and Pawns
Epilogue

The feds released Posey for burial three weeks later, and on a stormy July morning, Cassandra, Marva, Anthony McGann, and Joyce Strost gave her a sweet and simple send-off. The service was held in Posey's favorite outdoor spot, the apothecary garden. She left specifics in her will that Gretchen reviewed with the planners, one of which was the location.

The service would be short, with the four planners alone invited to say something meaningful about Posey. Anthony, Marva, and Joyce knew her the longest and shared their fond and humorous stories about her. When it was Cassandra's turn to speak, she offered unembellished gratitude to Posey for taking a chance on her, then finished her message with a quote from Shakespeare.

"It is fitting to say farewell to Posey here in this garden, the place she loved. She was a flower in never-ending bloom, bringing joy to all, making the world beautiful with her generous heart. Sadly, her petals fell too soon. We celebrate her today and will remember her in the season of flowers."

As Cass read the verse from *A Winter's Tale*, she scattered blossom petals into the rising wind.

"Here's flowers for you;
Hot lavender, mints, savoury, marjoram;
The marigold, that goes to bed wi' the sun
And with him rises weeping: these are flowers
Of middle summer, and I think they are given
To men of middle age."

Before the coffin was closed, Cass rested one of her treasured seashells, a sand dollar, on Posey's bosom and whispered, "May the tiny birds inside carry your spirit on the wind."

Malcolm Hunt placed a folded note below one of her hands with a private goodbye or wish, Cass didn't know. Malcolm choked on tears throughout the service with nobody to lean on. Bay stood beside him to offer any comfort she could. The circle of mourners was modest in accordance with Posey's instructions. In her words: "I don't want any pretenders at my service, just true friends."

After the coffin was sealed, Posey was wheeled to the back of the property within a grove of maple trees. Wild and isolated, few people knew a small burial ground existed. Posey's mother, Ramona, and father, Lionel were buried beneath gleaming marble markers. Posey selected a space between her father and an unnamed marble headstone with serene angels perched atop. Below the carved upside-down torch, the words "Siempre Recordado" were carved in Spanish. Anthony told Cass the translation: "always remembered." Cass knew the inverted torch symbolized a life cut short too soon—her father had the same symbol carved on Penelope's headstone.

The mourners paraded inside as thunder crashed and lightning cast white jagged streaks in the dark sky. Malcolm Hunt remained in the maple grove when the rain began to fall. He placed an extravagant wreath of Tudor roses on top of Posey's coffin, recalling her wish that Tudor roses were real, rather than an artistic rendition.

The flower combined the red rose of the Lancasters and the white rose of the Yorks, the two families fighting for the English crown during the War of the Roses before Elizabeth the First ascended to the throne. She wore the Tudor rose brooch to symbolize unity among the families. Dressed as Shakespeare and Queen Elizabeth, Malcolm and Posey entertained the fantasy of living in such a unified world, too.

"Rest in peace, my queen." Malcolm kissed the flowers, adding his tears to the white linen pall covering the coffin.

Posey requested an after-party featuring an abundance of comfort food, even if it was pizza from Angelo's and donuts from Sunrise Café. She didn't want fuss, just "belly-buster grub", as she put it. Beer and wine flowed freely to accompany the playlist she left behind of fiesta favorites. Maybe months from now, the merrymaking would be authentic. Today it was forced, done for Posey's benefit.

After Posey's funeral friends left, Marva, Fanta, Sage, and Cassandra were alone in the quiet. The sisters stayed to help clean up, offering Cass a chance to talk to Sage.

"Sage, I've been wanting to ask you something. You knew that Ophelia was hanging around the bluff, didn't you? I'm guessing you allowed her to borrow a horse from the Devane's stables. My sister and I saw her riding around the trails."

Sage bobbled the dish she was putting away and sputtered, speechless for a minute. "I missed her. It was such a shock to see her again. When she asked if I could somehow help her, I knew I could tell one of the grooms to get a horse ready and keep it a secret. I didn't want any trouble for her."

"How did you recognize her? She looks completely different from the photo you showed me."

Sage smiled wanly. "She looks like her mother. Ophelia told me she was hiding, that she'd had her face altered. You must think I'm a terrible person, and I know what she did was wrong, but I hope now she can find some peace."

Marva finished sweeping the kitchen and untied her apron to hang up. "Cassandra, come with me please."

The two walked into the pantry, and Marva handed her a brown padded envelope with something bumpy inside. "Posey left this with me to give to you in case anything happened to her. That was two weeks before she…" Marva's voice broke off as a lump in her throat prevented her from finishing the sentence.

Cass took the envelope and walked down the hallway to the atrium. The storm had passed, but a gray curtain cloaked the day in hazy shadow. Cass stood by Posey's favorite jacaranda tree and opened the envelope. An ornate silver key on a blue ribbon hooked onto Cassandra's finger, then she slid out a sheet of Posey's stationary scented with lilac and thyme and was overcome with the woman's presence, even before she began reading.

My dear Cassandra,

> *You and I are sisters of the sacred earth, daughters*
> *of the midday sun and the full moon, and I am grateful*
> *for the time we were planted together in the same soil.*
> *Please take my book of remedies from the summer*
> *kitchen and keep my spirit alive by remembering me*
> *when you craft them. This will be justice. As a witness*
> *to my indiscretions, I beg you not to judge me too*
> *harshly. None of us want to be in calm waters all our*
> *lives. Your friendship is assuredly the finest balm*
> *for the pangs of disappointed love. But do not miss*
> *your chance at happiness. You are the bravest person*
> *I know—not since my father have I known someone*
> *so brave. You asked me often about the past. The*
> *answers are here, in the treasure I left for you. The*
> *key will unlock it. Seldom, very seldom, does complete*
> *truth belong to any human disclosure; seldom can it*
> *happen that something is not a little disguised or a little*
> *mistaken. —Posey*

That evening, Cass dangled the ornate key in front of Bay and read the cryptic message Posey left behind.

"Do you know what it means?" Bay asked.

"No, but I'll have time to figure it out. Posey's estate will be tied up for months or longer. There are scads of unanswered questions, Lulu, and I intend to uncover all of them." Her blue eyes were white-hot fire.

Her mind traced questions in a continuous loop. *Why was Posey being blackmailed? Would Anthony tell her now that Posey was gone, or was he keeping a secret about himself? Who was buried in the unmarked grave at Spirit Gardens? What about Posey and Malcolm— what is their story?*

Bay understood. She wanted answers, too. If nothing else, she wanted to learn about the underpinnings of federal operations. Moreover, she intended to dig deeper into McNelly and his secrets. Could he be a federal asset, too? On the other hand, Bay was relieved to see her sister would occupy her grief with a worthy mission.

Before Posey's funeral, *Shakespeare's Couch* enjoyed a popular run at Carillon Tower Park, and donations for the arts at Flourish poured in. The deans were ecstatic, jokingly declaring "All's Well that Ends Well" at the cast party, a cheeky reference to the Shakespeare play. Bay thought it was tactless considering the hoard of crimes tainting the show's success.

Despite the federal secrecy, Bay pressed for information about the fate of the Kingsleys and Knights. In confidence, Downing said Peter and Ophelia would receive new lives under new identities until Joanna's trial concluded or the entire drug ring collapsed. It could be years before the Kingsleys were truly safe.

And what about Ginny and Henry Knight? Nobody was willing to tie Henry to any of the crimes, leaving him free from further prosecution. Bay was satisfied, but wondered how Ginny might feel, losing the possibility of a new life with Peter Kingsley.

The directors and players of the Shakespeare show were

pawns on Joanna's and Ophelia's chess board, and both players shared blame for Talon's death as far as Bay was concerned. Bay was heartened to see the cast rally around each other in the wake of the turmoil they'd endured. Their sincerity to put aside their differences renewed her optimism. She was pleased too that Desmond Carver decided to follow Claire to Ohio, where she was offered a faculty position. The course of true love might not run smooth, but at least some still chose to stay on board. Furthermore, Bryce Downing came to three out of the four performances saying he wanted to better understand the language of The Bard, and Bay was pleased to see her sister and Anthony McGann together in the audience.

At last, Bay could relax and enjoy the fruits of her labors and long summer days. The promised boat ride on a lake materialized one perfect July morning. Dressed in her water-resistant capris and sandals, Bay slathered on sunscreen, packed an insulated tote, grabbed her bucket hat and sunglasses, and drove thirty miles to Skipper Sam's marina on Three Witches Lake.

She pulled up next to Downing's car, where he waited with a smarmy grin on his face.

Seeing him dressed in a sky-blue shirt printed with sailboats and swimming fish thrilled her, and the sunglasses made him look carefree and mysterious at the same time. She gathered her things from the car and locked it.

"What's all this?" He hoisted the insulated tote in one hand, while he carried a plastic cooler in the other.

"Snacks, drinks. A good book to read."

He laughed. "I have snacks and drinks, too. We'll see how the offerings stack up."

She laughed as their competitive banter began, but she stopped cold after she followed him down the pier to his boat. From Downing's description, Bay had pictured an aluminum boat with a motor, something modest and rustic, not the boat anchored to the dock.

Downing helped Bay board the cabin cruiser, then he handed her the cooler and the tote. He hopped up and took her by the arm to show her around.

"There's plenty of room on deck whether you want sun or shade. Let me show you below."

A dining booth with benches lined one wall opposite a galley kitchen. A narrow door led to a bathroom, while the main room tapered into a bedroom with built-in cabinets. The polished teak wood smelled homey and the red, white, and blue nautical fabrics were welcoming. Bryce set Bay's tote on the galley counter, then opened the cooler.

"Corona and Guinness, depending on your mood. I also have tortilla chips, salsa, mixed nuts, and these." He held up a plastic bag of green grapes.

Bay snickered. "You certainly know how to impress a woman." She pulled an elegant bottle of white wine from the tote, a corkscrew, and two travel wine glasses. "It's an Italian Pinot Grigio. Crisp with notes of citrus." She reached in for the food items: brie, dried apricots, walnuts, assorted crackers, fresh berries, hummus, cut-up veggie dippers, and chocolates.

Downing chuckled. "I guess you didn't trust me, huh? Is that anything new though?"

Bay took his hand, then placed her index finger over his lips. "I'm learning to trust you."

"You win the food competition, Bay." He squeezed her hand.

She smiled. "You get the trophy for the best surprise, though. This boat is a wow, Bryce."

"It's not called *My Piggy Bank* for nothing. I squeeze every extra penny into this piece."

Bay laughed. "What is it with you and pigs, anyway?"

"How about you open that fancy wine while I get this boat ready to cruise." He pushed his sunglasses up and down on his face to tease her.

"Nope. What's fair is fair. Teach me how to get this boat undocked." She scrunched up her face. "Is that the right terminology?"

"Oh, let's not spoil the day with technicalities." He twirled her around like a dancer, pulled her in against him, and held on tight.

❦❦❦❦❦

Poetry Slammed
A Bay Browning Mystery
BOOK 3

The Browning sisters flex their mystery solving muscles as they muddle through a maze of secrets and conundrums in *Poetry Slammed*.

Bay's department colleague, Vivian Rossi, vanishes after hosting a poetry slam night at the college coffee shop. All that remains of the eccentric professor is her handbag, cell phone, and a trail of blood leading nowhere. As Bay unravels the ballad of Vivian, she finds herself tangled in the professor's hidden life—one more peculiar than any rhyme scheme. Between foreign students and the discovery of an unknown Dickinson poem, the docile Vivian is mixed up in a dangerous quest.

Meanwhile, Cassandra is still reeling after the death of her mentor and is bent on digging up the past to find answers to the present. Driven by her spiritual connection to Posey, Cass won't rest until the truth is revealed, even though all she has is a cryptic note and ornate key to guide her, and of course, her extra sensory powers! How far will Cass go to get answers, and what price will she pay to find them?

About the Author

Joy Ann Ribar is an RV author, writing on the road wherever her husband and their Winnebago View wanders. Joy's cocktail of careers includes news reporter, paralegal, English educator, and aquaponics greenhouse technician, all of which prove useful in penning mysteries. Her cozy **Deep Lakes Mysteries,** feature baker/vintner Frankie Champagne, who moonlights as an investigative reporter. Joy's **Bay Browning Mysteries** blend edgy, traditional, and paranormal elements twisted around classical literary themes. Joy loves to bake, read, research wines, and explore nature. Her writing is inspired by Wisconsin's four distinct seasons, natural beauty, and kind-hearted, but sometimes quirky, people.

Joy holds a BA in Journalism from UW–Madison and an MS in Education from UW–Oshkosh. She is a member of Mystery Writers of America, Sisters in Crime, Blackbird Writers, Cozy Crime Collective, and Wisconsin Writers Association. Her writing has received awards and recognition from WWA, PenCraft Book Awards, Book Fest, Reader's Favorite, and Chanticleer Cozy and Not-So-Cozy awards.

See more at *https://joyribar.substack.com/about*

Also by Joy Ann Ribar

DEEP LAKES MYSTERIES

Deep Dark Secrets, BOOK 1

Deep Bitter Roots, BOOK 2

Deep Green Envy, BOOK 3

Deep Dire Harvest, BOOK 4

Deep Wedded Blues, BOOK 5

Deep Flakes Christmas–
A Nisse Visit, PREQUEL

BAY BROWNING MYSTERIES

The Medusa Murders, BOOK 1

Shake-speared in the Park, BOOK 2

 Poetry Slammed, BOOK 3

Acknowledgments

Thank you to my creative team, including editor Kay Rettenmund, cover and interior designer Terry Rydberg at Fine Print Design, and my husband, LJ Ribar. You are all artists in your own right and candidates for sainthood for accepting my quirks and potentially unreasonable requests at times. Where would an author be without her street team? Thank you to my ARC readers: Jinny Alexander, Anne Louise Bannon, Valerie Biel, Laurie Buchanan, Christine DeSmet, G P Gottlieb, J. Ivanel Johnson, Sherrill Joseph, Margot Kinberg, Sharon Lynn, Tracey S. Phillips, Saralyn Richards, T.K. Sheffield, Carolyn Wilkins, and Kelly Young. I cannot imagine sharing a creative landscape with better people than these authors. Please check out their books and be prepare for thrills and enjoyable escapes.

In this mystery, I journeyed through The Bard's works and Elizabethan time period to research party foods, fashion, and social norms. The research was almost as enjoyable as crafting the story. If you have read, studied, or seen a Shakespeare play, I hope you discovered the universal themes of love, power, justice, self-awareness, lost innocence, struggle, good and evil—to name a few. These themes run rampant in this mystery, too. Humans, past and present, encounter the same types of conflicts and emotions life brings. For me, revisiting Shakespeare's plays was donning a familiar cloak, reminding me of old wounds, joyful memories, and strong connections to people who come and go in life. I will always marvel at his characters, his intense conflicts, and finally, his words.

What brings immortality to The Bard—to string together words like colorful gems, to piece them into lines of powerful prose, to craft a feast of mere words that we all may dine at his table—that is immortality.

Joy Ann Ribar

www.ingramcontent.com/pod-product-compliance
Lightning Source LLC
Jackson TN
JSHW080028190225
79074JS00004B/125

* 9 7 8 1 9 5 9 0 7 8 2 7 2 *